STAIRWAY TO THE

"Well, Isobel Winter," ⟨...⟩ ⟨...⟩ said, "Do we have a deal?" The handsome Hollywood agent rested a finger under her chin and raised her face to his.

Isobel wet her dry lips with her tongue. "Yes, Davis," she said firmly, "we have a deal."

"Good," Davis said and slowly reached out his hand, but not to shake hands. He touched her breasts, the span of his fingers wide enough to touch both at once. He nodded. "All right, Isobel—take off your clothes."

Obediently Isobel shrugged out of her tanktop and brief white shorts. Davis glanced at her almost casually, then in one swift movement half-knelt and ran his tongue across her breasts, a slick, warm caress against her hot and cold skin, and Isobel felt the tension building unbearably in her body.

"Oh, Isobel," Davis said softly, "we're going to do some great things together. . . ."

"All the right stuff: intriguing characters, sex, adventure and glamour."
—*The Jackson Daily News*

"A fantasy world bound to please romantics."
—*The Chattanooga Times*

WINTER WOMEN

MARY-ROSE HAYES

AN ONYX BOOK

NEW AMERICAN LIBRARY

PUBLISHER'S NOTE

NAL BOOKS ARE AVAILABLE AT QUANTITY DISCOUNTS WHEN USED TO PROMOTE PRODUCTS OR SERVICES. FOR INFORMATION PLEASE WRITE TO PREMIUM MARKETING DIVISION, NEW AMERICAN LIBRARY, 1633 BROADWAY, NEW YORK, NEW YORK 10019.

ONYX TRADEMARK REG. U.S. PAT. OFF. AND FOREIGN COUNTRIES REGISTERED TRADEMARK—MARCA REGISTRADA HECHO EN DRESDEN, TN.

SIGNET, SIGNET CLASSIC, MENTOR, ONYX, PLUME, MERIDIAN and NAL BOOKS are published by NAL PENGUIN INC., 1633 Broadway, New York, New York 10019

First Onyx Printing, January, 1989

1 2 3 4 5 6 7 8 9

PRINTED IN THE UNITED STATES OF AMERICA

For Patrick, Juliette, and Nicholas

Part One

1

1985

Isobel Wynne sat on a dirty tenement step munching an apple. She wore denim shorts cut up to the hip-bone, tight as a coat of varnish, embroidered cowboy boots with very high heels, and a scarlet bikini top that barely contained the lush swelling of her breasts. It was a mercilessly revealing costume—every surplus inch showed—and Isobel constantly had to remember to suck in her stomach. No matter how hungry she was, an apple was all she dared eat for lunch.

Isobel was on location in a decaying neighborhood in South Los Angeles, making a film called *Roper's War*. She was playing a tough but sexy cop posing undercover as a prostitute in an attempt to expose a narcotics ring. She liked neither the role nor the script and had not wanted to make the film in the first place. To add insult to injury, she would have to take second billing to Carlo North, reigning monarch of mayhem and violence.

Worst, the horrible irony was that she was making the movie for Hart's benefit, and *Roper's War* had utterly destroyed their relationship. . . .

Isobel took another bite of apple and stared resignedly at the growing crowd, now numbering in the hundreds. The word was out in the neighborhood: there would be a great stunt to watch—any time now!

The block was closed to through traffic, and the intersections at both ends seethed with the blue uniforms of cops, although only about half were real-life police officers—the rest were actors.

They were bored too. Everybody was bored with waiting; the new setup for lights and cameras seemed to be taking forever. But when all was completed to the director's satisfaction and he finally yelled "Action!" then the stunt car parked around the corner would hurtle down the block on screaming tires. The driver would be visible briefly, a voluptuous, scantily clad, dark-haired woman (presumably Isobel), before the car smashed explosively through the plate-glass window of the corner liquor store. Of course the glass was not really glass at all but spun sugar, and the brickwork was painted Styrofoam blocks, but it would all look authentic enough on the screen.

The stunt driver would collapse unconscious over the wheel.

"Cut!"

She would then climb from the battered car. Isobel would take her place and assume the same slumped position.

"Action!"

Isobel, unconscious, would be dragged from the wreck. Et cetera.

She had no idea where the incident placed in the film and did not even remember reading it in the original script. She assumed it was a later rewrite to beef up a sagging few minutes without a shooting, a stabbing, or a rape.

She decided she not only disliked *Roper's War*, she hated it.

Hart Jarrow had always hated it. Hart was an Academy Award–winning screenwriter who possessed not only great talent, but integrity and good judgment as well—an exceedingly rare combination in Hollywood.

Isobel and Hart had been together since April, and for the first time in her life independent Isobel, who had always prided herself on not needing a man, at least not one particular man, had guardedly been considering marriage at last.

Hart was good for her in every way; he was even advising her on her career. Over *Roper's War* he had raised heavy eyebrows in wry disbelief—"They can't be serious. It's exploitative garbage!"—and sent the bound script skimming across the room like a Frisbee to fall just short of the wastebasket.

"That bad?"

"It's shit," Hart said dismissively. "You can't afford to get involved. Forget it."

So, "No way," Isobel told her agent next day, lunching at Ma Maison on smoked salmon and Perrier. "It's not for me. And I shouldn't need another film this year anyway." Surely not—she had been working steadily for eighteen months, and she wanted and needed a vacation. A long one. She had been thinking about South America. She had never been there. These days it seemed she never had time to go anywhere. Isobel had always longed to see Rio de Janeiro, and perhaps this fall she and Hart could go.

But her agent had other ideas. "Think again. *Roper's War*'s going to make a bundle. You shouldn't pass this up."

Her business manager agreed. "You can't afford to, either."

"What do you mean, can't afford?" bristled Isobel, who had grossed more than four million dollars just the year before.

"Well"—a shrug and a deprecatory gesture of the hands—"I wouldn't say you're exactly *broke*, Isobel, but there've been some extremely heavy expenditures lately. And I did warn you about buying the Ferrari."

"Don't tell me I can't buy a goddam car!"

"And then these other items . . ." He waved papers at her. "I'd like some explanation."

"What other items?"

"The Thacker and Freibourg stud. $22,470."

"Palomino ponies. It was the twins' birthday, but the price includes equipment and full livery."

"And this one: I. Magnin, Saks Fifth Avenue, and Neiman-Marcus in San Francisco, totaling $46,000. Really Isobel, isn't Rodeo Drive enough anymore?"

"That wasn't for me," Isobel said promptly. "That was for my sister."

"But *your* money. And surely a best-selling novelist like Arran Winter can afford to buy her own clothes."

"Well, of course, but"—how to explain that without direct intervention, Arran was quite likely to appear on "The Tonight Show" or "A.M. America" wearing an unraveled sweater and dirty jeans? that she, Isobel, was enormously proud of her sister and wanted her to look smart?—"she never has anything to wear, and she hates to go shopping. . . ."

A sigh. "I see. . . ." Then the resigned tone suddenly turned grim. "Now, the Ardmore Galleries in Beverly Hills. A small item of $250,000."

Isobel's face softened. "Oh, yes. . . ." A Guido LoVecchio bronze, for Hart. A surprise for Hart's birthday. A magnificent horse, all muscle, flared nostrils, and thunderbolt hooves. The moment she saw it, she knew it belonged rightfully to Hart, who loved horses. "It's a piece of sculpture. A gift." She looked him in the eye, suddenly angry. "Surely I can buy a few presents for my family and friends?"

"You're a reckless spender, Isobel. And I have to warn you that your affairs are precarious."

"But I want a vacation. I *need* one."

"Well, go, by all means. But I suggest it be *after Roper's War.*"

When she finally had the nerve to tell Hart she had agreed after all to make the movie, he was as angry and uncomprehending as she had known he would be. They had their first real fight.

"You're throwing yourself away on this trash just for the fucking *money*?"

She wanted so badly to tell him about the LoVecchio horse, but she knew what he would say. "That's crazy, Isobel. Risking wrecking your career over a goddam piece of sculpture." It would spoil everything. Of course, once he saw it he would understand. Then he would agree that a compromise had been in order.

"I *need* the money," Isobel said finally.

"Not that badly."

Isobel sighed. Hart, a purist in his art form, would never understand that, for her, acting wasn't everything, that her ability to be generous, to have the power to fulfill people's dreams, was almost as important. It helped to make up for all the ugly impoverished years growing up in those grimy cities across the midlands and in the north of England.

She had given him an edited version of those days. He had not been particularly moved. Perhaps one day she would tell him the truth.

But not now.

"Isobel," Hart went on with vehemence, "you're hardly some ignorant little starlet letting big money go to her head. But you still buy more clothes than you'll ever wear, enough cars to open a European import showroom, and you spoil those kids rotten by giving them too many toys and horses they can't ride."

"Hart, I just want them to have everything I never—"

"And this pretentious white elephant of a house eats money like—"

This, for Isobel, with frayed nerves and a sullen, nagging headache, was suddenly too much. "If you don't like it, then leave!" she cried angrily. "Just get out!" She could accept criticism about the clothes, the cars, and the children's ponies, even agree, but no one was allowed to criticize her beautiful house, not even Hart. It was the realization of *her* dream, everything within it so carefully chosen, from the ancient brass-studded Indian dower chest, to the handwoven Peruvian rugs in Mark's and Melissa's rooms, to the David Hockney painting above the marble fireplace.

But paintings, rugs, and Indian chests did not have warm arms that held her closely in the night.

Hart took her at her word and left. He had not called her since.

Isobel had never felt so miserable. She tried to convince herself she was better off without him, but it was hopeless. Who did he think he was, anyway? What right did he have to preach about how much she spent? It was her money. How dare he as good as tell her she was prostituting her career? Of course, she would then remind herself viciously, even if he had won an Academy Award, he had been born to hick farmers on a small Idaho ranch and retained all of his narrow-minded hick attitudes. What did he know about *anything*? My God, thought Isobel, when he comes back I'll show him!

But she never had the chance to show him anything because Hart, with his Idaho rancher's stiff pride, had not come back.

She hadn't seen him in three weeks and missed him desperately. She missed everything about him. His deep, gravelly voice, his sudden gusty roars of laughter, his springing energy, his big, powerful body, the touch of his hands . . . The house seemed so enormous, so cold and empty, without Hart, and soulless—the way she supposed it always had been, more like a museum than a home.

It was always tidy now, too. No more wet footprints and soggy towels flung on the bathroom floor. No more empty beer cans left on the kitchen counter. It was glistening and empty, like a magazine photograph, and this was discouraging. But it was more than sheer emptiness that tore at Isobel—a sense of safety and belonging was gone.

Every day Mark and Melissa, eleven years old last June, asked where Hart was. They had seen many men come and go, but Hart had become someone special to them. With Hart, they behaved like real human beings instead of juvenile terrorists.

"Where's Hart, Mom? When's he coming back? Is he coming soon?"

Isobel told them he was working.

"But he always comes on weekends."

"He has a deadline."

They knew better though, and their eyes grew evasive and blank. There would be hell to pay, Isobel thought, if Hart didn't come back soon, and she shivered slightly.

Even the maids were depressed.

But I'll be damned if I'll call him first, Isobel thought fiercely, her hands curling into fists, the long manicured nails gouging painful red crescents in her palms. I've never crawled after a man in my life, and I won't start now!

With a bleak grin, she considered the irony of her situation. Here she was, Isobel Wynne, idol of the eighties, the goddess who had it all, sitting on a dirty, decaying step in Watts, California. Bored, miserable, and lonely. Hungry, too . . .

"Ms. Wynne? Excuse me—"

Isobel looked up into the awed, eager face of one of the gofers, a child fresh from film school who just *knew* she would be a famous director some day. She made Isobel feel, at thirty-three, absolutely ancient. "Ms. Wynne, there's a phone call. From England. It's your mother, Mrs. Winter—she says it's urgent."

Elizabeth Winter's news should have been shocking.

"Isobel—your father is dead. . . ."

It should have meant something, but it didn't.

Instead, Isobel heard herself say, "I'm so sorry, Mother—that's terrible." As though her father were only a distant relative or a casual acquaintance.

She had not seen her parents for years now, her mental images of them fading over time and distance to the substance of old, blurred photographs, but as their reality decreased for Isobel, so did the old anger and bitterness. Her only regular contact was at Christmas, when she would send expensive, carefully chosen presents and in due course receive a brief, rather vague thank-you note from Mother. It was much the best way for all of them.

"Can you hear me properly, Isobel? He's *dead!*"

"Yes, Mother, I can hear you."

A whisper—"I don't know what to do. . . ."

Death was hard for Isobel to take seriously. Just this morning a dying gunshot victim had flung himself repeatedly to the sidewalk in numerous retakes of a fight sequence. Yesterday Julio Sanchez, a Mexican character actor, had been doused with gasoline and torched. He had died in front of Isobel's eyes in screaming, writhing agony, but there he sat in the commissary later the same afternoon, munching a doughnut and reading *Variety*, impatient to go home to his daughter's seventh birthday party. "She won't blow her candles out unless Papa's there," he told Isobel and roared with laughter.

Mother shouldn't be so upset, Isobel found herself thinking reflexively, for Father, too, would surely get up again and go about his business.

"Don't you have anything else to say? Don't you want to know how George died?' Her mother's voice wobbled dangerously. "He was so young—he wasn't even sixty."

Isobel blinked and gave herself a mental shake. Her father was *dead* for God's sake. . . . "Yes, Mother" —and again—"I'm so sorry. What happened—was it an accident?"

She hardly heard her mother's shamed, bewildered whisper: "No, he killed himself, Isobel. He took his own life. . . ." Then hurriedly, making a desperate excuse: "He'd been drinking. They found an empty bottle beside him. He wasn't himself."

"Oh God!" Immediately outside her trailer, the props man was handing out automatic weapons to a group of young men wearing dark glasses and Italian-style suits, while an assistant made notations on a clipboard. "Did he—did he shoot himself?"

"Shoot? No. He—gassed himself. With the exhaust pipe of my car"—and as though Isobel herself were somehow to blame—"the one *you* gave me! And it's all so *horrible*. All the talk and the publicity and these awful reporters. They know about you now, of course, and about Christian and Arran. It's so undignified. He would have hated it. I don't know what to do. I can't bear to talk to them. Isobel, you *must* come home. I need you. I'm sure you're busy, but please. . . ."

"It's okay, Mother," Isobel said, thinking about walking out on a thirty-million-dollar movie in midproduction. But tomorrow was Friday, and surely she wouldn't have to be gone for long. They could shoot around her for a few days. "I'll be there as soon as I can. I'll get the first flight out in the morning."

"Oh, Isobel, thank God. And please, would you call the others? I don't even know where Christian *lives* these days."

"Yes, Mother."

"Tell them to come. I want you all here. . . . There's something you three need to know. . . ."

Too late, thought Isobel. There's nothing you can tell me now.

She called Arran in San Francisco and left a message on her machine. When Arran was writing, she never answered the phone until after 5:00 P.M.

Then she tried to call Christian. Until very recently, neither Isobel nor Arran had been able to reach their middle sister, who would contact them occasionally from distant places with exotic names.

A year ago Christian had simply walked away from her jet-set society life, disappearing one day before her much publicized wedding to Sam Stark, billionaire developer, racing yachtsman, and America's Cup hopeful. Leaving only a short, polite note of regret in an envelope also containing Stark's huge diamond engagement ring, Christian had left her glittering world for a gypsyish life on a sailboat with a mysterious man named Ludo Corey. Isobel and Arran had not seen her since. They knew nothing about Ludo whatsoever, except that Christian was wholly and blissfully in love with him.

Now Isobel had to leave a message for Christian at a marina somewhere in western Puerto Rico with a man whose English was marginal and who sounded drunk. Oh, Christian, Isobel thought ruefully, what do you think you're doing with your life? Certain that her headstrong sister had taken up with a drug smuggler, "What else could he be?" she had worriedly asked Arran.

Then she pushed such thoughts away, coolly practical once again. She called her travel agent to arrange a first-class plane ticket to London and a suite at the Dorchester Hotel.

She returned to work. She conducted the rest of her afternoon with great efficiency, completed her scene with a minimum of problems, and went to watch the dailies with the director and her costar.

Later, back home, Isobel organized the running of her household during her absence, promised Mademoiselle a vacation the moment she returned from England, and told the twins that no, they could not come with her this time, which precipitated an exhausting argument.

Christian returned her call, shocked and angry to hear the news. Half an hour later so did Arran, sounding as remote and cool as Isobel herself must have when speaking to her mother. However, to Isobel's relief, they both finally agreed to meet her in London. How good it would be, she thought, to see them again—especially Christian. It had been so long. . . . So much had happened. . . .

The impact of her father's death did not hit her until she began to pack. She laid out her clothes on the bed and found herself completely and uncharacteristically indecisive over what to take with her.

Then, kneeling on the floor beside the bed, staring at her clothes, Isobel found herself trembling uncontrollably.

George Winter was dead. Her father was dead.

Instinctively, she reached for the photograph in the heavy silver frame that stood on her night table. It always brought reassurance and support when she needed it, and a reminder that she was not alone. In the photograph, the three little Winter sisters, aged ten, nine, and seven, all brushed and tidy, posed self-consciously against a department-store studio backdrop for a birthday picture for Father.

Herself—black curls, blue eyes, pink cheeks, dimples; Christian—tall for her age and uncomfortable with her height and her too-big hands and feet; Arran—wide-eyed as a fawn, peering from under straight-cut bangs, one sock wrinkled around her ankle. Mother had been so upset about that sock—she said it quite spoiled the picture.

Years later, Isobel had found the photograph where Father had tossed it—in the garbage bin under the sink. She rescued it, smoothed it out, kept it, and treasured it. She had always loved that picture—far more than the later shot of the three famous Winter sisters in *People* magazine, all hiding now behind their well-trained professional smiles.

What would Father's death mean to them all? To her, personally?

And what would happen now? The reality of just how George Winter had died struck her with numbing force.

The emotion she felt was not grief. Isobel's early love and then hatred for her father were long burned out. Nor could she feel sad for him, for in George Winter's case death could only be a blessing.

There was no surprise, for the news itself was not particularly unexpected; she could even wonder why he had waited this long. What she did feel was sudden, debilitating fear.

Strong-minded Isobel, supposed to be so sensible and pragmatic, had never felt so terrified in her life.

2

Christian Winter Petrocelli sat beside Ludo Corey at a window table in a small restaurant in western Puerto Rico six miles south of Mayagüez.

The restaurant was unpretentious. The light was fluorescent and garish; the floor linoleum; the chrome and formica tables each decorated with a beer bottle containing a plastic daisy. Americans never went there because there was no atmosphere, and the place was packed with Puerto Rican families—mothers, fathers, children, grandmothers, and babies. The noise level was punishing. Everyone shouted, and salsa blared from the radio. The food, however, was excellent, and the prices less than one-third those of the picturesque restaurant next door, which catered to tourists.

Christian and Ludo were eating fresh-caught dorado grilled in butter and garlic and drinking Corona beer. Their table faced the ocean, or, strictly speaking, the Mona Passage. The water tonight was a smooth, iridescent lavender, the long lines of the gentle swells edged with scarlet. The sky was a depthless salmon pink. Just beyond the horizon, where the bloated, blood-colored sun was now sinking, lay the rugged mountains of the Dominican Republic.

Christian thought she had never been so happy in her life. Two minutes earlier, Ludo had said that he would definitely be quitting, that he would not be making any more trips, that yes, he felt the time had come to start his charter business. With the connections he had in the big hotels and with two boats—the other skippered by his good friend Miguel—they could be in business right away.

"After all, I'm getting old," said Ludo, "and it's quite a turn-on, thinking about a steady job, a home, that kind of stuff."

Cautiously, Christian pushed the thick chestnut hair from her tanned forehead and studied Ludo. She asked carefully, not daring to believe it yet, "Are you serious? *Really* serious?"

He nodded. "Yep. It's time."

Christian's face grew radiant. Her tawny eyes glowed gold. She whispered, "Oh Ludo, that's wonderful." She was thinking of those long, lonely days and even lonelier sleepless nights, when she had waited for him and feared for his life. He never told her where he went or what he was doing. He just melted away like vapor into the Caribbean Basin. At such times, he would slip effortlessly into his other skin, his Latin persona; dyeing his thick, blond hair black, he would once again speak the gutter Spanish he had spoken throughout his childhood in the decaying San Juan barrio below the fort of El Morro. Then she could barely even recognize him because, even more than the jarring change in his hair color, the use of Spanish altered him. The planes of his face shifted as different muscles came into play. He walked and held his body differently. He somehow looked leaner and more wiry— and dangerous. Christian knew that Ludo Corey no longer existed. He was Ludovico Jimenez—as he had been born thirty-eight years ago—and Ludovico Jimenez carried a gun. . . .

Christian never asked where he went and what he did. She did not want to know. Superstitiously, she was somehow certain that if she asked any questions it would, one way or the other, be the end for them.

So Ludo would disappear, and Christian would try to put that hard-eyed stranger out of her mind, telling herself that Ludo had merely gone away on business like other people, that it was no big deal.

But now, she would be able to sleep at night. He would be safe.

The sun dropped out of sight, and the waters of the Mona Passage tonight so deceptively languid, turned a deep velvety maroon. Ludo smiled across the table at Christian. It was a glorious smile. He never smiled at anyone else like that. The harshness of his face softened, and his eyes, which she had seen flash as dangerously as the steel points of twin daggers, glowed with love. Because he did love her. He did not tell her so, because Ludo never would—he did not know how. But he loved her, she knew. And she loved him desperately. She owed him everything. He had given her back to herself. Finding Ludo, she had stopped running, and she knew she would never run again.

She wondered whether to tell him about the baby now and decided it would be better to tell him later, back on the boat, when they would be sitting in the cockpit drinking wine, staring up at the night sky laden with those incredibly bright stars, listening to the gentle gurgle and slap of the water around the hull. There was even a bottle of champagne on board somewhere, Christian remembered. They could toast their new beginning as a family—a safe family. Her heart fluttered with happiness. Oh, how she prayed Ludo would be pleased about the baby. But he would be. Of course he would.

As they walked slowly down the dark country road together, hand in hand, back to the small sportfishing club where the boat lay docked at the marina, Christian pictured a child who would look like Ludo—a strong, sturdy body, tough little face lighting up with an impish grin, sun-bleached hair, and clear gray eyes. Or perhaps he would have her eyes. He might have dark brown hair like hers and light eyes. Perhaps it would be a girl, with blonde hair and . . . Christian smiled in the darkness, imagining the face of her precious new child. Surreptitiously, she touched her flat stomach. She did not show yet, but she would soon. He, or she, inside there, was already more than three months old.

They had almost reached the gates to the club, where a light shone and a watchman dozed in a small hut. The voices of cicadas and tree frogs rose in deafening nighttime concert. Ludo pulled Christian gently into the darkness under a huge stand of oleander, slowly unbuttoned her blue gingham shirt, and slipped it off her shoulders. Very deliberately, he ran his hands over her exposed breasts. Christian did not wear a bra; she did not need one, for her breasts were high, firm, and beautiful. Ludo bent his blond head and voluptuously licked first one straining nipple and then the other.

"Oh God, Ludo," Christian gasped, "don't—not here . . ." The relentless heat swamped her body, and each cell of her skin screamed for Ludo's touch, her breasts more on fire than ever, perhaps because of the baby. "Oh, Ludo," she moaned, thinking that never, nowhere could there have existed such a sensuous man. She had lived with Ludo for a year now, and it had been a year spent in a state of almost constant arousal. She had only to look at him, at any part of his body—the arches of his feet, the wide curve of his shoulders, the white-gold hairs on his muscular forearms—to flood instantly and heavily, to feel that thick, warm sexual tightening. . . .

"Don't button your shirt," he said. "I want to watch you while you walk. Your breasts move so beautifully."

"No, Ludo." Her hand moved to cover herself, to fumble with buttons, but he tucked it firmly under his arm.

With a chuckle in his voice, he said, "Nobody'll see you except me."

And Ludo was right, of course. The watchman was asleep inside his hut, and the whole place was as quiet as the grave, the little clubhouse deserted, one light burning in the office. They walked softly past the two tennis courts, the white lines glimmering faintly, then past the barbecue pit, the swimming pool, and across the lawn and down to the marina, where a line of sportfishing boats and several sailboats—one of them Ludo's thirty-foot sloop *Espiritu Libre*—shifted and creaked softly at their moorings.

As Ludo bent his head and whispered in Christian's ear, "How many times are you going to come tonight?" he rubbed the palm of his hand teasingly over the hard points of her naked breasts.

Christian gasped. "I—" Then she broke her stride and halted. She gripped Ludo's wrist. "There's someone on the boat."

Ludo thrust her behind him.

In a split second, the flick of a switchblade, he had slipped into his other skin, his other life. She heard the small, gentle exhalation of breath, which she knew came from anger at himself for not being on his guard.

On *Espiritu Libre*, a small, bright flame flickered, then was extinguished, leaving in its place a soft, steady red bead of light. A man coughed.

Christian felt Ludo's taut, bunched muscles relax slightly.

He called softly, "Who's there?" his voice flat and hard.

A voice replied, "Ludo? Hey, man"—a slight note of alarm—"it's me. Beto."

Christian found her hands were trembling. She buttoned her shirt and followed Ludo down to the boat.

On board sat Alberto Torres, club manager, Ludo's friend. Nothing to worry about.

He was there because there had been an urgent call for the señora, long distance. "I thought you'd be back soon, so I come down and wait," Beto said. "You so quiet, you scare me, man. Now you can give me a beer."

He handed a message slip to Christian. From Isobel, in Los Angeles.

After that, the day was ruined.

Isobel wanted Christian to leave Ludo at once and go to England. Their father was dead. She was needed.

"I can't, Iso," she said from the phone in the club office. "I just—can't." How ridiculous she felt, still to be so afraid of Father, even though he was dead. But she had always been afraid of him and of that breathless tension he dragged with him wherever he went until the atmosphere in the close little brown rooms they lived in was thick with it. Then, the young Christian would run away in suffocating panic, running down long featureless streets of identical houses where eyes would be watching through blank-faced windows, leaping at last onto a bus—any bus, so long as it took her away. . . .

"I know how you feel, Chris," Isobel said. No! Christian thought; nobody could know, especially not Isobel, who has never been afraid of anything or anyone in her life. "But Chris, Arran and I will be there. It'll be all right. We can't leave Mother to handle it on her own. And she said she has something to tell us. . . ."

There's nothing she can tell me about Father, Christian thought numbly as she felt the walls closing in and her breath shortening; but she found herself reluctantly agreeing to go. Iso and Arran would be with her.

Tomorrow morning early then, Beto would drive her to the airport in Mayagüez, where she would take the half-hour flight across the island to San Juan, and from there to London, where Isobel had reserved a suite for them at the Dorchester.

At least there was the baby. Thinking about Ludo and the baby and their new life together would give her strength. Christian reminded herself that she was no longer on her own—she was creating a family. She felt a sudden warmth and a glow of confidence. There would be something to live for in the grim days immediately ahead. However, when she told him her news, as if the day had not already brought horror enough, Ludo stared at her in bleak silence.

Finally he said, "A baby?" The air shimmered with cold surprise, and a steel curtain seemed to drop between them. "How?"

"Careless, I guess," Christian muttered wretchedly. She could not bear it. He did not want the baby after all. He was angry. Furious. Her heart felt as cold as stone.

"Are you sure? How far along are you?"

"Three months."

Ludo began, "You could still—" He fell silent at

her quick, indrawn hiss of breath, but the unspoken suggestion hung murderously in the air above them.

"No," Christian said.

"Well then"—Ludo shrugged heavy shoulders—"there's nothing I can say."

"I guess not," Christian replied, aching with hurt.

And so they went to bed, carefully not touching each other, and Ludo now lay asleep beside her, very quiet and very still as he always was, his arms serenely at his sides.

Christian lay on her back staring up through the open rectangle of hatch at the cluster of stars that suddenly seemed too bright, too big, comfortless and mocking. Her tears had dried stiffly on her cheeks.

"When do you think you'll get back from England?" Ludo had asked.

"A week. Perhaps two."

A pause. "You'd better take a hotel room then," he'd said finally. "I'm not sure where I'll be."

Christian had known at once what that meant. Because of her father's death or the baby or whatever, he was breaking his promise.

She left for England the next morning with the terrible premonition that she would never see him again.

3

Arran Winter, celebrated author, had spent the early part of her afternoon interviewing Chief Rufus Mahoney, San Francisco Fire Department, at the Washington Square Bar and Grill.

Chief Mahoney was forty-five years old, six feet five inches, and weighed well over two hundred pounds. He clearly enjoyed his enormous platter of calamari fritti and the basket of sourdough bread. He also appeared to be enjoying the interview itself.

"If they are trapped in the back of the building on the top floor," Arran said, fixing him with huge, serious eyes, "with the fire on the lower three floors and access blocked to the stairs and the fire escape, how would you get them out?"

They had already covered most aspects of fire fighting in this particular instance—arson in an old, wood-frame, four-story apartment building—and Arran had picked up some authentic-sounding phrases such as "ventilating the roof," "superheated gases," and "Scott air packs." Now, Chief Mahoney explained the mechanics of the pompier ladder, used for exceptionally tricky rescue work, and drew a picture in her notebook. "It's a goosenecked device, shaped like a fish bone, which you hook over the edge of the roof . . . like so."

He also promised to arrange a visit to a firehouse so Arran could examine all the equipment for herself and get a feel for background. "It's my pleasure," he said. "I'll do all I can to help," giving her shoulder a fatherly pat.

Arran sighed. He had already told her how clever

she was to write all those books—and she surely not much older than his own daughter Maureen, now a junior at Mercy High School. Hearing the familiar words, Arran felt her usual stab of exasperation. She hated her appearance. She had a fine, unlined forehead, a flawless English complexion, wide, expressive eyes the color of rain, and baby-soft, impossible to manage brown hair. She was thirty years old but actually *could* have been taken for sixteen, a thoughtful, rather shy high school student. In an attempt to look more mature, she had recently bought a pair of spectacles with nonprescription glass lenses and heavy tortoiseshell frames. They actually changed nothing. She now looked like a shy high school student wearing glasses and was still regularly asked by cynical bartenders to show her ID. But they made Arran feel more self-confident, especially when confronting older, formidable people like this enormous veteran fireman sitting across the table grinning at her. She was always slightly amazed when such people, experts in their own fields, patiently granted her their time and expertise to answer her no-doubt foolish questions and make sure she got her facts right. She was even more surprised when they actually seemed to enjoy doing it.

Chief Mahoney drove her home in his red fire chief's car. Arran found childish delight in driving in it and wished he had been able to put the siren and the flashing red light on for her.

Then, after a squeeze of the hand and a jolly wave, he was off, back to department headquarters, and Arran climbed the three grubby flights of stairs to her apartment, where she would spend the remainder of the afternoon typing up her notes.

Arran rented the entire top floor of a ramshackle Victorian building on lower Telegraph Hill. At street level, there was a cozy, rather dingy bar where jazz was played on Friday and Saturday nights and where aging beatniks from the fifties occupied their regular barstools, nursed their drinks, and reminisced into the small hours.

A whiskered crone, Mrs. Giancaccio, shared the

second floor with Rory "The Rabbit" Gulhane, an octogenarian ex-bookie. On the third floor, five serious-minded Asian students crammed into one unit; the other was occupied by a barker at one of the North Beach strip clubs who spent his daytimes at the local community college studying computer programming.

Originally, Arran had shared the top floor, but with success and her newly acquired wealth, she had been able to take over the other apartment when the tenant moved out and to persuade the owner of the building to put in a connecting door.

The building itself was dilapidated and in sad need of new decoration, plumbing, and wiring. It faced a noisy street and had no view. Arran could actually have afforded to live anywhere now; had she wished, she could have bought a mansion in Pacific Heights. But moving never occurred to her. The building had nurtured her and been a refuge through good times and bad. She enjoyed the 2:00 A.M. bar stories about Lenny Bruce, Mort Sahl, and Jack Kerouac. She liked drinking bourbon out of jelly glasses with Rabbit Gulhane while he pored excitedly through his mounds of ancient racing forms and did not in the least mind picking up Mrs. Giancaccio's prescriptions from the drugstore, even though her regular reward would be a stream of senile abuse.

For Arran, these people were almost family. The old building was home.

She lived a contented and hardworking life nowadays, among piles of books and mismatched pieces of furniture, and once a week she was bullied into a semblance of order by Rita, her Salvadoran cleaning woman, who changed her sheets, did the laundry, scrubbed the kitchen and bathroom, and shopped for the necessities of life, which Arran would have forgotten about. Rita had been foisted on a very unwilling Arran by Isobel, who had been appalled once too often by her youngest sister's haphazard life-style.

Here, Arran felt safe and contented. At last her life had smoothed out for her, thanks to her own hard work and to her unbelievable good fortune in meeting

Devlin, who had brought her not only peace of mind, but freedom from that humiliating, witless, febrile compulsion that would descend on her like the screaming Furies in times of stress and demand to be satisfied.

At 5:00 P.M., she finished typing her fire-fighting notes. Suddenly feeling the effects of the unaccustomed large lunch with wine, she flopped onto the bed to take a nap. The phone rang twice, but she ignored it.

At 7:15 P.M., after a cup of coffee, she switched on the machine for messages.

She heard Isobel's voice, and a shock like a seismic jolt went through her. The ground was falling away. . . .

When her hands stopped shaking, she tried to reach Devlin.

Dev was her lifeline. "Call me anytime," he had said, smiling that peculiar smile he had, a smile that told you that he had seen everything there was to see in people, from the very best to the very worst, that nothing could surprise him, ever, and that always if you looked hard enough, sometimes in the strangest places, you would find joy. To Arran, Dev was hope. "I mean it, day or night," he had told her and given her his private number.

But finding him this time of the evening was always next to impossible.

In her need, she conjured up his image as he had looked that first night they went out together: drinking beer at La Rondalla, a Mexican restaurant in the Mission District where the dusty strings of Christmas decorations stayed up year in and year out, Dev watching her quizzically, his face, so youthful and unmarked, belied by his thatch of white hair and ancient, kindly dark eyes.

He had liked her. She was sure he had. And in his own way, he was attracted by her. Later, in his shabby Volkswagen squareback, she had flung herself at him, body thrusting toward him, hands all over him, mouth voracious. After the shock of the initial onslaught, he had held her successfully at bay, gripping her wrists with surprising strength for he was not a big man, while she fought, swore, and finally wept in shame.

"You're a beautiful girl, Arran," he had told her then, quite calmly, "an enticing one, and quite, quite drunk. I'm going to take you home now; you're going to sleep well; and tomorrow, or whenever you feel ready, we'll talk." There had been no disgust in his voice, nothing judgmental, only kindness, concern, and recognition of her own particular demon. "I know them all," he might have said. "Every single one."

Arran had slept well that night. She knew she would because Dev had said she would.

Oh, if only she could find him now. She needed him so badly.

I'm frightened, Dev. I'm frightened of myself. I thought I'd be different now, but I'm not, and it's still there, as bad as ever. . . . Her hands began to shake again, and she felt the mounting heat of her body as the dreaded, welcomed, lurid images crowded one by one into her head. Dev, help me!

But Dev was nowhere. He was not at the office, the clinic, the center. She left messages everywhere, urgent messages, feeling more and more distraught.

When the phone rang abruptly under her hand, she leaped with relief.

But it was Isobel again, with travel arrangements, and Isobel would never be able to help, even if, unthinkably, Arran confessed to her, which she knew she would never do in a thousand years. How could she possibly tell her degrading secret to her beautiful, admired eldest sister. She imagined the scorn she would see on Isobel's face, the contempt in those gorgeous, iris blue eyes. It never occurred to her that of all people Isobel would be the most understanding, that she might even have a shameful secret or two of her own.

Arran restlessly paced the room, her mind a jumble of emotions.

Dev, where are you? I can't wait much longer. She could feel the tide building inside her.

Of course she had known all along how Father

would end up—it was the only logical way for him. But how terrible and frightening it was to know how right she had been. Arran felt immersed in dread and foreboding, as though something ominous and dark were reaching up from her innermost self to catch her, drag her down, tell her that yes, of course, this was the way it had to be, and she'd known it all along, hadn't she?

She was a person condemned. She knew what she had to do.

She didn't even change her clothes. Flinging into her purse all the cash she had and, on impulse, her passport and alien registration card, she ran out of the house in her good little gray suit—the one Isobel had bought her last month at I. Magnin, which she had chosen for her interview with the fire chief. Down the block and into the alley, where she claimed her car from Anunzio's garage, ineffectually telling herself to drive with some vestige of care as she tore around three sharp corners and rocketed down Broadway toward the Embarcadero. Don't be an idiot, her fading sense warned; you'll get yourself killed. . . .

By the time she passed the freeway on ramp at Sansome Street, she began to wish she were dead. It seemed to be the only way out, the only way to stop herself from doing what she was doing, going where she was going. As she swung right onto the Embarcadero and headed for the South of Market district, she had begun to cry with rage and helplessness.

How *dare* Father do this to her? If he wasn't dead already she'd do the job herself. Then the black humor of it hit her, and by the time she parked her battered tan Toyota in a vacant lot on Eleventh Street between Folsom and Harrison, she was almost hysterical.

With a shaking hand, she rang a carefully concealed bell that she had not rung in a year now, knowing that a pair of coldly appraising eyes would be watching her on video.

A metallic voice spoke from above her head: "Sorry, closed for remodeling."

"Knock it off," snapped Arran, who, to her dismay,

found she had forgotten her membership number. "It's me. It's Arran—"

"Can't help," the voice insisted. "Too bad. Closed for—"

"Don't give me that shit," Arran cried, her panic rising. "It's me—I'm—oh God, I'm—five-seventy-six." Surely that was right; please let it be right. "Now open the fucking door!"

A pause. She wondered what she would do if they refused to let her in. But then the buzzer sounded, and Arran almost fell through into a small, dark hallway. Immediately in front of her, stone steps descended steeply to a cellar, where a reddish light gleamed. There were many rooms in that cellar, which spread under two adjoining warehouses, and Arran knew them all and what went on inside them. Below the cellar was a subbasement with a soundproofed door in which Arran had not yet been. What might lie beyond that door both fascinated and terrified her. . . .

The huge-shouldered man at the desk said, "Hey, it's you. It's been quite a while."

"Yes," Arran nodded, feeling much calmer, her breathing slowing almost to normal, standing quite still, absorbing the atmosphere of the place. It was exactly the same as she remembered. A fantasyland of shifting light, a slight but pervasive feral odor, and muted sounds—distant, pulsing music, murmured pleas and demands, and the whispered susurration of naked, coupling flesh.

A towering man strolled past, his oiled body muscled like a wrestler, his head completely shaven, nude except for a studded harness and bulging black leather jockstrap.

"Yeah," the man at the door said as Arran turned to watch, "Gus's still around. You want him? Remember Gus?"

Arran nodded and ran her tongue over dry lips.

He studied a roster on the desk. "Then we got a new boy—Mexican kid with a lotta good tricks. Mean son of a bitch, just what you like, and hung like a fucking python. You want to try him after Gus? I could see who's around for later. . . ."

"Sure," muttered Arran. The tension drained from her body to be replaced by the old numbing anticipation. She would have them all. One after the other . . .

"That'll be five hundred up front," the man said. "Visa or MasterCard's okay."

He watched her as she strode away to stash her clothes in the locker room, and he shook his head. Honest to God, he thought, it took all kinds.

4

London sweltered in the throes of a late summer heat wave.

Isobel gazed out of the window of her suite at the blaring traffic in Park Lane. Beyond, she saw the parched grass and drooping trees of the park.

She had expected coolness, soft greens. She wished now she had gone to another hotel, one overlooking the river, where at least the water might offer the illusion of freshness.

She rubbed her aching eyes and crossed to the refrigerator, which was discreetly hidden in an alcove and camouflaged by orchids and roses. There was a bottle of Moët et Chandon champagne chilling inside, along with the half-pound of Beluga caviar always produced for Isobel's pleasure when she stayed at the Dorchester. Today, however, she wanted neither champagne nor caviar. Just a fast belt of vodka to try to feel human again.

She plunged a fistful of ice into a glass and filled it to the brim from the bottle of Stolichnaya she had brought from Los Angeles. Then she sipped it gratefully, feeling the groundswell of panic subside a little, wishing her sisters were there, although it was only eleven o'clock in the morning and there was the whole day to get through before Christian and Arran could be expected to arrive.

Isobel stared at the already melting ice cubes in her glass. As weary as she was, she was certain she would not be able to sleep. Then, on impulse, she reached for her maroon leather overnight case and upturned it haphazardly on the bed.

From among the tumbled assortment of hurriedly packed cosmetics, toiletries, underwear, and unread paperbacks, she picked up the silver-framed photograph of herself and her sisters and set it carefully on the night table.

Looking at it made her feel a little better.

Christian and Arran, she prayed silently, please hurry. I need you.

Christian arrived in the late afternoon. The ex–jet set celebrity had flown by hedgehopper plane from Mayagüez to San Juan; by 727 to New York; by wide-bodied jet to London, crammed in economy class among noisy tourists and whining, sticky-faced small children. In her private turmoil, she was oblivious of her surroundings and had quite forgotten that her last trip to London had been by Concorde.

"Iso, oh my God! I can't believe it's been so long!" Half laughing, half crying, she enveloped her smaller sister in her arms. "Oh Iso, I've missed you and Arran so. It's so good to—good to see—" Christian pulled away and raised trembling hands to her face. Her shoulders shook. "Sorry," she muttered through her fingers. "Just overcome, I guess . . ."

"Come on, Chris, sit down. Relax. You'll feel better with a drink. Then we can talk." Although Isobel thought she had never seen Christian look better—her tan a deep olive, her hair much longer than before, falling thick and lustrous to her shoulders—she could not help but notice that Christian's eyes were deeply shadowed and her face stiff with strain. Well, Isobel knew what her sister must be going through. . . .

Christian smiled hesitantly and said in a brittle voice, "Do you know, it's hotter here than in Puerto Rico!" She perched on the edge of one of the luxuriously overstuffed armchairs, kicked her worn sandals off, and curled her bare toes in the rug with the relief of one unaccustomed to wearing shoes. She pushed the heavy hair away from her neck with a quick nervous gesture Isobel did not remember and gratefully accepted the proffered drink.

Christian sipped, abruptly set the drink down, and wrapped long, slender arms tightly around her knees. "Have you talked to Mother yet?" She longed for the reassuring sound of Isobel's voice, the comfort of the plans she would have made. Isobel was so efficient, so practical, and as always Christian felt calmed listening to her sister relating mundane details about rental cars and the pros and cons of hiring a driver for the trip to Sheffield. Without Isobel, and Arran, who surely must arrive soon, Christian felt that she would be all alone in the world.

Arran arrived just before midnight.

She should have been there much earlier, but she had passed out in the basement on Eleventh Street and missed the plane.

When she finally checked in at San Francisco International, she found her passport had expired three months before. Arran always lost track of details like that. There had been endless delays until, ready to scream in frustration, she at last managed to persuade the reluctant immigration officials to let her board; then there had been more delays at Heathrow Airport on her arrival in England. "I'm so sorry, Iso," she apologized miserably. "I feel such a fool. . . ."

There had been no time for a shower before leaving. She had spent the first half hour after takeoff in the lavatory trying to scrub herself clean with paper towels, but she still felt filthy and wretched and certain her depravity was clear for the world to see and condemn.

She plopped down onto the rug, a disheveled waif in a crumpled Saint Laurent suit, and assumed her customary cross-legged pose.

At least she was safe with her sisters now, and she could trust Iso to take care of everything. But oh, damn Father to hell! *Why* had he done it?

"He was drunk," Isobel said wearily. "Mother said he'd drunk a bottle of gin."

"He's been drinking for years," Christian objected. "You know that. We all knew . . ."

"Alcohol wasn't the reason he did it, though," Arran said. "Just the—the trigger."

There was a taut silence, each remembering what she knew, none knowing what to say.

Arran noticed the photograph on the night table, absently picked it up, and found herself staring down at that long-ago picture of herself, Isobel, and Christian, the poor little Winter girls, who against all odds had succeeded so magnificently in the world—a Cinderella story in triplicate. But then she began to shiver with distress because oddly, despite their closeness and despite their love, for the first time she received no comfort from her sisters and suspected that in turn they received none from her.

The detached, writer part of Arran, the professional observer, tried to analyze the feeling in the room. There was grief, yes, and anger and guilt and all the other inevitable emotions engendered by violent unnecessary death. There were individual burdens; she could sense quite clearly that both Isobel and Christian labored with unspoken trouble, just as she did herself. There was something else, something insidious and secret, but what was it?

"Can anyone tell me," Arran asked abruptly, breaking the silence, "why we're all so afraid?"

Part Two

1

1970

The giant aircraft shuddered and roared as it moved
down the runway and hurtled into the sky, and eighteen-
year-old Isobel felt the goose bumps prickle on her
forearms.

It was happening after all. Right up to this moment
she hadn't dared believe it, but nothing, surely, could
stop them now. She and Christian were on their way
to California.

It was a miracle. For years, she, Christian, and
Arran had prayed for a miracle, and finally it had
happened in the form of an invitation out of the blue
from Mother's old friend Margie, now married to a
man named Hall Jennings III in Los Angeles.

"But she doesn't even know us," Isobel had protested, not allowing herself to believe that the invitation was neither a mistake nor a misunderstanding.

Margie Jennings was someone with whom Mother
exchanged Christmas letters and family photographs.
Margie's photos came every year, showing a pleasant-
looking blond couple, a little stouter each time, posing
with their daughter Stewart (Isobel's age exactly) beside a gaudily decorated Christmas tree, under which
lay a heap of prettily wrapped gifts. Stewart, with
golden curls, blue eyes, and dimples like Shirley Temple's, was always wearing a new, elaborate Christmas
outfit.

Isobel, Christian, and Arran all thought Stewart
looked too smug for words, but she did have the most
wonderful clothes. They had personal experience of
Stewart's clothes, because many of last year's outfits
would be packaged and sent to the Winter household

in time for the holiday parties to which Margie wrongly surmised the girls were invited.

"Stewart must go to parties every day," Isobel would gasp enviously, stroking the stiff folds of a gold satin skirt or the richness of a maroon velvet bodice. "Is everyone rich in America?"

"Of course not," Mother said vaguely, not really paying attention. It was almost time to put on the kettle for Father's tea. But then, Isobel wondered, what did Mother know about it? Mother's world focused entirely on Father. Certainly she had never been to America. "Though I must admit Margie did marry well in the end," Mother ventured, on her way out to the kitchen.

Margie had indeed. Hall Jennings III was president of Orient Pacific Airlines, whose head office was in Los Angeles. He was also the scion of a very old New York family with investment banking, brokerage, and shipping interests. The Jenningses were a large clan; Hall had brothers, sisters, cousins, nephews, and nieces galore, all of whom seemed to be continually involved in elaborate and profitable weddings with other rich old families at which pretty little Stewart was frequently invited to be a bridesmaid.

"The very fancy ones must be bridesmaid's dresses," Christian observed.

Father hadn't liked Margie to send "hand-me-downs." "It makes one feel like some kind of poor relation." ("Well, what else are we?" Isobel muttered.) He had wanted Mother to return them immediately and tell Margie not to send any more, but for once Mother had overruled him. He never mentioned the matter again, but the next Christmas, when Isobel rushed downstairs to model the sky blue taffeta gown Stewart had worn to her cousin Ames's bridal dinner at the Plaza Hotel in New York, he turned on his heel and left the room without a word, taking much of the pleasure of the gift with him.

"Well, we won't let him spoil it," Isobel had said firmly, though her lips threatened to tremble. Why couldn't Father just once tell her how nice she looked, or at least say something kind? "We'll wear them just for us."

Certainly, there had been nowhere else to wear the dresses, because unlike Stewart Jennings, they never went to weddings or parties.

The sisters often discussed their plight. "We never go anywhere," Isobel would sigh with frustration, staring at her pretty reflection in the mirror.

"Nobody ever asks us," Christian would observe sensibly.

"How can they?" Arran always demanded. "We don't know anyone."

And so the daydream had taken root and flowered: the dream about going to America, where everybody was happy and rich.

"If only we had money," Christian said wistfully.

"Perhaps somebody will die and leave us some," said Arran.

"Who?" scoffed Isobel. "Nobody except the Jenningses even knows we're alive anymore."

Which certainly seemed to be true. It was because of Father, although they tried to be understanding because he had been wounded in the war. They would all remember that long-ago November night, sitting as close to the sputtering gas heater as they dared, when Mother had explained why Father was not like other fathers. Because of his wound, he had become completely antisocial, a recluse, refusing to see people from the outside world.

"How was he wounded?" Isobel had promptly asked. "And where?"

"In the head," Mother told her, and then added, voice low and dramatic, "The surgeon took fourteen pieces of shrapnel out of his brain!"

"Gosh!" said Isobel, impressed. Christian looked sick.

"So we must always be very, very kind to Father, do what he wants, and make him happy."

Certainly, Mother lived by her word. To make Father happy, she had gradually dropped everybody, and even the most stubbornly persistent friends and relations at last faded from sight in the face of such total lack of encouragement. The fact that the Winters moved so much was further isolating. Sometimes they moved twice a year because, although reclusive, Father was also endlessly restless. The girls did not realize until much later that Mother was partly responsible for the moves as well; she did not want the neighbors to find out the truth about Father. The only person she did keep up with was Margie Jennings—"Because she lives so far away," Isobel observed astutely.

Isobel was the most frustrated by the Winter family's way of life. One October, she had been awarded the lead in the Christmas play at school—a startling achievement for a first-year student. But in the midst of rehearsals, Father had decided with almost hysterical urgency that they must move at once to Birmingham, and so they did—to another shabby, genteel neighborhood where the girls entered yet another school and where Isobel would have to start all over again in her striving for recognition, in her desire to prove that she was not just another anonymous face, that she was *somebody*.

With each move, Christian would suffer through a regular cycle of hope, disillusion, and despair. She would wonder whether just perhaps, this time, the new house, town, and school would be better than the last—but even though nothing was ever better, there would always be a honeymoon period at the beginning when Father's mood would be lighter, his anger level lowered to mere intermittent rumblings of discontent, and Christian would not feel so frightened.

She would even dare to dream of playing out a whole season on the tennis team. Christian, who loved tennis, had a sad record of either arriving too late in the summer term to qualify as other than a replacement or playing the first few weeks of the summer before being forced to quit.

The initial period of relative tranquility never lasted, however. There would be an escalation of tension, leading to Father's dreaded outbursts of fury at everything and everyone—his home, his family, even Mother.

Arran, of course, had always had her own defense. She would withdraw into the richly populated world inside her own head, where the characters and situations she created were so much more exciting and interesting than those of her everyday reality. Arran had been in the habit of writing stories, happily alone in her bedroom, since she was six years old. At age eleven she wrote a full-length novel about children and horses—an amazing feat of imagination since she had seldom seen a real horse, much less ridden one.

"Nothing ever bothers you," Isobel would say enviously. "I wish I was like you."

"Me too," echoed Christian.

"Don't be silly," said Arran. "Of course things bother me."

"But not real things," Christian pointed out. "And you're not even frightened of Father—or of never having a *life*!" She sighed dismally. "Oh Lord, what on earth are we going to do?" Then she and Arran looked confidently at Isobel, sitting on the bed dressed once again in Stewart Jennings's taffeta gown. Isobel was the leader. She made decisions. She could always be counted on to think of *something*.

Isobel had no idea, but she knew what was expected of her. She looked from one to the other of her sisters. "Why," she said purposefully, "we've got to make a plan." And playing for time, she made a great show of arranging the stiff blue folds of the dress around her. "We've got to get away somehow. Things can't go on like this."

Christian and Arran waited expectantly.

And Isobel did not let them down. "We'll go to America," she said suddenly, wondering why she hadn't thought of it before, "and then we'll get terrifically successful! You can do anything in America."

"America!" cried Christian ecstatically. "Of course! But how?"

"If we want it enough," Isobel said firmly, "then it will happen. It always does." She just *had* to believe that.

"But how will we be successful?" Arran asked.

"How? Why, we'll have *careers*!" Isobel had always known what she would do with her life. Her eyes brilliant with determination, she announced, "I'm going to be a famous actress, or a model on television."

"And I'll be a writer," Arran said excitedly. "I'll write a best-selling novel and sell it to the films and Iso can star in it."

"But what about me?" Christian looked from one to the other. "I'm not beautiful, like you, Iso, or clever like Arran. What can I do?"

"You?" Isobel scoffed. "That's easy—you can be a tennis champion and win Wimbledon."

"I don't think I'm good enough," Christian said uneasily.

"Then you can be like Margie," Isobel announced breezily. "You can marry a millionaire like Hall Jennings. You can be the *rich* Winter sister! When you're rich, you can do anything in the world you want. Think what you could do for Arran and me!"

That night, therefore, it was all decided. They would go to America, where they would naturally become successful and famous.

All they needed was a means of getting there. . . .

And one day it happened, just like that.

"Stewart goes off to college in the fall," Margie wrote, "and we're spending the whole summer at home for the first time in years. It would be so great if the girls could come over. I can't believe they're nearly grown-up and I've never even seen them! Don't you remember how we promised ourselves we'd get Isobel and Stewart together—so long ago now! We mustn't wait any longer. Stewart will be so excited if you say yes. . . ."

And here they were, off to America at last, for six whole weeks.

Father had been angry—there had been more about the poor relations being thrown a bone by the Yanks—but he compromised in the end. Isobel and Christian could go, but not Arran. She was too young. As for the cost, no problem—thanks to Hall Jennings, the airline president, they would fly free, first class.

*   *   *

"We're going," Isobel muttered now, as the plane soared into the sky. "Oh Chris . . ." Christian sat in the window seat with her nose pressed flat against the glass, hands white-knuckled on her seat belt. Isobel, who had worried about Christian being shut in the plane with everything tightly closed, took her hand and pressed it—"Chris, are you okay?"—but Christian was rigid with excitement. The plane was quite all right. It was taking her away to freedom. She turned to Isobel and grinned with joy.

The cabin slanted at an impossibly steep angle. They saw dim, greenish gray fields and endless rows of dirty redbrick houses lurching and wheeling below them in a fading circle before disappearing into a veil of cloud.

Then everything blanked out. Thick swirling gray, streaks of moisture on the windows, until with dramatic suddenness they broke through the cloud cover into brilliant blue sky and the sun was brighter than they had ever seen it before. It was a symbol, a promise.

"We're going to California!" Isobel cried. "We're really going. . . ." For six glorious weeks, she would see no more dingy, depressing streets and dirty gutters; no more boxlike rooms filled with dull brown furniture; no more net curtains stiff with the unrelenting city grime; no more ugly linoleum or rust-stained bathtub; no more of Mother's decomposing dried flower arrangements.

"If only Arran could have come too," Christian said guiltily. "Fifteen *isn't* too young. And she's much older than she looks."

"It won't be so bad for her," Isobel pointed out. "Father likes her much better than he likes us."

That was certainly true. Father was not fond of either Isobel or Christian. "You don't like it here, do you?" he had demanded. "You don't like being at home with Mummy and me. You want to go away." When they looked at one another in embarrassed silence, Father had taken it as assent. "Then to hell with you," he had yelled, and he had marched into the small room off the kitchen, which he used as an office, slamming the door behind him.

"Yes," Christian said now, "he does like Arran. And she's always able to get away, sort of. She never notices anything around her when she's writing."

"Well, when we're rich and famous, we'll make it up to her," Isobel said comfortingly. "I'll bring her out as soon as I get my first part," never doubting for a moment that this would happen very soon.

And then the flight attendant wheeled up the drinks cart and offered them cocktails. Isobel ordered a gin and tonic, pretending that she did it every day and that this was not the first time she had ever drunk real alcohol apart from the small glass of cooking sherry allowed at Christmas dinner.

"Iso!" Christian hissed nervously, "you'll get drunk!"

"Phooey!" Isobel said scornfully and took a long swallow of her drink, ice cold but warming at the same time. She marveled at the sensation that swept glittering to her head like a trail of diamonds. "Oh *boy*!" She stretched luxuriously in her soft, comfortable seat. "Chris, this is the life for me."

By the second sip, she had put her entire past behind her. She had forgotten Father, Mother, the mean little house, and even Arran. She was Isobel Winter, eighteen years old and beautiful. She was going to California and her life was beginning.

By an incredible stroke of luck, she had been given one chance, and she was going to play it for all she was worth. She was going to California, and somehow, some way, she was going to stay there. Isobel vowed that minute that she would never go back.

2

Christian, seventeen and five feet nine inches, her thick chestnut hair swinging, strode into the passenger terminal at Los Angeles International Airport alert as a pointer after game, her nostrils flaring in pleasure at the sharp, cool, canned air, her senses tingling with delight as she absorbed the exciting scene. Nothing would ever again affect Christian as did her first impression of California. Eagerly, she drank everything in, gazing entranced at the chattering, shouting travelers streaming in all directions: at hard-faced young servicemen returning from Vietnam, shouldering duffel bags; at chanting groups of hippies brandishing antiwar posters; at saffron-robed Hare Krishnas with tambourines; at young people in tattered jeans, beads, embroidered vests, gypsy dresses.

"Oh," Christian sighed happily, "I'm going to love it here! Love it, love it, *love it*!"

Margie and Stewart were there to meet them.

Greetings and hugs from Margie, instantly recognizable, looking just the way she did in her photographs, wearing a flowing emerald and turquoise muumuu. How strange to think that this vast, friendly woman in the brilliant Hawaiian print was the best friend of pinched, colorless Mother!

"My dears, I can't believe you're really here! Hope you're not too exhausted! Isobel, honey, you are the absolute *image* of George when he was your age—I can't believe it!"

Eighteen-year-old Stewart, whom they would not have recognized from her photograph and who no longer bore the slightest resemblance to Shirley Temple, wore a hot pink mini-dress that barely covered her behind. Her legs were endless. Her tan golden. Her manner cool. "Well, hello there."

Stewart, far from being excited, had not wanted Isobel and Christian for the summer at all. "Oh Mom! Jesus!"

"I won't have that language, Stewart."

"Yeah, but—I mean, come on now. For the whole summer?" she had whined plaintively. Stewart had plans for the summer. She had just graduated from Rosemary Hall, her Eastern prep school, and planned to spend July and August partying, lying on the beach, and smoking a lot of grass. She did not want to waste her time baby-sitting these two English wimps. And they were wimps. By God, were they ever. She looked with distaste at their clothes—nobody had worn pleated skirts and white oxford shirts since the Dark Ages. They were both square as shit, and probably even virgins. Stewart sighed audibly, knowing it would be terrible.

After the cool of the terminal, there was a brief blast of heat and a dim vision of a pallid sun trying its best to shine through layers of brassy smog; then Isobel and Christian were in the air-conditioned comfort of a dove gray limousine, which took them in silent and elegant comfort to Bel Air, where the sky was blue.

Elaborate wrought-iron gates swung soundlessly apart; the limo swept grandly through, past banks of flowering shrubbery and an emerald lawn where sprinklers hissed, and pulled up at the pillared entrance to the Jenningses' plantation-style mansion. Isobel thought it the most beautiful house she had ever seen. Inside, drinking in the splendor of the wide marble foyer, the soaring staircase, the paintings, the flowers, she promised herself she would own a house just like it. One day. One day soon!

She and Christian were to share a room overlooking a rear patio. Beyond the patio, behind more banked shrubbery, they could glimpse the sun-spangled turquoise of a pool. Beyond the pool a landscaped walkway led to the tennis court. "A tennis court," Christian muttered in bliss. "Iso! A tennis court!"

"If you're not too tired," Stewart said politely, knowing that her mother was within earshot, "change into your suits and come on out and swim." She hung around the doorway waiting to see whether the rest of the clothes Isobel and Christian had brought were as bad as what they were wearing. They were.

"Why don't I lend you each a suit?" Stewart said hurriedly, not out of charity, but knowing how embarrassed she would be if someone—Davis Whittaker, for instance—came over and found two pale wimps in her pool wearing navy woolly one-pieces. He'd think they were *her* friends, for Christ's sake.

Christian did not want to wear Stewart's suit. She knew perfectly well that Stewart did not like her or want her there, and she felt ill at ease. But Isobel, who would never turn down an opportunity, said, "Thanks." The bikinis Stewart brought were very stylish. Startled, Christian stared at herself in the mirror, at her long slender shape and gently swelling young breasts, enhanced by three small triangles of blue fabric, and thought with total surprise that here she looked *right*. She had never thought of herself in any other terms than as beautiful Isobel's plain, too tall, too dark younger sister; but here she was not too tall after all, and her un-English olive skin seemed appropriate. Oh my God! thought Christian, I look *pretty*!

In a plain black bikini, Isobel was spectacular, her magnificent breasts barely contained within the sleek black material, the shape of her nipples prominently visible. "Iso," Christian said with awe, "you really look sexy in that." And with satisfaction, she added, "Stewart's going to be *mad*!"

By the end of the day, Stewart, a spoiled princess who had been granted her every whim all her life, realized that Isobel was a force to be reckoned with and felt annoyed with herself for being deceived. Isobel had balls, thought Stewart over the next few days, with grudging respect, and quite possibly was not a virgin after all. Certainly she was no wimp. However, to Stewart's disappointment, Isobel had little interest in listening to her rambling, self-obsessed monologues and appeared unimpressed by Stewart's friends, who all drove expensive cars, owned expensive clothes, sound systems, sports equipment, and other toys, and spent their time lounging on the beach or around the pool, indulging in casual sex play, getting stoned, and laughing inanely.

Stewart had no idea that Isobel, already a competent actress, was playing a part.

Because of course Isobel was impressed. How could she not be? She was as impressed as hell, never having believed such a life-style existed. In her wildest imaginings, girls and boys her age and younger could never afford to own sleek continental sports cars and to drive them recklessly between beach, country club, and parties at one fabulous mansion after another. She was also bitterly angry at the injustice of it all and at the stupid waste, for Stewart and her friends took all of it for granted. She decided she *hated* Stewart! Isobel gritted her teeth with anger, determined that Stewart would never know how badly she wanted it all too. Never!

At night, she had a recurring dream: after a long flight from some nameless fear down an endless murky gray road between high walls, she would find herself standing in a doorway in the wall, which opened onto a brilliant, sunlit garden. She wanted to go in so badly, but no matter how she tried she could not force her body through that door. She would wake up in tears of frustration and then lie sleepless for hours, listening to Christian's soft, even breathing across the room, watching the shifting reflections of trees and moonlight on the ceiling, thinking frenziedly and helplessly of how fast the time was passing. And she still had so much to do!

She *had* to stay here. She refused to go back—back to smoky, dingy Birmingham, where this fall she was supposed to get a job in a shop, or as a typist or receptionist. Better to run away to London and be a streetwalker, Isobel thought, with only the haziest idea of what a streetwalker actually did. She could not bear the thought of working in a store or an office. She would die. All she had ever wanted to do was be an actress.

"It's a nice idea, dear," Mother had said with a faint, distracted smile. "Quite impractical, of course. One does have to eat."

Isobel knew she was being selfish going on about it. She ought to give in with good grace and take a job to bring in a little more money. But, "I could be good, Mother. I *know* I could be good."

"Well, of course you could, dear. You were so sweet in *Alice Through the Looking Glass*. But all girls want to be actresses at your age."

"I'll never want anything else, Mother. I swear I'll never be anything else."

"*Look* at me, Mother!" Isobel had wanted to scream in utter frustration. "Look at me! Everybody does—everyone except you and Father." This was true—even wearing her drab school uniform, Isobel's progression down any street was marked by a wavelike turning of male heads and whistles of appreciation. But she wanted to do so much more than just turn heads. . . .

Given a chance, thought Isobel, what couldn't I do for all of us! Thrashing restlessly in her pretty, white guest-room bed, she knew she was responsible not just for her own future but for those of Christian and Arran. Then she reminded herself that she *had* been given her chance. Miraculously, here she was in the City of Angels, a scant mile or so from the movie capital of the world. This was it. Now it was up to her. . . .

But, as in her dream, she had come so close only to have it all remain still out of reach. Margie and Hall Jennings, middle-aged and complacent, were in no way even remotely connected with the movie business, and none of their friends appeared to be either. Isobel met a succession of other nice, respectable, wealthy people—

bankers, stockbrokers, property developers, or doctors whose attitude toward the movie colony generally seemed to be one of wariness. It was all fascinating, they admitted, but only at a distance.

Please God, help me, prayed Isobel. Let me meet a producer, director, agent, screenwriter—anybody who can get me in through the door. But God had not obliged her, at least so far.

To do her justice, Isobel did not let her frustration show and was a polite, appreciative, and properly enthralled guest when Margie took her and Christian to see the sights: Disneyland, Marineland, and finally, at her urging, a tour of Universal Studios.

She was tempted to confide in Margie. Could she be made to understand the urgency? Margie was very fond of her, and she thought there was a chance.

Isobel timed her approach carefully, choosing a lunchtime beside the pool when Stewart had left the house on an errand.

Before long, however, Isobel knew Margie would never be forthcoming and guessed the real reason Margie was so fond of her. It was because she looked so like her father, with whom, to her stunned surprise, Isobel discovered that Margie had once been passionately in love.

"You were in love with *Father*?" Isobel, bemused, noticed that the sunlight through the green and yellow beach umbrella over their heads turned Margie's florid cheeks a stridently mottled orange. "But Margie, I didn't think you ever met him. Mother never said anything about . . ."

"Oh yes, Iso. Of course, it was a terribly long time ago, but once the three of us were practically inseparable. We did everything together. Liz and I were both in love with him. . . ."

Margie's face grew vague and dreamy. She dug around absently in her avocado salad, withdrew one shrimp, examined it, and set down her fork. "It was just before the end of the war. The summer of 1944—the most beautiful summer for years, or perhaps it just seemed that way to us."

Isobel sat absolutely still, listening to Margie's story in astonishment.

"We even managed to forget the war," Margie said. "It was always there, of course, everybody in uniform and everything, from food to clothing, so scarce, but it was summer and we were only eighteen. All so close, even though we were so different. I was—well, just me I guess, the same big, jolly old me. Haven't changed a bit, though I was a little thinner then. Elizabeth was the serious one—always taking things to heart and wanting to save the world. She worked on committees and things, for prisoners of war, refugees, and war orphans. And George. Oh, George—I can see him now. . . ." Margie stared abstractedly into space. Isobel waited, holding her breath.

"George was so terribly handsome—thick black curly hair and those wonderful blue eyes, just like yours, Iso dear. And he was so, so brilliant. He'd been accepted at Oxford. He wanted to be a poet. He wrote wonderful poetry. But of course instead, he got his call-up papers, and soon after that it was all over. He was hurt—right at the end of the war, when it was practically over. It was so terribly *cruel*. He was in the hospital a long, long time . . . over a year. My parents wouldn't let me see him. I was heartbroken. . . ." She sighed gustily, then pulled herself up and smiled across the table at Isobel. "But all's well that ends well. Later on I married Hall, Stewart was born, we were happy, and the rest, as they say, is history!"

Good God, thought Isobel, she's *still* in love with him! But how *wet* she must have been. How very pathetic. If I'd been in love with somebody, I wouldn't care *what* my parents said. I'd have gone to see him!

"I never saw George again," Margie went on ruefully. "But Elizabeth was much better for him than I would have been. She stuck by him through thick and thin; I guess she took him up as her most important cause. . . ."

The Mexican maid removed the salad plates and brought a cut-glass dish filled with sliced peaches. Margie nodded in automatic thanks, her mind clearly still thousands of miles and several decades removed. Finally, she brought her reminiscing to a close: "And that is why I was absolutely determined to keep in touch, my dear, no matter what Elizabeth said. I wasn't going to let George's children slip away out of my life. It was such a joy being able to send things for Christmas—I felt almost as though I was part of the family again!"

That was when Isobel knew beyond a doubt that Margie would never help her. In her mind's eye, George Winter was the handsome young student of a quarter of a century ago whom she loved. She would never do anything to upset him, and she would never never be able to understand what he was like now.

Margie took Isobel shopping for clothes on Rodeo Drive. She also took her to have her hair professionally styled. She would have taken Christian too, but Christian really wanted only to play tennis. She was in paradise, playing on a beautifully surfaced court and using Stewart's new metal racket—lent willingly, since Stewart never bothered to play. With her long legs and wide reach, teenage energy and accurate eye, she blossomed quickly into a formidable player. Instead of shopping expeditions, Margie took Christian to the Bel Air Swim and Tennis Club and introduced her to some of the young people.

Isobel envied Christian; part of her would have liked to relax and play tennis and fool around too, but her driving, determined side would not let her, for there simply wasn't time and she had to be ready if and when opportunity knocked.

Studying the other women at the beauty salon and at Gucci, I. Magnin, and Neiman-Marcus, Isobel realized that to get anywhere in Los Angeles one had to be tan, thin, and at least look rich. Every day she stared critically at her naked body, pinching the flesh around her hips. She was overweight and too pale. She put herself on a stern regimen of exercise and carefully timed sunbathing sessions, while eating only meat, fruit, and vegetables. By the end of her second week, Isobel had lost five pounds, firmed up the softness around her hips, and acquired a light golden tan.

And it all happened just in time. On their third Saturday, Margie gave a party in her and Christian's honor, and Isobel met Davis Whittaker.

Stewart was in love with Davis. Since he never seemed to call or take her out, Isobel gathered that the feeling was not reciprocated. "He's really cool," Stewart confided. "Even *you're* going to think so," she said, determined to impress Isobel somehow. "Though he's old, you know. He's twenty-six. He was in Vietnam. He's graduated from Yale Law. He was supposed to go into partnership with his father in Hartford, Connecticut, but he couldn't stand it, you know, working in some stuffy old company which has been around since B.C. He came to L.A. instead and went into the Industry. His father was pissed. He said he'd cut Davis out of his will. Can you imagine?" Stewart picked at a flake of marijuana caught between her teeth. "Silly old fart—Davis had *always* wanted to work in the theater. He was stage-mad in school. Parents are so dumb! Here, have a toke," she invited, passing a brown, soggy-looking joint.

Isobel declined. "No thanks."

"You're really square," Stewart said. "You know that?"

Isobel turned over and conscientiously rubbed her stomach with Hawaiian oil of aloe. She'd give it twenty minutes, then turn over again. "Doesn't bother me if it doesn't bother you."

"I guess not." Stewart shrugged. "I mean, it's your own thing."

From behind the oleander hedge came the crack of hard-hit tennis balls—Christian was playing with some bronzed young athlete from the country club, and she was probably beating him.

Isobel yawned. She was starting to feel sleepy, all warm and oiled, and the sun was so bright it was hard to keep her eyes open. "Is Davis an actor?" she murmured politely, without much interest, for Stewart's friends were all so boring and so much the same.

"God no," Stewart said, drawing smoke deep into her lungs. "Mmmmmh—ahhhhh! This is great grass. You sure you won't change your mind? No? But he should be. He's so groovy looking." Stewart squirmed on her air mattress, poised on the very edge of the pool, reached out one foot, and agitated the water. "Oh God, how I could get it on with Davis Whittaker! I bet he's great in bed! Iso, are you on the pill?"

"No."

"You should be, you know. I've been on it for three years. . . . Anyhow, he's tall with this great body, and he has eyes you wouldn't believe. Kinda brooding, with these real sleepy bedroom lids, you know?"

"What color are they?"

"Huh? Oh"—Stewart giggled—"I dunno. Kinda brown, I guess, but sexy."

"Great," Isobel said, very drowsy now. "So what *does* he do if he isn't an actor?"

"Talent agent," Stewart said dreamily. "Isn't that the worst waste? Handling other people when you look like Davis . . ."

Isobel suddenly felt very wide awake.

"Anyway, you'll meet him on Saturday at the barbecue," Stewart said. "*If* he decides to come, that is."

Davis Whittaker very nearly did not come to the party. He did not want to see Stewart, whom he did not like and whose ignorant, pseudohip speech drove him mad, nor did he particularly want to meet the English girls, Margie's guests of honor, who would be plump, sweet, naïve, and wearing pastel prints.

But he did come, because he was broke and eating other people's food instead of buying his own made a lot of sense. For a good meal, he would be polite to the English girls and even to Stewart. Davis grudged spending money on himself, even to eat, because every penny he owned went into the Whittaker Talent Agency. He slept illegally in the storage area behind his office, where he brewed coffee and heated soup on a portable Coleman stove. His client list, which was sparse, was made up of aspiring young newcomers who could find no one else to represent them, an occasional referral from an old college buddy, now a junior executive with M-G-M, and dropouts from other agencies, such as the spaced-out actress who had been let go by the William Morris Agency and an aging soprano who sang at bar mitzvahs and weddings when she was sober. He needed good clients desperately, but good clients did not need him.

However, Davis was an optimist and a survivor. He quelled the panic that threatened to overwhelm him each time he thought of his rent and the good clothes he needed to wear to look convincing as a rising young agent, gritted his teeth, and hung on. He refused to give in, determined to prove to the old man that he could make it on his own, even if it killed him. Sometimes, in dark moments, he thought it probably would; paranoid with depression, he would grow certain that the world was out to destroy him. But something would always happen at the last minute to stave off total disaster for one more day. A client would land a commercial or a walk-on in a soap. Or there would be an invitation to a party where he might make a lucky contact. . . .

On Saturday afternoon at five-thirty, Isobel was modeling for her sister.

"How do I look, Chris?" she asked tensely.

Christian turned, then stared. "Different," she said uncertainly.

"What do you mean by different? Do I or don't I look all right?"

"You look sensational." This was the absolute truth. Isobel had spent the afternoon at the hairdresser having her thick black curls styled to float deceptively naturally from her head. But it was not just the hair, thought Christian. Perhaps the dress? It was new—very simple, very short, a coarse, cream-colored linen. Yes, it must be the dress that made Isobel look so sleek and glamorous—so *finished*. "Sensational," she repeated. "Really."

"Good," Isobel said, lightly.

But the way she said it made Christian realize it was not really said lightly at all; this was serious business. For Isobel, there was much more at stake than just looking pretty for a party. Christian wondered what it could be. Whom was Isobel dressing so carefully for? Whom did she expect to meet here? But when the party started, she put it all out of her head. Everything was so perfect it seemed ridiculous to worry.

Christian could never have imagined such a beautiful party. The patio and pool area were decorated with flowers and strung with colored lanterns; bottles of white wine and imported beer chilled in barrels of ice; a mariachi band strolled among the guests singing and playing while waiters passed huge plates of hors d'oeuvres: giant shrimp dipped in hot sauce, guacamole, juicy pieces of chicken on sticks, mushrooms wrapped in bacon—all quite ordinary fare for the Jenningses and their crowd, a simple weekend family barbecue, but to Christian it all seemed impossibly exotic.

By the time the steaks and chickens were flung onto the glowing coals and brushed with sauce by the three hired barbecue chefs, Christian was in love with everything: with the velvety night, the opulence, the beauty, the gardens, the food, the wine—with life. She wished Iso would relax and enjoy herself too. Iso took everything so terribly seriously.

However, by the time the steaks were finally served, Christian had forgotten about Isobel. She had found even more to be in love with: Tommy Miller, the boy she had played two sets with at the country club yesterday, a muscular, sun-bleached Apollo who to her thrilled surprise asked her to be his partner in the junior open tournament.

"If you're *really* under eighteen," Tommy said eagerly, "then shit, we can fucking well clean up!"

Isobel knew she was a winner the moment she stepped through the french doors onto the patio. A hush fell, eyes turned, and in a very few seconds she was surrounded by males of all ages: teenage boys, young men in their twenties, fathers, even Hall Jennings. So far she had seen little of Hall, who worked hard and returned home late, when he would retire to his den for peace, a glass of bourbon, and a comfortable sojourn with *The Wall Street Journal.* "Hi, Isobel. How are you today? Hope you're having fun" was his normal vague greeting, to which Isobel would respond appropriately. But tonight he was effusive. "You're looking marvelous, my dear—simply radiant. I've never seen you look so good!" Even as inexperienced as she was, she could read the naked admiration in his eyes. She smiled inwardly with satisfaction and mentally filed her discovery.

Davis Whittaker stood on the outer perimeter of the group, talking with Margie. He had of course seen Isobel the second she had appeared. He thought that even if he closed his eyes he would still see her, her image imprinted on his eyelids as though she were radioactive.

". . . so glad they're having such a good time," Margie was saying of her young guests. "They're such dears, so appreciative. It's fun to spoil them. Their parents and I were best friends . . . grew up together."

When Margie wandered away to circulate among her other guests, Davis was free to study Isobel, having first made sure that Stewart was safely ensconced in a group of her tiresome friends, but he did not make his move until the steak plates had been cleared away by the help, and the party became mobile once again. Then, suddenly, he and Isobel stood beside each other at the bar. The move had been engineered as much by Isobel, although Davis was unaware of that.

"I hope you're enjoying California," he said politely, holding her wineglass for the bartender to fill.

"Thank you," Isobel replied. Her voice was low pitched, with a slight huskiness and a breathtaking English accent. She looked up at him, and Davis received the full impact of her eyes for the first time. They were a clear blue, ringed with indigo. Amazing eyes. Then she smiled. Her lips were full and lush, a deep dimple showed in each cheek, and Davis's glance was drawn irresistibly to the cleft in her chin, which somewhere he had heard meant sexual insatiability.

He rocked slightly on his feet, thrown momentarily off balance by a rush of what could be described only as lust in its most primitive and demanding form; then, with a wide-angled, slightly glassy stare, he took in the rest of her body. Skin like a ripe peach. The cliché appalled him, but it was the only description that fitted. A deep, dark inviting cleft between breasts that would be hard and soft to touch at once. But Isobel was more than lovely eyes, a great figure, and a cloud of tousled black curls that, Davis guessed quite correctly, for all their casual perfection, had cost a lot of money to style. Isobel was a presence. In a crowd of sixty people, she was the only person he saw. She was magnetic. Unromantic, even cynical, knowing more beautiful girls than he could count, Davis Whittaker found himself shaken to the core.

He suspected he was staring at her like an idiot, shook his head, and hurriedly drank some wine. Normally articulate and beguiling with women he wished to impress, he now could think of absolutely nothing to say. The silent seconds ticked by until in a rush of desperation Davis finally asked Isobel what she thought of California wines.

Isobel said she thought they were very good, though she did not drink much.

Then he asked whether she had had a chance to do much sightseeing. Isobel said yes and told him about Disneyland and Universal Studios. He wondered what else to ask her, terrified that he was boring her, wanting only to keep her by his side.

He need not have worried. Isobel was going nowhere. In fact she was not listening to a word he said; she was studying him as intently as he was studying her.

First, she had to admit Stewart was right. Davis was very good-looking: dark-haired, with eyes that were a striking shade of amber. They were hooded, sleepy eyes, although Isobel was certain that his heavy-lidded glance missed nothing. However, good looks aside, he had a strong face. Studying those covertly watchful eyes and that hard, determined mouth, Isobel thought with satisfaction that Davis Whittaker could probably be tough and, from the little information she had been able to glean from Stewart, that he wanted success almost as badly as she. . . .

All she had to do now was make him want to help her, and she had a feeling the battle was already halfway won.

Davis took her lightly but firmly by the arm and led her out to the pool. Isobel was aware of Stewart's baleful eyes fastened on their backs as they walked away between the oleander hedges. Her lips curved with wry amusement. Poor Stewart! Her desire to impress Isobel with Davis Whittaker had certainly backfired.

They stood side by side on the tiled edge of the pool, looking down into the turquoise, flower-strewn water.

"When do you go back to England?" Davis had to ask.

"In about three weeks."

Three weeks. So soon . . . "Back to school? You're Stewart's age, aren't you?"

Isobel stated emphatically, "I've finished school."

"What, then? What will you do?"

She moved a hairsbreadth closer, and Davis could smell the fragrance of her perfume and sense the heat of her body. He listened to the heavy thudding of the blood in his ears. Jesus, he thought, I could take this girl back to my bed, strip that designer dress off her back, force her down, and fuck her till I was so goddam exhausted I'd fall unconscious onto those gorgeous breasts and sleep until I woke and fucked her some more. I could drown in that beautiful, sleek body; I'd suck every inch of her skin.

But there was so much more . . . I want to know her, thought Davis, really know her through and through. I want to see her smile at me in the mornings. I want to own her and keep her. . . . And she's leaving in three weeks.

He realized it was the first time in a long while that he was looking at a woman and seeing just the woman. Normally, he assessed each new woman with an agent's eye, regardless of whether they might become clients, much as a photographer might automatically take note of bone formation, shadow, and flesh tones.

Isobel turned to face him, her breasts almost brushing his rib cage. She smiled radiantly and Davis felt his mouth go dry.

"You'll laugh if I tell you," she said wryly.

"Try me."

She looked at him a moment longer. "I want to act," she said with determination. "And not just act. I want to be a star. And I don't, absolutely *don't* want to go back to England." She looked up at him with sudden defiance. "Now go ahead. Laugh."

It was as though a megawatt bulb flashed on inside his head. Against his torrential images of lust, a cool professional voice in his mind was saying, of course she'll be a star. And if *you* feel this way about her, how do you think every other male in the country will feel? In the world?

Jesus Christ, he'd watched every man at the party watch Isobel, guessing that inside each pair of pants was an actual or imminent erection. Not even Hall Jennings was immune, and Davis could safely bet that Jennings had hardly ever looked at any woman but Margie in his whole married life, or wanted to. . . .

Davis could hear his heartbeat now, booming uncontrollably inside his chest. He felt quite breathless. Very deliberately, his arms unnaturally heavy, he reached forward and put his hands on her shoulders.

He stared into her face. Isobel stared back, her eyes narrowed and determined.

Davis said very quietly: "I don't hear anyone laughing."

3

Bel Air
15 August 1970

Dearest Liz:

Here's the latest update on your girls' impact on the U.S.

Thanks and thanks again for letting them come—I can't remember when we've all had such a good time. I don't know what I'll do with myself when they go home, although of course you must be missing them dreadfully. This is the first time they've been away, isn't it? Though next time George must be persuaded to spare Arran as well. She'll be old enough then.

We gave a small party for them last Saturday—family and friends and assorted young people. Isobel was *quite* a hit and bowled everyone over, even poor darling Hall—he says he finds her *fetching*—isn't that sweet! But thanks to Isobel he's started coming home on time for a change, and we've been having some nice family dinners at a civilized hour.

Stewart's nose has been put out of joint a bit. However, the experience has been good for her as I'm afraid she was getting a bit too big for her boots. There's a little of the green-eyed monster involved too, as one of the boys Stewart likes—not a boy, actually, since he's about twenty-six—has become rather smitten with Isobel and keeps dropping by to see her. Isobel, tactful child, has not gone out with him alone as she doesn't want

to hurt Stewart's feelings. The romance is hardly
likely to get serious though as the girls go home in
just over two weeks now. Dear Isobel—she's
such a pet and so like George at the same age. I
nearly died of shock when I first saw her!

Christian is having a fine time too. We don't
see her much as she spends all day playing tennis
at the club. Between you and me she has a boyfriend also—a sweet boy named Tommy Miller.
He goes into his senior year September at Thayer
Academy. They're playing in the junior open tournament together—my goodness, Christian is a
strong player! They could even win!

Dearest Liz, rest assured I watch over them
both like a real old mother hen and nothing's
going on that "Auntie Margie" doesn't know.
Don't worry about a thing. Just relax and look
forward to having them home with you before
you know it.

Give all my love to George and a big hug to
Arran. Tell her we hope to see her for sure next
time!

Very, very much love to you too!
Margie

At 2:15 on a blinding hot Saturday afternoon,
Christian and Tommy met Angie Schwartz and Larry
Stevens, reigning champions, in the finals of the junior
open.

The week had been one of mounting excitement for
Christian. Each day had seen another round successfully won; each evening Tommy had bought her a
Coke and a hamburger or a pizza and had delivered
her, flushed with triumph and happiness, back home
before nine o'clock: "Gotta get her beauty sleep, Mrs.
Jennings—in training, ya know. Another big day
tomorrow!"

Last night he had kissed Christian for the first time
and said with confidence, "We're a great team, partner. We're going to knock 'em dead!"

Now, her world shrunk to blinding heat, a red composition court with dazzling white lines, and across the net, the threatening presence of Angie, blonde and muscular and grimly determined, and Larry, six-three, with thighs like tree trunks and a first service like a bullet, Christian knew she was about to make the most monumental fool of herself. She felt as though she would throw up the lunch she had not eaten. Winning this tournament meant such a lot to Tommy; he was depending on her—and she was going to let him down. She knew it. He would be polite—he did have good manners—but he would be cold and angry in his disappointment, and she would want to die. She would crawl away somewhere and kill herself. . . .

Thank heavens Isobel was here, sitting in the front row beside Margie Jennings. Christian didn't dare turn to look at Isobel, but she conjured up her face in her mind, saw those blue eyes, which could radiate the warmth of a summer sky or glint like polished steel. "Go for it," said Isobel's voice. "Don't be so wet. You can do it. You can!"

And thank goodness Stewart was *not* here. Stewart intimidated Christian, and she did not want to make a fool of herself in front of her. She was grateful for the last-minute invitation that had sent Stewart scorching off to Malibu in her little white Alfa Romeo.

A crack like a rifle shot, and Larry's first service hurtled down the center line. Christian automatically bounded into a deep crouch, flexed, swung, and returned the ball hard and deep into Angie's backhand. Angie scrambled her return as Christian loped forward to join Tommy at the net. She caught Angie's shot neatly, aiming a crosscourt volley at Larry's feet. Larry scooped it up on a half volley, which Tommy intercepted and put decisively away. Love, fifteen.

Tommy turned to Christian and flashed her a brief grin. Christian grinned back in surprised delight. Well, maybe she could do it after all!

At 3:15, the sun seemed fixed, motionless in a white-hot sky, immediately over their heads. The boys' shirts hung sodden and dark on their bodies. Angie's shoulders, arms, and forehead glistened with sweat; her straight, blonde hair clung wetly to her scalp. Christian alone looked reasonably fresh and neat, moving tirelessly about the court, well into her stride now, flushed across the cheekbones but otherwise showing few signs of wear. At three games all in the second set, she and Tommy having won the first, all she was aware of was that hot red court and the bright green balls that were smashed to her from the other side of the net and that she must return. . . .

The afternoon wore on. The heat only grew worse.

Angie and Larry won the second set six games to four, and the match went into the third and final set at 3:45 P.M.

The sun seemed as fixed in the sky as ever. The crowd was thinning; one by one the spectators had moved into the shade or sought refuge in the air-conditioned clubhouse. Plump Margie, loyally keeping her seat in the almost empty front row, fanned her perspiring crimson face with a paper napkin and sent the waiters running regularly for iced drinks. Beside her, Isobel leaned rigidly forward, hands gripping the edges of her chair.

Christian felt herself weakening. Her shots were losing their accuracy. Once again she started to panic. She was going to make a fool of herself. She was going to lose the match for Tommy. . . .

But if she was making mistakes, so were Angie and Larry. It was still anybody's match. Even though she and Tommy seemed to have to fight grimly for every point, they were hanging on. And they held on doggedly, agonizingly, until the score was six games all.

A tiebreaker. The final, decisive game, the four of them serving alternately depending on who won the point. Angie would serve first. "I've got to pull myself together," Christian muttered fiercely; "we've got to win." But now she was sure they would lose. Angie and Larry were too determined, and her feet seemed leaden. She could already see Tommy's face, so disappointed in her, so politely dismissive as he said good-bye—forever. She lost the first point. She was off balance for the shot and watched, frozen in dismay, as her ball sailed out beyond the stands. Tommy won the second; she lost the third. Tommy won the fourth; she lost the fifth. It was match point to Angie and Larry.

But Angie double-faulted.

Christian, now breathing hoarsely through her mouth, sickeningly aware of how she had almost thrown away the match, took heart. Perhaps she and Tommy were meant to win after all.

In her mind, Isobel said, "You stupid twit, watch what you're doing!" Christian mentally squared her shoulders.

Angie's first service flew powerfully over the net; Christian smacked it on the rise, hard down the center line. Larry retrieved; there was a short and violent exchange between Larry and Tommy; then back to Christian, who swatted the ball in a high lob over Larry's head so that it landed out of reach in the far corner.

Deuce. Tommy grinned and gave her a thumbs-up sign.

Christian to serve. Please God, make it a decent one, she prayed.

And it *was* a very decent serve. Angie hit it in the net.

Another match point—this time to Christian and Tommy.

Christian serving again. Oh God, please let me not double-fault. Not *now*!

And she didn't. Her first service was in hard and clean. Larry swiped it directly back to Christian, who returned it with force, aware the moment the ball left her racket that it was a fraction too low. With doomed resignation, she heard the *crack* as the ball hit the tape, then miserably watched as it rolled along the top of the net—Angie and Larry scrambling desperately— and dropped, softly, miraculously, to the other side. Christian could not believe it.

She and Tommy had won.

Oh God—they had won. . . .

Tommy crushed her in a hot, wet embrace. Christian's knees suddenly felt like limp spaghetti, and if Tommy hadn't been holding her up, she would have slid to the ground. She could feel her legs tremble as she walked to the net to shake hands. The overheated blood roared in her ears; she could only vaguely hear people cheering, and Isobel's voice, close by, saying, "You were wonderful, Chris! Chris, I'm so proud! You *will* win Wimbledon! You'll show 'em!"

Then Tommy's arm was around her again. He kissed her wildly, on her ear, her nose, her shaking lips.

The club president was congratulating them. There was to be a party later—dinner, dancing, and an awards presentation.

"You clever dears!" cried Margie.

"Fantastic, Chris!" beamed Isobel, hugging her.

"Wow," crowed Tommy, "are we ever going to party tonight!"

Tommy picked Christian up at the Jenningses' house at six-thirty, driving the black Mercedes convertible, lushly upholstered in scarlet leather, that his mother had given him for his birthday. Now that he had won the tournament, he hoped she would follow through on the Porsche Targo she had promised, for he had decided the Mercedes was a little too staid to suit his image.

"Have a great evening, kids," Margie smiled, congratulating herself. What a wonderful time Christian was having, and what a nice, wholesome, well-mannered boy young Miller had turned out to be.

Tommy took Christian possessively by the elbow to lead her into the clubhouse. Christian was very aware of his presence. She could smell the clean smell of baby powder, shampoo, and after-shave and feel the warmth radiating from his body. He wore skin-tight white jeans and a loose white-cotton lawn shirt, half unbuttoned over his broad, tanned chest. She thought he looked magnificent.

What a wonderful day it had been, and it was end-

ing with the most thrilling evening of her life. She had
dressed carefully under Isobel's eagle eye. She wore
Iso's new dress from the Courrèges boutique on Rodeo Drive—a black, space-age creation, all zippers
and pockets, and Isobel had put makeup on her for
the first time, quelling all Christian's nervous objec-
tions. She had thinned Christian's heavy, almost ferocious brows and elongated her dark eyes with brown
eyeliner, while rubbing purple shadow into the crease
of the lids.

"There," Isobel had said with satisfaction, "you look
super. Quite exotic. Egyptian, almost. Where *do* you
get your skin? I'd give anything to tan like you!"

The only sad note for Christian was that Isobel
would not be at the party to see her receive her prize,
for Isobel had a date with Davis tonight. Underneath
all Isobel's sisterly concern that Christian should look
her best had been a current of tension. Obviously the
date with Davis was important.

Christian floated through the evening on clouds of
exhilaration and triumph.

She ate barbecued ribs outdoors on the terrace among
a crowd of admirers, Tommy at her side, forever ready
to fill her plate and glass, fetch her dessert, fulfill
every wish. Christian felt like a princess.

She danced with him to the music of the Beatles,
the Rolling Stones, Jefferson Airplane, and Carlos
Santana. At the prize-giving, with stumbling, confused
thanks, she accepted a little silver-plated statuette and
a gift certificate for one hundred dollars at a place on
Wilshire Boulevard called Stan's Sporting Goods. Christian was overcome with excitement; she had never
expected to see so much money in her life.

Oh, she thought, what a gorgeous night. She was
intoxicated with the excitement, music, good food,
adulation—and always Tommy, charming and handsome at her side. Yes, she guessed she was really and
truly in love with Tommy; she didn't want tonight ever
to end.

The lights dimmed. Tommy drew her into his arms

again on the dance floor, and Christian could now feel that telltale swollen hardness against her lower abdomen. She had felt it last night too, standing beside the Mercedes in the parking lot, when he had kissed her properly for the first time, using his tongue. Then, it had seemed as though lights exploded in her head while warm tingling tides swept through her body.

Now she felt Tommy's lips brush her temple and melted with pleasure as she heard his voice, very softly, whispering in her ear: "Chrissy, I want to be alone with you. Can we get out of here? Go for a drive?"

Oh, how she wanted him to kiss her again. She could kiss him forever. . . .

"Hey," he said impulsively, "we'll go to my house, okay? It'll be cool. . . ." He led Christian down the shadowed pathway to the parking lot, paused briefly, kissed her swiftly on the lips, and murmured: "You've never seen my house. You'll like it."

The crimson sun spread across the western horizon. The sky was darkening behind them. Lights were coming on, burning spectrally through the low-lying smog.

It was still very hot. Isobel had never known what heat was before she came to Los Angeles—solid heat, which enfolded you like a blanket, which you breathed in through mouth and nose. This afternoon at the tennis club, it must have reached the nineties. Here on the beach in Santa Monica, where she sat with Davis over the remains of their picnic supper, it was not much cooler. The sand was still hot to touch. Surfers were still lying on their boards, riding the swells in the gathering dusk.

The picnic had been a broiled chicken, coleslaw, potato salad, french bread, and a six-pack of Coors, all of which Davis unpacked from a Safeway bag and laid out on the blanket. "Nothing fancy," he had said with a grin, "just plain, down-home, summertime American cooking!"

A beach picnic was the obvious choice for such an evening, Isobel had gratefully thought as they drove down the sweltering San Diego Freeway in Davis's old

Buick, the air conditioner of which had long ago failed. What a good idea . . .

But Davis's choice had actually had little to do with the weather. He was obeying an impulse to keep this evening low-key. He did not want to take Isobel to a restaurant, where a lot of strangers would stare at her and intrude on his sense of possession. This evening would mark a milestone in both their lives, and he wished for there to be as few distractions as possible.

As he watched her eat, digging into the picnic food with a hearty appetite, he wondered yet again whether he had gone out of his mind, whether he was making a crazy mistake, picking up a young English tourist at a party and deciding to indulge her in her ambition to be a star.

Then he decided that no, this was not where his craziness lay. There must be thousands of young women in this city who were more beautiful than Isobel and who also wanted to see their names on the marquees of movie theaters, but they would probably fail and Isobel succeed because she was special. Unless he was much mistaken, Isobel would one day be very big box office. Not only had she all the prerequisites—face, figure, and determination—but also, he was sure, she possessed that extra magical ingredient, the elusive X factor impossible to buy or to learn because one either had it or one did not. It had been described variously over the years as sex appeal, charisma, or simply "It."

Star quality.

He looked at her dispassionately as she drank from her beer can, watching the sliding movement of her throat muscles, the slight lifting of those perfect breasts so precisely outlined by her thin black tanktop. Her pretty but still too rounded legs were curled, catlike, beneath her. He estimated Isobel had to shed another seven to ten pounds to look really great on camera, but that was nothing.

Davis decided he was not crazy at all. In fact, what did he have to lose? Nothing. . . .

She turned her head, and her eyes met his. Her lips glistened in the last rays of the dying sun. She grinned and clinked her beer can against his. "Cheers, partner!"

. . . And everything. He had allowed himself to fall in love with Isobel, knowing perfectly well that for her he was merely a resource, the first rung on the ladder to success, that she did not love him, although she would need him for a while.

He allowed himself one bleak glimpse of his future, deciding he could write the scenario himself. He would train Isobel, promote her, package her, and launch her, and she would take off like a rocket to be a star among stars, making him, incidentally, extremely rich in the process. He could taste his success now; and it tasted like Dead Sea fruit in his mouth because he would see Isobel with other men, read about her affairs and romances in the columns, and perhaps even go to her weddings.

He already wanted to kill those other, unknown men.

"Oh *shit!*" said Davis aloud.

"What's wrong?" Isobel asked anxiously.

"Oh nothing, just thinking"—Davis stretched out long legs and kicked at the warm sand with his bare feet—"about what's going to happen to us."

"Yes, me too. I'm so excited I could die." Then, with a chuckle, she said, "Davis, I'm going to make you terribly rich! With ten percent of everything I make, you're going to be a millionaire in no time!"

"Great," said Davis without enthusiasm.

"What's the matter?" demanded Isobel. "Isn't that what you want? Then you can tell your father to shove it, and you can move out of that dirty little office and open something really grand. You can hang pictures of me all round the walls. . . ." She rested her fingertips on his tanned thigh and ran her hand down to his kneecap. Davis felt a quiver of lust inside his groin and wondered how it was possible for someone to be so insensitive. Didn't she know how he felt? Couldn't she guess?

"Yes, Isobel, of course I'm excited," he said in a calm voice, sitting up and clasping his hands in his lap to hide the sudden erection swelling the front of his navy blue shorts.

He opened the last can of beer and drank thirstily.

"Well, then, what's the problem?"

"Problem?" For a split second, Davis almost told Isobel what his problem really was. It was so tempting—but love was not what she wanted, and he suspected he would drive her away if he told her. "Oh, nothing in particular, just details," he said at last. "Boring stuff like what we use for money for your rent and classes. That kind of thing."

"Oh, that—don't worry about it," Isobel said off-handedly. "I'm taking care of it."

"How?" demanded Davis, a breath of premonitory jealousy crawling in his belly. "How're you getting money? Who's giving it to you?"

"Never you mind," said Isobel. "I'm working on it."

"I can't help you out at all with money," Davis had said during one of their long, preliminary phone calls. "You're going to have to take care of it somehow. I know you can't get anything from home. It's tough, I know, but if you really want it that much. . . ."

"Don't worry," Isobel had said, then as now. "It's being taken care of. I'll surprise you."

But no, he would not be surprised. Somehow, Isobel would find someone to stake her. Davis had no doubt that Isobel could do anything. His part would be purely mechanical—lining up dance, voice, and drama coaches; scheduling photography sessions and test shots; arranging for Isobel to be seen, appropriately dressed, by the right people in the right places. They had decided together on her new name—Isobel Wynne. It had a good, upbeat sound to it. And for the marketing—something with class and simplicity. Using the English angle, probably. None of the sexy, wet T-shirt stuff. Isobel must be known as an actress, a personality, and a star—but never, spectacular though they might be, as just another pair of tits.

He would have to find her an apartment, too. She could not continue to stay with the Jenningses.

"Stewart's getting suspicious," Isobel had said uneasily. "She must know something's going on."

"Does that matter?"

"Of course. She'll be angry. She loves you."

Davis sighed. "I've never given Stewart any reason to think I'm in love with *her*. Anyway, she'll be going away to school in a couple of weeks. What can she do?"

"She could do plenty if she finds out too soon. Like talk to her parents . . ."

"Does that make a difference?"

"They could send me back to England tomorrow. Please, Davis, trust me. I don't want Stewart to know anything until it's all arranged. It's important." Because it was to Hall Jennings that Isobel was going for money.

She didn't feel good about it, but what choice did she have? It would have to be Hall. With an instinct as old as Eve, she had recognized the glint in his eye during the past week when he watched her, thinking she did not notice him watch. Yes, he was approachable.

It would not be a sexual approach. She guessed quite rightly that this would shock and repel him. No, she would be entirely businesslike.

Hall Jennings liked good food and good wines. Isobel planned to invite him to lunch at a restaurant he would enjoy, wearing something understated but smart to make him proud to be seen with her. During lunch, she would invite him to invest in her. It must be phrased just right. She was not asking for a loan, but offering an investment opportunity. And he would get his money back, every penny, doubled in spades. She would see to that!

She still didn't like it; it meant going behind Margie's back. It was a betrayal when Margie had been so good to her. And even if Davis didn't care for Stewart, Stewart cared for him and had confided in Isobel. She no longer hated Stewart. She even felt a bit sorry for her.

But damn and shit, thought Isobel, what else can I do? Her own future and that of her sisters hung in the balance. She would do what she had to do.

Isobel tore a drumstick off the chicken carcass with a rending determination that made Davis wince as she chomped the meat between even, very white teeth.

Delicately, she raised the last forkful of coleslaw to her mouth and washed it down with another mouthful of beer. Then, as she had long ago trained herself to do at such times, she put the uncomfortable matter from her mind. She had learned that if one postponed problems long enough, they sometimes resolved themselves.

She sighed, stretched out on the blanket, and closed her eyes.

Davis slowly repacked the paper bag with the debris of their picnic and patted her lightly on her gently rounded stomach. "Had enough?"

"Mmmm. It was wonderful. Just perfect."

"Good." The sky was darkening to purple over their heads. A few stars had appeared. Davis rested his hand on Isobel's stomach a moment longer, feeling the heat of her body, listening to the beat of his own pulse.

Then, for the first time that evening, a dark, deep confidence broke through his mood of introspective gloom.

He reminded himself that Isobel was Stewart's age, just eighteen years old. For all her outward sophistication, she was an inexperienced, naïve young girl, in a foreign country without resources or friends save himself and the Jenningses.

Soon she would be out on her own, except for him. She would need him. She would be vulnerable. And she had barely even had a date, much less a lover, in her life. Davis recalled her hearty appetite for food, suspecting that unfulfilled sensuality and lusty appetites lay elsewhere too. He was not a conceited man, but he knew he was very good in bed. Given such inexperience, such untried virgin material, he could lay his imprint on her indelibly, *make* her not want anybody else. . . .

And what better time to start than now.

Davis stood up and gently nudged her with his foot. "Come on, sleeping beauty, time to hit the freeway."

4

Christian leaned happily back against the red leather seat and watched the stars wheeling across the sky as Tommy took the little car in punishing turns up a steep canyon road. Up, up, and up again until the road leveled out, and they roared at eighty miles per hour along a straight ridge, the lights of Los Angeles unrolling below them like an endless magic carpet.

They drove through majestic gates, then pulled up in front of a long, low, traditional-looking ranch-style building whose massive carved doors might have come from a Spanish colonial cathedral.

"Here we are," Tommy said jauntily. "Home."

"It's lovely," Christian said admiringly.

"Wait'll you see inside! My mother had it absolutely gutted."

He held the huge doors open for her, and Christian stepped through—to stand rooted on the threshold gasping in shock. She had never seen anything like it, never imagined a house like this. It didn't even look like a house, the interior as vast as an aircraft hangar and two stories high.

There was no furniture—at least in the traditional sense—no chairs or sofas, but sunken white carpeted seating areas like moon craters surrounding abstract chunks of metal that presumably acted as coffee tables. Far away on the left was a black-and-white tiled dining area, the table a large, irregular slab of greenish marble suspended by copper wires. Above a massive fireplace on the right glistened a somehow evil-looking oil painting in reds, oranges, and black.

Immediately in front of her, fifteen-foot plate-glass windows overlooked the Los Angeles Basin.

"Oh!" breathed Christian faintly. "Oh my. Oh Tommy . . ."

"It's great, isn't it," Tommy said happily. "None of that traditional shit."

Christian couldn't restrain a small shudder. Iso might like it, but personally she found it cold and frightening. She also felt a trace of vertigo, staring through that huge glass wall into nothing, as though she were hanging in space. It was not a comfortable feeling.

She followed Tommy toward the dining area. "Get the view," he said casually, as though it could possibly be missed, and waved a powerful arm. "And you can see the pool now." Yes, thought Christian nervously, you certainly can. There it was indeed, on the upper deck of the house, cantilevered and immense, a jutting prow shape thrusting out over the edge of the cliff like a ship about to sail over the edge of the world.

"If there was an earthquake and it broke," she began, "the water would—"

"Yeah, I guess," said Tommy, unconcerned, now playing his fingers over a recessed control panel in the wall. "Watch this, now—this is neat. . . ."

As though they were in a theater, the house lights dimmed, while ghostly green illumination rose in a vast, circular fish tank built into the adjacent wall, the fishes' eyes gleaming bulbous and startled. "Piranhas," Tommy said cheerfully. "We feed the little suckers live mice."

"Ugh!" shuddered Christian, while another section of wall slid soundlessly to one side, like moving scenery, to reveal a sparkling, businesslike bar.

"Champagne," Tommy cried. "We need to celebrate!" He rummaged inside the refrigerator and withdrew a bottle of Piper Heidsieck. Then he expertly untwisted the wire, maneuvered the cork out, and filled two crystal flutes without spilling a drop. Christian, still disgusted about the mice, felt a twinge of dismay at his nonchalant skill. It was almost impossible to believe that this callous, oversophisticated young

man was her partner on the tennis court, her darling
Tommy, seventeen years old, just as she was. She
recalled with embarrassment how before arriving here
she had imagined a cozy home with Mr. and Mrs.
Miller sitting in a pretty, chintz living room rather like
the Jenningses' living room, drinking coffee and perhaps reading the papers or watching television. They
would have said something like "Well done, you two—
you certainly played a good match!"

"Where are your parents?" Christian asked.

"Drink up," Tommy said, tipping back his glass.
"Parents?" he said, as though the word were unfamiliar. "Oh, yeah. My stepfather's back East somewhere
on a trip, and Julia's at the Farm."

"Oh," said Christian, "you have a farm? I thought
your father was a—a lawyer or something. Is Julia
your sister?"

"My mother," Tommy corrected absently, pouring
more champagne. "And no, we don't have a farm.
The Farm is a—I guess you'd call it a—a nursing
home. She's a lush. She's gone to dry out."

"I—I see," Christian said faintly. "So we're by ourselves?" She told herself to stop being stupid—this
was Tommy, but he wasn't the Tommy she thought
she had known, and she felt thoroughly uncomfortable
with him.

"Sure we're by ourselves," Tommy said. "All alone.
The servants live out. . . ." He approached her jauntily, caught her around the back of the neck with one
large, strong hand, and drew her against him. "Hey,
loosen up, partner!" He bent his handsome blond
head and kissed her hard on the mouth. It was an
awkward kiss; their noses were jammed together and
Tommy's eyes, too close, distorted and bulging, reminded her of the piranhas.

"Aaaah . . ." He drew away slightly, champagne spilling from his carelessly held glass and slopping down her
dress. He stared into her face. "Oh Chrissy . . ." Then
his mouth was on hers again. His glass fell, and as
it smashed into splinters on the tiles, Christian felt

his teeth cut into her lips, his thick tongue thrust into the soft recesses of her mouth. He dragged her tightly against him again, hurtfully, and she began to struggle.

"Don't fight, darling little Chrissy, don't fight. . . ." Tommy scooped her up in his muscular arms as though she weighed nothing at all and announced thickly: "Hey, house tour!" He sank his teeth playfully but painfully into her neck. "You ain't seen the bedrooms yet."

This was not how it was supposed to be. Christian, Arran, and Isobel had endlessly discussed what really happened when one lost one's virginity. They had read books, talked to friends, and even tried to ask Mother what it was like.

"Of course it will hurt a bit," Isobel said practically, but with a caring lover the hurt would be negligible, and they all looked forward to a tender, romantic experience.

Now, facing the actual moment, Christian felt trapped, frightened, and revolted. On his own home territory, Tommy was no longer the charming, well-mannered boy of the tennis club but an arrogant bully. He wouldn't take no for an answer. And there was nobody to help.

They were in Tommy's parents' bedroom. "Neat, huh?" he said. "Julia's into a jungle phase."

The carpet was brilliant green. The bed was the biggest Christian had ever seen and was heaped with exotic animal skins. A jungle mural occupied one entire wall—vast trees, livid, knife-bladed grasses, carnivorous-looking flowers with sinuous, fleshy petals and wide throats that looked as though they demanded live creatures for breakfast. Through the tangle of lurid vegetation, she could glimpse peering yellow eyes, the undulating scales of a monster snake, the striped hindquarters of a tiger, and a hairy tarantula the size of a puppy. Live plants, almost as obscenely luxurious as those in the mural, twined and twisted around the rest of the room.

The ceiling was painted black.

With a flick of the wrist, Tommy readjusted the lighting, and then the room was dark, the ceiling an overwhelming night sky filled with impossibly huge stars and a bulging, bloodshot tropical moon. The sounds of crickets rose in crescendo, punctuated by the whoops and wails of monkeys, coughs of leopards, and assorted other nighttime jungle sounds.

"Sexy place," Tommy announced, flinging Christian down on some zebra skins on the bed, then stripping off his jeans and shirt with one lithe movement. He loomed over her naked, all bulging muscle.

Christian stared up at him speechlessly, her mind numb to anything save the panic rising steadily inside her.

Trapped! She couldn't get out. Tommy wouldn't let her go. He was going to strip her dress off and throw himself on top of her, and then he was going to ram that—that—Christian hardly dared look at his swollen penis, which glinted threateningly crimson in the lurid light of his mother's artificial moon—that *thing* up inside her.

She couldn't breathe. Her lungs seemed paralyzed. Gasping for air, she croaked, "Tommy, I can't—I can't—I don't *want* to! Not like this—"

"Ah, come on," Tommy said impatiently.

Sweat broke out on Christian's face and back, and in one terrified flash she knew what it would feel like to have that thick, frightful-looking organ tearing through her against her will, but that was only part of it.

Then Tommy was on her, pinning her down on the bed in the jungle darkness. She heard her dress rip, felt his greedy, grasping hands on her breasts, and she couldn't breathe—she was trapped in a dark box with no air and the lid screwed down tight and she had to get away, had to, had to. . . .

In mindless panic, Christian began to fight. She had to get out *now*!

"Chrissy," Tommy gasped, half laughing, "c'mon,

Jesus, partner, what's the *problem?*" Then he gave a
strangled grunt as she hit him wildly in the throat.
"Jesus, *fuck!*"

She twisted violently under him, her knee thrusting
into his tight, engorged testicles. Vaguely, she heard
him scream. She struggled out from under his writhing
body, leaped to her feet, and stared down at him
where she lay retching on the bed.

Then she was away like lightning, her bare feet
soundless on the soft, deep rug. Through the bedroom
door, along a passage, up the stairs, crashing through
the heavy front doors and away down the driveway,
not noticing the sharpness of the gravel cutting her
feet. Out on to the road at last and then running,
running, running through the night . . .

She ran until she couldn't take another step. The
road curved sharply here, steeply downhill to her left.
On her right loomed a high stone wall topped with
broken glass. Into this wall was set a pair of ornate
wrought-iron gates.

Christian collapsed panting into a thick clump of
purple ice plant at the foot of the wall, linked her
hands loosely around her knees, and rocked gently
until she felt the dreadful suffocating fear subside. She
was alone in the dark, and she had no idea where she
was. She had lost her shoes. She had no money and
her dress was torn. But that was all right. Being alone
and lost in the dark did not worry her. She was free.
She could breathe again.

She was not sure how long she sat quite still in the
ice plant, gratefully feeling herself relax. It might have
been ten minutes, or it might have been an hour. But
suddenly she felt the hairs prickle on her neck and a
quite different fright invade her.

She wasn't alone.

In the darkness, someone or something was watching her.

Davis's office was on the top floor of a narrow, old
four-story building that was sandwiched like a poor
relation between two modern, steel-and-glass high rises.

He shared the building with a number of small, marginal businesses, including an organization for famine relief, an Asian import company, and Madame Giorgio, a practicing clairvoyant. There was a faint but pervasive smell in the hallway of Lysol, dust, and urine. The bottom half of the walls was painted the institutional green of certain public lavatories, schools, and prisons.

"Welcome to the palace," Davis said, lifting his eyebrows ironically, as he ushered Isobel out of the shuddering elevator and held open a scabrous door whose frosted glass panel announced WHITTAKER TALENT AGENCY in fresh black paint.

"It's lovely," Isobel said wryly, taking in the battered steel desk, the sagging swivel chair behind it, and the two beige Naugahyde armchairs for clients, placed side by side against the wall.

"The inner sanctum is even more exotic," Davis told her, showing her a room not much larger than a closet, containing a folding cot, a pile of books, two telephones, a very small utility sink, and a tiny alcove with a cord strung across it for hanging clothes.

"I'm not supposed to be living on the premises," Davis explained, "so you must excuse the temporary look. Come on in." He ushered her inside and nudged the door closed with his foot.

Isobel found herself staring with fascination at the narrow little cot. It looked flimsy for what she knew was shortly to take place upon it. Although nothing had actually been said, Isobel knew what would be expected of her. Now was the time to seal their bargain . . . but like this? . . . in such a hot, ugly little room . . . on *that*? It was hardly the romantic deflowering about which she had fantasized.

"Well, Isobel Winter," Davis said, turning to face her, "do we have a deal?" He rested his index finger under her chin and raised her face to his. "Are you going for the big time? Are you going to put yourself in my hands?"

On his own turf, Davis seemed tougher, more confident, almost jaunty, and Isobel, who had begun to dismiss him as easy to manipulate, felt the stirrings of reappraisal. Also, in this ridiculously small room, he looked bigger and taller than he had on the beach, and his shoulder blades rested firmly against the panels of the closed door. She could even feel slightly afraid of him, and her breath came a little faster. . . .

His hands hung loosely at his sides. He had long-fingered, strong-looking hands. Isobel imagined what they would feel like, any moment now, against her bare skin, what they would do, and then trembled slightly, uncontrollably agitated.

She wet her dry lips with her tongue. "Yes, Davis," she said firmly, "we have a deal."

"Good," Davis said and slowly reached out his hand, but not to shake hands. He touched her breasts, the span of his fingers wide enough to touch both her nipples at once; then his hand traveled with deliberate slowness across her ribs, down her abdomen, to come to rest, a gentle, warm but insistent pressure, against her already damp groin.

He dropped his hand. There was silence. Isobel found she was holding her breath. Then he nodded casually. "All right, Isobel—take off your clothes."

Obediently, her fingers unnaturally stiff and clumsy, Isobel shrugged out of her tanktop and brief white shorts. She touched her breasts nervously; they felt cold and hot at the same time, hard and heavy. Davis glanced at her breasts almost casually, then in one swift movement half-knelt and ran his tongue across her erect nipples, a slick, warm caress against her hot and cold skin, and Isobel felt the tension building unbearably in her body.

"Oh, Isobel," Davis said softly, "we're going to do some great things together. . . ."

The stark overhead light glared down on their heads. No, Isobel thought once more, with a twinge of nostalgia for her fantasy, this was not how she had envisioned the Great Moment—losing her virginity in a squalid, stifling little cubbyhole on a rollaway bed in a fourth-rate office building where the only window overlooked an air shaft. Where was the champagne, the moonlight, the satin sheets, and the gentle, romantic lover? But this was the way it was going to be, here and now with Davis. It was business. With a twinge of self-congratulation, she thought she must now be a real woman of the world.

Methodically, he stripped off his own clothes and tossed them casually into the corner under his row of pre-Vietnam, New England suits, bought when he still had money to spend on suits and which were now all too narrow in the chest and shoulders.

Isobel crouched naked on the cot while Davis undressed, feeling shy, intimidated, and even ashamed of the voluptuousness of her body. She asked almost timidly, "Could you turn the light out?" It was so harsh, everything so uncompromisingly detailed, Davis's naked body too blatantly masculine and hairy. A mat of glossy black hair covered his wide chest, trailed down over his lean, hard-muscled abdomen, and erupted in the thick hair of his groin.

He did not answer. He knelt down on the narrow bed, which creaked alarmingly under his weight, knees touching Isobel's, his penis lying fatly along his thighs. He kissed her for the first time, and Isobel forgot about the light. She forgot about everything.

Davis's kiss was long, deep, and very practiced, his hands teasing her nipples as his tongue fought with hers. He reached far up between her legs, his fingers stroking the downy base of her spine. Then he drew his hand slowly, slowly down the silky cleft of her buttocks and gently but firmly separated the moist, swollen folds of her vagina.

He took his mouth away from hers. "You *are* a virgin."

"Yes."

"You know how I want you?"

"Yes."

"Are you *sure*?"

"Yes. Oh Davis, for God's sake—" His hand, wet with her, was back on her breast, her nipple held lightly between his thumb and index finger. Her breast now felt impossibly tender, and her whole body ached with need of him. "Davis, please."

"All right, then," Davis breathed, "all *right* . . ."

"But the light?" Isobel whispered into his neck. "Please, turn it off."

"No," Davis said with finality. "The light stays on."

He was a dark silhouette above her, edged with brilliant fluorescence. Damn him, thought Isobel furiously as he began to enter her. She struggled automatically against the stretching discomfort that soon became pain. Davis moved one arm and pinned both her wrists behind her head. Isobel bit her lip and arched her body against his. "Relax," Davis said gently, "for God's sake, don't fight me now."

She refused to cry out. She wouldn't. Nothing would make her cry out, not with him watching her—but then she realized that the pain, intense as it had been, was suddenly gone. She opened her eyes wide in surprise. She wasn't a virgin anymore. Davis had released her hands, and he was kissing her and stroking the hair back from her sweaty forehead. She could feel his length and hardness up inside her body, and it was all as good and as exciting as she had guessed it would be.

But it was over far too soon.

After a final punishing, thrusting spasm, and a gasping cry, Davis sprawled limply on top of her, his eyes closed, his thick lashes wet, his hands compulsively caressing her breasts and shoulders. "Oh, Isobel, oh, Isobel, my love . . ."

Then his hands lay still, his face rested quietly against her hair, and he appeared to be asleep.

Isobel lay still, enfolded in his heavy arms, feeling hot, sticky, and increasingly numb, but also proud of herself. She had done well. Now she was back in control. She had Davis's measure all right. She had seen him spent and vulnerable, and he would never intimidate her again.

She shook his shoulder gently. "Davis? Okay if I take a shower now? It's probably time I went home."

He roused at once.

His eyelids flew open. He propped himself on one elbow and looked at her, the corners of his mouth curving into a lazy smile.

"A shower? Go home? But oh my darling star, did you think the show was over?" He touched his forefinger to the cleft in her chin and his hooded amber eyes gleamed. "It's only just begun. . . ."

5

She wasn't alone.

Someone was watching her.

Christian turned very slowly, unable to hear anything save the exaggerated creaking of her neck muscles and the betraying thunder of the blood in her veins.

What was it? Who? Had she imagined that furtive, shifting rustle?

She peered around her, her eyes raking the stretch of glass-topped wall to her immediate right, the tall iron gates guarding the darkness of the driveway beyond, the moonlit road curving abruptly away downhill, the steep hillside falling below her. Was that a dark shape, creeping soundlessly from bush to bush? Did it move, or was it her imagination? Surely on such a steep stony slope nothing could move without rattling pebbles and clawing noisily at shrubbery.

Christian strained her ears, but all she could hear, far below, was the muted drone of a powerful car, the sound rising and fading as the car traversed the steep hairpin bends.

Christian had decided she had imagined the whole thing when—there it was again: a sliding rustle, accompanied by a faint sigh.

Her hair prickled on the nape of her neck, and she rose from the ice plant into a half-crouch, prepared to run.

Then she saw, with a sickening shiver of fright, that the great iron gates were swinging soundlessly open. Whatever was behind them would now come after her. . . .

Her breath caught in her throat. She leaped out into the road, then reeled backward, blinded by the sudden sweeping glare of gigantic headlights.

The car came to an abrupt halt in front of her, the engine idling in an expensive, rumbling purr. From behind the lights, a faintly amused male voice asked: "Good God! What have we here?"

He might well have asked. Christian looked wild, one hand thrust forward, warding off danger, the other thrown up to protect her dazzled eyes. She might have been a gypsy, barefoot and tousled in her brief, torn dress.

The lights dimmed, but Christian could still see nothing but swimming green blotches. Helpless, she heard the heavy thud of a door and light footsteps approaching. She shrank back in fear.

"Don't be scared," the still invisible stranger said in a soft voice in which Christian sensed an undertone of threat. "I didn't mean to frighten you. But would you mind telling me just who you are and what you're doing sitting outside my house in the dark?"

"I—" began Christian, and she licked her dry lips, unable to speak. She felt the pressure of pent-up tears behind her eyes. "I—I'm sorry. I wasn't doing anything."

"I'm delighted to hear it," said the stranger, who, now that her sight was returning, appeared to be a pale-haired, slender man of medium height, wearing formal evening clothes. He held something casually in his right hand, a hard-edged metal object that glinted dully in the muted light. With a numb lack of surprise, drained of emotion, she realized it was a gun.

She began to explain, "I was running away. . . ."

"Really?" He gestured with the barrel toward his car—now clearly visible to Christian as a massive, vintage Rolls-Royce— "Well, obviously you can't run any farther. You've hurt your feet, you know." He shifted the gun to his other hand, beckoned to Christian, and held the passenger door open for her. "Get in, my dear." Wearily, Christian obeyed. "And what's your name"

"Christian. Christian Winter."

"Very pretty, too. Judging from your accent, you must be British." The stranger's voice also held the trace of an accent. He was almost certainly not American.

"Yes."

"How intriguing." He climbed into the car beside her. She heard him whistle a weird two-note call between his teeth. Then he opened the glove compartment and, to her relief, put the gun away.

Christian asked nervously, "Was it loaded?"

"Of course," he said. "Whatever's the use of an unloaded gun? But I don't need it anymore, now."

He switched the headlights back to high. And there, a massive sentinel between the high gateposts, black on black save for the gleaming reflections on smooth musculature, stood a giant Doberman.

Christian shivered. "Oh! *That* was it. I knew something was there, watching me. I was so frightened. . . ."

"No need," the man said comfortingly, "unless you'd tried to break in. Then Hansel would have overpowered you and held you until I came back. But he's an excessively polite and well-trained dog. He wouldn't have hurt you. He would simply have waited for me to tell him what to do. Then he would have released you. Or," he added matter-of-factly, "killed you, of course, if I thought you dangerous enough."

In the brilliant sweep of the headlights, Christian watched the powerful rhythm of Hansel's steely haunches as he bounded ahead of them. She cast a terrified glance at the calm profile beside her and said in a small voice, "But I'm not dangerous."

Her companion shrugged. "The sweet, pretty young things who murdered so brutally for Charles Manson last year didn't look dangerous either. Close by, too— not more than a mile away. So one carries a gun now and employs these ludicrously elaborate security precautions. Such a pity—" he sighed. "But it's the way the world turns."

They drew up at the brightly lit entrance of a Georgian-style, white stone house. The front door opened, as if on cue. A male figure wearing black trousers and a white jacket stepped out onto the porch.

Her new companion ushered Christian out of the Rolls, took her lightly but firmly by the arm, and led her up the front steps. Hansel trotted unnervingly close by on her other side, almost bumping her hip.

"Good evening, sir," said the manservant.

"Good evening, Pierre." And to Christian he said, "Come on in, my dear."

Hansel stopped short of the front door; at another whistled command, he wheeled around, and Christian caught a last glimpse of steel-sprung black haunches as he bounded away into the darkness. "Hansel stays outside, you might be glad to know, doing his job. Now then, Pierre, I have a guest, as you see. Would you please bring brandy, my medical kit, and some warm water to the small study. And don't bother to put away the car. I'll be needing it later."

"Yes, sir." The manservant bowed slightly from the waist and vanished soundlessly into the nether regions of the house.

"And now, my dear"—the stranger leaned forward and swept Christian up into his arms, deceptively strong arms for so slightly built a man—"please don't think me forward, but that is a silk Bokhara you're bleeding on." For the second time that night, Christian found herself carried off by a man, but this time she was not afraid. Amazingly, she was able to appreciate the beauty of the hall, furnished even to her uneducated eye with enormous taste and imagination with European antiques and lovely old rugs.

He carried her down a short passage, through a door, and into a small, comfortable room lined with bookshelves.

"There." He dropped Christian neatly into the depths of a huge, maroon leather armchair and drew up a matching ottoman for her feet. He stood beside her, watching her quizzically. "In just a moment, you can tell me who you were running from and why. I have to admit you're quite the most intriguing thing to happen to me in a long time, and I'm very grateful. I was at the most exceptionally boring party tonight."

Christian looked up at him curiously, wondering why, after the initial shock of their meeting, she had not been afraid of him despite the gun, the terrifying Hansel, and her virtual kidnapping. However she now felt quite unthreatened, whereas an hour or so ago with Tommy she—once again she tasted the remnant of that fear and shuddered.

Perhaps it was because this man had told Pierre not to put the car away. Perhaps it was because he was old. . . .

Despite his lithe figure and young man's strength, he was at least sixty. Christian studied the immaculate black dinner jacket, white starched shirtfront, and black bow tie, then moved upward to the chiseled face, narrow-bridged, slightly hooked nose, and thick silver hair. There were deep laugh lines around his eyes. He exuded comfort, well-being, and security. For a second, Christian found herself wishing she could have had a father like this man. She never noticed that his eyes were watchful, the very pale blue of a winter sky reflected on ice.

"How rude of me, my dear," he was saying now. "I know your name and you don't know mine. I am Ernest Wexler. You are most welcome to my home. I propose to do something about your poor feet, give you a brandy—you still look quite shaken, you know, and a brandy will do you lots of good—and then drive you to wherever you would like to go. You may of course stay here if you wish, but you are a very young, beautiful girl, and I imagine that whoever is in charge of your well-being will be anxious. Ah, Pierre, thank you. On the table, if you please, and hand me the bowl."

With poker-faced aplomb, as though this were a routine affair, Pierre placed on the table a silver tray bearing two delicate Baccarat brandy snifters, a bottle of Courvoisier, scissors, Band-Aids, a bottle of Mercurochrome, and some gauze. With a juggler's skill, he also produced a yellow plastic bowl half-filled with warm water, which he handed to his employer.

Wexler set to work. "Very obviously," he remarked, after Pierre had bowed, withdrawn, and closed the study door behind him, "judging by the state of your rather attractive dress—Courrèges, is it not?—and your general condition, you have had a bad tussle with some assailant—your boyfriend?—and you ran away over gravel." He studied her dirty, bleeding feet and expertly dabbed at them with cotton. "It is unfortunately embedded, you know. Now, this will sting a little. There—sorry—can't be helped . . ."

Christian winced as the Mercurochrome touched her cuts, then relaxed as Wexler's delicate, clever fingers applied gauze pads and Band-Aids. "There," he said after a while, with satisfaction, "you'll be quite all right now, but you'll have to stay off your feet for a day or two. No running around the countryside anymore." He poured a small amount of brandy into one of the snifters and handed it to her. "Now, you'll feel much better with a drop of this inside you." He raised his own glass in a toast. "To you, my dear. To the gold at the end of the rainbow. Sip carefully.".

Christian felt the brandy explode marvelously in her stomach while the fumes coiled hotly and sinuously in her head. "Mr. Wexler," she said timidly, "thank you very much for being so nice to me. I don't want to be a nuisance."

Wexler smiled at her and said courteously, "It's my pleasure. Now that we're comfortable, I'd appreciate knowing a little more about you. Who, for instance, is this tedious young man—I am right, am I not?—who's made such trouble for you? I imagine he must be a neighbor of mine."

"I suppose so," Christian agreed. "I probably didn't run all that far, really. He's named Tommy Miller. He's my age. Seventeen."

"He isn't by any chance the blond-haired young lunatic who drives the black Mercedes?"

Christian nodded. "Yes, he—"

"In that case," Wexler said with grim satisfaction,

"he probably won't be around very much longer to bother people." He raised his glass, swirled the cognac inside with great care and regard, bent his elegant head, inhaled, sipped, sighed with pleasure, and put the glass down. "How are you feeling now, my dear? Better?"

"Oh yes, thank you."

"I met his mother once," Wexler reminisced with some distaste. "Dreadful woman. She used to be a nail model. She has married often and increasingly advantageously. What in the world were you doing with young Miller? We'll start there, and work back. . . ."

"I thought he was nice," Christian said. "He was awfully kind to me, at first. I met him at a party where I'm staying. We played tennis together, and we were in a tournament this afternoon. . . ." Only this afternoon, yet it seemed like years ago. "We won. But afterward. . . ." The memories flooded back. Images of a crystal champagne glass smashed on black-and-white tile. Tommy's mother's awful bedroom. Herself struggling with Tommy on the bed, then running through that house in the dark. And then—"Oh, Mr. Wexler, I"—the tears suddenly flooded from Christian's eyes as she remembered more. "Oh, Mr. *Wexler*." She gave a small cry of distress.

"Oh my dear!" He leaned forward anxiously and gathered up her hands in his. "Was it so very bad? My dear, tell me. That wretched boy should be shot. Better yet, *castrated*!"

Christian gulped and shuddered, and her tears splashed down onto their clasped hands. "No, no, it wasn't—I mean, we won the *match*!" She moaned through her sobs. "We won!"

Wexler smoothed the tumbled hair from her hot forehead. "So you said, which was very clever of you. But—"

"But I won a prize! I—" She took a deep, shuddering breath, remembering her little purse lying there on that huge, cold dining room table, which reminded her now of a grass-stained tombstone.

Wexler hurriedly poured more brandy. Christian took

a large slurp and choked. He patted her on the back. "There, there. Now then, try again. You won . . ."

"A—a lovely little silver trophy. And a—a gift certificate for Stan's Sporting Goods. For a hundred *dollars*! I've *never* had that much money," wailed Christian. "And I left it in his house and now I can't go back there and get it, not ever!"

Wexler sat back on his heels and eyed her impassively; then he began to laugh. He was obviously extremely amused. "Oh my," he said, as Christian snuffled her way back into a semblance of control, "how pleasant if all our problems could be so easily solved!"

Solved? She blinked at him with swollen eyes, not daring to hope. "You mean you might be able to get it back for me?"

Wexler regarded her with a wry smile. "Certainly I can. You'll have it tomorrow."

"Oh, Mr. Wexler! If you knew how much it meant to me!"

"Think nothing of it, my dear. I assure you it will be my pleasure." He smiled again, and his eyes, for a second unguarded, glittered coldly.

Although she was not sure why, Christian almost found herself feeling sorry for Tommy Miller.

Isobel climbed the stairs very slowly. She had never felt so tired in her life. There was not a muscle in her body that did not ache. She was like an exhausted animal fleeing for the safety of its own burrow in which to recuperate and marshal its strength.

She hoped that Christian was not awake and waiting to tell her all about her evening with Tommy. Right now, Isobel couldn't take it. Please God, she prayed, let Christian be asleep. Then she, Isobel, could be alone in her clean, cool bed. She could close her eyes and forget everything until tomorrow. But it was no good. Unwillingly, once again, Isobel remembered it all.

The second time, Davis had set out deliberately to arouse her. His searching hands had been everywhere on her body, probing, unfolding, doing things Isobel had never dreamed of and from which she initially shrank until Davis overcame her prudishness and she writhed against his hands, hot and eager and slick with sweat. He had parted her thighs and kissed her where he had hurt her, his tongue reaching deep inside her until Isobel found herself moaning his name, gripping convulsively at his hair, and thrusting herself up against his mouth. Afterward, he had wanted her to do the same for him. And while she hesitatingly complied, he had played with her body so tantalizingly that, almost against her will, she had come again herself.

Isobel blushed hotly in the darkness. She felt overwrought and overwhelmed. She didn't understand her feelings. She was now struggling with a whole new range of emotion, as though she had been turned loose in a bizarre new landscape without a map. She felt raw inside and wanted to cry. Too much had happened to her too quickly. She did not *want* to feel sensual, tender, and soft inside, with this unexpected urge to give herself. She did not want any of it. Such emotions were infinitely threatening and would undermine what she had set out to do, although the part of her that had never been loved wanted it all so much. . . .

Isobel felt torn in shreds. She told herself it was useless trying to understand it now. At least she could sleep knowing she was now a client of the Whittaker Talent Agency. It was what she wanted, what she had worked for. She was on her way at last, and love was a luxury that would have to wait. In any case, her life had not been so sheltered that she had never heard of the casting couch. Isobel reminded herself coolly that what had happened tonight happened all the time in Hollywood. She must not make such a big deal out of it. To Davis Whittaker, she was just another pretty girl whom he would screw and then promote and who might make him some money if he was lucky. To him, tonight meant nothing but the confirmation of a business deal.

For herself, she must start planning how to raise the money she needed. But not tonight. She would work on that first thing in the morning.

She padded down the passage on leaden feet, noting the line of light under her bedroom door. Oh no, Isobel thought wearily, Chris is awake.

She opened the door.

But Christian was not there.

"All right, you bitch," Stewart said, staring up at her with hard, hot eyes, "what the fuck have you been doing with Davis?"

Isobel blinked in shock. She stood in the doorway, staring at Stewart, who ought to have been at the overnight beach party in Malibu. "What are you doing home? Where's Christian?"

Stewart ignored her. "That was Davis's car outside. I saw you. Where've you been? You weren't at the club. I went there and they said you'd left right after the finals, around five."

"Yes, I suppose—" Isobel shook her head wearily. "Stewart, I'm awfully tired. Could we talk about it tomorrow?"

Stewart stood up. Her eyes glinted menacingly. "You seem to have forgotten that Davis is *mine*, that *I* want him, and that this is *my* house."

"All right," Isobel said soothingly. "Listen, I'll tell you—we went to the beach for a while to cool off—a whole bunch of us—and then we went to—to a party. Somewhere in the hills. Davis gave me a ride home."

Stewart looked her up and down cynically. "Sure."

Oh God, Isobel thought, did it show? Could Stewart somehow tell what she'd been doing? Hurriedly, she wondered whether she had overlooked some telltale trace. Of course, she had been unable to take a shower. Davis used a fetid little bathroom with crumbling tile at the end of the hall. Unfortunately, the inadequate light from the naked bulb had been adequate enough to reveal a skittering cluster of cockroaches. Isobel had closed the door again with a small shriek of disgust and been forced to wash herself as well as possible in Davis's little sink. She had done her best, and she had combed her hair very carefully. Surely nothing showed. But—

"You've been doing it," Stewart cried with certainty. "You have! You fucking bitch—you *know* I love him! I told you myself, and you go sneaking after him behind my back."

"Stewart, stop it. Stop it right now. You hear me? I wasn't—"

"No? Then turn around. Go on, turn around." Stewart took Isobel roughly by the arm. "Look. Look at yourself."

"What?" Isobel stared at herself in the full-length mirror, seeing with dismay the red spot on her white shorts. "Well, so what? I just got my—"

"You finished a week ago," crowed Stewart. "I *know*. You were a virgin after all, but you aren't any longer. You were with Davis all night. You can't con me. Know how else I know?"

Isobel stared at her, frozen with horror. Stewart went on: "You *smell* of it! Didn't you know sex smells?"

"Shut up!" Isobel said tightly. She was starting to feel sick. Her knees began to tremble and she sat down heavily on the bed.

"You bitch," Stewart said, "screwing me up, going after what isn't yours. I want you out of this house. I hate you. You can't do this to me. I hate you, do you hear? I'm going to talk to my father and have you sent back to England . . . tomorrow!"

Part Three

1

Christian leaned her head forlornly against the window, chin propped in her hand, gazing down at the roiling tops of thunderheads.

She was somewhere over the Kansas prairies at thirty-six thousand feet. Alone at last, she was able to think for the first time in two days, although she did not want to have to think very much, because soon she would have to worry about explaining to Father.

Why she was back ten days early. Why Isobel was not with her . . .

"Chris, I'm staying." Isobel had looked pale and determined, a defiant glint in her eye. "Davis is going to be my agent. He's starting me with a voice coach right after Labor Day. Isn't it great? It's really going to happen, and I'd been so scared it never would. . . . I'm not going back with you, Chris."

So Christian would have to break the news by herself.

Oh, God.

She closed her eyes, and at once the kaleidoscope of the last two days flickered wildly through her tired brain.

She slept late the morning after the tennis tournament, waking to find the house empty except for herself and Margie.

Hall Jennings had left early for his usual Sunday morning golf game. Strangely, Isobel had gone with him.

Christian knew Isobel did not know how to play golf. . . .

"And Stewart was so *angry*," Margie said worriedly.

"She wanted to see Hall before Isobel did. Christian, dear, whatever has happened? I've never seen Stewart so furious. She went driving off in an absolute frenzy." She clasped plump hands together in distraction. "I do hope she doesn't do anything silly. She was driving so fast."

Christian did not know what to say. How could she? "Gosh, Aunt Margie, I don't know. Iso was asleep when I came home. I haven't seen her today at all."

She waited anxiously all morning, but Isobel did not return.

At noon, Mr. Wexler drove in through the gates, presented Christian with two dozen yellow roses and a package containing her purse and her trophy, then swept her into the Rolls and off to lunch just as she was, in shorts, unlaced sneakers, and oxford shirt with the tail hanging out.

"But I can't come like this," Christian had cried.

"Why not?" Wexler had asked blandly, pulling up outside the Caprice on Beverly Drive, his Rolls just one of a lineup of automobiles the value of which, together, would account for the national debt of the average Central American country. A white-jacketed valet had driven the Rolls away somewhere; Wexler took Christian by the arm and led her into an airy establishment of white wicker, green tablecloths, white napkins, fragrant smells, flowers, and obsequiously bowing waiters.

Wexler was so supremely confident that his place in the world was right up there at the top that his easy confidence was transferred to Christian. She held her head high, limping slightly as she passed between the banked arrangements of orchids and all the staring people.

Lunch was delicious, and, to her total surprise, Christian found herself telling Mr. Wexler all about herself. He didn't seem to be bored at all. She told him about Father and Mother and about how it was at home, about Isobel and Arran, even about how she dreaded having to go to the technical college in the fall to take a business course so she could be a secretary. "I'm not like Isobel and Arran. I don't know what else to do, you see. I'm not very bright."

"That's entirely your opinion," Wexler said dismissively, "and a most inexperienced one at that."

"But everyone says so."

"Then everyone," he said calmly, "is foolish. As you will prove soon enough."

Christian hadn't believed him, of course, but it was good hearing it, and she basked in the warmth of his approval.

After lunch, they went to Stan's Sporting Goods and chose a racket and a new tennis outfit. In addition, Mr. Wexler bought her a navy blue velour warm-up suit with white piping down the sleeves. She had tried to say no, but somehow one didn't say no to Mr. Wexler.

However, she suspected that the most valuable present he had given her was the small engraved card that she carried in her purse:

ERNEST HENRY WEXLER, ESQ.
Le Clermont
Avenue Hector Otto
Monte Carto

Below this address were printed three phone numbers in different countries. He had circled the one in London.

"I'll be in London in early February next year," he told her. "I expect I'll stay several months. If you would like, give me a call. I'd enjoy hearing from you."

Christian couldn't help but wonder why he was being so nice to her, dull Christian, whose only claim to fame was winning a tennis tournament. She didn't understand, but such attention was so exciting and flattering that she reveled in it moment by moment.

Margie had seemed suspicious. She had been full of anxious questions.

Who *was* this man, who looked like an elderly Paul Newman? How was it possible that Christian had met him? Surely she hadn't met him at the tennis club party. Why had he taken her to lunch? And whatever had happened to poor Tommy Miller? Julia had just called, back from the health farm a day early. Tommy's room had been disordered, clothes scattered in feverish abandon, his car gone, deep ruts in the gravel driveway. No message. Christian had been the last to see him—what did she know about it? Christian honestly knew nothing. The last time she had seen Tommy Miller, he had been groaning on his mother's bed, clasping his bruised testicles, but she remembered the expression in kind Mr. Wexler's eyes and Mr. Wexler had been to Tommy's house. . . .

Julia had called again, later in the afternoon. Tommy was in Aspen, Colorado, staying with his father, who was vacationing with a new girlfriend. Tommy hated his father, who could hardly, under the circumstances, have been delighted to see his son, either. She wanted to know what the hell was going on.

"I'm sure this Mr. Wexler is nice," Margie had said worriedly, "but I don't like it, Christian."

She had asked around and found out very little about Ernest Wexler, other than that he was a citizen of Monaco, spent part of each year in California, and was extremely wealthy, although nobody knew the source of his money. He reputedly had friends in the highest government circles.

"I feel I must tell your mother, dear. I am responsible, you see, while you're with us."

As it turned out, however, Margie forgot all about it because at that moment, Davis Whittaker drove up, with Isobel beside him. . . .

A stewardess, elegant in the high-collared, sea green uniform of Orient Pacific, offered champagne. Christian accepted, sipped, and reflected that this was the third time she had drunk champagne in the space of three days. She could not help but wonder, staring down into the dark heart of the prairie storm, when she would ever drink it again. With a dismal little pang she wondered, yet again, what would happen now.

Suddenly, the captain's calm voice was warning of

turbulence and politely requesting that those moving about the cabin return to their seats.

Turbulence, thought Christian. That perfectly described the last two days. . . .

"Chris, I'm not going back. Mr. Jennings has said he'll put up the money."

And later, a terrible argument between Stewart and her father in his study. Before the door had fully closed, Christian had clearly heard Stewart screaming, "But you can't *do* this, she's destroyed my *life*!"

Half an hour later, her face set and white with rage, Stewart had slammed out of the house carrying a suitcase, and Christian had heard the violent roar of her car as it tore down the driveway, scattering gravel and mud.

Yesterday, Margie had wandered about the house distractedly redoing already perfect flower arrangements.

Isobel spent the morning packing. She told Margie, "I'm so terribly sorry to be so much trouble. I think it's best if I leave right now, don't you?" Margie had said yes.

Davis Whittaker had picked her up before lunch. Christian had said good-bye to her sister quite calmly. It had all happened too fast for her to take it in properly. Isobel had been far more upset. She had hugged Christian tightly. "I'll get you back here as soon as I can—and Arran too. Oh, Chris, I'm going to miss you. Take care of yourself. . . ." Davis was waiting quietly in the car, eyes hidden behind dark glasses.

Then the hammerblow fell. Christian was to go home at once.

"I'm really sorry, dear, but I think it would be best," Margie had said wanly. "Mr. Jennings will arrange a flight for you tomorrow." She had added with a rueful smile, "You Winter girls are quite a handful, aren't you?"

Christian's ears popped. They were beginning their descent. In fifteen minutes, the captain's voice informed her, they would be landing at Kennedy Airport.

She watched the floor of dark clouds rising toward her; the light grew murky; great sheets of rain smashed against the thick window.

New York. A change of planes now to a London flight. She was halfway to England.

She felt very lonely and frightened going home without Isobel at her side to protect her.

She tried to remind herself that she was a tournament winner who lunched at expensive restaurants with sophisticated men, traveled first-class, and drank champagne, but it did no good.

She felt young, scared, and helpless.

Arran leaned out the window, anxiously waiting for the postman.

Until this summer, she had never bothered to watch for the mail as there was never a letter for her, seldom anything at all save a bill or advertisements, which the postman used to announce with a cheerful *rat-a-tat-tat* on the door knocker until Father had stormed out and shouted at him to shut up and leave them alone.

Now every week there was a letter from Christian, and once even a scrawled postcard of a giant Mickey Mouse from Iso. Arran had heard all about the Jenningses, their home, Stewart, Disneyland, the party—and Davis Whittaker. She devoured each word, filling in the gaps from her own prolific imagination, fleshing out the experiences and all the new people in her sisters' lives until, almost, she might have been there herself. Almost . . .

Arran had bitterly resented not going. She had miserably asked God over and over, how could Father do this to me? She would think of Iso and Chris out there in the world while she was still stuck here in this wretched little house, and it would be all she could do not to cry.

Although crying would do no good.

Father was Father.

Arran sighed. Sometimes she thought she had always known the truth.

"Yer dad's naught but a bluidy loonie," cried Bert

Pullin, the greengrocer's son, so long ago now. When had it been? Where? Liverpool? Manchester? Strange how Arran remembered that little scene. She had been seven, and Isobel ten. Isobel, who loved Father fiercely, was outraged. "You shut up, you little twerp," she had yelled at Bert Pullin, who had laughed at her. "My dad's different 'cause he got wounded in the war. He got shot in the head. He's a *hero.*"

"Bollocks," jeered Bert, who hated Isobel because she was so pretty and would never look at him.

Isobel had burst into furious tears and slapped Bert across his thin, spotty cheeks. "He's got *medals!*" she had yelled at him, as she took Arran firmly by the hand and marched stiffly and proudly away. "*Lots* of them!"

Back at home Isobel had pleaded, "Mother, please, I want to see Father's medals. Show me the medals again." And to Arran she had said, triumphantly, "There, see?" as Arran stared silently at the small strips of colored silk and the tarnished stars, arranged carefully in their battered leather case. The Burma Star. The Distinguished Service Order. "Father and I went to Buckingham Palace," Mother said, her eyes misting, "and the king himself pinned it on Father's chest. It was the proudest moment of my life!"

"There!" cried Isobel. "Don't you listen to that filthy little liar."

But medals or no medals, soon not only Bert Pullin was calling Father a loonie.

The women were talking about it in the shops, about that poor downtrodden Mrs. Winter with those three kids and the barmy husband. It was all so stupid, of course, Isobel would insist in furious loyalty. Father was nothing like poor Mr. Simpkins, a tattered old wreck in a stained mackintosh who thought he was Jesus. Father just got upset and angry and confused and shouted at people.

Very soon afterward, they moved again, to a different city.

8:15 A.M. Any time now. Arran leaned out the window. Father had been bad again, especially since Isobel and Christian had left. There had been sudden tight little silences, uncalled-for rebukes, occasional flares of wild anger. Arran was glad her sisters were coming home soon.

The postman came whistling down the street, delivering the mail, *rat-a-tat-tatting*, but did not stop at their house.

Instead, moments later, the red mail van pulled up outside. Across the street the lace curtains shook slightly. Within the hour, the whole street would know about it and be agog.

Telegram at the Winter house. And a telegram *always* meant bad news.

CHRISTIAN ARRIVING LONDON HEATHROW WEDNES-
DAY AUGUST 19 10 AM PAN AM FLIGHT 235 STOP
ISOBEL NOT REPEAT NOT ACCOMPANYING STOP LETTER
AND DETAILS FOLLOW STOP MARGIE

Catastrophe. Arran thought Father would scream his throat raw with anger. She hid in her room for the rest of the day.

The night was quiet because Mother made him take his pills.

Next morning the house was in chaos again, Father stamping up and downstairs shouting at Mother, who was leaving early for London to meet Christian's plane.

"I won't have it!" he yelled after her. "Do you hear me, Elizabeth? No, I will not!"

The taxi came. Father followed her outside, unshaven, disheveled, and barefoot, his bathrobe flapping. He shouted to the quiet, early morning street, "She's got to come home. I order her to come home. I'm her *Father*!"

Windows slammed shut, others flew open.

An irate voice yelled back, "You belt up, cantcha!"

Arran lay quietly in bed, staring at the ceiling, wondering how she could ever wait for the night, when Christian would tell her what had really happened.

It was late morning. Father brooded and sulked in his

office. To pass the time until Mother and Christian returned, Arran determinedly went to work on her current story. Writing, she managed as usual to put everything else from her mind. She was absorbed until, with a small start, she realized she was no longer alone. Father stood in the doorway watching her. He was a tall man, his unkempt black hair prematurely streaked with gray, his once handsome face loosely fleshed, his eyes confused and lost. His body, unexercised, was thickening rapidly. Father would be fat soon, Arran thought dispassionately.

"Writing again, Arran?" he asked gently in his beautifully cultured voice.

"Yes, Father."

"Might I read some of it?"

"I don't think you'd like it."

"But may I? Just the same?"

Arran shrugged. "Yes, of course."

"And you can read mine. I was writing a lot of poetry, you know. It kept my mind off things. A most pleasant antidote for war. If I hadn't—you know" —Father rubbed vaguely at his head—"I'd have read English at Oxford. I was going to Magdalen College."

"Thank you, Father. Yes, I'd like that," replied Arran, who had frequently had this same conversation with Father and been presented with his collection of poems written in meticulous copperplate script. The pages had been much handled since 1945; the paper was brittle and the ink was turning brown. The poems themselves were unabashedly derivative of Rupert Brooke and Siegfried Sassoon.

Father came into the room and closed the door. Tentatively, he touched her soft hair. "You don't hate me, do you Arran? Because I didn't let you go to America?"

"Of course not," said Arran. It was almost the truth, now that Christian was coming back.

"Do you love me?"

"Of course."

"Would you say it? Out loud? I want to hear you say it."

"I love you, Father."

"And you won't ever leave me? Not like the others?" Father did not wait for an answer, but fell to his knees, buried his face in her lap, and clasped her around the waist. "You're not like them, though," he told her confidently. "Isobel and Christian don't love me at all. They just want to go away. . . ."

At five o'clock, the taxi pulled up outside the house. Arran watched Mother climb out, anxiously scanning the front of the house, chewing on her lips.

Christian followed, a new, extraordinarily sleek Christian, but gray with fright and fatigue under her glowing California tan.

Arran stood beside her sister in the hall while, trembling, Christian handed Isobel's letter to her father.

2

Westwood Village
August 25, 1970

Darling Chris,

I hope it wasn't too dreadful for you, breaking the news. I felt simply terrible leaving you alone to do that—Chris, I'm so *sorry*! There was never even a chance to tell you what was really going on.

It would all have worked out well without Stewart, but as you know she's insanely jealous of Davis and me and said some absolutely horrible things. She was going to try and have Mr. Jennings send me straight back to England, and I couldn't, wouldn't risk that happening.

I stayed awake all that night (no, I wasn't asleep, Chris), got up at dawn, dressed in my best, and was waiting for Mr. Jennings when he came down. I got him to take me out for breakfast before golf. We went to a place called the Country Kitchen in Santa Monica. I was feeling sick and just had coffee. Mr. Jennings had a whole stack of pancakes, with bacon. No wonder he's getting fat. Anyway, I said my piece, about how badly I wanted to be an actress and how Father would never let me. I went on a bit about Father. I have the tiniest feeling Mr. Jennings is jealous because he knows Margie's always been in love with him. Then I told him about Davis being willing to represent me, but how I couldn't afford to stay here. I told him I wasn't asking for a loan but for him to think about making an investment in me. I don't think he expected me to say it quite like that, and I think he was even a little bit impressed. Anyway, he said he'd think about it while he played golf. We arranged he'd pick me up at the beach about 12:30.

Honestly, it was the weirdest feeling, sitting on the beach by myself at 7:30 in the morning in exactly the same spot where I'd sat with Davis just twelve hours earlier. There were some very funny people around who'd been sleeping under the pier.

Mr. Jennings came back at 12:30 like he said, took me to lunch up the coast, and we had the nicest talk. He was very kind. He said he'd have to talk with Davis too, so we all had a meeting together that afternoon and it was settled! He and Davis are now business partners. Can you *imagine*!

I've moved into a little studio here. It's quite nice. I found a cheaper room, but Mr. Jennings didn't like it. He said he'd feel bad thinking of me being there. And guess what—he's bought me a *car*! It's fabulous—a 1968 Mustang convertible, fire-engine red! He said I couldn't possibly live in Los Angeles without a car. I tried to say no, but he wouldn't listen. The only problem is, of course, that I can't drive! Mr. Jennings couldn't believe it, that I could be eighteen and not know how to drive, so he's paying for driving lessons too. What a sweet man!

I feel awfully guilty, though. Margie is very upset. She feels she's failed in her responsibility and nothing I could say would make her feel better. Stewart is being an absolute bitch. I told her I wasn't in love with Davis, but that just made it worse. Thank God she's going back east to college next month.

I have absolutely *begged* Mr. Jennings not to tell anyone about the car. I think that would finish them off.

I start all my classes right after Labor Day: voice, ballet, yoga, and God knows what else. I can't wait for it all to begin! And for the work to start pouring in! And for you and Arran to come to California. . . .

Love, love, and love again,
Isobel

"A car!" Arran said with awe. "Iso's got her own *car*!"

"Everyone has their own car there," Christian said absently, thinking about Isobel sitting on the beach in her best clothes for five hours, waiting for Hall Jennings to finish his golf game.

By mid-September, the blue skies and golden beaches of California seemed a faraway, impossible dream.

Christian could hardly believe she had been there.

Reality was the Birmingham Technical College.

Christian hated the technical college even more than she had thought she would. It was bleak and old-fashioned, blackened with soot. Inside, the corridors were long and dark, lined with brown linoleum. The rooms were tall and barracklike, filled with scarred desks fashioned with sunken wells for the typewriters she quickly learned to loathe.

She was an inept typist, and shorthand befuddled her. Bookkeeping and data processing fulfilled her wildest nightmares. As gray October merged into dark November, she felt more and more like a prisoner, her mind escaping whenever possible to California, to Isobel, to the tennis club, to Ernest Wexler. Tommy Miller, in retrospect, became an ordinary, impulsive teenager, not without charm.

Would she ever go back there again? Would Isobel really pull it off?

The only good part about the technical college was that Arran went to classes with her. Arran had decided not to return to high school, and gentle Arran's decisions were generally immutable. "They can't teach me any more English, and I want to learn to type."

Christian admired Arran's dedication more than she could say. Arran knew exactly what she wanted from life—she wanted to be a writer—and Christian did not doubt for a moment that she would be successful. She had the same confidence in Isobel.

But what about me? she wondered miserably.

Father held her firmly to blame for Isobel's defection and made her life a misery. He lost no chance to chastise or belittle Christian, seizing on her poor performance at college, scornfully assuring her she would be lucky to find a job as a junior file clerk. He referred to her regularly as "Miss Mediocrity."

Christian began to have regular nightmares. She would find herself crouching in a small, dark box whose lid was grinding down, down on her unprotected head while Father's derisive laugh echoed through the walls.

After school, faced with going home, she felt her stomach clench and her breathing become rapid and irregular. Sometimes, unable to stand it, she would board a bus, any bus, and ride to the end of the line in distant, unknown parts of the city. There, she would peer through the steamy windows of transport cafés, watching clusters of West Indian drivers and bus conductors drinking tea from thick white china mugs, wishing she were one of them.

When she returned home, Father would slap her and scream at her for her disobedience, spittle flecking his chin.

Arran would do her best. "Leave her *alone*!" Useless.

"Don't you dare talk to your father like that!" Mother would cry.

"Don't let him see you're afraid of him," Arran would later warn her. "You make him worse."

Christian did not know what she'd do without Arran or without the sustaining thought of Ernest Wexler, whose card she carried in her pocket at all times.

"Let's talk about your Mr. Wexler," Arran commanded, sitting cross-legged on the bed.

She had been thrilled to hear about Christian's adventure and had made her tell it over and over again in case some important detail had been left out. "Gosh!

Tommy really would have raped you if you hadn't had one of your fits!" And: "They really and truly have bedrooms like that in Hollywood! How super!" But it was Ernest Wexler who caught her imagination the most. "Do you think he's in the Mafia?"

"He's not Italian. He's from Monte Carlo."

"Well, perhaps he's an international gangster. Oh, Chris, wouldn't that be exciting!"

"He carries a gun, of course," Christian reminisced. "But that's for self-defense—because of Charles Manson."

"Phooey," said Arran. "I'll bet there're hit men with contracts on him." After a thoughtful pause, she went on: "When he comes to London in February, you ought to ask him for a job."

Christian stared at her sister, stunned. "A job? But I can't do anything."

"Don't be so wet," said Arran. "And don't listen to Father. I keep telling you."

"It's all very well for you and Iso. I can't even learn to type. I'm Miss Mediocrity."

Arran rolled her eyes to the ceiling. "You make me want to scream. Listen, Chris, tell me—why are you keeping Mr. Wexler's card so carefully and crossing the days off your calendar until February?"

Christian looked uncomfortable. "Because I'll feel better just knowing he's in England."

"When he gets here," Arran said firmly, "you're going to phone him."

"He won't remember me."

"Then remind him. Of course he wants you to phone him. Why else would he have given you his card?" A thought struck her. "Chris! Perhaps he wants you to be his mistress!"

"Good God! Me?" snorted Christian, then howled with spontaneous laughter for the first time in months. "Oh, Arran, that's *funny*!" She was certain Ernest Wexler's mistresses would all be exotic and sultry with gaunt cheekbones and husky, smoky voices; they would smell of Joy perfume and always wear slinky black cocktail dresses.

"You never know, though," Arran said calmly. "Listen, it'll be February in six weeks. You've *got* to call him, Chris. You've got to. It's your big chance." She said ruthlessly, "Your fits are getting much worse, aren't they."

For a second, Christian's head was filled with a dark roaring. She looked at the floor and nodded.

After a pause, Arran said determinedly, "If you don't phone him, I will. You can't stay here."

1971

Christian left home for good on February 14, 1971.

She would never have done it without Arran, who had planned it all carefully, including the date.

The technical college was seething with lust and intrigue. There would be chaos. Arran herself had received an anonymous valentine with a tersely printed message inside: I'd like to fuck your brians out! She giggled all the way to the station.

"Fuck my brians, oh, Chris, fuck my brians!" She had to laugh at something or she thought she'd cry and never be able to stop. "A magazine, Chris. You've got to have something to read!" She bought a copy of *Vogue* and thrust it into her sister's hand, then snapped abruptly, "For God's sake, come on or you'll miss the bloody train."

The two girls trotted briskly to the platform gates, their breath smoking in the cold, sooty air. It was twenty-five degrees, and although it was almost nine in the morning, the light filtering through the leaden clouds was uncertain, more like dusk.

They paused under the departure notice board, where Christian's train was listed: LONDON KING'S CROSS 09:50 PLAT-FORM 7

When'll I see you again? wondered Arran miserably. Far up the platform, the guard was walking purposefully toward them slamming compartment doors one by one. She thought there were few sounds quite so final as the slamming of those doors.

"Come on, luv," said the ticket collector from his booth at the gate. "If you want the train, better 'urry."

She's never coming back, Arran thought.

Christian suddenly burst into tears. "Oh, Arran—" She flung her arms around her sister's neck.

"It's okay," Arran muttered awkwardly. "Stop it—please—" Her eyes ached with the pressure of unshed tears. "Go on, now, Chris, go on! For heaven's sake, don't be such a drip. It's your *chance*! Take it!"

"I *can't*!"

"Balls!" said Arran rudely. "You *can*. And you've got to or I'll never speak to you again!"

The train hissed a blast of steam, then jerked backward, its gears engaging with a sudden shrieking clash of metal.

"Buck up there now, luv," the ticket collector said.

"Oh, Arran—"

"Get on!" Arran shoved Christian through the gate. Christian shot her one last anguished glance, wiped her nose on the back of her hand, and turned as the guard blew his whistle. Arran watched her running athletically down the gritty platform and leaping into the first carriage. The guard banged the door shut behind her. Then, with a laborious grinding and shuddering, the long train started to pull away.

Arran stood at the gate watching the train move out of sight, carrying her sister to London, to Ernest Wexler, and to her future. She never noticed how the tears were rolling down her cheeks.

" 'ard thing, saying good-bye. I'd go get a nice cup of tea, luv, if I were you," the ticket collector advised kindly. "It'll make you feel ever so much better."

3

For months now, Isobel had worked harder than she believed possible. By the beginning of the new year, she was growing impatient. Surely Davis could send her up for something! But Davis steadily shook his head. Not yet, he would say, she wasn't ready.

At the end of January, however, something happened to make him change his mind, although he wouldn't tell her what it was. One Thursday afternoon he had her dress carefully and took her to the Polo Lounge at the Beverly Hills Hotel on Sunset Boulevard, "to test the water," he said thoughtfully.

Isobel knew all about the Polo Lounge. It was a power arena, a place to see and be seen, where men with deep tans and hard eyes talked into phones at their tables, made deals, put together packages, and perhaps, with the flick of a pen and a signature scrawled on a cocktail napkin, committed millions of dollars to a mere idea.

She was thrilled. She knew that she looked great and that she and Davis made a striking couple. They would certainly be noticed! Davis wore a well-cut cream-colored suit over a black silk shirt; she wore a short, simply cut white shift and high-heeled sandals. She wore little makeup, save for around her eyes. Her skin glowed with natural health. She did not wear a bra, and her breasts stood out high and firm.

She looked immediately in front of her, but she knew people were watching them cross the room to their banquette. Inwardly, she shivered with excitement.

Davis ordered daiquiris. "Stay cool," he told her.

A squat man with thinning black hair passed their

table, paused, and turned. "Hey, Davie boy, long time no šee! Where've you been, for crissakes?"

"Around. How're things going?" Davis asked with a lazy smile. He did not introduce Isobel, who looked up with an expression of polite reserve. The man was wearing too tight sharkskin pants and a maroon velour sweater with a deep vee, displaying two gold medallions and a Star of David twinkling in a nest of black chest hair. His smile was wide and toothy. His black eyes were in constant motion, darting from Isobel's breasts to her face, resting a second on her cool blue eyes, then darting, once again, over her head and around the room, back to her breasts, returning finally to Davis.

"El Jerko," he accused. "You been holding out on me. Who's the gorgeous chick?"

Davis made perfunctory introductions. "Sol Bernstein, Isobel Wynne."

"Isobel Wynne?" Davis could see the computer in Sol's mind searching its memory banks and coming up with a negative.

"Nice to meet you, Mr. Bernstein," Isobel said politely.

"Sol, baby. For you, plain old Sol—hey! You're English. . . ." Data would now be flashing across that mental screen: English. New in town. English actresses sure hot right now—look at Julie Christie, Vanessa Redgrave, Sarah Miles.

"Just arrived from London," Isobel agreed and offered a number four smile. Polite, but cool. Cool . . .

Davis was giving nothing away right now, either. Sol Bernstein left their table with his curiosity unsatisfied, puzzled and titillated, eyes still darting. "Well, you guys, gotta run. Gotta go earn a buck. Davie, baby, I'll give you a call next week. We got lots to talk about. Let's have lunch."

"Sure," agreed Davis pleasantly. "Let's do."

Bernstein's maroon back veered away. "That's one numero uno shit," Davis remarked in a placid voice. "He'd sell his grandmother for a quarter. But he's big at Viking Studios, and he's got a big mouth. Now he's going to call around everywhere and try to find out who you are." He smiled. "Last week, he wouldn't have given me the time of day. Now, he even remembers my name. . . ."

Over the weekend, Davis gave her the script of *Free Fall*.

"Read this," he told her, handing her a thick wad of typewritten pages. "A friend of a friend made me a copy. I'm not supposed to have it. Don't tell anyone you've seen it. Read Addie's part, and tell me what you think."

Free Fall was the story of Avatar, the greatest rock star in the world, who had become controlled by his predatory manager, Portia Glaze, through the constant, cold-blooded administration of drugs.

Addie, a young British groupie, was in love with Avatar. She had some good scenes: a steamy encounter with her idol on the bus during his final, disastrous nationwide tour, and a ferocious encounter with Glaze at the party following the San Francisco concert.

"It's being touted as a serious film," Davis said, "and they're going after all the hot issues: feminism, corruption in the rock music industry, the drug culture . . . you name it."

Isobel took the script home, handling it as if it were made of glass. She read it over and over. Who is Addie? she asked herself. How does she feel? Where does she come from? Where does she think she's going?

"Addie is very young," advised the directive in the screenplay. "She is beautiful, with an earthy, sexy, but somehow naïve quality. Desperately in love with Avatar, she has run away from her working-class English home to follow his band, which has become her whole world. . . ."

Davis called her in the evening to ask her what she thought.

"It's me," said Isobel with certainty. "I'm Addie."

"Good," said Davis. "The casting call is in two weeks."

Isobel felt a thud in her stomach, as though a mallet had struck an anvil.

It was happening. At last.

He scheduled her first photograph session. "Got to get your book together, now. . . ."

Refugio Ramirez was the best photographer in Los Angeles. In the country. The world. Maybe the universe.

So he assured Isobel with total certainty, as he followed her up the steps to his studio. "If Whittaker wants the best, then he calls me, natch," he exclaimed vehemently, watching the movement of her buttocks under the tight blue denim of her washed-out jeans. "The Ram is numero uno. El ultimo!"

He was also the most expensive. However, Davis had not balked. "Don't worry—he'll do it for free. He owes me. I saved his goddam skin, once."

And it seemed that Ramirez had indeed not forgotten that night five years ago in the Saigon bar when, without the fast intervention of Davis Whittaker, the feisty, drunken Chicano news photographer would have been carved to small pieces in an argument over a pretty little golden-skinned prostitute.

That was why he was giving up his whole Sunday and working for nothing on Whittaker's protégée, and it was why he wasn't even going to lay a finger on the gorgeous rump bunching and straining so deliciously under the tight fabric just inches in front of his eyes, no matter how much his fingers itched and his private parts throbbed with excitement.

He was not resentful, however, because the girl really was gorgeous. Whittaker might have something special here, just as he thought—although they wouldn't know how she photographed until they saw the contacts. Davis did not know what kind of look he was after, either. "Just keep shooting," he said. "Then shoot some more."

To Isobel, he gave this warning: "He's a dirty-minded, horny little toad, but he's truly great. If anyone can do it for you, he can."

Ramirez actually did look rather like a toad, Isobel thought. He was short and squat, with spatulate fingers, long hairy arms, and bandy legs. He had thick lips, bulging eyes, a squashed-in nose, and kinky black hair plastered with oil.

He was one of the ugliest little men she had ever seen.

Setting down her garment and tote bags in a corner of the cluttered studio, Isobel found herself stifling a giggle as she recalled something else Davis had said: "You'll find it hard to believe, but he's made love to nearly every beautiful woman in Southern California. Watch out! He's not called 'The Ram' for nothing!"

Now Ramirez poured a cup of powerful black coffee for Isobel, strong enough, she suspected, to strip the scarlet paint off her Mustang—"none of that watered-down gringo shit here, baby"—and when she had drunk it, made her walk up and down and around the studio, sit, stretch, and dance to a Rolling Stones record while he brooded, chin in hands, and smoked a pungent-smelling black cheroot. Then he had her stand beside the wide window so that he could study her face in natural light, tilting her head this way and that, aligning neck, jaw, and shoulder, minutely examining her face, laying the flat of his hand on her cheek as he studied shadow angles. "Son of a bitch," he muttered over and over. "Son of a bitch."

He scrounged among the clothes and props she had brought with her and discarded everything that was neither black nor white. "A feel," he mumbled. "Just a feel. Something maybe coming together . . ."

He added props of his own: a black-and-white-striped Mexican serape with long fringes, a floppy straw hat, a man's white shirt, and a black lace shawl. He piled it all in the middle of the floor and stood back pensively, puffing on his evil-smelling cheroot, his body so still he might have been in a state of deep meditation. The phone rang; he ignored it.

When the phone finally stopped ringing and the echoes died away, Ramirez snapped forefinger and thumb together and announced: "Okay, babe, let's hit it."

For the next two hours, he shot close-ups of Isobel. He angled shots from front, side, below, above; tied her hair back in a youthful ponytail; pulled it loose and forward; rolled it in a knot on top of her head; changed her neckline; added scarves and jewelry, then took them away again. Throughout he talked to himself in Spanish, with rising excitement.

By 1:00 P.M. Isobel was hungry. Her stomach growled. She felt tired and stiff. Her feet hurt. Her neck ached.

"So what?" demanded Ramirez. "Who gives a shit?" He flung garments, props, and accessories into a bag, scooped up cameras, light meters, and lenses into another, grabbed Isobel by the wrist, and dragged her forcibly down the steps to the street. "I don't eat when I'm working and it's going good. If you're on a roll, baby, you don't fuck it up. Here"—he opened the door of a sleek black Maserati and thrust her into the passenger seat—"get in. And hit on this—it'll take your mind off your problems."

He nonchalantly lit a joint and handed it to her. "Three tokes, babe—no more . . ."

They roared north toward Malibu. When the speedometer clocked eighty-five miles per hour, Ramirez leaned across, took the joint from Isobel's fingers, and pinched it out. "For later, baby. For after, when you've been a good girl."

At the beach, he had her put the shirt on, knot it around her waist, stride with the tails flapping, and pose hands on hips, cocky, the straw hat pushed rakishly to the back of her head. "Nice, nice," Ramirez cried encouragingly. "Now, move it, baby." His camera clicked and clicked. "Okay, hold it. Try the shawl now—the black one—whooooee!" He chatted incessantly and compulsively. "Let it go off the shoulder. Yeah. *Awright*—let it go all the way. Never mind what's showing, trust me. . . ." And he went on yelling, in a rising crescendo of mingled Spanish and English: "Whittaker's crazy, man. Tells me no tits, and I tell him sonofabitch, with tits like those she should be proud, she should show the world. They should run 'em up a fucking flagpole. . . ."

A crowd started to gather.

Isobel heard snatches of comments and questions.

"Who's *she?*"

"This a fashion spread?"

"You seen that girl before?"

"Who . . . ?"

"Must be really something—that's Ramirez!"

Isobel immediately picked up on the energy from the crowd and began to work the audience. She twisted, turned, and stretched, smiled and frowned, moving gracefully, for them. "Hey, great, baby! I love ya!" Ramirez shouted, clicking away. The February shadows were lengthening now, but the crowd still grew, craning their necks to watch. The wind started to rise.

The fringes of the serape flew like pennants. Isobel's hair streamed across her face. She reached up a hand to brush it from her forehead, spinning around fast, pivoting on one foot, enjoying herself thoroughly, eyes glinting wickedly, carefree as a gypsy.

Ramirez shot his final roll as the crowd, sensing the end of the session, moved excitedly toward Isobel, their heads and shoulders and outstretched arms making long foreground shadows on the sand.

There had to be a downside, though she hadn't realized that it would be so intense or that she would feel so depressed.

"I suppose it went all right," Isobel said wanly to Davis when he arrived at her apartment. "Ramirez said he'd call later. He was in a hurry to get back."

She had felt so high this afternoon, so terrific. Sure she could do anything, be anything; she had even felt she could fly.

But now, she felt utterly flat and almost tearful.

"Soon's I know what we got, I'll give a call," Ramirez had shouted from his car. He had not seen her to the door, or asked to come in, as she had half-expected he might. He wanted to get rid of her as quickly as possible. He wasn't interested in *her*—just in the image he would develop on paper.

"If he was in such a hurry," Davis said, "then he must think he has something good."

Davis had brought take-out Chinese food for their dinner, the four white cartons standing in a row on her dresser. He was opening the lids and peering inside. He was hungry. "We'd better eat this while it's hot."

Isobel, who had not eaten all day, now thought she'd be sick if she ate anything. How could Davis be so insensitive as to be hungry? She decided she hated him.

She felt depleted, unhappy, and used, convinced that all Davis really wanted of her was a successful client, one who would make him rich so he could show his father that he could do it on his own. She sat slumped on her studio couch experiencing the full reaction to her afternoon's triumph, thinking how badly she wanted his arms around her, the sound of his voice comforting her, telling her that she was beautiful, that the pictures would be great—and that he loved her.

In her warm, half-waking, half-sleeping fantasies, she would conjure up that moment when she first saw Davis Whittaker, standing outside her circle of new admirers at the Jenningses' party, staring at her with a peculiarly intense, speculative expression. She could feel the touch of his fingers still vibrating on her wrist as he led her away toward the pool, where they could talk alone. But then, after their agreement to work together, it all changed. He seemed not to care anymore for her as a person, even though his lovemaking always had the power to break her into small, quivering pieces.

Even now, watching the curve of his back and the movement of his shoulders as he carefully arranged paper plates, forks, and small containers of hot mustard and soy sauce on her coffee table, she felt a nearly unbearable, gut-deep craving for him.

Oh, damn him!

She glowered at Davis, who no longer saw her as a real person. He had told her so himself, just last week. He had told her to strip, then walked coolly around her, his expression serious, with no hint of the lover in those brooding amber eyes. "You've put back on at least a couple of pounds," he had said warningly. "With a photo session in seven days, you've got to cool it with the pizza. And stick with diet sodas or plain water."

"You're talking as though I'm a side of meat."

He had looked her straight in the eye then and said, "Exactly, Isobel, though we prefer to say 'product.' That's you, now. Isobel Wynne, product."

Oh God, the nerve of it! "The sooner you understand that, the better, and the less hurt you're going to be. You're a package of talent and looks. Those people out there aren't interested in you as a person, just in the product. They buy if they think you'll make money for them. If you're a pro, you'll give them what they want; then you'll make money too. You'll be rich and famous. That's what you want. Isn't it?"

"I think it's the most cold-blooded thing I've ever heard," Isobel had hissed angrily.

Davis had shrugged. "You'll have to get used to it if you want to survive. It's for your own protection. You have to learn to separate personal from professional. Even learn to laugh at it all." And then, watching her stormy face, he said, "Trust me, Isobel. I care about you."

Bullshit, thought Isobel. Of course you don't care. I'm just product. . . . I don't exist. To Ramirez, I'm just an image, more real on paper. . . .

In retrospect, the Polo Lounge was now just a meat market where she, Isobel Wynne, product, had been put on display and paraded in front of sleazebags like Sol Bernstein. She felt humiliated. She hated it all. . . .

Suddenly, she thought longingly of the joint Ramirez had given her. It had made her feel wonderful. But Davis would have disapproved had he known about it, because he was very down on drugs. He wouldn't let her drink booze, either. A little wine, now and then . . . that was all.

"Come on, Isobel," he was saying now, sounding

paternal. "I know you're tired and it's been a big day, but you have to eat. You know you enjoy Szechuan cooking." He handed her a plateful of cashew chicken and delicate strips of Mongolian beef. Isobel nearly gagged. Instead of eating, she refilled her glass from the jug of Red Mountain chablis on the coffee table. Davis took it away from her at once. "No more wine. Come on, Isobel, eat a *little*. . . ."

"I don't *want* it," Isobel said with a childish pout. Why couldn't he understand that she didn't want food, just someone to love her and tell her how terrific she was. Immersed in a sudden wave of homesickness, she longed for her sisters and loathed Davis, who seemed to control her life as ruthlessly as Portia Glaze controlled Avatar's.

She wanted to go home and forget the whole thing.

Then, still thinking of her sisters, she remembered why she was here. They depended on her, and she wouldn't let them down.

Later, in bed with Davis, his arms around her at last, but much too late, she cried his name over and over, her hands twisting in his thick hair, kissing his lips, his eyes, his throat, while her body merged into his, ecstatically sharing his flesh, skin, and substance. Naked in bed, they shared a language and a purpose.

Now Isobel was able to forget that the moment they parted it would all be different. She writhed against Davis, welcoming him inside her, murmuring throatily with satisfaction. She pressed his hands against her hard, aching breasts, feeling the familiar tension growing, spreading, rippling through her body, forcing herself to wait, wanting so badly to let it all go out from her, groaning with the urgency of her need, Davis's lips on the soft flesh below her ear, his teeth biting suddenly at her lips, his wonderful, wonderful monumental hardness. . . .

They were moving together in rising urgency. Isobel's eyes were wet. She saw spinning colors and jagged starbursts of white. She gasped and felt herself borne over the edge into the roaring darkness of pure sensation.

"Yes," gasped Davis in her ear. "Oh yes, my darling, yes, yes . . ."

And then three things happened all at once.

Davis burst inside her, crushing her against his chest in a convulsive spasm, as Isobel screamed aloud in triumph.

Somebody pounded wildly on the door and shouted: "Will you kids cool it? People want to sleep around here. It's three o'clock in the fucking morning!"

And the telephone rang.

"Goddam it!" cried Davis.

It was Ramirez. He sounded stoned. "You guys better get your asses over here," he said in an odd, tight voice. "Right now. You're not gonna believe this. . . ."

The little Mexican met them in the doorway to his studio, stuttering in excitement, exuding a feral smell of sweat and tension.

"Look at this!" he shouted as Isobel and Davis bent over his light table to examine the contact prints. "Look at this one, and this one, and that. I tell you, man, with this girl you can't *take* a bad picture. Each shot, even the lousy ones, are fucking terrific! And with this one—see, I pulled one print just to see. Careful, it's still wet. . . ."

They stared down at Isobel on the beach, innocent, provocative, radiant, youthful, one hand clutching at the billowing serape, the other tossing back her wind-blown hair, and at the clearly delineated foreground shadows of heads and shoulders, raised arms, pointing fingers, reaching hands. . . . It was a once-in-a-lifetime shot.

"With this one, I make history," Ramirez said with awed solemnity.

4

Christian sipped a dry sherry and watched the birch logs crackling merrily in the Adam fireplace of the bar in Tanner's Club, just off Bond Street. A very old man wearing a suit of well-cut but thoroughly lived-in tweeds stood with his back to the fire, the tails of his jacket hiked up, frankly and unabashedly warming his behind. This was the earl of Petersham, Ernest Wexler had told Christian, down from Yorkshire for directors' meetings.

An hour ago, she had been sitting chilled and apprehensive in a third-class railway compartment. Then, at the station, she was met by Ernest Wexler, impeccable in a black cashmere overcoat with velvet collar and brushed bowler hat, who transported her to Tanner's— one of the most exclusive private clubs in London—in a chauffeur-driven, bottle green Jaguar. The ride had been as swift and smooth as a journey by flying carpet.

"Your table's ready, my lord."

Christian looked up. A distinguished gentleman in club livery had approached the earl, who blinked, nodded, and agreed. "Yes, thought so myself. Shocking, what?"

Inches from the aged, furry ear, the maître d' yelled, *"Your table's ready, Lord Petersham!"*

"No need to shout, what?" complained His Lordship, and he allowed himself to be led, grumbling, toward the dining room.

"Ninety-two and all his faculties but one," Ernest Wexler commented on his return from the telephone.

"I've never seen a lord before," said Christian. "Not

that I know of, anyway." And, impulsively, she added, "This is a *lovely* place!"

"It's very pleasant," Wexler agreed. "I use it a lot when I'm in London. They have a first-class chef and various other facilities. There's a rather expensive backgammon game in progress upstairs right now. Ah—I see our table's ready too. After you, my dear."

It was a curious replay of the Beverly Hills lunch, adapted to an English setting in winter. A beautiful setting, impeccable service, and a clientele who were all well bred, elegant, successful, or just plain rich. Christian sat in her Chippendale chair wearing her pleated navy blue school uniform skirt and matching cardigan over a white oxford shirt, studying the beautiful women with their lovely clothes, well-coiffed hair, and graceful, manicured hands. She could not help but be aware of her own reddened fingers, blistered with chilblains—but it didn't seem to matter, sitting with Mr. Wexler. He's above all that, Christian thought worshipfully, and settled down to enjoy the first really good lunch she had had since leaving California.

Smoked salmon came first, followed by a marvelously tender rack of lamb flavored with rosemary and a touch of garlic. To accompany the lamb, Wexler ordered a Beaulieu cabernet sauvignon. "We'll be nostalgic, shall we, and have a California wine? This must be one of the only places in London that carries it."

Christian refused to think about what would happen later. Martin, the chauffeur, would be back with the car at 3:00 P.M. Then what? If her future had not been discussed, she would have to return to King's Cross station in time to catch the Birmingham train.

"Christian, my dear," Mr. Wexler had said on the phone, "how delightful to hear from you. Yes, of course come to London. We'll have lunch. We have a lot to talk about."

By the end of the main course, however, all they'd talked about was Mr. Wexler's business trip to Southeast Asia the past month, which he had illustrated with gently hilarious anecdotes to make her laugh, and reminiscences of Los Angeles and that night when she had risen like a dryad from the ice plant in front of his house and how scared she had been of Hansel. "Poor Hansel can't come to England, of course," Wexler observed. "He'd have to spend six months in quarantine at Heathrow. He'd find that too degrading." Christian murmured politely, delighted that Hansel had been left behind. "Pierre, of course, is with me. We have a lease on a nice little house in St. James's. Now tell me, what do you hear of your sister? Has she taken Hollywood by storm yet?"

Christian brought Ernest Wexler up to date on Isobel's progress, as much as she could. "She doesn't have time to write much, of course."

"Naturally . . ." From Isobel, they brushed lightly over other apparently unrelated topics. Christian had no idea that she was inadvertently revealing much information about herself or that she was being very skillfully probed and interviewed.

Nor could she guess how clearly her desperation showed to a man like Ernest Wexler. Wexler had known desperation once himself. He could recognize it instantly in others and knew very well how to turn it to his own ends. Properly manipulated, it was a powerful tool.

"And so, my dear," he asked gently, at last, over coffee, "what are you going to do now?" He knew perfectly well what awaited Christian unless her future changed suddenly and drastically. He envisioned the imprisonment of a wild creature—a drab life behind a desk or a counter, for which she was blatantly unsuited and which would eventually destroy her.

She set her cup down on the table and gazed directly at him, her brown eyes stark. "I don't know, Mr. Wexler. I don't have any plans."

"You don't, for instance, have a defined ambition, like your sisters?"

Christian laughed wryly. "How could I? I'm not beautiful, and I'm not clever. Just good at tennis. I don't have any other talents."

"I wouldn't say that," murmured Ernest Wexler.

"There are other things in life. For instance, you speak French. You did well in French at school."

Christian stared at him in surprise. "How do you know?"

"Because you told me." Then, in impeccably accented French, Wexler asked, "Have you ever been to France?"

"Non," Christian replied. *"Je n'ai visité jamais en France."*

"Not bad," Wexler applauded. "By any chance do you know German? A useful language, German."

Christian shook her head. "They didn't teach it. I only know French."

The waiter refilled their cups from a silver coffeepot.

Then Christian caught sight of a clock. Two-forty-five. A cold finger touched her spine. The car would be outside in fifteen minutes.

The sheer foolishness of it all struck her. What *had* she and Arran been expecting to happen? Why in the world would Ernest Wexler offer her a job? She didn't even know what his business was. Even if she did, what could she possibly do to be of any use? And then—had she seriously thought that he would supply her with a place to live as well? "Perhaps he wants you to be his mistress," Arran had said. Looking around her at the beautiful, sophisticated women in the dining room, aware of her own shaggy, unstyled hair, ugly clothes, and dreadful hands, Christian felt like howling with wretched laughter.

She decided she must have been mad.

But it *had* been a lovely lunch, and if she left now to catch the train she would be home before she was really missed. Mr. Wexler would probably not mind lending her the fare. Ernest Wexler, who had noted the direction of her eyes and the suddenly depleted look on her face, said gently, "Yes, Martin will be here very soon. Then I must go back to my office for a while. I'm flying up to Manchester this evening."

Christian swallowed bravely. "Oh yes. Of course. I should be leaving too. My train leaves about four, I think."

Wexler leaned forward, cupped his chin pensively in his hands, and studied her face. "Tell me frankly, my dear. If you were offered an alternative to going home— the opportunity of a job, say—and it was an attractive offer, perfectly legal, what would you do? Would you take it?"

Christian turned very pale. "Oh yes," she blurted. "I—I would. Of course I would."

"Good," Ernest Wexler said, "because I have a proposition for you. Quite a respectable one, so you don't have to worry."

She stared at him, eyes wide.

She didn't look as though she would be able to speak, so he continued gently: "If I'm right, and I know quite a lot about you now, you know, your expectations are minimal and your home life is destructive and threatening to you. You have no resources of your own and no alternative at this moment."

Christian began, "When Isobel starts working, she's . . ."

"Yes, yes," Wexler said impatiently. "Of course Isobel will come to the rescue when she gets her big break, and Isobel's intentions are undoubtedly good, but a career doesn't blossom overnight. For now, Isobel has to put herself first. You cannot rely on Isobel."

"But—"

Wexler signaled for more coffee. The hands of the clock now stood at precisely three o'clock. Martin would be outside with the Jaguar.

Wexler sipped his coffee and leveled his index finger at Christian. "Listen carefully, my dear. I'm going to make a suggestion."

He had her total attention. Long ago, Ernest Wexler would have felt very sorry for Christian, but he had learned that pity, like many other virtues, could be a hindrance to survival. Instead, he had learned to capitalize on the circumstances that prompted the pity in the first place.

"Now, I am a businessman," he began carefully. "Very basically, I buy and I sell. Often I buy goods in one country and sell in another. My head office is in

Monaco, for tax advantages since I deal in extremely costly high-profit merchandise. It is also usefully situated geographically. I have clients throughout Europe and in the Middle East and Africa. I also maintain an office here in London and one in Los Angeles, from which I conduct my U.S., Asian, and Latin American affairs. I—Oh, John! How good to see you, dear fellow. I had no idea you'd been lunching here too."

Wexler rose to shake hands enthusiastically with a tall, dark-haired, dark-eyed man of around forty. His face, compared with the February pallor of others in the room, was startlingly tanned. "Join us for a coffee."

The stranger shook his head. "Sorry, Ernest, love to take you up on it, but I'm in one hell of a rush, actually."

"We shan't keep you, then. But John, meet my friend Miss Winter. Christian, my dear, this is John Petrocelli. You'll have to become better acquainted some other time.

John Petrocelli was impeccably dressed in a charcoal gray pinstriped suit over a creamy silk shirt. She could have felt exceptionally shabby in her old school uniform, but John Petrocelli did not seem to care. He looked her over keenly, glanced at Wexler, then smiled at her with apparent approval. "Good to meet you, Miss Winter."

"The skiing must have been good," Wexler observed.

"Couldn't have been better. Perfect weather. See you on the slopes sometime, Ernest."

"Nonsense! Skiing's for young bones and warm blood!" Wexler waved him a cheery good-bye and settled back into his chair. "Nice fellow. We do business together—most pleasantly, too. He's a partner in Steinberg, Petrocelli."

Christian, who did not know of the famous Italian Swiss bankers, smiled politely.

"If the name means nothing now, it will. But to return to more pressing matters—we don't want to keep poor Martin waiting in the cold indefinitely."

Christian fixed her eyes once more on the urbane face of her companion and waited.

"I flatter myself," Wexler said, "on being able to recognize certain abilities in people. Such as yourself."

"What abilities?" Christian blurted. "French and tennis?"

Wexler smiled. "It's a good start. For the rest, you have great potential, and you can always learn."

Christian was lost. "Potential?"

"You have natural style and elegance; you are not easily intimidated by your surroundings; and you have freedom of spirit. I was most impressed by your comportment the night we met. A person of inferior mettle, having suffered attempted rape, been terrorized by Hansel, and abducted by an armed man, would have handled herself with much less poise. With some minor adjustments, you could also be a very beautiful young woman."

"Thank you."

"You're welcome. Now, in my line of work," Wexler went on, "I always need people such as you, who are intelligent and quick witted and who do not become flustered under stress. There is much pressure. Shipment to deadlines. The handling of clients, who can sometimes be most temperamental. Foreign negotiations and sales—"

Christian looked aghast. "Mr. Wexler, I'd never be any good as a salesgirl. . . ."

"Please, Christian. Hear me out." He held up his hand in admonishment. "We're not discussing the sale of trinkets or toiletries over the counter at Woolworth's. In any case, you do yourself an injustice. You are an extremely good saleswoman. You have presented yourself to me very successfully. Otherwise I would not now be making you this offer."

"That's different."

"Of course it's not. Now Christian, my dear, let me give an example of where you might be useful to me. With my type of business, which fluctuates depending on current world affairs, I rely on goodwill and repeat orders. My clients pay a good deal of money for our particular commodity, and it is to our advantage that they get up from the table happy. That's just an expression, my dear," he said, at Christian's puzzled look. "You'll be hearing it often, I expect. Now"—he folded his hands together and leaned back in his seat—"in certain instances, with a little imagination and applied psychology, a customer can be induced to increase an order with the utmost willingness. It can be very advantageous during negotiation and consolidation of the sale to have on hand an elegant, sophisticated young woman with a command of languages."

Christian seized on the only aspect of Wexler's speech that she understood. "But I only speak a little French. . . ."

"Then you'll have to study hard, won't you."

"And I'm not elegant."

"A few shopping trips and a visit to Elizabeth Arden can fix that up quite easily."

"Or sophisticated."

"You are naturally sophisticated."

"But, Mr. Wexler, I don't have anywhere to live."

"Some of my London employees live in our house in St. James's Court. There happens to be a nice vacant room, attractively decorated, overlooking a mews. Provided you approve, you are most welcome to it. As to other problems you think you have, you are legally of an age to leave home, and you will make quite a handsome salary."

Christian's mind spun. She knew it was all impossible. This kind of thing simply never happened.

She tried to pretend she was Isobel. What would Iso do? What would Iso say? What was the catch? Was she supposed to sleep with all these foreign clients? That would be something Iso would ask, but Christian was too shy. Such a sordid possibility did not fit, however. Mr. Wexler was so personally fastidious. She could not believe he would demand such a thing of her.

Her mind raced. She realized suddenly she didn't even know what his business was. Iso would have found that out long ago; she would have demanded to know the nature of Mr. Wexler's valuable merchandise. Christian tried to think of the most expensive

THE WINTER WOMEN 139

items in the world. Gold? Silver? Jewels? Paintings? Racehorses, perhaps? Fur coats? Ships? Sports cars? He had said it was legal, so it couldn't be drugs. What, then? She asked him.

"Arms," replied Ernest Wexler urbanely.

Christian looked at him, puzzled. "What?"

"Guns. And heavier stuff, of course. Mortars, tanks, missile launchers, whatever's available."

"Oh," said Christian, adding faintly, "is that really legal?"

"Certainly. I deal with governments and legitimate military and police forces. I also have a few private clients, mostly in the Middle East."

"I see," she whispered.

"Actually, we sell to anybody, provided we can get an export license and there's a legitimate end-user certificate."

"You make it sound so ordinary," said Christian.

"And so it is. No different, really, from selling coffee or automobiles, only much more lucrative. Weapons, you see, are always in demand, and somebody will always be there to supply them. It might as well be me. Well now," Wexler said briskly, "time's getting on. We'd better relieve poor Martin and run you over to St. James's. You may then have an hour or so to think this over. If your decision should be negative, as is your perfect right, then Martin can run you home to Birmingham in the Jaguar. It'll be good for the car, and he'd enjoy the drive."

Crossing Piccadilly, Martin weaving expertly through a wall of taxis, cars, double-decker buses, and frantic pedestrians, Wexler asked her casually, "By the way, what did you think of John Petrocelli?"

"He was quite nice," said Christian.

"Good, because I expect you'll be seeing quite a lot of him."

Wexler smiled to himself. Yes, she would indeed. In the not so distant future, she would be marrying him. . . .

While Christian was in London eating a delicious

dinner of coq au vin and salad by herself, Isobel was parking her Mustang in the cavernous garage at Century Park East, Los Angeles. She sat for a moment, hunched over the wheel, listening to the thunderous noises her heart was making inside her chest.

She took ten deep breaths, the way her voice coach had taught her to do at such times of stress, and wished she had allowed Davis to come with her, as he had wanted.

She had been firm. "No. I want to go alone. You'll make me more nervous." Now, she thought how silly she had been. How could she possibly feel more nervous than she was already?

To make matters even worse, it was raining. Not English rain, gently pattering, but California rain, falling heavily in straight vertical lines. There was a leak in the Mustang's vinyl roof. Rain had dripped steadily down her neck as she sat in the worst traffic gridlock she could imagine on Wilshire Boulevard. She felt wet and sticky and sweaty under her rakish black raincoat with the yellow stripe down each sleeve. She had a headache, a sore throat, too. She wouldn't even be able to speak.

She peered into her rearview mirror, expecting to see a ravaged face with haunted eyes. Instead, her usual, really quite attractive face looked back at her. Isobel felt a bit cheered; at least her terror didn't show. She gave a tentative smile. The mouth in the mirror smiled back. There!

Resolutely, Isobel climbed out of her car and made her way toward the elevator, realizing as she punched the button for the thirty-ninth floor that she had forgotten to make a note of her car's location. The garage was so huge. Would she ever find the Mustang again? This seemed irrelevant, however, since she could not make herself believe that there would be a life after the audition.

The elevator smelled of wet raincoats with a trace of cigar smoke. Isobel thought how important this audition was for her—and for all of them—and her mouth tasted of dry cotton.

The outer office of Lausch and Lord, Casting, was filled with beautiful girls. Isobel's heart lurched with dismay. She had never seen so many beautiful girls in one place at one time. She had not known there were so many beautiful girls in the world, all, surely, much more gorgeous than she was, and each of them determined to be Addie.

She marched toward the reception desk, feeling herself the object of a dozen hostile eyes. Her journey seemed to take hours. The receptionist was whip-thin, sleek, and so polished she might have been cut from metal. She wore a silver dress with white cuffs. Her pale, gleaming hair was pinned behind her head in a French twist. She was talking on the phone. Another call came in, with a flash of red light on the switchboard and a courteous, dulcet chime. Isobel had never heard a chiming phone before.

The receptionist put the first caller on hold and murmured something to the second. She snapped her fingers, manicured with silver polish, at Isobel, and held out her hand. "Photo."

Embarrassed by her ignorance of procedure, Isobel fumbled in her new portfolio, took out an eight-by-ten glossy, and handed it to the receptionist, who laid it on a stack of other photographs without looking at it.

Behind her back, Isobel thought she heard someone giggle.

The receptionist pointed a silver nail toward a beige velour couch and ordered "sit" as though talking to a recalcitrant puppy.

Isobel scowled. God, what a bitch! But the rush of anger made her feel better. After a few moments, when her fury had subsided a little, she discovered that the other girls in the room did not look so formidable after all. Some, she thought with satisfaction, were very unsuitably dressed to be Addie. Addie would not wear slinky black, like that teased-out blonde who had to be twenty-five if she was a day, nor would she wear three elaborate hairpieces and display her boobs like the tall redhead.

Isobel had put together her audition outfit very carefully. She wore a twisted yellow bandana around her black curls, a black vinyl miniskirt, and a yellow T-shirt with a Grateful Dead logo across the chest. She thought she looked just right.

An hour passed. Isobel tensely turned the pages of trade magazines without making sense of a single word and waited. The phones chimed sweetly. Girls came and went. A young man wearing violet-tinted glasses, with a scraggly blond beard and long mousey hair secured behind his neck in a rubber band, escorted them one by one into a back office.

Once he picked up a handful of photographs from the reception desk, Isobel's included, and disappeared with them.

Well, at least her photo was terrific.

Isobel recalled that bizarre night last week when she and Davis had been so violently interrupted, at such an inopportune moment, by people yelling, phones ringing, and then that rush through predawn darkness and rain to Ramirez's studio.

Davis had stared silently at the photo for several minutes. Finally he had said, gravely and somehow sadly: "You're going to be a star, Isobel." And to Ramirez he offered: "It's great. Thank you."

"What the fuck did you expect?"

"I mean, really great."

The little Mexican shrugged. "It'll make history. . . ."

The blonde in the black dress was called. There were only two girls left in the room now. The receptionist was arguing with a dark-haired girl who was pleading, "Shit, I came all the way in from the Valley in this weather. I *have* to see Mrs. Lord."

"Leave a picture," the receptionist said coolly, "and we'll get back to you if we can use you."

"Isobel? Isobel Wynne?"

Isobel looked up, startled. The mousey-haired man said, "If you're Isobel, follow me."

She stood, and followed him across the room, wondering why she was no longer nervous. He held a door open, and she stepped inside.

Everything was perfectly all right, now.

Four people—two men and two women—were facing her across a wide desk strewn with papers, photographs, Styrofoam cups, and well-used ashtrays. These people weren't frightening at all. She saw a fat woman with frizzed red hair and a face that was all drooping lines like an exhausted bloodhound—the legendary casting ace, Meg Lord. Then there was her assistant, a pale girl in a nondescript dress and glasses, who had protruding front teeth. The two men were from the studio: one balding, overweight, in a black suit and conservatively striped tie; the other man younger, around thirty-five, with a lean, intelligent face.

Isobel smiled at them all. She wondered why she had been so frightened.

Both men smiled back.

"Good afternoon," she said confidently. "I'm Isobel Wynne."

"Miss Wynne—oh yes," said Meg Lord in a surprisingly high-pitched, breathy voice. She handed Isobel's picture to the heavyset man on her right.

He studied it and glanced up at Isobel. "Very nice. Did Ramirez do this?"

"Yes, he did," said Isobel, feeling quite in control now and perfectly calm. She was sure these people were on her side. They liked her picture. They wanted her to be Addie. She could feel it. Unruffled, she took other pictures from her portfolio to show them. She answered all their questions just as she had rehearsed with Davis. Yes, she was from England, newly arrived in Los Angeles; before, she had been doing repertory work in theater. Birmingham Rep, actually. She was represented by the Whittaker Talent Agency. Yes, she did have a working visa and had her green card with her, which she could show them if necessary . . . and yes, the pictures had all been shot by Refugio Ramirez. . . .

Shelley Pearlman, the balding man, who was associate producer of *Free Fall*, handed her a script bound between orange plastic covers. "Miss Wynne, read the marked speech for us—Addie's speech, the one beginning 'I'm Addie . . .' "

Isobel took the script and pretended to read the page from top to bottom. She glanced around the table, listening to the expectant silence. Then she became Addie. She was a little English groupie in headband and T-shirt. A simple working-class girl with a rough accent. She didn't have much education, but she knew what she wanted. She wanted Avatar. She loved him. She would die for him. . . . She smiled down at him, where he lay staring angrily up at her from among stained satin pillows. It was a tender smile, protective and full of female wisdom, ignoring his anger, her mouth still soft with the imprint of his kiss.

"I'm Addie," she told him gently, the corners of her mouth lifting. "I live here on the bus. I've always loved you. . . ."

When she finished, there was a short intense silence. Then, "Thank you, Miss Wynne, that's enough," came the breathy voice of Meg Lord.

Isobel blinked, momentarily displaced. No longer in the swaying bus staring into Avatar's drugged and hostile face, but back in Century City, in an overheated room staring across a littered table at four people whose decision might change her life.

"You do the accent pretty well," the young man said.

"Thank you, Miss Wynne," Pearlman said in a neutral voice. "We'll be in touch with your agent if we need you again."

Isobel nodded. She smiled calmly and inclined her head. "Thank you."

Moments later, eyes closed, she leaned against the faintly vibrating steel of the elevator and whispered "Thank you," again, from her heart.

She was going to be Addie. She knew it.

It took her forty-five minutes to locate her car in the dank, dark garage.

Outside, it was raining harder than ever.

By evening, five expensive homes would have slid down canyon walls in tons of cascading mud.

Isobel neither knew nor, if she had known, would

have cared. A few hours later she had a fever of 103. She stayed in bed the next five days and refused to see Davis until the night he appeared at her door to tell her she'd been called back for a test.

"If you do okay, you're probably going to be Addie," he told her. Oddly enough, he didn't sound very excited.

5

George Winter's face was flushed, and even from the doorway Arran could smell the gin on his breath. He closed the door behind him, crossed the room, and sat down on the bed beside her. "Christian's gone, hasn't she. She's not coming back."

"I don't know, Father."

"She's like Isobel. She won't come back to Mummy and me." His eyes were red rimmed. He had been crying. "Why? Why did she go away?"

Arran looked down at her hands, embarrassed.

"I want a family," he said petulantly. "A family stays together."

"Christian's grown-up now. She's eighteen."

"She won't ever come back. I know she won't." George Winter pushed his lips out in a bewildered pout. "There's only you left now, and Mummy, of course. . . ."

Arran sighed. "Well, you know how Mother loves you."

"And you, Arran? What about you? Do you love me?" His voice pleaded, face glistening with sweat.

"Of course."

"Come to me—" He held out his arms to her. "Make it all up to me. I need you, Arran. You're all I have left. . . ."

At four o'clock one Friday afternoon in April, Arran walked down the grimy steps of the technical college in a particularly grim mood. Two months had passed since Christian had leaped on the London train and been carried out of her life. Nine since Isobel had flown to California and not returned.

News had been very sparse since Christian left. Arran had felt abandoned and miserable—until her discovery that Father was intercepting the mail and destroying the letters from her sisters; a postcard from Isobel had lain shredded into tiny pieces beside the front door.

Now they both wrote to her c/o Mr. Bates, landlord of the Dog and Whistle, the pub down the street. Mr. Bates was understanding about Father and felt sorry for Arran.

Arran no longer felt abandoned, but she was still miserable—and bitterly lonely. She crossed off each day on her calendar in heavy black pen—there was nothing to look forward to, but at least another day was gone.

The weather was no help. April should have brought gusty warm breezes, blossoms, and hope. Instead, it was a cold, dank month of biting easterly winds and slashing rain. Today the wind keened down the dingy street like a fretful animal trapped between the rows of tall, sooty buildings, while thin dun-colored clouds raced by overhead.

Arran shivered and clutched her coat collar tighter around her neck. A surge of students clattered down the steps past her, shrieking and complaining at the cold.

Arran followed slowly in their wake. She was in no hurry, despite the raw chill. She did not want to go home.

She gazed blankly straight ahead, not seeing the scurrying, bundled figures, the traffic inching down the clogged street, or the brightly lit window of the chemist's shop until, with a shock of almost physical impact, her eyes locked with the cool green stare of a young man sitting astride a motorcycle at the curb.

Arran stopped dead, as though hitting an invisible wall.

He was one of the ugliest men she had ever seen.

His heavy-browed face was wind roughened and

brutal; his nose had obviously been frequently broken; a red, half-healed scar curved around his unshaven chin; his hair was a tangled mass of oily, brown curls. He wore a metal-studded leather jacket, tight leather trousers, and steel-toed boots. His gauntleted hands rested negligently on the handlebars of a hulking black BSA.

Hideous, thought Arran, evil, violent, and hideous—except for his eyes, which were the clear, beautiful green of seawater over white sand.

"Hiyuh," he said.

"Are you talking to me?" Arran bit at her lower lip. Despite the chill, she felt suddenly feverish.

"Bet yer fuckin' boots I'm talking to yer. Want a ride?"

Arran stared into the narrowed, light green eyes and sighed deeply. Her gaze ranged from the crown of his greasy curls, down over his battered face and powerful torso, and then rested for a moment on the bulging muscles of his leather-clad thigh.

"Mike up yer mind. Ain't got all dye." His accent was not local. He was a cockney. A native Londoner.

She nodded slowly. "Yes. Okay."

His wide mouth stretched in a predatory grin. " 'op on, then—mike it quick." He kick-started the motor and beckoned to Arran. She swung one long leg over the seat, drew up her knees, and clung to his muscular waist. Then, in an acrid cloud of smoke and with a throaty roar from twin exhausts, they were away. Behind them, Arran heard an enraged female voice scream, "Blackie! Well, bleedin' 'ell, whatcher think yer—"

She hung on, hands gripping the heavy muscles of the man's abdomen, her face pressed against the skull printed on the back of his jacket. The cold wind streamed her hair. The powerful bike throbbed between her thighs. She felt alive for the first time in months.

Blackie Roach had determined at a very young age not to emulate the depressing and, to him, degrading lives of his parents. His father, a railway porter at Paddington Station, spent his free time and the family's entire disposable income betting on the dogs and the horses and swilling beer with his cronies in the local pub. His mother, an office cleaner, was a worn-out wreck of forty-five who looked closer to sixty.

Blackie and his five siblings had been raised in hopeless poverty, and by the age of sixteen he had decided enough was enough.

By eighteen, he had built up a successful business dealing in amphetamines, Quaaludes, and cocaine at the transport cafés and roadhouses up and down the motorways of Britain. He was a familiar figure on the M1 between London and Birmingham, roaring down the fast lane on his black BSA, helmetless, his long, tangled hair whipping in the wind, lips drawn back in a frozen, grinning snarl.

Through the spring and early summer of 1971, he was not alone on his wild rides; a slender, big-eyed girl would often be perched behind him, her cheek snuggled against his leather-covered shoulder.

Arran quickly grew familiar with most of Blackie's haunts. Waiting at the counter, or at a table among a cluster of bikers or truck drivers, she would drink cup after cup of coffee while he did business in a succession of back rooms or toilets with drivers such as Otto from Hamburg, Germany (Mercedes eighteen-wheeler); Marc from Lyon, France (Berliet); Murphy from Liverpool (British Leyland).

Arran became almost a legend in her own right on the motorway. She was treated with care and a degree of awe. A woman—child, really—so careless of life and limb as to ride regularly with Blackie Roach must be touched either by God or by the Devil.

Blackie himself came to accept Arran in his life with astonished gratitude, and after their first night together, he asked her just two questions. He dared ask her nothing more, certain that if he did she would leave him flat. He never understood why she wanted him when obviously, with her fragile, elfin beauty, good education, and clearly middle-class background she could have had almost anybody, but Blackie Roach had never been a man to look a gift horse in the mouth. Ride it while it lasts—that was his motto. Scorch up and down the M1, make his back-room deals, take the money, spend the money, live from moment to moment because any one might be his last. Blackie had no illusions. Tomorrow he might be in prison. Or dead . . .

In the meantime, he gave Arran what she seemed to want. To the end, he never knew her last name. He took her with him on countless wild, illicit journeys and made his score. Then, his pockets heavy with wads of grubby five-pound notes, triumphant, the front of his leather trousers swollen, for nothing turned Blackie on so hard as the sudden possession of lots of money, he would snatch Arran roughly away from her place at the counter or table, take her out to the parking lot where the long rectangular shapes of the trucks lined up under the blazing fluorescent lights, unlock a door with a key lent by tonight's cooperative driver, and throw her inside.

They would struggle there together across the front seat, or, if they were lucky, behind the seat there would be a snug compartment with a mattress.

The first time, excited beyond bearing by a combination of the money in his jacket and the thought of sticking it to this lovely, extraordinary, crazy girl, he had frightened himself by his own force. Her arms and shoulders felt so fragile under his big hands, her breasts so soft and small, the nipples like tender little buttons. He had rammed into her so hard he had panicked that he might have hurt her badly, and she, to his belated amazement, was a virgin. She had made no sound, just clawed her long fingers into his straining buttocks and dragged him into her even deeper.

Then, week by week in the roiling, sweaty darkness, she would beg for it harder. "Oh yes, harder, for God's sake, Blackie, don't stop now, fuck me, Blackie, go on go on *go on* . . ." Now, there was nothing she would not do, no punishment he could mete out that she would not take. Her fragile, slender body seemed made of steel, and she outlasted him each time.

By June, he could sense her disappointment in him, for by now he was occasionally refusing to meet her demands. As Arran's experience grew, so did her taste for the violent and bizarre. "No," Blackie would say flatly, "I won't do that. I'll hurt you." For all his wildness, he had a conventional, even romantic streak when it came to women. It bothered him that Arran, so classy and so delicate, would want him to do such things to her. When the initial ferocity of their coupling was spent, he would discover an unexpected tenderness, an urge to gather her in his arms, to protect and caress her. "Why do you want it?" he once asked in bewilderment, running his hand gently over the long, smooth lines of her naked body, angry and ashamed now with himself for some of the things he had done to her. And later, the second question: "Arran, why do you like it?"

Arran said something then that shocked him. "It makes me feel clean," she said in a remote voice. He never asked her anything ever again.

That summer, Arran was not unhappy. Her life hung together in a peculiar, three-way equilibrium.

There was her writing life.

She was methodically keeping notebooks now in which she would write down thoughts and record feelings and ideas for stories. In the long light evenings after supper, she would work on her stories, praying for no interruption from Father. She began to submit them to magazines and to receive rejection notices, some polite, some not so polite. The more kind, sometimes constructive rejections she read carefully and saved. Painstakingly, she was gathering experience and laying the foundations of the style that would make her one of the most successful novelists of the eighties.

She kept all her records and private work under a loose floorboard in her room, together with her letters from Isobel and Christian, knowing that Father regularly went into her room and searched through her things while she was out. She tried not to think about Father's invasions, for if she did, she felt sick with rage.

There was her life at the library.

Arran walked out of the technical college and into her first job the week after she met Blackie. She had learned to type well enough to meet her requirements, and she decided there was no point in staying. The public library was an obvious place to work in order to widen her horizons, and she was accepted there as an assistant, to exchange people's books and generally make herself useful on a week's trial period. The pay was meager; the hours very long. She worked Monday through Saturday, with Wednesday afternoon off.

By the end of her first week, Arran had become indispensable. She was pleasant with the customers and actually knew something about books. Her advice was sought more and more often. "What's this one about, dear?" "Would I like her new one, do you think?" "What was the name of the man who wrote . . ." By the end of her third week, she had acquired a small following.

Miss Stoatley, a tall, hatchet-faced woman in hairy tweeds who taught mathematics to the lower grades at the local comprehensive school, looked forward to Saturday mornings, when she could talk to Arran. She even found herself confiding half-buried details of her unhappy childhood—how it had felt growing up plain, gawky, and much too intelligent, endlessly and humiliatingly sitting on the sidelines at parties waiting to be asked to dance.

Nurse Timms, fat and fiftyish, had a passion for florid historical romances with lurid covers showing well-endowed heroines in decorative disarray. The books would frequently be returned coverless, with a garbled excuse that water had spilled on them or the puppy had chewed them.

"Don't worry, Nurse," Arran would say gently, instinctively knowing, she was not sure how, that the cover in question now adorned Nurse Timms's bedroom wall or had been carefully saved in a scrapbook. "It's really quite all right." And Nurse would look pathetically grateful.

Colonel Thwaite, D.S.O., Ret., dropped by regularly to choose a boys' adventure story from the children's section for his grandson, Ben. Ben's favorite was the once famous Biggles series, featuring Captain Bigglesworth, flying ace, and his irrepressible sidekick, Algy. "Ripping yarns, these," the colonel would inform Arran eagerly. "The little chap just eats 'em up." By his third visit, Arran had correctly deduced that there was no young Ben. Colonel Thwaite, lonely and out of place in today's world, yearned for a simple world of black and white, of heroes and villains, as provided by the clean-cut adventures of Biggles and Algy.

There were others—so many lonely people, for whom the library was a refuge filled with the security of dreams.

Then there were the children, a steady stream of them in the afternoon after school. "Me Mum don't like me 'ome alone 'n says to come 'ere." Arran organized afternoon story hours for them. "You're ever so good with the kiddies," said Miss Truelove, the head librarian, who dreaded the daily arrival of the noisy, nasty little brats. "Really, Arran dear, you ought to find some nice young man, get married, and have some of your own." Arran would think of the only man she knew, Blackie Roach, and smile wanly. "Not yet, Miss Truelove."

So her summer continued.

She managed it all remarkably easily, even the trips with Blackie, which turned out to be simple to arrange. Mother and Father were in bed by ten, and Father would take his pill. Arran would then climb from the bathroom window to the tarpaper roof of the neighbors' toolshed, swing herself to the ground, and meet Blackie beside the public phone booth at the corner.

Then they were off: streaking through the night down the motorway in a world of glaring lights, raging noise, and wind-lashed speed, a world of garish truck-stops, rough men and women, harsh voices, and smells of exhaust, diesel, sweat, beer, and sex.

She rode with Blackie two, sometimes three nights a week. He was a dark, grimly thrilling secret.

It couldn't last, though.

One night Blackie did not come.

Arran waited for him for half an hour. If he was later than half an hour, Blackie said, then forget it—he'd fucked up. He wouldn't make it.

So far he had never failed her.

Arran waited and waited in the dark, ignoring the steadily dripping rain, longing for Blackie, for the touch of his oil-stained hands, the vibration of the heavy machine, and the heat, darkness, and urgency in the cab of tonight's truck.

Finally she returned home. She found it difficult to climb onto the toolshed without Blackie's boost from below. So she scrabbled and kicked her way onto the tarpaper roof, her hands sliding on the slimy wetness, soaking her clothes and grazing her knees. She did not sleep well.

The next day she learned why he had not come.

TRAGEDY ON M1
MOTORWAY SHOCKER
9 DEAD IN M1 PILEUP

screamed the headlines in all the papers.

It had been one of the worst motorway accidents ever.

A truck had blown a tire at eighty miles per hour and swerved into the passing lane. The motorcyclist riding in the fast lane at an estimated ninety-five miles per hour had had no chance at all. An observer had seen him hurtle through the air for a hundred feet, skid along the asphalt for another fifty, and end up under the rear wheel of the jackknifed truck, which by now blocked all the northbound lanes. A total of thirty-five vehicles were involved; nine people were killed outright; three more would probably not survive their injuries; fifteen were hospitalized.

The motorcyclist had been crushed and mutilated beyond recognition.

It must have been fast, though, she told herself. Blackie must not have known a thing.

6

Christian would do anything for Ernest Wexler. His age did not disturb her in the least. Neither did his profession. That was how she knew she was in love.

She lived for the sound of his light tread on the stair, his melodious, slightly ironic voice with its trace of a European accent, asking, "How are you today, my dear?" in whichever language he happened to be thinking, and the sight of his distinguished face with the high cheekbones and enigmatic, icy eyes.

Lying sleepless in her high bedroom, she would wonder despairingly how she could ever learn everything quickly enough to please him. But then the challenge of her new life would grip her again, and she would lie trembling with excitement, silently mouthing her determination into the darkness. She would do what he wanted if it killed her, for she loved him.

She dreaded displeasing him. Once, she had unwittingly made him very angry, and the memory chilled her.

The door had not been quite closed, and unthinking, she had burst into his private office uninvited, flushed with some small personal triumph.

". . . acute personal inconvenience should be adequate," Mr. Wexler was saying to an unexceptional-looking brown-haired man wearing a gray suit.

"I'll give him a Friday deadline," the man said. "Six P.M. After that . . ."

"I'm sorry," Christian said. "I thought you were alone."

Two pairs of eyes examined her intently in silence, Mr. Wexler's pale and glittering with anger, the other's brown and quite expressionless. For a reason she didn't understand, Christian found this very ordinary man utterly frightening.

"Out, Christian," Wexler said in a voice that cut like a whip. "And never, never come into this room again without an express invitation from me."

She fled to her room and cried.

That night he had left for Los Angeles for three weeks without saying good-bye to her.

When he returned, however, he seemed to have forgiven her. He never mentioned the incident again. In fact, he was so pleased with her progress during his absence that he decided to put her to work at last.

"You and I are going to entertain tonight," he announced cheerfully.

It was midnight at Annabel's, a dim grotto underneath Berkeley Square catering to the rich and fashionable, the patrons tonight including a duchess, a prominent French film actor, a notorious call girl, a cabinet minister, and the ruler of a small, oil-rich state on the Persian Gulf.

The latter, Sheikh Abdullah Aziz al Fehd, shared a small table discreetly set back from the dance floor with Ernest Wexler and Christian Winter. Christian, in a sleek black evening gown by Balenciaga, had become an earl's daughter for the evening.

"Our friend al Fehd," Wexler had explained, "is a terrible snob. He has an awe bordering on the fanatical for the British ruling class, and it is his eternal frustration that for all his oil and all his money, to say nothing of the very well equipped personal army at his disposal, he can never be mistaken for an English gentleman. It doesn't help that he can neither speak the language nor look right in the clothes.

"Which is your cue, my dear. . . . Tonight, you are the Lady Christian Winter, daughter of an English earl. Whom shall we honor? Petersham? I'm sure the old satyr would be proud. . . ."

The sheikh was short and stocky, and he wore an

extremely expensive suit from a Savile Row tailor. The suit did not hang at all well. Christian thought he would look infinitely more impressive in robes and a burnoose. They conversed in French because, as Wexler had warned, his command of English was negligible.

He was very gratified to be sitting beside an earl's daughter and set out to impress Christian with descriptions of his Italian sports cars, his racing stable, his yacht, which spent all but two weeks of the year berthed at Cannes, and his wife's shopping forays to London, Rome, and Paris.

Christian smiled until she thought her cheeks would split, exclaimed admiringly at appropriate moments, and looked aristocratic.

Sheikh Abdullah drank copious amounts of champagne and demanded to see her again. "Perhaps Lady Christian and I will take a country excursion tomorrow." Ernest Wexler said he thought that could certainly be arranged.

At eleven the next day, Christian called for the sheikh at the Ritz Hotel, Martin driving the Jaguar and practicing addressing her as "Milady."

The sheikh was ready and waiting, looking forward to the trip with childish expectation. He wore a bulky country tweed suit in hideous russet checks that lent a greenish cast to his sallow face, as well as brand-new oxblood shoes that clearly gave him acute discomfort. Christian thought he probably wore sandals back at the palace.

At Wexler's suggestion, she took him to the Compleat Angler in Marlow, a historically famous and extremely expensive restaurant on the banks of the Thames some twenty-five miles outside London. It was a good choice. The sheikh found the view of green meadows and gaily decorated riverboats exceptionally English and did full justice to his luncheon of fresh trout, strawberries and cream, and Stilton cheese.

Afterward, he demanded a walk along the towpath. It was now raining lightly, but he squished heroically through the mud for a full half-mile until the new shoes were hopelessly stained and he was beginning to limp.

He looked exhausted when Christian deposited him at the Ritz at five o'clock in the afternoon. She wondered whether he really had enjoyed himself, but surmised that a certain amount of discomfort was expected as the lot of an English gentleman and that he would have been disappointed without it.

She was proved right.

It seemed that for several hours Sheikh Abdullah Aziz al Fehd had realized all his fantasies.

He was suitably grateful. His order included not only the English antiriot guns and American machine pistols but all ten cases of the Russian assault weapons for which Wexler had recently concluded negotiations in Singapore. Wexler International would reap a profit of more than one million U.S. dollars.

"I knew you'd do it, my dear," Wexler said cheerfully. "It must have been the walk in the rain through the mud."

The San Francisco warehouse was located in a decaying industrial area south of Market Street. It was a huge maze of scarred pillars, rusted iron girders, and vast pieces of half-ruined machinery. A hundred feet overhead, above the sagging galleries and twisted metal walkways, moonlight struggled through the decades of crusted grime on the long skylight.

The warehouse had been abandoned since the late fifties, the loading bays empty, the obsolete equipment quietly rusting, trash and debris accumulating on the concrete floors, the only sounds the wind moaning through broken glass, the scuffling of rats, and the wheezing of an occasional wino sheltering from the weather.

Tonight, however, the place had come to life. There was a party going on. Hall Jennings had never been to a party like this in his life.

A rock band was playing; the lead vocalist, a bare-chested young man wearing skin-tight black leather pants and a barbaric necklace of feathers and bones, howled into a microphone at zero range as though he would swallow it. His thick mane of straw-colored hair shimmered in the bright light. His lean, almost ascetic face was pale and sweating. He looked drunk, stoned, insane, or perhaps on the verge of a major epileptic seizure. Hall Jennings could not decide which.

A group of party guests wearing outlandish clothes— or nonclothes, their bodies painted with arcane shapes and colors—were dancing manically to the music. A long trestle table offered a sumptuous banquet of cheeses, salami, sourdough bread, apples, delectable black grapes, and an enormous ham, which had been ripped apart as though by animals.

Beside the table, a very young girl wearing little but a violet T-shirt decorated with a lightning bolt severing a heavy chain and the legend FREE THE PEOPLE! in crimson was carefully tossing grapes into the air one by one and attempting to catch them in her mouth. Beside her a young man with a ginger beard was violently shaking a bottle of Moët et Chandon champagne—oh no, thought Hall Jennings, shocked, *not* Moët et Chandon—and shrieking with pleasure at the resulting explosion of foam.

Around the perimeter, between the looming machines, people lay comatose on mattresses amid drifting clouds of dope and cigarette smoke.

The focus of attention, however, was on a hostile confrontation between two women. The taller woman, auburn haired, about thirty, stood poised in spread-legged aggression, a wide leather belt wrapped around her hand, the heavy butterfly-shaped buckle swinging threateningly. The younger girl was unarmed. She wore a loose white blouse of Indian cotton, one sleeve half-ripped from her arm. Her black hair was wild. One side of her face was horribly discolored and swollen, imprinted with a vicious welt.

"You're killing him!" she was shrieking. "You're bleeding him to death—just for the *goddam money!*"

The older woman swung her belt. Had the blow landed, it would have been crippling, but it misfired and wrapped ineffectually around her wrist. . . .

"Cut!"

Bud Evers, director, strode out onto the floor.

Silence fell.

The vocalist broke off in midphrase and stood sullenly, swinging the mike by its cord. The musicians came to a ragged halt. The dancers stood still. The only sounds were muted scuffles and sighs from the people on the mattresses, who were not professional actors but street people recruited from Haight Ashbury by the set designer to provide an authentic atmosphere.

"Pammy, dear," said Evers crossly, "for God's sake don't swing your arm like that. You know that thing doesn't have any heft to it. You have to bring your arm up and through—like so—" and he demonstrated. "Otherwise you'll screw up again."

"Isobel!" Evers roared at the younger girl, who was now rubbing her cheek. "Leave that the fuck alone! How often do I have to tell you? Makeup! Get your ass over here and touch up Ms. Wynne's cheek. Again!"

Bud Evers was as famous for his irascibility on the set as he was for his perfectionism, but it still jarred Hall Jennings to hear him speak to Isobel like that.

"And another thing," the director went on, still annoyed, "don't cringe when she swings at you. You're far too mad to worry about it hurting. You want to kill her. And anyway," he concluded wearily, "you know as well as I do that it's only Styrofoam."

The makeup girl dabbed at Isobel's cheek. Pamela Peterson, playing Portia Glaze, grimaced and took an experimental swing with the belt.

"Okay everyone, let's take it from the top."

"You mean we gotta run through the whole fucking song again?" Charlie Dark, British rock idol, who, as Avatar, was starring in his first dramatic role, blew a farting noise into the microphone.

Evers ignored him. "Positions, please," he ordered. "Isobel, you're too far over. A foot to the left—you're off your mark." Then, to the cameras, he said, "Roll it."

A skinny boy rushed to the middle of the set with a clapper board. "Scene thirty-five, take five."

"Action."

The band swung into their song. Charlie Dark alternately growled ferociously into the microphone and gibbered in a manic falsetto.

The sound mixer huddled over his console, convulsively twisting dials.

Isobel approached Pamela Peterson with the deadly purpose of a stalking lioness. "Ms. Glaze, stop right there. Ms. Glaze, I wanna say something to you. . . ."

Hall leaned back against a pillar, safely behind the bank of technicians and cameramen but still commanding a good view of the scene, and thought how much he was enjoying all this! It was idiotic, even decadent, to squander so much time, energy, and money in such a silly way when it could have been used for cancer research, energy exploration, or putting men on Mars—but it was all such fun! He had never been involved with the movie industry, despite living in Los Angeles for so many years. He had even despised the whole thing. But now, against all likelihood, he was a partner in a talent agency, watching his prime investment as she performed.

Sometimes he thought he must be mad. He found it hard to believe that he would do anything so impulsive, that he would ever live his life on two such totally unrelated levels. It was difficult now to separate the real from the fantasy. He had to force himself to remember that it was all acting, that Isobel was not really hurt, that that young singer who looked so ill would soon wipe his makeup off and return to his hotel suite for a large, healthy dinner.

This was the second time he had visited Isobel on the set. The first had been back in Los Angeles, in the studio, for her bus scene.

She and Avatar had made love on a tiny couch in a half-shell of a bus set on casters, which periodically set it rocking. Hall had marveled, watching, that they could possibly act at all under such artificial conditions. And it all looked ridiculously uncomfortable.

"Isobel, you're not in shot. Move an inch closer to Charlie—half an inch more—that's better." And the camera was surely not more than six inches behind her head.

It was grindingly boring work, and it had taken all afternoon. Hall was hot and sweaty after one hour; how must Isobel and Charlie be feeling, working so close beneath those glaring, hot lights for so long?

However, later, viewing what Hall was informed were called "the dailies," he saw, magically, a couple making love with sensuous eroticism in a moving bus. It affected him strangely. He had felt hot all over again, in quite a different way.

When the cast and crew moved to San Francisco to shoot the concert and party scenes on location, he could not resist the excuse of quite unnecessarily attending a local meeting of Orient Pacific so that he might watch Isobel again. He told Margie the meeting would probably run over the next day; he would have to spend the night. He said nothing about the movie.

He felt wicked, guilty, but adventurous and, above all, *young*. His venture was even likely to be a financial success.

The Whittaker Talent Agency was starting to get off the ground at last. Isobel's success had created a small stir, and suddenly potential new clients were calling. Studios and casting agencies were calling. Davis opened a new office on South Beverly Drive and hired a secretary named Charlene Hoover.

Charlene was half black and half Iroquois Indian—"a slave/brave cocktail," as she described herself with a sneer of her thin lips. She stood six-one and had skin the color of burnished copper. She wore her straight black hair in a severe knot at the back of her head and covered her eyelids with iridescent silver-purple shadow. She ruled Davis's office with the determination of a drill sergeant, and Hall found her both exotic and terrifying.

He felt rather as though he had boarded a raft on a fast-flowing river that was whirling him at increasing speed through wild, white-water rapids, and, his journey started, he was helpless to get off. He wished he could share his exhilarating but frightening new experiences with someone. He used to confide in Margie. Until Isobel came along, he would tell her everything . . . but not now. Not this.

Margie had been upset enough hearing he had backed Isobel, knowing it had been against George and Elizabeth Winter's express wishes. She felt she had betrayed her dearest friends. But at least she knew only about the money. She did not know about the car—although of course Isobel had to have a car in L.A. and compared with Stewart's Alfa Romeo it cost nothing—and she did not know about Hall's visits to the set. Nor would she, please God.

Hall could not really feel bad about his daughter.

Although she might have thought herself in love with Davis, Davis certainly had never been in love with Stewart, and in any case, he was far too old for her (it never occurred to Hall that Stewart and Isobel were exactly the same age). In turn, Isobel was certainly not in love with Davis. She was only interested in her career. Stewart might still get Davis in the end, Hall thought, if she still wanted him.

So Hall reassured himself, congratulating himself smugly on being really "with it" for a man his age. On very special occasions, he even allowed himself to fantasize about taking Isobel to bed.

That night, after the dailies, he invited her for dinner at Trader Vic's. Daringly, he flirted with her for the first time, and Isobel, flushed with the success of her big scene and Evers's grudging praise, flirted right back. It was all rather charming and innocent.

"You're a fascinating young lady," Hall ventured after most of a bottle of private-reserve cabernet.

"You're a marvelous man," replied Isobel, giving Hall a smile that turned his legs to jelly. "I don't know what I'd have done without you, and I think that you're very attractive."

Afterward, dizzy with the knowledge that he *could* if he wanted, thinking how wonderful it was to hear a young woman like Isobel tell him he was attractive, but resisting temptation because of poor dear Margie,

Hall took Isobel back to her hotel and, in the lobby, kissed her good night on the cheek.

Later, he was to wish devoutly that he had taken Isobel to bed after all and been hung for a sheep as a lamb.

He had been seen in Trader Vic's by at least two acquaintances of his and Margie's, who had both scrutinized his glowing, loverlike attitude toward the very young, very beautiful, well-stacked brunette. By the next morning, the news had traveled back and forth across the continent, as fast as ATT could deliver it. At Wellesley, Stewart was angrier than she thought it possible to be. Isobel, treacherous bitch, had taken first her lover and now her father! God, how she hated her.

Late that night she stood in front of her mirror staring into her own coldly furious blue eyes and promised aloud: "You're going to be very sorry for this, Isobel Winter!"

7

Westwood Village
July 16, 1971

Darling Arran,

Well, here we go again, another epistle c/o the pub. Oh God, I hate for you to have to do this. Father must be getting worse and worse. He never used to search our rooms. Darling, we must get you out of there. If it was only a question of money, I'd send you a ticket tomorrow, but you'd never get a visa and I can't ask Hall to help— there was the most god-awful stink over that dinner we had together in San Francisco during *Free Fall.* It's terribly embarrassing and everyone's talking. Nobody believes nothing, absolutely *nothing* went on. If I saw Margie, I don't think I could look her in the eye. Everyone believes I screwed him in the first place to get him to put up the money. I *hate* people!!!

The rotten thing is the gossip hasn't hurt the film at all. Lots of free pre-publicity, and I've done an interview for *Silver Screen,* who calls me "sexy Isobel Wynne" and says I "talk in a husky contralto." Davis is sending me to read next week for a really terrific supporting role in a cult flick—I play a young girl who falls in love with a nice young man and gets yanked off to a weird ranch in the desert where everyone dresses in animal skins and worships him. It's very topical—weird religious cults are popping up all over the place now—this really is freak city! Keep your fingers crossed—I need that part so badly! I'm totally broke.

Chris's Mr. Wexler phoned last week, over on business. What does this guy do for a living, anyway? He says Chris is fine and seeing a lot of John Petrocelli. What does that mean? And do you realize that it's *the* Petrocelli, of Steinberg, Petrocelli, one step away from the Rothschilds? Wow! Our little Chris has come a long way. . . .

I saw a darling sweater in Bullocks yesterday, just your color, and I've sent it in a separate package. Hope you like it. . . .

Avenue Hector Otto
Monaco
20 July 1971

Dear Arran,

Sorry not to write last week but was cruising on Archimedes Spathis's yacht. It's two hundred feet, with a helicopter in the stern. I'm serious. Lovely furniture and full of flowers. It doesn't seem like a boat at all but more of a posh hotel. I had a stateroom to myself—very grand. Mr. Wexler was in America so couldn't come. I was so disappointed. John Petrocelli came instead. He's quite nice and taught me how to water-ski. There's a speedboat on board too—you can't imagine! I'm tanned again now. The food was very good.

Mr. Wexler came back last night, thank goodness, because I missed him so much. I'm staying in his house, which is actually his head office though you wouldn't think so from the outside. It's pink stucco with tiled roof and flower boxes just like the other houses, but inside it's all Telex, phones, and computers, with a storage room in the back for the inventory. The shutters look like wood, but they're really steel with a wood veneer. I don't like the house much, actually—it feels a bit like a prison—but it's not too bad because we go out so much.

Yesterday Mr. Wexler took me to dinner with the Shah of Iran at the Hotel de Paris. They're doing business together. The shah is quite nice.

Mr. Wexler is going back to Los Angeles tomorrow. I wish I could go too—I miss him so much and it'd be lovely to see Iso—but he says John Petrocelli will take care of me so I won't be lonely. He's taking me for lunch to a restaurant up the hill in a village called La Turbie. That's in France. The French border is only a few hundred yards from my bedroom window—isn't that funny?

Oh Arran, I love him so much. I can't tell you how wonderful he is. He's taught me so much and changed my life. And the best part—he's promised he'll help you, too. He says if things work out the way he hopes, definitely in September. . . .

It was a marvelous surprise, getting two letters in one day. Arran hid them carefully under the loose board in her room along with all the other letters and photographs and Isobel's gifts—a smoky blue silk shirt from Neiman-Marcus, a Hermes scarf, a Gucci purse. Next there would be a sweater from Bullocks. She wished Iso would stop spending all that money. When could she ever wear these things, anyway?

Late at night, when it was safe, Arran would take her presents out and look at them, stroking the soft, expensive fabrics and sniffing the brand-new leather of the purse. Then she would study the photographs Isobel had sent of herself and Davis Whittaker at a beachfront restaurant in Santa Monica. How handsome he was. Was Isobel in love with him? She never said, and Arran did not like to ask her. She had a strong intuition Isobel did not wish to be asked.

Certainly, there was no doubt Christian was in love, despite the irritating sparseness of her letters—"The shah is quite nice"—oh, *really*, Chris!

How exciting and romantic their lives were, thought Arran wistfully. She never knew what to say in her own letters beyond describing the small events at the library and trying to make them interesting, which was difficult. She would never tell them about Blackie Roach. Not even how he died. How could she possibly offer Blackie Roach against Archimedes Spathis, the Shah of Iran, and Davis Whittaker? Her sisters would think it all so squalid; she could imagine how Isobel's lip would curl in disgust, hearing about what they had done together in the trucks. And she barely mentioned Mother and Father and how it was at home now. . . .

Father's increasingly frequent visits to her room grew more and more unbearable. "Never leave me," he'd cry. "I don't know what I'd do if you left me. Promise you'll never leave me." Then he would read his dreadful poetry to her and stroke her hair and his hands would tremble. "Here's the one I wrote that night at Ludgate Manor," he announced one time. "It's a wonderful old place—been in Lord Warfield's family for hundreds of years. We took it over for the officers' mess, you know—told you that, didn't I?"

"Yes," said Arran, who had heard all the stories many times before—only sometimes it was Warfield House in Kent, sometimes Foxworth Hall in Essex. The name of the aristocratic owner would vary too.

"Used to write my poetry in the window seat looking out over the croquet lawn. I can see it all now, as though it were yesterday. Old Binky Peters would be playing Noël Coward on the piano and singing. Lots of talent in the old Ninety-second Squadron. Poor old Binky bought it, poor old sod—shot down over the North Sea. Like so many of the chaps—never came back . . . D'you love me, Arran?" His mouth pressed against her shoulder; his breath smelled of gin. "Please, Arran, say you love me."

Shrinkingly, she would answer, "Yes, Father, of course I love you."

"You're not like the others," Father would say next. "You understand me. You love me. . . ."

Christian's latest letter was unusually thick.

Arran tore it open impatiently. Inside, in addition to the expected letter was a crisp rectangle of light blue paper and a second sealed envelope with her name on the front.

Opening it, Arran found herself staring down at a formal wedding invitation. Christian Winter and John Petrocelli requested the pleasure of her company at their marriage on September 18, 3:00 P.M., at the Brompton Oratory, London. The reception following would be at the Savoy Hotel.

Christian was to be married! In three weeks . . .

The blue paper was a money order for one hundred pounds.

Arran's head spun with bewilderment. She leaned for support against the corner phone booth where once she used to wait for Blackie, unfolded Christian's letter with slow deliberation, and began to read.

". . . he told me he fell in love when he first saw me in the Tanner's Club last February," Christian wrote. "Hard to believe as I must have looked awful." And, as though needing convincing, she added: "It's all rather romantic, isn't it?"

Arran shook her head and read on. "He's much older, of course—forty-five actually, though he looks younger."

She would never have said that about Ernest Wexler. She never thought about his age at all.

"And he's been married before, though it was annulled. His first wife walked out on him right after the wedding. He's being very nice and says I don't have to become a Catholic if I don't want, even though we're being married in the Oratory. Very grand . . ."

There was no physical description of John Petrocelli. It wasn't enough just to know he looked young for his age. Arran read feverishly on.

"But oh, Arran! Mr. Wexler is bringing Iso over from L.A. to be a bridesmaid, and you are to be one too! He says now that I'm marrying John, he'll do all he can for you—and being Mr. Wexler, that means a lot! He'll pay for you to go back to California with Iso and can arrange for your visa too because of some government contacts who owe him favors. Isn't that wonderful? At last! I think Mr. Wexler would do anything for me right now because he's so pleased about the wedding. He's smiling all the time. He says he's always thought of John as his son, and of course he's very fond of me.

"Please, Arran, phone me as soon as you can. . . ."

Father must have suspected something was going to happen. Arran tried to school her face to show no emotion or excitement, but Father's intuition was almost eerie. He searched her room on a daily basis for some signs of a defection. Whenever she approached the house, he would be watching for her at the window, his face a pale blur through the lace curtains. Each evening he would interrogate her relentlessly. In a tight, cold voice, he would demand a moment-by-moment account of her day—whom she had seen, what she had thought. She'd been wishing she could go away, hadn't she? he queried. She was just like the others after all. . . .

Arran would remind herself that she could leave now. There was a hundred pounds upstairs under the board in her room. She could go to London now. . . .

What was she waiting for? Did she somehow believe that things might change? That she would be able to say, "Father, Mother, Christian's getting married," and have them be pleased and excited and come to the wedding with her, where she and Iso would be bridesmaids? Was she fooling herself that after all these years of fear and anger, they might after all be a normal family, even if just for a few hours? Was she waiting for the right moment to confide in her mother— "Christian doesn't love John Petrocelli, and I'm worried . . ."?

The night of September 7 she found Father sitting on her bed reading her latest story. He turned to face her, smiling and jubilant. "This is sheer rubbish, Arran. No wonder they keep sending your stories back. I think you ought to give up this nonsense, don't you?"

Something inside Arran shivered and recoiled. She tried to remind herself that he was crazy, that his judgment was meaningless.

When he at last left her room, she studied her reflection in the mirror, very carefully, wondering whether Father's disease was hereditary and whether some metaphorical shrapnel might destroy her mind, too, when she was eighteen. She reread her work. Maybe it really was as bad as Father said. Perhaps it was as terrible as his own poetry. How would she know? I don't believe it, Arran told herself. I won't let myself believe it. My writing's all I've got. . . .

The next night, when Father came to her room again after supper, she repelled his cloying advances and pushed him away for the first time. Something had hardened inside her. "Leave me alone. Get out of here!" She could hear his shocked, outraged panting. Then he reared over her, a bulking, heavy figure in the darkness, and Arran was suddenly afraid of him. He was mad and he had been drinking. What would he do now? Whatever he did, she knew Mother wouldn't help; she would say it was Arran's own fault.

"How dare you!" Father roared. "You don't talk to me that way. I'm your *father!"* And he lashed out at her with heavy fists.

Arran threw herself sideways with a small sob of despair. She heard a crunching thud and a scream. Father had missed her; his hand had crashed into the wooden headboard of her bed. The door flung open. Mother stood silhouetted against the bright landing. She never asked what Father was doing in Arran's room in darkness with the door closed. She called, "George! Oh God, George, what is it?" And Arran watched her father rush into the safety of her arms to be comforted like a little boy.

The next morning, Father stayed in bed. Arran ate her breakfast under her mother's coldly condemning eye. Poor Father was hurt. He might have cracked two fingers.

Arran went to her room and waited until she heard her parents leave for the doctor; then, hurriedly, she dragged up her floorboard, pulled out the things she had kept there—a folder containing her stories, Isobel's and Christian's letters, Isobel's presents from

Los Angeles, and ten crisp ten-pound notes. She packed it all in two plastic shopping bags from Sainsbury's supermarket.

She walked to the corner bus stop without looking back.

She was on her way to London, and after Christian's wedding she was going to Los Angeles with Isobel.

It was her seventeenth birthday.

Christian was a beautiful bride.

She wore an ivory silk wedding gown by Chanel, the lines simple and flowing. Her veil was a froth of antique Brussels lace. She carried a cascade of yellow and white roses.

Ernest Wexler, who gave her away, wore a yellow rosebud in his buttonhole.

Arran and Isobel, bridesmaids, wore coronets of yellow roses in their hair. Arran's kept slipping sideways over one eye. Isobel had done her best when they dressed for the wedding, but Arran's hair was too fine and slippery to hold the coronet securely. Oh God, she thought anxiously, worrying that her pantyhose were wrinkled or her slip was showing, I hope I don't look too much of a mess. But she supposed it didn't matter. Nobody was looking at her. Everybody was watching Christian—and Isobel, of course.

Isobel looked sensational; she was even more beautiful than Arran remembered. Isobel had a part in a new film. She was a success even before her first film was in the theaters. She had worried about seeing Isobel again, so gorgeous, successful, and sophisticated, but her fears were needless; Iso was no different inside. She had taken charge as usual, the bossy older sister Arran adored, supervising the fitting of Christian's veil and sighing despondently, "Arran, what *are* we going to do about your hair?" It might have been old times.

Isobel had flown over for the weekend. It stunned Arran, the thought of someone coming six thousand miles for a weekend! "But I wouldn't miss it for anything," Isobel cried happily. *She* apparently did not doubt that Christian was doing the right thing. "Oh, Chris, what did we say would happen? Look at you! The *rich* Winter sister! And he's so *nice!*"

The service seemed to be very long, even though, since Christian was not a Catholic, there was no nuptial mass. Arran's feet hurt. She stared at her sister's elegant back and wondered whether this was really happening. Was she really standing in Brompton Oratory watching her sister marry one of the wealthiest men in Europe? Was Isobel really a movie actress? Was she, Arran, actually going to board a plane that night for California?

No. She couldn't believe it. She had to be dreaming. Christian felt the same. "I'm going to wake up tomorrow," she had said while Isobel arranged the veil, "and none of this will have happened."

Arran defiantly took her foot out of her shoe and scratched her left calf muscle with her big toe. If this was a dream or was for real, who cared? She didn't know any of these smart people, and she'd never see them again after this afternoon.

"I do," Christian was saying in a tone of mild surprise, and John Petrocelli, his velvet brown eyes glowing, was slipping a ring onto her finger, turning up the folds of her veil, and kissing her lips.

She was no longer Christian Winter. She was Mrs. John Petrocelli. She was a married woman. She need never be afraid of Father again. . . .

The reception at the Savoy Hotel was spectacular. It would be written up in all the society columns. Isobel and Arran stood in the receiving line for more than an hour greeting and shaking hands with hundreds of well-dressed, smiling, curious strangers, until Arran's own smile felt stiff and pasted onto her face. Her feet ached terribly. She had never been to a wedding before and did not know what to expect, but this, surely, was more of a social circus than a wedding. It was artificial. It wasn't right. Christian ought to love John Petrocelli. Father and Mother ought to be here.

Then she thought about them standing beside Christian in the receiving line and felt chilled. Father would be drunk, enraged, and shouting, while Mother, drab and anxious, would be clasping his arm protectively, murmuring, "It's all right, George. It'll be over soon. Then we can go home. . . ."

Arriving in London, she had sent them a telegram and written a long letter of explanation. Mother had written a dreadful letter back, accusing her of trying to kill her father.

John Petrocelli had written a letter too, expressing his desire to visit, but had not received a reply at all.

"Don't go," Christian had begged. "It'll just make things worse."

Isobel did not dare visit. "If only they had a phone, I could at least call."

The receiving line duties were over. Everyone had arrived. All five hundred of them. Waiters passed champagne, caviar on little pieces of toast, smoked salmon. Arran wandered among the glamorous people, overhearing fragments of conversation. Everybody seemed to be talking about money—about tax shelters, about offshore investments, about Philippe, who was condominiumizing his property in Majorca. Arran did not understand any of it. She felt depressed, hot, and thirsty and steadily sipped her champagne. She wondered how her glass always seemed to be full.

Suddenly, coming unexpectedly face-to-face with Isobel, she burst into tears. "Oh my God!" Isobel took one look at her sister, flushed, glassy-eyed, with rakishly slipping coronet, and rushed her to the ladies' room just in time.

"You'll feel better now," she said ten minutes later, as Arran sat wearily on a stool and stared into the mirror at her wan face.

"That's right, dear," the attendant said comfortingly from behind a redoubt of hairpin trays, sanitary napkins, bottles of spot remover, and aspirin. "There's nothing like having a good sick. Better out then in, I always say." She added tactfully, "It'd have been the heat done it. It's ever such a close day."

*   *   *

Three hours later, Arran was completely recovered.

The wedding was over. Christian had left for her honeymoon in Switzerland. She was married—for better or worse, she was Mrs. John Petrocelli, and nothing could be done about it.

Arran stood beside Isobel outside Terminal 3 at Heathrow Airport, listening to the shriek of jet engines, shouts of baggage handlers, blasting horns of impatient traffic, and drone of flight announcements. She inhaled a heady breath of diesel fumes and jet exhaust and felt a billowing airiness inside. It was all happening. She was really going. . . .

"Right then, girls." Martin came up with a trolley and loaded their luggage onto it. "Have a good trip." His eyes lingered hungrily on Isobel's beautiful face. "Don't wait too long before you come back and see us."

Arran stared at the receding taillights of the Jaguar until they merged into the heavy flow of traffic leaving the terminal. Then Isobel's voice cut briskly into her jumble of thoughts with the only one that really mattered now. "Come on, Arran. Pull yourself together. Wake up! You're going to California!"

8

Christian lay on the bed in the luxurious Hotel Metropole in Geneva, staring up at the intricate molding of the ceiling. Outside the window, moonlit lawns and rose gardens meandered down to the glimmering waters of Lake Leman.

It was her wedding night. She kept reminding herself of that, because it did not seem like a wedding night at all—more like a pleasant evening with a polite, considerate friend.

She did not feel like a bride. But how could she?

"It would make me so very happy, my dear, if you and John were married. . . ."

She had stared at Ernest Wexler in dazed surprise, sure she must have misunderstood. "Marry *John?*"

"I think mid-September would suit everyone," Wexler went on, unperturbed. "And naturally we'll arrange for your sister to fly over from California. Arran must also come. Of course, you'll want them both to be bridesmaids. Now, regarding Arran," he said slowly and carefully, "I see no reason why she could not return with Isobel after the wedding."

"I don't love him," Christian had said slowly, fighting a feeling of dizziness.

"Naturally," Wexler agreed. "But you must admit it is a great opportunity for you. As a Petrocelli, John is not altogether ineligible. And you have always told me how badly you want to help poor Arran."

"But why should he want to marry *me?* And he doesn't seem to love me, either. . . ." In fact, throughout the summer, he had never attempted to do more than kiss her at appropriate moments and hold her

briefly in a chaste embrace. He was always very dignified, his manner and bearing appropriate to his position as one of Europe's leading bankers. She could not
imagine him ever mauling her as Tommy Miller had.

Smiling, Wexler merely observed, "It's an excellent
match, my dear, and emotion is always adjustable."
Then he added, "Your sisters will be so very pleased
for you!"

From that moment on, although she had never actually said yes, she was committed to marry John
Petrocelli.

And now that it had actually happened, she would
have to get used to the idea.

John had come out of the bathroom and was smiling
down at her. He was wearing plum-colored pajamas.
The color suited him. With his dark eyes and olive-
toned skin, heightened by a Riviera summer to near
swarthiness, he looked almost exotic.

"My little bride," he said tenderly. He had a full-
lipped, sensitive mouth and perfect white teeth. Christian tried to imagine that mouth on hers and couldn't.

He knelt beside her on the bed.

Now, Christian thought. It's going to happen to me
now. Oh my goodness, he's going to make love to me!
But she felt curiously detached. Her primary thought
was that now Isobel wouldn't be able to act so superior anymore.

"Call me from Switzerland on Tuesday," Isobel had
ordered, clutching Christian by the upper arms, "and
tell me if it's any different if you're married! Send
John out somewhere, and tell me *all* about it! On
second thought, he can stay and listen if you're going
to brag!"

Now, John took her in his arms and kissed her
gently. Christian's lips stayed closed. He made no
attempt to part them.

"I thought that tonight," he said seriously, "we
might just lie quietly beside each other. It's all been so
hectic, hasn't it? I expect you're quite exhausted. We'll
hold each other. . . ."

Christian, who was eighteen years old and not ex-

hausted at all, nevertheless was relieved that she would
not, after all, have to experience the ultimate joys of
matrimony tonight. Perhaps tomorrow she would feel
more like a bride. Perhaps tomorrow she might want
him. Later, lying beside him, listening to his even
breathing, feeling the warmth of his body, she felt
grateful to him. John understood how she felt and was
thoughtful and considerate. Perhaps in time she *could*
learn to love him.

The next day Christian and John drove along the
shores of Lake Leman, past the fairy-tale villages of
Coppet and Nyon, then up the steep mountain road to
the fashionable resort of Gstaad, where John owned a
chalet.

Now, the honeymoon would start. The setting was
idyllic. High up in the Alps, nestled in a lush green
valley, the town was picturesque beyond belief. It
even had a medieval castle with a crenellated keep—
now a grandly renovated hotel and restaurant. John's
chalet could have been an illustration from Hansel and
Gretel, with steeply pitched roof and gables, gingerbread
trim, gaily painted and carved wooden shutters, and
window boxes filled with bright geraniums. Inside, it
glowed with warmth and sparkled with cleanliness,
from the scrubbed pine floors to the gleaming copper
pots in the kitchen.

"It's my country retreat," John said, "somewhere to
go for peace and quiet. Here we can get to know each
other. We've had no time for that, have we?"

That was Sunday. By Tuesday, they still had not
made love. Although they shared the same bed, John
had done no more than stroke her shoulders and kiss
her with undemanding affection.

When Christian called Isobel in Los Angeles, she
lied.

However, she was beginning to feel more relaxed
and affectionate in return. It was hard not to feel
affection for someone so kind and so warmly approv-
ing. John would regularly tell her how proud he was of
her and compliment her on her clothes. He noticed

and praised each outfit she wore. She was so young, he would tell her, but so accomplished—she dressed so well, spoke French so well, and was such a credit to him.

Each morning while John spent several hours on the phone to various parts of Europe and the United States, Christian would walk far up into the high meadows through the sweet-smelling grass and Alpine flowers. Her body needed the long walks—her muscles ached for exercise. She would sit sometimes and listen to the chime of the cowbells—impossible to tell how far away the cattle were grazing, for the sweet sound of the bells carried on the clear, cool air for miles—and think sadly and romantically about Ernest Wexler.

Then she would return to share with John a light lunch of baguettes, saucisson, salad, fruit, and a bottle of pleasantly dry white wine. In the afternoons, they would stroll through the village or take short excursions in John's Daimler. In the evening, there would be cocktails, dinner in town, and, later, bed and peaceful sleep. They fell into a routine that was comfortable and seldom varied.

Until their seventh night in Gstaad.

John seemed different, his attentions toward her more marked, his body continually in contact with hers.

Tonight, Christian thought, it'll happen tonight. . . . And to her surprise, she found herself not exactly on fire with anticipation, but not unready either. For the first time, she looked at John as a man and a potential lover. He was not unattractive. She wondered how his hands would feel, touching her ardently, all over, and found herself blushing. A definite sexual tension built between them during dinner at the restaurant. Everything John said somehow seemed to hold special secret meaning for her. After the meal, he ordered Grand Marnier and drank a toast to her and to their marriage, touching his glass to hers, his dark eyes looking meaningfully at her lips. Christian felt a twinge of excitement. He would be a sophisticated lover. He was forty-five years old; he must have known a great many experienced women. She wondered how he would begin, what he would do, how it would feel having him inside her. He rested his hand on her knee all the way home.

Back at the chalet, John propelled Christian up the narrow stairs to their bedroom with barely controlled urgency. Christian couldn't help but respond. With shaking hands, she began to undo the buttons of her Saint Laurent blouse.

"No!" John ordered her, gripping her by the elbows. "No, no. Not yet—not here." His voice was taut with excitement.

"What—" Christian began, as her husband, raising one hand for silence, turned and burrowed in a drawer. He took out a small, wrapped package.

"Wear these," he begged. "Change in the bathroom and put them on. Then come out and show me."

Obediently, Christian took the package and retired to the bathroom, closing the door. It would be sexy underwear, she thought with a sudden wild giggle, black lace panties, with a frilly garter belt and mesh stockings. Quickly, she untied the package. To her utter astonishment, far from yielding naughty lingerie, the package contained a typical English schoolgirl's uniform: navy blue pleated gym tunic, white aertex shirt, and sensible white cotton knickers with elastic around the legs.

Following immediately upon her heightened emotional state, it was too much. Christian crammed both hands into her mouth to quell the sudden, uncontrollable, hysterical laughter.

"Put them on," her husband called through the door, his voice high-pitched and strained. "Please, Christian—quickly."

Christian's laughter faded. Whatever would Iso say? Then she shrugged good-humoredly. She could think of no reason why she shouldn't dress up like a schoolgirl if that was what John wanted. Although wearing the bizarre clothes, so reminiscent of what she had been wearing when she first met John Petrocelli at Tanner's, she felt ridiculous and uncomfortable.

The tunic was too short. If she bent over, she would show her knickers. The white double-knit shirt was skimpy and too tight across her breasts; she could see the dark circles of her nipples through the thin fabric.

When she opened the bathroom door, John was sitting on the edge of the bed, eyes bright and expectant, waiting for her. His legs were spread. He had opened his fly, and as she stood in the bathroom door staring at him, he began to massage himself eagerly. "Come here," he commanded in a husky voice. "Christian, come to me!"

She approached the bed reluctantly. He positioned her between his opened knees. His full lower lip was flaccid and wet. "Oh Christian, my lovely Christian, my little bride . . ."

"John," Christian began, feeling at a total loss, "what are you doing? I—"

"Oh God!" her husband groaned, rolling himself fiercely in his hands. "Oh my little girl, my little Christian, pull your skirt up, my darling, pull it right up, let me see . . ."

Christian stared at him blankly, her hands hanging at her sides. She did not understand what was wrong with John, why he would want to look at the ugly cotton knickers. Resigned, she pulled up her skirt. John's gaze focused hungrily between her legs. "Pull them down," he begged, hands still working busily. "Take them down for me. Let me see it! Oh, please . . ."

Christian flushed in discomfort. Every instinct warned that she did not need to do this. Should not. But he was her husband, and he had been so kind to her. She was grateful to him. Obediently, she pulled her knickers down to her knees.

John gazed raptly at her. Then, his face tightening into an expression of near panic, he slid one hand between her legs with unbelievable swiftness, his index finger thrusting inside her vagina. Christian shrieked involuntarily and hopped backward, nearly falling onto the pretty hand-loomed rug, but John held her firmly.

His face became smooth and his lips trembled with gratitude. "Virgin," he muttered with breathless excitement. "Oh yes, a tight little virgin—my little virgin . . ."

He pulled the knickers down around Christian's ankles and ordered her to step out of them. Then, as she watched in horrified fascination, he wrapped his penis in the knickers, apparently oblivious of her presence, clenched his hands in so tight a spasm she was afraid he would injure himself, gave an inarticulate cry, and fell backward on the bed, still clutching himself, his face white and sweating.

Afterward, matter-of-factly, he dropped the semenstained garment into the laundry hamper for the maid to wash, methodically brushed his teeth and showered, dressed in a fresh pair of royal blue pajamas, and wished Christian a pleasant good night. He told her they needed to get up slightly earlier in the morning to be in time for Mass.

Christian lay sleepless. She knew she would never tell Isobel about this. She wondered what Mr. Wexler would say, if he knew?

As though to welcome Arran, a brisk northeasterly breeze had dispersed the smog from the city. The huge HOLLYWOOD sign stood out clear and white up in the hills, and the sky was a fresh blue.

"You're going to love L.A.," Isobel promised confidently, gunning her scarlet Mustang onto the freeway. "Oh, Arran, I'm so excited you're here. I've missed you and Chris so *much!* We're going to have a ball!"

Isobel's new apartment was in a white, Spanish-style villa with red tiled roof, a driveway of marble chips, and lemon trees flanking the entrance. Isobel led the way upstairs. "Ta-*dah!*" she cried proudly, throwing open her front door and standing aside for Arran to enter. "What do you think?"

Arran stood still, staring. Her first impressions were of sunlight, space, polished wood floors, and flowers. "I think it's absolutely *beautiful,*" she whispered after a moment's stunned pause. "Oh Iso, it's gorgeous!"

Isobel hugged her, crowing with the excitement of

showing off her new home to her sister. Then she dragged Arran down a short passage to the bedroom she had prepared for her. "It's not much but it's all yours!"

Arran stared at a studio couch covered with a gaily striped quilt, a white lacquered vanity, two white basket chairs, a bright Navajo rug, and, on the wall, a framed print of red and green parrots. Through white louvered shutters, she glimpsed a small garden with flowering shrubs and more lemon trees.

"Oh Iso," Arran said, "I—" Then she burst into tears. "Sorry . . ." Isobel gathered her into her arms and held her tightly and protectively. "It's okay," she crooned huskily. "Okay. Everything's going to be all right now."

In the days that followed, Arran moved very gingerly in the whirling vortex of Isobel's life. To her relief, during the first few days of adjustment, Isobel was shooting a shampoo commercial. "Bread and butter, dear," she apologized. "One simply can't afford *not* to." And she whizzed off to the television studio in her little red car. However, during her time off, she took Arran sightseeing, rushed her to parties and lunches, and, to Arran's dismay, forced her to go shopping. "It's going to be such fun doing you over," she assured Arran confidently. "I'm going to buy you lots of new stuff. You could look fabulous, you know, if you put your mind to it."

Privately, Isobel was worried about Arran, appalled by her thinness and her indoor pallor. She had forgotten English people were so pale. She resolved to turn Arran as soon as possible into a healthy, bronzed California girl. However, here Arran was a disappointment. Isobel had forgotten how stubborn her serious little sister could be, and Arran did not want to be a typical California girl. She was not tempted by the glamorous boutiques on Rodeo Drive, and she resisted the use of cosmetics. With heavy misgivings, she grudgingly allowed Isobel to take her to the incomparable Mr. G. to have her baby-fine hair styled into a

flattering urchin cut. Then, to Isobel's acute embarrassment, she protested loudly about the cost. "Sixty
dollars?" Arran exploded, staring into the mirror. "For
that? It's *daylight robbery!*"

Mr. G., proprietor and *the* current arbiter of style,
was scandalized. Nobody had ever dared challenge his
prices. He looked Arran over quickly. There was that
characteristic shabby arrogance to the girl. He decided
that to have such nerve Arran must be Old Money.
"But, dear heart, it's absolutely *you*," he assured her
deferentially. "You look simply *darling.*"

Afterward, sitting over piña coladas in the Polo
Lounge, Arran and Isobel had a violent argument.
"No, Iso, I won't let you spend money on me like
this."

"Why not, damn it?" snapped Isobel, who hated to
have her gifts spurned. "Why shouldn't I? It's what
money's for."

"It's not right. I feel uncomfortable—" She looked
around her at all the glamorous, glossy people. "Iso,
I'm different from you."

In honesty, Isobel herself had to admit that this was
very true and that having Arran live with her was not
the complete joy she had expected. In certain small
ways, Arran was even difficult—and small things added
up. Though Isobel was immaculate, Arran was messy
around the house. She would often forget to tidy the
bathroom after herself, and she was inclined to leave
dirty coffee cups on the kitchen counter. Also, most
annoyingly, Arran never seemed to like the attractive
boys Isobel found for her; she preferred the company
of the most disreputable people. "That guy Sonny,
now—he's real low-life, Arran. He looks like a Hell's
Angel." She remembered Arran giving her a very
funny look, and she had wondered, at the time, what
was going through her sister's mind. But no one ever
knew what was in Arran's mind. . . .

"I love staying with you," Arran was saying now,
very seriously, "but you're doing too much for me. I
can't let you. When I find my feet, I'm going to look
for my own apartment."

At first, Isobel was shocked. But later on, thinking it over, she knew it was right. She and Arran would never be truly compatible living under the same roof. "You can't possibly leave yet, though," she admonished. "You don't know how to take care of yourself. . . . You're just a baby."

1972

In the end, Arran stayed with Isobel for eight months. Having decided it was a temporary arrangement, the sisters got along much better. By April, however, Arran knew she must move out. It was time to go to work. She was uneasy, not being able to work, knowing she never would be able to in Isobel's apartment. There were too many distractions: the phone rang too often; too many friends dropped by; there was always a restless air of impending crisis; and always she felt the disturbing presence of Davis.

Arran knew Davis wanted her to leave. He had been unfailingly kind to her, joked with her, teased her, and called her "Little A." But, she was sure, he couldn't wait for her to be gone so that he could have Isobel to himself again. She wondered if Isobel knew how much Davis loved her.

"If you're really sure you want to set up house on your own, we'll drive around and look," Isobel said.

Curiously, having made the decision to move, Arran was hesitant about going through with it. She saw several apartments that she really liked. But each time, she procrastinated until, by the time she made up her mind that it was the right apartment after all, it was gone. Perhaps she was not ready to be independent. She felt in an odd state of suspension.

In May, however, the problem resolved itself. Isobel took a week's vacation and drove Arran up Highway 1 to visit friends in San Francisco. Arran loved the drive. She was fascinated with everything—with Hearst's castle, where they did both the indoor and the outdoor tours; with the rugged scenery of Big Sur, where they lunched at Nepenthe in a dreamlike atmosphere of cliffs, mist, ocean, and wind chimes; and with the quaintness of Carmel.

But in San Francisco she found her spiritual home. "I'm going to stay here, Iso," she said firmly her first afternoon. This was what she needed; this was what she had been waiting for. Just as she could not live comfortably under the same roof as Isobel, neither, she knew now, could she inhabit the same city. No matter where she lived in Los Angeles, Isobel would be dropping by to give her presents and take her to a party or to the beach or out to lunch. She would forever be arranging dates for Arran with clean-cut young studio executives or eligible UCLA graduates. Much as she loved Isobel, she must be on her own. The break must be a clean one.

Predictably, Isobel was horrified. "You can't decide something important just like that!"

"Why not?"

"Because you can't. Anyway, San Francisco's great to visit, but I wouldn't want to live here. It's cold, dirty, and full of weirdos."

"I think it's beautiful," Arran said stubbornly, thinking, I fit in here!

The next day she found a place to live: a room in a small hotel in North Beach—a raucous, bohemian neighborhood, home to topless bars, Italian grocery stores and delicatessens, jazz clubs, restaurants, bookstores, and coffeehouses.

Isobel hated Arran's room. "Oh really, now. This is the *pits.*" She noted with dismay the flaking plaster, stained hand basin, scarred bureau, and ratty carpet. A peek out the window yielded a view of an alley, complete with garbage cans, scrawny, pillaging cats, and a spaced-out hippie propped against the wall staring intently at his dirty toes.

Arran beamed. "I like it!"

Isobel did not say anything else, but looked distressed and anxious. Arran thought of the pretty little room in Los Angeles that Isobel had made so nice for her and felt horribly guilty. She remembered all the willing help, the love and the trouble taken, and the good intentions. For a moment she wavered; but she held firm. Roaring in her head was the urge to be separate, to be free to live her own life the way she wanted.

"I'm sorry, Iso," she said gently. "Please try and understand. I'm so very different from you. I want different things. . . ."

"It's so far away," said Isobel.

"Yes." Far enough away to make her own mistakes without Isobel flying to her rescue.

"Promise you'll call at once if you need anything at all."

Arran nodded. At the final good-bye, waving to Isobel as the bright red Mustang roared away down Broadway toward the Embarcadero Freeway and the Bay Bridge, to connect ultimately with Interstate 5 to the south, she felt bereft and nearly cried. But then, right on the heels of her sadness came exhilaration. She was on her own and she was not afraid.

And her real life was starting, as of right *now!*

Part Four

1

1973

"You knew all the time, and you never told me."

"For the most obvious reason: you'd never have married him," Ernest Wexler replied blandly. "But Christian, my dear, need we be so melodramatic? Does it really matter so much?" He crossed one leg over the other and studied the knife-edged crease in his white flannel trousers. He was looking particularly dapper today, Christian thought angrily, in a white Egyptian cotton shirt and Brooks Brothers blazer, his thick silver hair neatly trimmed and brushed, a brand-new mustache adorning his upper lip. "After all," he went on, "it happens comparatively seldom, and you have to admit it's a relatively harmless aberration."

"Perversion."

Wexler clicked his tongue irritably. "If you like."

"Yes, I do." Christian had been married for more than eighteen months now. She was still a virgin, but no longer innocent. She stared at Ernest Wexler for a long moment, a challenging stare, but as usual the challenge was lost on him and she let her eyes range, instead, over the blue sparkling waters of Lake Annecy. She and Wexler sat together over coffee on the vine-shrouded terrace of L'Auberge du Port. Out on the glittering waters, a black-haired girl in a yellow monokini, bare breasts as tan as the rest of her body, swooped back and forth behind a water-ski boat like an exotic dragonfly.

The medieval town of Annecy, set on the borders of this enchanting mountain lake in the French Alps, was just an hour's drive from Geneva, where John Petrocelli was attending a board meeting of his bank. He would join them in late afternoon.

Christian felt a rush of breathless anger, before reminding herself that it was futile to be angry.

"You sold me to him."

Wexler did not contradict her. "A bit brutal, but yes, if you care to phrase it that way."

"John Petrocelli received a virgin child bride in exchange for ten Cobra gunships."

He nodded. "Steinberg, Petrocelli might have advanced me the money for them without you as an inducement, but I couldn't take the risk. An opportunity like that doesn't come twice, you know."

"It must have been expensive," Christian said drily. "I'm glad I didn't go cheap."

"Naturally," agreed Wexler. "There was the purchase price to my agent in Laos—not exactly peanuts—and payoffs all down the line." He ticked the items off on his fingers. "Money for the pilots who obligingly flew them over the border—at great personal risk. And then money for stripping the armament, temporarily converting the gunships into crop dusters, shipping them across an ocean, and packaging and shipping the arms as machine tools, in a separate vessel. I tell you, my dear"—he passed his hand wearily across his brow—"it was a nightmare of logistics."

"I can't feel too sorry for you," Christian said. "You netted twenty million dollars."

"Grossed," Wexler corrected vehemently. "Good God, my dear. Grossed!"

"Excuse me. Incidentally, who was the buyer?"

"A group in Central America. Who remains anonymous."

"Anonymous? Why?" Christian stared across the lake at the mountains, now pale and indistinct in the midafternoon haze. "Surely you only deal with legitimate governments, military or police forces?"

Wexler raised one eyebrow. "Do I detect a note of sarcasm? You're growing up, my dear. No longer the naïve child. Naturally, it was not a legitimate government, or they could have bought military matériel from the United States through legal channels, at much less cost."

"I see."

"However, for all I know, soon they'll *be* legitimate. I don't imagine the present government will last much longer."

"Thanks to you."

"If they hadn't bought from me, they would have gone to somebody else. There are other suppliers. Why shouldn't I turn a profit when I can?" Ernest Wexler reached into an inside pocket of his blazer and extracted a Havana Corona cigar. He lit up comfortably, settled back in his chair, and watched the fragrant blue smoke rise lazily in the warm air.

He was so pleased with himself, thought Christian, it was disgusting.

"Of course, the bank did very nicely, thanks to their iniquitous interest charges. And naturally, may I remind you that, as the wife of the senior partner, you benefit as well, my dear." He closed his eyes, leaned his head against the back of the chair, and allowed the filtered sun to play across his face. Watching him, Christian thought for the first time that he looked old. His skin, normally ruddy, was pale and had a yellowish cast. There were gaunt hollows in his cheeks and dark, bruised-looking patches under his eyes. She wondered whether he was ill and felt a flood of anxiety. But then she hardened her heart. How could he have deceived her so badly? She had worshiped him, but he had merely used her. He had offered her as a bribe. He was a grasping, amoral old man. Her disillusion was crushing, and she hated him.

"You can hardly expect me to thank you," she said bitterly. "What you did to me was a terrible thing."

"Nonsense," said Ernest Wexler, sounding very tired. "Should I have allowed you to remain where you were? Being driven half out of your mind? Your life was intolerable, or have you forgotten? To say nothing of your sister . . ."

"If I hadn't married John, would you still have arranged for Arran to go to Los Angeles?"

"To be frank, I doubt it. Who knows? But consider, my dear, is your life really that bad? Is it so very much to ask, when such a great deal is given to you, that you give your husband pleasure by dressing occasionally as a schoolgirl? There are much worse things, you know."

"Yes," said Christian. "I'm finding that out."

Wexler's eyes flicked open. "Surely he hasn't become violent?" he asked, with a tinge of anxiety.

Christian sighed. "Not exactly, but . . ." The uniform and masturbating into her underwear were no longer sufficiently titillating. In an expressionless voice, she related how he was now fascinated by watching her urinate. Lately, he had wanted her to urinate onto his hands. "He's sick," she concluded. "He needs a psychiatrist."

"Of course he does," murmured Wexler tiredly. "But you must understand that John is extremely conservative and rather narrow-minded. To him, psychiatrists are only for crazy people. He does not for one moment consider himself crazy. Merely slightly eccentric."

"And I want a divorce."

His eyes shot open and his small, neat body became galvanized. "My dear! You mustn't even consider such a thing."

"An annulment, then. It shouldn't be difficult. His first wife got one. I suppose for the same reason."

"Don't be a fool," Wexler commanded. "You'd be throwing away everything for a prudish whim. As Mrs. John Petrocelli, you have an entrée anywhere in the world. As the ex-Mrs. John Petrocelli, you're nothing. Think."

There was a tight silence. Against her will, Christian thought of their houses in London, Geneva, and Gstaad; the apartment in Paris; the sleek-hulled forty-foot yacht *Chrisophile,* which John had given her for her birthday; her own silver Jaguar XK-E, which John called "the Silver Bullet"; the seats at the center court during Wimbledon; the tickets to the steward's enclosure for Henley Regatta; the royal enclosure for Ascot Race Week; the box at the Paris Opera; and, most recently, the skiing at Chamonix and Val d'Isere, which she had adored. . . . She felt deeply ashamed of herself. How *could* she be so crass? Why, she was becoming, in her way, just as amoral as Mr. Wexler.

"Well?" demanded Wexler.

She colored. "Money and power aren't everything."

He studied her face, his expression almost amused. "Aren't they?" he asked, after a moment. He gave a small, brittle chuckle. "You'll learn. But I hope not the way I learned. I hope you'll never see your family murdered or your country obliterated. And I pray that you'll never be beaten and starved in prison. When one is completely helpless, Christian my dear, one discovers that power is of the utmost importance and that power is money—there really is nothing else."

Christian looked into his cold, pale eyes. She wanted to go on hating him, but could only feel horribly sad.

"Don't do it," said Ernest Wexler. "Don't divorce him yet. Give it one more year."

She looked away. "All right."

Arran had never been so happy in her life.

She felt as though she had come home.

She loved San Francisco.

She would wake each morning excited to start the new day, pull on her T-shirt and jeans, and stroll down the block to the Caffé Trieste for breakfast, which was two cups of powerful espresso, a pastry, and the morning *Chronicle,* which would have been left on one of the tables. She would read for an hour or so and chat with whoever was there.

Sometime after ten-thirty—the exact time didn't matter much—she would go to work.

She had found a job her first Monday morning.

Walking down upper Grant Avenue, in love with the whole scene, she passed a bookstore with an eclectic, jumbled window display: an elderly dog sprawled casually asleep across a pile of paperbacks and a yellowing HELP WANTED sign. Arran went inside.

The store was narrow but surprisingly deep. The floor was wide, bare pine boards; a coffeepot steamed invitingly on the counter; two old ladies, a hippie youth, and a little girl sat reading on enormous, sagging old sofas. Shelves and shelves of books stretched back endlessly into the farthest reaches of the store. The old dog raised its head, looked at Arran through rheumy eyes, and gave one sharp bark.

Arran wandered around the stacks, stepping over piles of books on the floor and circumnavigating piles of unopened crates until, toward the rear, she found a tubby, middle-aged man, bald save for fluffy tufts of reddish hair sticking out over his ears, hanging a sign over one of the sections: MYSTIC AND OCCULT.

"Excuse me," said Arran, "do you work here?"

He turned to look at her in surprise. He wore large, round glasses that must have been very strong, for his eyes seemed abnormally huge. He reminded Arran of a large, disheveled owl. He replied, "Yep."

"I've come about the job."

He blinked at her warily. "That so?"

"Yes. I'd like it."

"Why?"

"Because I like books, and I need the money."

"It doesn't pay much money."

"That's okay. I don't care."

"Two dollars and fifty cents an hour."

"Sounds fine."

The man blinked at her again; then he grinned. He held out his hand. "Good enough. What's your name?"

"Arran Winter."

"Mine's Helmut Ringmaiden. I'm the owner. When could you start?"

"Now, if you like."

The grin grew wider. "Good enough," repeated Ringmaiden. "Welcome aboard!" They shook hands on it.

It had been as simple as that, and now Arran was one of three employees of Mogul Books. Her hours were from roughly ten-thirty in the morning to somewhere around ten-thirty at night, to be shared between herself and a lanky twenty-two-year-old dropout named Freedom. Freedom wore a straggling brown beard and

a permanent semidazed expression. He had been hit
on the head a year ago by a policeman's billy club
during a riot on the Berkeley campus and had never
been quite the same.

There was also Bones, Helmut Ringmaiden's fifteen-
year-old mixed-breed dog, who spent his days snooz-
ing in the warmth of the sunny window and was trained,
in the absence of a bell, to give a warning bark when a
customer entered.

Arran soon found that of her two co-workers, Bones
was much the more reliable. Freedom was forgetful,
easily distracted, and would occasionally stroll casually
out of the store in the middle of serving a customer.
However, he was the undisputed master of the cranky
old coffee machine, which both Ringmaiden and Arran
found unmanageable. "How I groove on that caffeine,"
Freedom would cry happily while convulsively grinding the Colombian beans he bought by the ten-pound
sack. He refused to operate the cash register, however, because he said it freaked him out. It was very
old, huge, and black, and Freedom swore that its
fading design of garlands and roses turned into snakes
with evil red eyes when he wasn't watching. It also had
a disconcerting trick of shooting its cash drawer out
with such violence that an unsuspecting operator would
be struck hard in the stomach.

Arran took over the cash register, feeling unthreatened by the snakes, and by the end of the week was
beginning to handle the book ordering as well. She
was also given the chore of taking Bones for his noon-
time stroll along Grant Avenue, where he would head
determinedly for the kitchen entrance of Luigi's Café
and wait stolidly until Pietro, the chef, appeared with
the customary tidbit.

Helmut Ringmaiden, released from the more tedious chores of running his business, was free to sit
reading in the back of the store or wander down the
aisles contentedly rearranging the shelves. Just as Miss
Truelove had before him, he wondered how he had
ever managed without Arran.

Arran adopted Mogul Books as a home away from

home, and Ringmaiden, Freedom, and Bones became her new family. She fit comfortably into their gently crazed world and as at the Birmingham Public Library, found herself attracting a variety of lonely misfits and eccentrics. They would drink Freedom's pungent coffee, lean on the counter, and talk and talk, attracted by her sweet smile and gently uncritical presence. Seldom would they leave without buying at least a paperback or a greeting card.

After a month, Helmut Ringmaiden raised her salary to three dollars an hour.

Arran moved out of the hotel and found a cheap room down the block. It was about as unappetizing as the hotel room had been, but she didn't mind. She spent very little time in it.

She began to write again. After the store was closed, she would pound away on Ringmaiden's old Underwood typewriter in the small, littered office until long after midnight. Periodically, he would read her stories and offer careful and well-considered advice. Helmut Ringmaiden had once worked in the public relations department of one of the largest New York advertising agencies. To Arran's work, he brought a long unused but still valid perspective. "If you expect to sell your work," he told her one night, slightly bleary from three glasses of Strega at Luigi's, "people have to like your characters. Ever notice how shitty all your characters are and how your main themes focus on confinement and abuse? It's depressing." Under the table, Bones whined in his sleep and farted noisily. "Let the light in," Helmut Ringmaiden advised tipsily, "and one of these days you'll have something you'll be proud of. You can do it. You have the talent."

"You really think so? You think I'm really good enough?"

He stared at her, looking more like an owl than ever. "Do I think so? Yes I do, but for Christ's sake, little girl, write about somebody we can all like for a change. . . .

It was too good to last. One morning, a month later,

Arran woke without her normal happy anticipation at starting another exciting day. For the first time in San Francisco, she found it hard to get out of bed. In an unaccountably sullen mood at work, she snapped at poor Freedom and was even rude to Helmut Ringmaiden. She didn't understand what was wrong because everything was going so well for her.

The next day she felt slightly better; but by mid-afternoon the depression had crept back as strong as ever, accompanied by a persistent feeling of impending doom. She told herself it was premenstrual tension, but later that week her period came and went as usual and nothing changed. She dreaded waking up, because each morning it was a little worse.

The day she met GianCarlo Vaccio in the Caffé Trieste, the feeling had coalesced into a hard, breathless ball of panic in her chest. During the past months, Arran had sometimes seen GianCarlo on the street. He worked as a bouncer at one of the strip clubs on Columbus Avenue and on slow nights would occasionally be lounging in the doorway watching the action outside. On duty he wore a shiny, ill-fitting black suit that strained and bulged over his huge shoulders and thickly muscled arms and legs. As Arran walked by, she would feel his cold black eyes study her, but she never turned her head.

Now, looking up from her cup of coffee and sandwich, Arran saw those predatory eyes watching her again. She stared back at him, unable to look away, feeling a warm, heavy flowering somewhere deep inside her. Across the table, Freedom looked up from his copy of the *Berkeley Barb*. "Arran? What is it?" Very slowly, as though sleepwalking, Arran rose to her feet. Freedom caught her by the sleeve. "Hey!" Under the table, Bones suddenly growled. "Arran," muttered Freedom, distressed, "what are you *doing?*"

Arran ignored him. She walked slowly across the café. Freedom watched the hulking bouncer reach out his big hairy hand and take Arran by the wrist. He said something to her, and after she paused, Freedom saw her nod. Then the man rose too. He tossed money on the table, took his leather jacket off the back of his seat, and left the café, pulling Arran after him. Freedom shrank back in his seat in incapacitating distress. He returned to Mogul Books totally distraught. He pawed desperately through his shabby backpack for his bottle of Valium. "What's wrong?" Ringmaiden demanded. "Where's Arran?" But Freedom couldn't speak, much less tell him what Arran had done . . . where she had gone, and with whom. . . .

Arran trotted at GianCarlo's side down the street, around the corner, and onto Columbus. When they arrived at the club where he worked, he pushed aside the heavy curtain covering the doorway and pulled her in after him. Her eyes temporarily blinded in the darkness after the bright street, Arran could see nothing but a bored-looking blonde gyrating under a reddish spotlight, shaking her immense silicone breasts in rough time to the music.

GianCarlo held her tightly by the elbow. "C'mon through." He led her between tightly packed but nearly empty tables to a door in the back marked EMPLOYEES ONLY. He shouldered his way through the door and dragged Arran down a brightly lit passage, where a cocktail waitress wearing little but a pair of snagged mesh tights was arguing vehemently with a busboy over tips. Somewhere a typewriter was clacking; a telephone shrilled.

Through another door, and up a steep flight of narrow stairs covered with worn, crimson carpet. Through a labyrinth of doorways, passages, and more stairs to a final door, right at the top. During their journey, GianCarlo said just two things to Arran. "How old are you?"

"Eighteen."

"You better not be fuckin' lyin'."

GianCarlo's room had sloping ceilings, badly stained with moisture. Old-fashioned wallpaper displayed cupids holding cornucopias spilling lavish showers of fruit. The bed was unmade. His black evening suit lay tossed over a straight-backed chair. An array of bottles and lotions—after-shave, cologne, shampoo—filled a glass shelf over a tiny sink. A used condom lay among lipstick-stained cigarette butts in an ashtray on the night table.

GianCarlo released her elbow and eyed her slight figure up and down. "You don't hafta take your clothes off," he said in the bored voice of one surfeited with an endless display of available female flesh.

"I want to," Arran said, pulling off her jeans.

GianCarlo shrugged. "Suit yourself," he said indifferently and lay down on the bed. He unzipped his pants, and his huge organ lay fatly against his hairy stomach, reaching almost to his navel. He casually freed the bulging testicles from the confines of his jeans, caught Arran by the arm, and drew her forward. "Okay, baby, what're you waiting for?"

Obediently, Arran slid the vast purple head of his penis between her lips and slowly swallowed him until he grunted with pleasure and writhed on the bed. "Great, baby, hey, do it, baby . . ." His big body heaved and twitched in pleasured spasms. Arran worked steadily until his grunts slowed to long rippling purrs of pleasure and she could feel the quiverings of imminent eruption. She took her mouth away and began to lick him, voluptuously, up and down. "All *right*," GianCarlo muttered appreciatively. "Hey, baby, you sure know how to give one hell of a blow job."

"Don't I," said Arran and then slashed at him lightly with her teeth, nicking the tender membrane and drawing blood. She stared him calmly in the eye. GianCarlo stared back, his mouth open in pain and shock.

"Jesus *fuck!*" He leaped to his feet, picked Arran up, and flung her across the bed. "You little cunt! You bit me. Jesus Christ, are you gonna be sorry. I'll teach you something you won't forget."

Arran watched him prepare to hit her. "For God's sake take your pants off," she said coldly. "You look stupid."

"Huh?" Caught off balance, GianCarlo dropped his hands. Then, very slowly, not once taking his black eyes from her cool gray ones, he tugged his tight jeans down to his ankles and stepped out of them. He was not wearing underpants. His erection thrust out under his shirt like the branch of a tree.

"Now then," Arran said softly, licking her underlip, "teach me. So I won't forget."

They grappled together for the rest of the afternoon, until the clouded panes of GianCarlo's west window turned pink with the setting sun. Hour after hour, he pounded into her, pouring into her tireless body the pent-up rage he had nurtured all his violent life. He came over and over again, in great shuddering bursts, while she wrenched and twisted her body under his great weight and thrust up at him or down onto him as though she could never get enough.

Finally, GianCarlo knew he was spent. He lay back limp and exhausted. She told him she wasn't satisfied, to go down on her please, but that he would never do—it seemed disgusting to him, to go down on a woman. In the end, he used his hand on her until she should have been wrung out and whimpering for mercy. At last, frustrated and furious as he could seldom in his life remember being, he took her by the shoulders and shook her violently, slapping her back and forth across the face, listening with vicious satisfaction to the thumping sound of her head striking the wall.

Finally, she came. She came in pounding, wavelike spasms, calling him Blackie, which pissed him off even more, for he was no nigger, for Christ's sake. Then she became very quiet and composed, staring at him solemnly with her wide, slate-colored eyes. GianCarlo felt uncomfortable now. Jesus, she couldn't be more than fourteen. Sullenly, he removed the tatters of his bloodstained shirt. She had made one hell of a mess of his back. "You'd better get dressed," he said. "Hurry it up, now."

Footsteps pounded on the stairs. A frenzied knocking at the door. A voice cried, "Gino, for fuck's sake get your ass up front—you're half an hour late."

"Sorry about your shirt," Arran said calmly. "I'll buy you a new one."

"Forget it," said GianCarlo. "Just get out of here."

Nimbly, she dressed, rinsed her face, and combed her hair. Apart from a slightly swollen cheek, the afternoon might never have happened.

Back at Mogul Books, Helmut and Freedom waited in fearful suspense. When she strolled through the door, her expression serene and happy, they both sighed with relief. Bones grumbled and sniffled in the window.

"You shouldn't have done that," Freedom cried reproachfully. "Man, you scared us. That's a mean guy. He's bad vibes."

Arran glanced at Freedom, and for an instant her wide, smoky gaze held the fixed, thousand-yard stare of combat veterans. Then she smiled rather strangely. "Don't worry. I won't need him often."

2

"Incidentally," Steve Romano said idly, tickling the pale soles of Isobel's feet as she floated in front of him on the twinkling surface of the dark blue pool, "are you and Whittaker fucking?"

Isobel's stomach knotted. She hated the way Steve said that, as though that was all there was to it—a mere momentary physical impulse, like a pair of dogs. . . . She buried her hot face in the wet plastic of the air mattress. After a choked moment, instead of the truth, which was that Davis had not touched her for months, she managed, "Does it matter?"

"Of course not," Steve replied nonchalantly. "Just curious."

Steve Romano was thirty-five, his body classically beautiful, his hair straight, thick, and charcoal black. His long, slightly tilted eyes were a protean hazel— sometimes brown, sometimes gold or green, and all shades between. His skin was a light, burnished olive. The star of Isobel's new film, *Ransom!,* he was one of the most bankable actors in Hollywood and his good-will was vital to Isobel. If he wanted her off the picture, it would only take one phone call.

Steve Romano always demanded approval of his leading actresses.

"It could be a very destructive experience," Davis had warned. "The guy's an egotistical, chauvinistic bastard. He regards women as toys. He won't play against any woman on the same professional level as himself, you know, just the up and coming who can't afford to kick back at him. He virtually demands seigneurial rights as a clause in his contract, and if he does not approve"—Davis drew the flat of his hand across his throat—"you've humiliated yourself and lost the picture too." He sighed. "Think it's worth it?" He looked at her searchingly. "Isobel, there'll be other parts. You're going to make it whatever happens. It doesn't have to be this one. . . ."

Isobel felt cold, but she said in a tight voice, "I want this one. I want it so badly. . . ." The part was Maria Collins, heiress to a broadcasting empire who was kidnaped by bandits while vacationing in Acapulco. While held for ransom in the Sierra Madre del Sur, she became obsessed with her captor, Enrique Diaz, played by Steve Romano. It was a story of systematic mind-changing. If she did well, her career would receive an unbelievable boost. It demanded really gritty acting, and it would be her first starring vehicle. "I'd do *anything* for this part!"

A pause. "You'll probably have to," Davis said, his voice hard and remote. "Good luck to you."

Why should he care? Isobel wondered forlornly.

Today, she had agonized all morning wondering what to wear for her lunch meeting with Steve Romano at his house. What would make her seem irresistible? Finally, she decided to look romantic and ethereal, surely something new for Romano. She selected a filmy white dress that draped softly at each shoulder and a wide-brimmed, pale blue straw hat that made her eyes glow like sapphires.

As it turned out, she needn't have bothered. Steve Romano answered the door himself, stark naked. As he led her directly through the house to the pool area in the back, he cast one eye at her billowing white voile gown and said casually, "You're not at a garden party, babe. Why don't you dump all that shit in the bedroom—through that door there." He pointed.

So much for romance. Isobel undressed and then, feeling awkward, stepped out through wide glass doors onto the trellised lanai beside the pool, where a poker-faced Asian servant wearing a black cotton jacket and trousers was arranging bottles and glasses on the bar—a white marble slab supported at each corner by a coyly smiling, enormous-breasted stone mermaid. The man-servant was creating immensely elaborate, pink rum drinks. He handed one to Isobel with a little bow, one to his employer, then bowed again and withdrew. "Thanks, Shiro," acknowledged Steve Romano. "You can serve lunch in about an hour."

Steve and Isobel solemnly clinked glasses. "Salud," said Steve as he eyed her lush body with calm interest. They drank, and then they swam. The pool was beautifully landscaped around the natural contours of the lot. Its edge was built of smooth, carefully chosen rocks, and the interior was unpainted so that the water was a deep, mysterious navy blue. At least, Isobel thought, Steve Romano had architectural taste.

Now, he caught her by the ankle and tugged his float alongside hers. "You're right," he said good-humoredly. "It's really not important at all about you and Whittaker. Who gives a shit!" He ran his hand lightly down the tanned curve of her back, then over and around her shoulder, before meditatively cupping her left breast in his long fingers. "You've got a great body," he allowed. "Hell of a body." He ran the point of his tongue over his lower lip. "I've never seen such tits."

"Thank you," Isobel said, nervously raising her eyes over the pillow of the mattress, hoping the servant wasn't watching. "And so do you . . ."

"Except for the tits," agreed Steve, then chuckled. "Don't worry about him—he's gone back to the kitchen. He won't come back for a while. But even if he did, what the hell. It'll make his day. Hey, loosen it up there a bit, can't you?"

Isobel shifted accommodatingly as Steve slid his fingers between her thighs. Then he spun her mattress around so that her head was level with his crotch, his muscular erection inches from her eyes. She felt his fingers slip inside her, and he rolled athletically onto one hip. "Eat it, babe," Steve commanded huskily, his hands all the while teasing, probing. "C'mon."

Awkwardly, Isobel circled his narrow loins with one arm, drew him against her, and swallowed him. His penis was cold and tasted of chlorine. She resolutely did not think about Davis. The mattresses rocked dangerously, and she clutched at him in sudden fright.

"So what does it matter if you fall off?" Steve chuckled happily, half sitting, his hands squeezing her breasts. "You're not going to drown!" At which he gave a spasmodic thrust of his hips, tossed Isobel into the water, and plunged with her, locking his strong legs around her neck, staying inside her all the way to the bottom of the pool.

Taken by surprise, Isobel had no time to draw breath. She choked as he thrust into her mouth and flailed at him with her arms. She was suddenly terrified that he was a real sadist who was going to drown her while the servant was innocently preparing lunch. The dark water turned black. Her ears rang. She thrashed helplessly through bursting, blinding bubbles. Then mercifully his legs were gone from her neck and her feet touched bottom. He withdrew his swollen organ from her mouth, and as her head broke surface into brilliant white light, she heard him laughing. She had not drowned, but standing at the edge of the pool in less than four feet of water, half blinded and completely disoriented, her soaking hair streaming across her face, she was furiously angry.

Steve Romano stood behind her now, cupping her body against his, entering her energetically from behind. Isobel braced her arms against the violence of his movements and tried not to hit her chin on the sculpted rocks. He went on and on. She stared down at the brown fingers kneading the white skin of her breasts, thinking that most women would give anything to be in her place, making love in a pool with Steve Romano. Only of course it was not making love at all—it was just fucking. For him it was all a power trip. And she suddenly thought of Davis and wanted to cry. Then he climaxed with such noisy gusto that she bit her lip with anxiety. Not only would the servant have heard, but surely the neighbors up and down the block. Look on the bright side, Isobel, she told herself firmly. It has its humor. You'll laugh about this tomorrow—especially when you're Maria Collins.

Steve gave her a splashy pat on the bottom, swung himself out of the pool, and knelt on the edge, a brown pagan creature with dripping hair, his heavy genitals hanging down between his thighs. "You ever fucked in a pool before?"

"No."

"Didn't think so. You gotta learn to relax more. You're awkward as hell. Go with it. Float into it. . . . But don't worry. You'll learn. All it takes is practice." He stood up and yelled, "Shiro!"

The manservant immediately trotted around the corner as though he had been waiting for the summons. "You can serve the lunch now," Steve said blandly. "And bring the Piper Heidsieck and the chardonnay we chose earlier."

Isobel felt strange sitting naked and disheveled at a formally set glass and wicker table, being served cracked crab, endive salad, and french bread, the immaculately dressed and impassively courteous Shiro periodically leaning across her naked right breast to fill her wineglass.

"There's quite an art to fucking in a pool," Steve said conversationally, unrolling a snowy linen napkin and tucking it around his muscled, hairy thighs. Shiro filled his glass, placed the bottle of chardonnay in a silver ice bucket, and bowed politely. Isobel watched his retreating black back with gratitude. "Pretend you're in bed," Steve continued. "Roll into it—just remember not to breathe. Jesus, how I want to suck on your breasts."

He leaned over her, bent his head, and drew the nipple and areola of her left breast into his mouth. Isobel felt the slick warmth of his tongue, knew her nipple was hard as stone, and felt a stab of hot pleasure coupled with equal stabs of fury and humiliation. She did not like Steve Romano. She hated Steve Romano. He was treating her like a prostitute, bought and paid for, and she did not want to want him. She would do whatever was required of her because she had to have the part of Maria—but she wasn't going to enjoy it.

Isobel forced herself to laugh merrily. "Come on now, Steve," she said in a teasing voice. "I'm not part of your lunch."

He took his mouth away, looked up at her through his tangled hair, and chuckled with genuine humor. "Of course you are, babe. But if you like, I'll save you for dessert. . . ."

For the next half hour, while they ate their crab and salad, he contented himself with caressing her bare leg with his toes and running his hand up and down her thigh. "They sure got me a good one this time," he said cheerily. Isobel ground her teeth in rage and remained in her seat through sheer willpower alone.

Eventually, Steve called for Shiro, who appeared on the double, removed the plates, brought out a bowl of long-stemmed strawberries, and, at Steve's order, opened the bottle of champagne.

Then it was time for dessert.

Steve took her hand, tugged her out of her chair, and led her to a wide green-and-white-striped cotton mattress lying under a trellis on the other side of the pool.

Isobel sat down, her expression guardedly mutinous. Steve sauntered back to the table and returned with the strawberries and a bottle of suntan oil. He placed the berries carefully on the ground, pushed Isobel gently down onto her back, then puddled about a tablespoonful of oil between her breasts. He knelt beside her and worked it into her skin with long, sensuous strokes.

It was three-thirty in the afternoon and very hot. She had had a lot to drink. His hands moved expertly on her body. She discovered she was feeling drowsy and lazy, and his hands suddenly felt very good. But whatever he did, she wasn't going to give in, Isobel promised herself defiantly. She wasn't going to come. She *refused* to come. She would have to appear to climax to satisfy the man's ego, but that was no problem. She was a good actress.

"You're quite a turn-on," Steve said. "I like the combination—a body that won't quit and a prudish little mind. It's going to be a lot of fun breaking you in." He reached over her and picked up a strawberry by its stem. "Okay now, open up."

Obediently, Isobel parted her lips. But Steve said, "Not your mouth, babe . . ."

Isobel stared up into his hot, hazel eyes. Her body felt jarred inside and her hands trembled. Slowly, she opened herself for him with shaking fingers while he stared greedily between her legs. Then, with deliberate slowness, he pulled off the stem and mashed the huge juicy strawberry inside her.

Isobel gasped in stupefied rage. "Needs a little topping off," Steve said calmly. He held her firmly with one hand and poured champagne.

"Oh my *God!*" cried Isobel as the freezing liquid fizzed and tingled against sensitive membranes. Then he was crouching between her legs, holding her thighs wide apart, licking, nibbling, and devouring the crushed fruit, sighing his pleasure, while Isobel writhed her hips in uncontrollable fury, then uncontrollable excitement, and suddenly, without warning and to her intense shame, found herself overwhelmed by the most shattering orgasm she had ever known.

Steve raised his head, his lips stained with strawberry juice, and nodded complacently, as though grading a test. "Good, good." Then he moved up to straddle her chest, crushing her breasts around his still rigid penis. "I've wanted to fuck your breasts all day. . . ."

Isobel did not remember a great deal after that. She had lain on the mattress, sticky with oil, sweat, semen, and strawberry juice, absolutely unable to move. She *did* remember being in the pool again, which felt numbingly cold. Then a rich sunset, black shapes of palm trees, more champagne, a wide bed, and lying face down, impaled, while Steve Romano popped an amyl nitrate capsule under her nose, chuckled, and told her she had a great ass as well as great tits. She remembered coming again, helplessly, in screaming spasms.

Then the pearl gray sky lightened to pink. Was this

dawn? Had there been a night? And a rushing of cold, desert air. Climbing steps to a familiar room . . .

Then nothing. Total blankness, until she woke in bright sunlight in her own bed. The phone was ringing.

Davis's voice was controlled and remote. "I guess you had a successful meeting with Steve Romano. He seems to think you'll be quite a compatible team. Congratulations. It must have been a good lunch. . . ."

"Morning, Miss Wynne." Charlene Hoover studied the number-one client, who looked as cool and polished and beautiful as always, wearing a new black linen dress and high-heeled, scarlet sandals, but who had new shadows under her gorgeous blue eyes, visible as soon as she removed her huge Christian Dior sunglasses.

"Hi, Charlene," said Isobel. "He's expecting me."

Charlene nodded and picked up the phone. "Miss Wynne's here," she told Davis formally, then told Isobel to go right on in. "He wants to walk you through your contract."

Isobel's heart crashed sickeningly inside her chest. She smiled pleasantly at Charlene, opened the door, and entered Davis's office with her head held high. Inside, she closed the door and leaned back against it a moment, staring at him across the long room.

Davis Whittaker had changed. He was a success now, and he looked it. He was nearly thirty. His thick black hair was carefully cut and styled. His mouth looked firmer, and his sleepy hooded eyes were colder and more calculating. He still dressed conservatively; he scorned the pastels, open shirtfronts, and winking medallions. Davis Whittaker was a rising young Hollywood agent, but in his bones he was still a New England aristocrat. And beneath that beige worsted suit and navy blue shirt, his body was as hard and fit as ever, Isobel guessed. She ached to touch him, but she did not dare.

He rested well-kept hands quietly on the top of his wide walnut and leather-topped desk, which was characteristically bare save for the folder containing her contract, the expensive pen and pencil set she had given him for Christmas, and two telephones—one black and one white.

"Well," Davis said softly, staring at her across the room, "how are you, Isobel?"

She licked dry lips. "Fine." Her voice came out as a husky whisper.

He nodded. "Good, good, you're looking well. Now come sit and we'll go through all this."

He looked as beautiful as ever, and now he looked powerful too. Isobel felt sick and furious, thinking of the afternoon and evening with Steve Romano. She flopped into the chair Davis held out for her so politely—no longer cheap brown Naugahyde but stainless steel and leather—and noticed miserably how he managed not to touch her.

Charlene brought in coffee. Davis thanked her, told her to hold calls, and then got right to work, leading Isobel scrupulously through the contract clause by clause, outlining, explaining, detailing, telling her how much money she would make and that she had star billing for the very first time—after Steve Romano, of course. After a while, Isobel stopped listening to the words—there was no point, for she trusted his judgment absolutely. All she heard was the remote tone of his voice, and she knew he didn't love her anymore.

"You'll want to take this and have your lawyer look it over," Davis was saying then, rising, holding out his hand. "Then get it right on back to me." He was looking at his watch. He was telling her he had a lunch date. She was being dismissed.

"Congratulations again," he said and gave her a wintry smile. "Now you're a real star."

Isobel inclined her head. "Thanks." And she felt her heart splinter like glass. She stretched her lips into a smile and acted, acted. "Thanks for everything, Davis. See you later."

She strolled nonchalantly through the outer office and said something polite to Charlene, airily swinging her scarlet leather tote bag, which now carried her first starring contract. Her composure lasted all the way down in the elevator and out to the parking lot, where, no longer needing to keep up her front, it broke.

The Mustang was parked beside Davis's chocolate brown Mercedes. Isobel leaned her forehead for a moment on the gleaming metal of his car's roof and felt the tears run helplessly down her cheeks. She thought about how crying would ruin her makeup and could not have cared less. She flung the tote bag savagely into the back of her own car, then slumped into the driving seat, buried her hot face in her trembling hands, and began to howl with misery.

Three cars away, the person who waited in the silver Porsche watched her calculatingly with hard blue eyes.

Unabashedly, Isobel wept on. She had never felt so alone. For a moment, Arran's face slipped in clear detail into her mind. Isobel saw Arran's wide, innocent gray eyes and gentle smile and on a sudden impulse decided to get out—get out of Los Angeles, get onto Interstate 5 and keep driving. All the way to San Francisco. Go to Arran, who loved her, and tell her . . . Oh God, thought Isobel, tell her what? About Steve Romano and fucking in his pool and on the patio and the bedroom floor and wherever else it had happened? Tell Arran what she had done to get the part of Maria Collins? Oh, really. How could Arran ever understand?

Shit, oh shit, Isobel thought wretchedly.

"There are other scripts," Davis had said. "It doesn't have to be this one. You'll make it whatever happens. . . ."

But she had wanted it all now, not later—and she had got it. She must make the best of it.

With hardening resolution, Isobel dried her eyes, squared her shoulders, and decided that she had paid so dearly for the part of Maria that she was going to make *Ransom!* and Steve Romano take her right to the top of the heap or die trying.

The driver of the Porsche waited until Isobel's car had turned the corner and disappeared, then climbed out, entered the building, and rode the elevator up to Davis Whittaker's office.

Charlene buzzed Davis, then told the visitor: "Please take a seat. He won't be long. He's on a conference call with New York."

The visitor smiled, crossing one slim leg over the other, and picked up a magazine.

On the other side of the door, Davis sat slumped in his expensive chair staring at the huge black-and-white matted photograph of Isobel on the wall. He was not on a conference call at all, as Charlene well knew.

After a moment, when the ragged pounding of his blood had subsided, he buzzed Charlene and told her to send in his visitor.

As the door closed, Charlene heard his greeting: "Stewart! I'm so glad you called. What a nice surprise!"

3

The Lord Mayor of London sat on a little gilt chair immediately in front of Christian. He wore white tie and tails and full decorations of office, including his resplendent gold chain. The Lady Mayoress sat to his left, in draped mauve silk and diamond tiara. To his right sat Princess Margaret, a plump, tiny figure in delft blue and too much jewelry. Christian could have reached out and touched her.

Christian was seated between her husband and Ernest Wexler in St. Paul's Cathedral, at a special performance of Berlioz's *Requiem*. Wexler, a staunch admirer of Berlioz, had insisted this performance not be missed, particularly with Colin Davis conducting the London Symphony Orchestra, augmented with two extra choruses and three brass bands.

The music poured majestically through the huge vaulted nave, and Christian, not usually especially stirred by music, was aware of a peculiarly charged urgency in the rolling cadences and, for no particular reason she could identify, suddenly felt afraid.

As the orchestra swung into the sinister opening chords of the Lachrymosa, she glanced to her right, where Ernest Wexler sat immediately behind Princess Margaret, his head thrown back, eyes tightly closed, new shadows apparent in his sunken cheeks. She watched his too thin hands draw into tense claws, where they rested on his elegantly tailored knees, and his thin lips tighten over his teeth. She watched as he reached inside his dinner jacket, took out a pillbox, and surreptitiously swallowed the contents.

After the long drawn-out Amen, with its soft harmony of interwoven strings and muted percussion, there was a moment of resounding silence, then waves of stunned applause, cries of approval, and bows from Colin Davis, triumphantly disheveled, clearly exhausted, but just as clearly still possessing the energy to do it all over again.

Then the long process of the departure of royalty. Princess Margaret was escorted down the endless, red-carpeted nave by the Lord Mayor and Lady Mayoress, followed by a bevy of attendants, ladies-in-waiting, and flunkies.

Free to leave. John, tall at Christian's side, offered his arm to her rather formally, now the husband she respected, handsome and dignified in evening clothes, the imperfections of approaching middle age neatly disguised by good tailoring. Here was the powerful banker, friend and advisor to heads of state and chairmen of international conglomerates, the aristocratic product of centuries of breeding among the finest European families. At such times, Christian could almost forget that whining, pathetic creature insisting she straddle his chest in the bathtub and urinate while he cried out and writhed in climax.

As he stood up, Ernest Wexler staggered once and clutched at Christian's arm for a brief steadying moment. Then he drew a deep breath, regained his balance, and strolled, debonair as always, at her side through the massive arched doors and out into the courtyard.

"I would enjoy a requiem like that being written for me," he said. "Provided, of course, that I was alive to hear it performed." He helped Christian into the back of the Jaguar. "Now we need a drink. Martin, we're going to Grosvenor Square."

The reception at the American Embassy was in honor of Henry Kissinger, who greeted Ernest Wexler as an old friend and chatted charmingly to Christian for several minutes, complimenting her both on her gown—an extravagant confection by Zandra Rhodes created from peacock-hued scarves with glittering gold borders—and on the excellence of her German. Christian liked him immensely but wished she had worn lower heels.

Wexler appeared to be rejuvenated by the reception. He wandered through the huge room, clearly enjoying himself, chatting with acquaintances, drinking quite a lot of champagne, and nibbling on hot hors d'oeuvres. Christian remembered that sudden, terrible fear she had felt in St. Paul's and decided she must have been, after all, simply overwhelmed by the music.

Within the hour, however, Wexler was at her elbow, restless, wanting to leave. He was very pale, with a spot of feverish color on each cheekbone. "I want to go to Annabel's," he announced in a slightly petulant voice. "This is boring—don't you think so? You look bored. . . ."

Back in the Jaguar, Christian wondered with wry amusement what she would have said if, three years ago, someone had told her she would meet Princess Margaret and Henry Kissinger in the same evening and be accused of looking bored. . . .

A good table waited for them at Annabel's, not too far from but not too close to the small dance floor, where the Beautiful People gyrated in gridlock proximity and near total darkness. A bottle of Dom Perignon rested in an ice bucket.

John held out Christian's chair for her, and she sat down. Her hands felt cold and her neck prickled. She felt terribly afraid again. For reassurance, she stared first at the soft reflection of lamplight glowing from the brass pillars separating the dining area from the bar and then at the deft hands of the waiter extracting the cork from the bottle of champagne. She willed herself to be calm.

Wexler raised his glass. "I wanted there to be a certain texture to this evening," he announced, touched his glass to Christian's, and then began to talk to her as though John were not even there. "I shan't be seeing you for a while, my dear. I'm not very well, you know."

"I know," replied Christian, feeling the fear coalesce into a hard ball in her chest. Forcing her tone to be light, she said, "I hope it's nothing too serious."

"No," Wexler said with a dry chuckle. "It's nothing that can't be easily taken care of. It's just such a bore, and rather undignified besides. I'm not used to being sick."

"Will you have to go to hospital?"

"Certainly not—I despise hospitals." He sipped appreciatively, then studied the bubbling golden liquid in his glass, stating firmly, "No one should be expected to live without champagne."

"Does that mean you're going to have to stop drinking? Is it—liver trouble?" Christian ventured.

Wexler looked at her and smiled. "No, my dear. My liver is quite robust—surprisingly so under the circumstances—and no, so long as I live I have no intention of giving up alcohol. But I see the writing on the wall and am going off for a very overdue rest."

"Where will you go?"

He continued to smile. "Somewhere warm, undoubtedly." And then he asked her to dance.

Christian would remember each tiny detail of that dance as though it had been burned into her brain. They danced just once, to Françoise Hardy singing "J'Attendrai." Wexler sang along to it, softly, in French. His arm around Christian's waist felt frail and delicate—no longer capable of carrying her across the hallway of his home so she would not bleed on his silk Bokhara. The girl in the disco booth had long, smooth, honey-blonde hair, and Christian could see her pink part when she leaned forward over her twin turntables.

Very soon after the dance, Wexler announced that he was tired—it was one-thirty in the morning, "and the champagne is all finished now. . . ."

Martin dropped Christian and John off at their house on Cheyne Walk on the Chelsea Embankment. Through the rear window, Wexler waved good-bye to them, his thin mouth curving in an ironic smile. Christian's last image of him was turning to direct Martin, and fingering his mustache.

*   *   *

"My very dear Christian . . ."

The letter had been brought up to her on her breakfast tray, along with three invitations, a bill from Harrod's, and a reminder from her dentist that it was time for a checkup. It was written in black ink on heavy vellum, in a decisive hand.

This is by way of an official good-bye. It is now impossible to ignore the intruder thriving inside me, since the medication level necessary to assuage the pain grows out of control. We shall therefore not see each other again. Certainly not in this life, and I have never been inclined to believe that there is anything afterward. If I am mistaken, then the long overdue rest I need will undoubtedly be spent in a warm climate, since by many standards my life has been somewhat reprehensible.

Be that as it may, I have no regrets—at least not for myself, although you gave me pause, my dear, last spring at Annecy. "Money and power aren't everything," you told me, and I assured you quite definitely that indeed that was all there was.

Perhaps I did you a gross disservice in marrying you to John Petrocelli. Faced unequivocally, and rather humiliatingly, with my own mortality, I have been doing rather a lot of thinking. I can only say in self-justification that I thought I was doing the right thing at the time. It did not occur to me that I was righting one wrong by imposing another, or that I was in fact substituting one form of entrapment for another.

I want to try to make it up to you, Christian, in the only way I know how, and you must excuse me if the way seems crass. Remember that I am just a decrepit old mercenary.

I have accordingly taken the liberty of opening an account in your name at the Credit Suisse, Zurich— details on the enclosed card—where you

220   Mary-Rose Hayes

must contact Herr Bernard Wertheim. He expects
to hear from you. It is a numbered account in
which I have deposited 3.5 million Swiss francs—
approximately one million dollars U.S. at the current rate of exchange.

This comes to you with my blessing, my dear,
for what that is worth, with no strings or restric-
tions whatsoever. You may leave John or not just
as you see fit. You are now free to live your life
however you wish, and I hope it is a long and
exciting one.

Good-bye, my dear, and good luck. Thank you
for granting me that last year of your company.
Incidentally, if I had ever been capable of loving
someone, it would undoubtedly have been you.

The letter had been mailed the day before. It had
been written long before what Christian would come
to understand was a carefully choreographed evening
of farewell, with the Berlioz *Requiem* chosen as a
suitably stylish personal tribute.

And it was now eight-thirty in the morning of the
following day.

Christian thrust her untouched breakfast tray to one
side, unmindful of the scalding coffee spilling across
her thigh, and flung on the first clothes she could find.
She did not stop to wash or to brush her hair. She ran
downstairs taking the steps three at a time, grabbing
up her purse from the hall table on the way.

Out through the door she raced, slamming it behind
her, running down the street and around the corner to
the mews garage as though pursued by demons. Her
only sustaining thought was the thin hope that somehow he had failed, that somehow she would be in
time. But she knew that Ernest Wexler never failed in
anything he set out to do and that she was far, far too
late.

Christian drove recklessly across London in her
XK-E, cursing the rush-hour traffic. However it was
only ten minutes to nine when she pulled up with a

screech outside the tall, narrow house and stared up at the rows of blank-eyed, inscrutable windows that told her nothing. She leaned on the bell, longing for Pierre's comforting arrival, Pierre who would answer the door any minute now and tell her that Mr. Wexler was safely upstairs eating his breakfast and talking on the phone to Monte Carlo, or Teheran, or Washington, D.C. But Pierre did not come, and with a chill Christian now remembered that he had been sent to Monte Carlo yesterday to put the house in order for Wexler's imminent return. . . . And the office staff would not arrive until nine-thirty.

She drew a deep breath and took the key ring from her purse. The house was a fortress; there were burglar alarms, combination and multiple locks—but Christian had lived in this house. She knew the combinations, and she still had the keys.

Behind her the steel-reinforced front door swung closed with a solid *thunk*. Christian stood alone in the dark hall and listened to the house. It was absolutely silent. She called: "Mr. Wexler! Mr. Wexler—it's me—it's Christian!" She shrank from the unnatural loudness of her own voice.

She glanced into the room on her right—the living room—and into the dining room, which, with its Telex and battery of phones, was used as a communications center. Then she peeked into the small office, where she had eaten her first dinner in this house—it seemed so long ago. . . .

Christian mounted the stairs with dragging feet, her hand sweating on the oak banister, leaving cold moisture on its polished surface. Her heart hammering in her chest, she forced herself to enter his bedroom.

It was empty.

She looked around very slowly. The room was totally neat, as she would have expected. A suit of paisley silk pajamas and a robe had been laid on the undisturbed bed, and a pair of small slippers were positioned neatly on the floor. The sheets had been turned down for the occupant, who never came. . . .

The curtains were drawn over the windows, and a bedside light was turned on, shining directly onto a small pile of newspapers and magazines.

A door stood open across the room. Christian walked through it into the dressing room. She saw an old-fashioned suit press and a fine mahogany wardrobe filled with suits of every weight and texture, to take him to any function in any climate around the world. There was a formal morning suit with charcoal tailcoat and gray striped trousers; white and black dinner jackets; velvet smoking jackets; blazers; tweeds; business suits in grays, dark blues, and pinstripes; and a rack of hats—bowlers, panamas, fedoras, even a beautiful curly-brimmed white felt Stetson.

She stared at long rows of highly polished shoes, at colorful cascades of ties, ascots, and foulards, and at the gleaming mahogany tallboy whose drawers would contain socks, shirts, underwear. She bit her lip so hard it bled.

There was just one more door, the door into the bathroom, and that was closed.

Christian opened it an inch onto an instant, potent odor of death.

Like a robot she opened the door wide—and stood there quite silently staring into Ernest Wexler's pale eyes.

A last flicker of determined denial told her that it was not too late if his eyes were open and he was looking at her. She took one step forward. But his eyes were lightless and dry, and had been dry for hours.

He was lying on his back in his enormous bathtub, still wearing his tuxedo. His shoes were placed neatly beside the tub—presumably he had not wished to scratch the porcelain. Christian saw—and recognized—the gun. She knew it was a .357 Magnum. Not particularly accurate, but devastatingly effective at short range.

Ernest Wexler's face was quite unmarred, his head, curiously flattened, resting peacefully against a pink shawl spread around the back of the bath. Only it was

not a shawl. It was blood, bone, and brain matter—
the back of his head was gone.

Christian noted all of it, still in a robotlike trance,
until, on the floor behind the tub, she saw the blood-
soaked towels that he must have arranged to protect
the carpet. Then she put her hands to her mouth and
began to make a peculiar, keening scream through her
fingers. She backed slowly and clumsily through the
door, bumping into the doorframe, knocking into furniture and into the walls. She staggered blindly back
into the bedroom, crouched like a crippled animal
beside his bed, buried her face in his silk bathrobe,
and froze there until, later, John came.

4

Arran rose very slowly to the surface through layer after layer of warm, enfolding darkness. She had been down there very deep. But she was being summoned. Something was forcefully intruding into her cozy cocoon of sleep. Something demanding and quite relentless.

Oh shit . . .

The final sheaves of sleep fell away, and she lay on her back staring at the shifting light patterns on her ceiling, feeling disoriented—and then gripped with foreboding.

The phone shrilled again beside her bed, seeming unnaturally loud, and at this time of night—3:30 A.M.—it was never good news.

The phone had rung at about this time exactly a month ago. It had been Christian, a shocked, trembling-voiced Christian.

"Arran, he's dead. . . . I can't bear it. . . . Please, please come. . . ."

She had flown to England in the morning, Christian's stunned whisper in her ears: "He had cancer—he refused treatment—what am I to do?" Thinking about Christian being a widow, she felt glad just the same that Christian had after all loved John enough to grieve for him.

But John Petrocelli, perfectly healthy, met her at Heathrow, and Arran learned that it was Ernest Wexler whom Christian had loved, and Ernest Wexler who had died.

Now, listening to the strident shrilling of the phone, she was afraid to answer it. She had left Christian on the road to recovery, about to leave for Zurich to arrange her affairs; but remembering how devastated Christian had been, and considering how prone her sister was to strange terrors and compulsions, Arran suddenly, sickeningly, feared the worst.

She picked up the receiver at last. "Hello?"

"How'd you like your clitoris bitten bloody?" a voice said loudly. "I'd make you . . ."

Arran dropped the phone as though it were red-hot. She stared at it lying on the floor, continuing to spew such filth as she had never heard, had never dreamed of. The phone looked like the head of an evil black snake. It even writhed slightly on its tight coils as it talked.

She couldn't bring herself to touch it. Helplessly, she heard the voice grating on and on. She was frozen. She couldn't think or act. She could do nothing but sit there and watch it and listen.

"What the hell's happened to you?" Helmut Ringmaiden demanded as Arran stumbled into the bookstore. "You look like death warmed up." Without much sympathy, he added, "Tough night?"

Arran looked at him with dazed eyes. She shook her head. She couldn't, *couldn't* talk about it. She managed, "I didn't sleep well. I was worrying about my book."

"Bullshit," said Ringmaiden. "You know perfectly well no agent's going to get back to you about the book for at least a month to six weeks. Why suddenly lose a night's sleep now?"

"It's been a month," Arran mumbled. "I mailed it just before I went to England."

"So what!" The pudgy bookseller slammed his fist down on the desk so that the dust and papers flew. "You know as well as I do you're not worrying about the book."

Arran said nothing and looked mulish.

"What the fuck did you do last night?" Ringmaiden demanded brutally. "Who, and how many?"

"I didn't do anything," Arran cried. "I was home. I didn't go anywhere. I went to bed early."

"Was it that creep GianCarlo?"

"I haven't seen GianCarlo for months." This was perfectly true. GianCarlo had grown clumsily possessive and Arran had at last sent him on his way. He was useless to her. For himself, his experience with Arran had been so traumatic his entire life had turned around. He was now married to a stout, placid Italian girl whose father owned a grocery store; he was driving a delivery truck and was expecting to be a father for the first time around Christmas.

Ringmaiden sighed deeply. "Well, whoever. Listen, Arran. I've warned you. I've warned you over and over. This is a rough town. So far you've been lucky. But sooner or later you're going to get yourself in big trouble. Jesus Christ," he said disgustedly, "do you expect me to believe you're looking like that because of your goddam book!"

"Yes I am!" Arran half screamed, eyes blazing and dark. "Now will you leave me alone! Don't preach at me. You don't know *anything!*"

She swung on her heel and left him to go and wait on a customer.

But each time the phone rang, all day, she would tremble with fright and refuse to answer it. Sometimes Freedom took the call, which was very brave of him, certain as he was that in the receiver dwelt evil spirits that would needle their way into his head and eat his brains. Mostly, Ringmaiden, exasperated, had to answer the phone himself.

Arran dreaded going home. She worked at the store as late as she could, and then sought refuge in the small jazz club down the street, where she had taken to stopping late in the evening to listen to the saxophone player, a lank-haired, mournful-faced girl named Rocky. She would enjoy the music, drink two glasses of red wine, listen to aging beatniks argue interminably about issues that were either long dead or insoluble, and chat with Fatso, the bartender.

Tonight, Rocky played her sax with heart-wrenching pathos. Listening, Arran began to feel soothed and calm and was finally able to tell herself she should not be so afraid. Last night's caller was just some unknown freak who had called her number at random. It was merely a disgusting accident that would never happen again.

Still, when the bar closed at 2:00 A.M. she was glad to let Fatso walk her home. Fatso was a lugubrious black man who weighed about one hundred and fifty pounds dripping wet and stood about six feet five inches tall. He was well on in his sixties and long ago had played trombone with Duke Ellington. Sometimes he could be persuaded to come out from behind his bar and jam with the band. Though Fatso was old and had arthritic knees and poor eyesight, in the dark he looked like a tall, mean dude, and with him Arran felt safe.

Now, sensing trouble, he not only walked her to her door but came all the way upstairs to her room and waited while she checked to make sure everything was all right—and disconnected her phone. He gave her his own number to call in case she had trouble. It didn't occur to either of them to call the police.

Arran lay sleepless in bed, eyes wide open, waiting. Nothing happened. She finally felt safe enough to go to sleep when the room grayed and took on detail, the garbagemen began their cacophonous dawn symphony, and the delivery trucks from the produce market groaned through the narrow streets.

It was daylight now, she was safe, and the dark night things had gone away.

Later, having slept well for four hours, she sat at her usual table in the Caffé Trieste reading the newspaper and munching on her croissant, enjoying the wonderful smell of freshly ground coffee. She felt heavy eyed but reasonably cheerful. The nightmare call seemed unreal now. She could almost imagine she had dreamed it.

The next night she disconnected the phone again and slept like a baby. And the next. The fourth night she didn't bother to disconnect it, and it didn't ring.

She decided she was safe. It had been a horrible shock, but it was over now. It had been a random piece of bad luck.

"It's okay now, Fatso, I'll go on up. Don't worry," she said at her doorway and kissed his wrinkled brown cheek. "Thanks a lot. See you tomorrow."

Arran went cheerfully upstairs alone, up three flights of peeling paint, faded wallpaper, and dim lighting from low-wattage bulbs on the landings. She opened her door and slipped inside, closed it, and slid the chain across.

The phone rang at once. It was 2:30 A.M.

"Can you *imagine* what I can do with a knife, Arran?" the same voice asked politely. "Imagine yourself tied to a tabletop, your legs wide open, and I fuck you stupid, and then I cut . . ."

Jesus, Jesus, Jesus.

Arran dropped the receiver to the floor, her hands feeling boneless, and vomited between her feet.

It seemed forever before she could steel herself to pick up that loathsome black *thing* and replace it on its cradle and take it off again immediately. In the meantime, the dreadful voice droned on and on telling her exactly what he'd do with her in the most graphic and disgusting detail. Fully dressed, she spent the rest of the night huddled in a ball under her bedclothes—waiting for footsteps on the stairs, waiting for slithery sounds at her door, waiting for the door to open, for *IT* to come in with a knife—because he would. He knows my name, Arran thought. He knows who I am and where I live. . . . It was not random at all. . . . He knew her!

At Mogul Books, shaking and white as a ghost, Arran shrank away each time a male customer came into the store, and every time the phone rang she blanched and hid behind one of the bookcases.

At noon, the phone shrilled, and Helmut Ringmaiden called her up to the front desk. "Arran, it's for you."

She approached with dragging feet and stared at the receiver he held out to her. She shook her head. "I can't. I—tell him I'm not here. I won't talk to him."

"It's not a him. It's Sally Weintraub."

"Who?"

"Your agent. Arran, your agent is calling you from New York."

Lost in her numb terror, sure that it was a trap, that it was her nighttime caller pretending to be a New York agent, she twisted both hands behind her back and shook her head.

"Go on, Arran. Take the damn phone!"

At last she forced herself. "Y—yes?" she whispered.

"Arran Winter?" The voice was, indeed, female, and briskly efficient. "This is Sally Weintraub. Now Arran, I've read your book, and I think it's really quite a good effort, particularly for a first novel." She paused, plainly expecting a delighted reaction.

"Oh."

"Uh, yes. I would definitely be glad to represent you. I would like to suggest a few minor changes before I send it out, though—not really necessary but they could make a difference—mostly involving a little cutting—"

Arran screamed. The receiver fell heavily onto the desk.

"What the hell!" Ringmaiden picked it up. "Sal! Sal, are you still there?"

Arran collapsed onto the floor and put her head between her knees, listening to Ringmaiden making placating noises. She could hear Sally Weintraub's voice sounding rightfully angry. "Now look, Helmut, all I did was suggest a few minor cuts, nothing drastic, and the kid screamed at me. That kind of ego I don't need. I won't work with it. The book's good, especially for a first shot, but *really*, Helmut, give me a break— Hemingway she's not! At least not yet."

Ringmaiden smoothly countered, telling Ms. Weintraub that Arran had recently had a personal shock quite unrelated to the book. "I wouldn't have sent her to you if I thought she couldn't deliver. Sal, she's got talent and guts. Give her a chance. . . . Yes, a personal shock and we're about to take care of it. . . . Yes, Sal, thanks a bunch. And to you. She'll be thrilled. . . . Yeah, bye now."

Then he hung up, grasped Arran by the wrist, and yanked her roughly to her feet. "All right, you. Enough of this shit. You're going to tell me what's going on, and you're telling me now."

Captain Moynihan of the San Francisco Police Department Sex Crimes Detail in no way resembled Arran's image of a police detective. He was middle-aged, overweight, with chubby jowls, and he had food stains on his tie. He wore a baggy gray suit that had worn shiny on the behind, and he moved as though he suffered from a combination of upset stomach, gas pains, and hemorrhoids. Arran felt sorry for him at once and wanted to make him comfortable. Not even Freedom felt intimidated, although Moynihan was a police officer and Freedom was understandably terrified of the police. Unasked he brought the captain a cup of coffee and waited expectantly to be told how good it was.

"Great coffee," Captain Moynihan said with obvious sincerity. Bones stumbled stiffly through the office door and fell across the captain's enormous, dusty shoes with a sigh of content, as though he had found a long lost friend.

After a few minutes of pleasant, inconsequential talk about dogs and then books, the captain said with intense admiration, "So you've written a book yourself. How wonderful. I wouldn't be able to write a book, not for a million bucks." He sat in Ringmaiden's chair, his ample buttocks overflowing each side, sipped his coffee, and looked almost sleepily relaxed.

"Nobody's going to pay me a million bucks either," Arran said. "Not that anyone wants to buy it yet . . ."

"And I don't suppose they will, if you can't bring

yourself to talk to your agent on the phone," Moynihan said gently. He looked at her somberly over the rim of his coffee cup. "Now then, Arran, why don't you tell me what's going on?"

He led her through the two phone calls, with many digressions and apparently unrelated comments that demanded comments in turn from Arran. Helmut Ringmaiden, whom Arran had asked to remain, could not help but admire the way in which Moynihan managed to extract a very complete history without appearing to do so and without Arran's realizing how much she was revealing.

"Since he knows your name," Moynihan said at last, "we must assume he either knows you or has heard of you—which is not surprising, considering your preference for violent sexual partners."

Arran stared at him in surprise. How had he known that?

"Tell me who you've been seeing."

Arran shrugged helplessly. "Just—some guys." She blushed. "I don't know their names."

"You must call them something."

She closed her eyes. Oh yes, yes indeed. There was Freezer, and Slats, and Butane—and Rabbitman. She looked like a twelve-year-old concentrating as she recited a poem. She thought for a moment and then added several more.

"These were all sexual partners?"

"Yes."

"Do you remember telling any of them your name?"

"No. But I might have. I suppose."

"And where did you meet these men?"

"At a bar—kind of a club, really. It's a biker hangout."

"Where?"

"In Oakland. East of Fruitvale." She gave an approximate address.

"I see. And then you'd have some drinks, and have sex—"

"Just a beer or something. I don't drink very much. And we wouldn't have sex there."

"Where, then?"

"There was this house, a run-down old house in Alameda. They'd take me there. . . ." She had a vague memory of a huge, decaying mansion, only she never paid much attention to the surroundings. She retained only a series of images: a vast, shadowy room with a splintery wood floor; stained mattresses; an enormous Nazi flag hanging on the wall—it must have been at least ten feet by six—blood red with a black swastika; a tray of kitty litter in one corner for the house cat, a scornful Siamese who would pick its way delicately among the writhing bodies on the floor. She thought they kept guns there. And there were drugs, of course. "But I don't do drugs. Ever."

"Could you find that house again?"

She shook her head. "It was on the corner of two big streets, and there was a—a vacant lot on one side. Grass and garbage—and a broken old pram."

"A what?"

"A pram—baby carriage."

"A big old house on a major intersection, with a vacant lot next door with an old pram. No problem— we'll find it. Good eye for detail, Arran, but then you're a writer, aren't you . . . ?"

Arran colored. "Maybe."

"There won't even be a maybe," Moynihan said, his voice hardening a trifle, "unless you take some responsibility for yourself." He surveyed her critically, and she saw that his eyes were gray and unexpectedly penetrating. "Now here's what you do." He methodically checked off items on his thick fingers. "Number one, disconnect your phone. Number two, get out of that apartment immediately. And I mean today. If you can't find a place to live at once, move in with a friend. Number three, make sure your new phone number is unlisted. Number four, find yourself a roommate—someone you can trust. Number five, and most important of all, get yourself some counseling. You are deliberately putting yourself at acute risk, and we have to be realistic. You have to make some changes in your life if you want to live long enough to enjoy being a successful author. I don't know why you feel you have to do this to yourself, Arran, and it's not my job to know. I take care of the effect, not the cause." He handed her a short list of names, all of them followed by Ph.D. "All of these are okay," Moynihan told her. "We've used them all, in the department. You get smart and call one of them right away."

"I'm going to Mexico tomorrow," Isobel said, her voice curiously subdued. "Who was that who answered your phone?"

"My new roommate."

"Oh. He sounds black."

"He is. His name's Fatso. He works as a bartender and plays the trombone.

"Oh," said Isobel.

Arran waited for a tirade of older sister concern and admonition. When nothing happened, she took pity on Isobel and said reassuringly, "Don't worry, Iso. He's pretty ancient, and we're sharing the rent—that's all."

"That's good," Isobel replied vaguely.

"Remember how I wanted a bigger place?" Arran did want to share her good news. "Well, thanks to Fatso it's all worked out. We've moved into the top unit in the building where he works, and we each have our own room! Oh and Iso, my agent likes my book. She thinks she can sell it."

"That's wonderful."

"I feel very good about everything right now. You'll have to come up to visit and meet Fatso when you get back from Mexico. You'll like him."

"I'm sure I will," Isobel said wanly. "Good-bye, Arran. I'll send you a present from San Blas."

"Have fun," said Arran.

She hung up, nonplussed and, despite herself, a little bit piqued. Isobel should have reacted more. Had Isobel in fact listened to a single word? Then Arran shrugged philosophically. Isobel was starring in a film and going to Mexico and had a lot on her mind.

Why complain? Especially since she, Arran, had been telling the truth, saying how good things were now.

She had done everything Captain Moynihan had said.

She was safe with Fatso and an unlisted number, and there had been no more phone calls.

The only thing she had not done was see a psychologist, but that she would never do.

5

Stewart was much too clever to bad-mouth Isobel to Davis, so she invited him to dinner and allowed her parents to do it for her. It was entirely natural that she should invite Davis to dinner; after all, her father was still his friend and business partner.

Hall Jennings was also still smarting from the humiliation of almost having made a monumental fool of himself. He had come so close, so very close to putting at risk his credibility, his life-style, and his long marriage to Margie. He was also uncomfortably aware that, although his actions might have been innocent, his thoughts, emphatically, were not. Occasionally at night, lying in bed beside the gently snoring Margie, he would curdle inside with embarrassment and shame. And he could not help but be angry with Isobel for having been the cause of such disruption in his life.

Margie, of course, was both hurt and angry, with an added ingredient of betrayal. She had taken Isobel into her home and her heart and had been repaid in such shabby coin. "Rather a deceitful girl. I couldn't help but feel thoroughly used."

As this closely paralleled Davis's own emotion regarding Isobel, he did not contradict her.

"Well maybe," Stewart said, "but I still think it showed guts, coming out here and going after her career the way she did."

Davis decided that Stewart was really a much nicer person than he had thought. Being with her was much less emotionally draining than being with Isobel. She had no driving ambitions to be a movie star; she was exceptionally attractive and just the opposite of Isobel in looks. Tired of New England winters, Stewart had just transferred home to UCLA and now, in her senior year, seemed far more mature. Davis found himself surprisingly pleased to see her, and there was the additional bond of a shared background, even of family ties (for several Whittakers were married to Jenningses back in Connecticut).

Davis felt at ease and more relaxed than he had in months. He was glad Stewart had called him that morning and invited herself for lunch.

Ransom! lurched into the final throes of preproduction with the usual threats of lawsuits, actual lawsuits, firings, and widespread paranoia customary in the movie business when a major motion picture gets off the ground. Damon Rutherford, the legendary Broadway actor supposed to play Drake Collins, Isobel's millionaire father, suffered a mild stroke and had to be replaced at the last minute. The original screenwriter was fired; a second and then a third were brought in with more threatened lawsuits and arbitration by the Writers' Guild. There were endless frustrations and delays with the Mexican government regarding permits, the hiring of local talent, and an escalation of payoffs.

However, a high-level interest in the movie was maintained by the exciting romance between the two stars, Isobel Wynne and Steve Romano, and the publicity department played it up for all it was worth. Tear sheets and clippings from newspapers and magazines arrived on a daily basis on Davis's desk. He would read about Isobel's being at a party with Steve, dining cozily with Steve at some plush night spot, snatching a weekend with him in Palm Springs, Big Sur, or Escondido.

Of course, he was well aware that a great deal of it was engineered for publicity; for all he knew, there was no romance at all. He was also well aware of the importance to Steve of power games and manipulation; Isobel might have no option but to go along with it all, for she could still find herself thrown off the picture. But just the same, there they were in all the photographs, faces close together, smiling. "This is love!" Steve reputedly told the *National Enquirer*. And fact or fantasy, it hurt just as he had always known it would.

He was thankful for the undemanding, comforting presence of Stewart. He avoided Isobel as much as possible, handling as much business as he could over the phone.

Once the film actually went into production, he barely saw her—until the departure for San Blas was imminent.

Isobel called early on Sunday morning. "Davis, do you know how to drive a boat?"

"Sure," he replied.

"Great," said Isobel. "I've rented a cabin cruiser for the day. For us. I'm bringing a picnic. Davis, I really want to see you. It's been weeks and weeks. . . ."

He found himself agreeing before he had time to think. He would never know how much she was counting on this excursion and how frightened she had been of calling him.

Isobel greeted him on the dock, smiling broadly. She looked fabulous, thought Davis, very un-movie-star, wearing jeans, a workshirt, and a dark blue floppy cotton hat. In one hand, she carried a duffel bag containing sweater, jacket, bathing suit, and towel, and in the other, a large wicker hamper full of food. The boat was a twenty-five-foot Chris-Craft with a small cabin and comfortable afterdeck. The weather was perfect: blue skies, calm seas, and a gentle westerly breeze.

Isobel herself took the boat out from the dock while Davis handled the lines. "The weather's so calm, and it can't be that much different from driving a car!" She had developed a passion for cars and was a good though too fast driver. She had sold the Mustang— "hated to do it; I really loved it; it was my very first car and a good friend"—but how she adored her new Maserati. She had *Ransom!* and Steve Romano to thank for that, Davis thought wryly.

After half an hour, Davis took over the wheel and headed them far out into the Pacific, until Los Angeles was a mere dirty blot on the horizon and the mountains had faded into a line of haze. He stood on the flying bridge in full sun, the wind lifting his hair, the heat dry and prickling on his naked shoulders. Suddenly, with a wild yell of glee, he opened the engine up to full throttle. The boat didn't ride the water particularly well, but it felt good. It felt more than good—it felt great, pounding violently into the low swells, feeling the vibration of the deck under his feet, and watching the white water foam around the bow. The tension and suspicion of the last few months now seemed ludicrous. Thank God Isobel had had the sense to arrange this day. He wished they had gas enough to push all the way to Hawaii. To hell with *Ransom!*, with fame, success, and money. Who needed them? He was on a boat on the ocean with food and beer on a gorgeous day—with Isobel. He felt young and irresponsible and defiantly happy! "Fuck the world!" Davis yelled, letting go the wheel and pounding both fists at the air. He hadn't had such fun in a very long time. Far too long . . .

They roared on for another half hour, Isobel at his side, hat lost, hair flying, until she announced she was hungry. Davis slowed and cut the engine. Suddenly, it was very quiet. The little boat rocked lightly. The sun beat down. Isobel unpacked the lunch. There was french bread, cheese, salami, ham, crunchy green apples, and a six-pack of beer. She settled herself cross-legged on the white plastic pillows, spread out the food, and unself-consciously took her bikini top off, spreading her arms luxuriously to the sun.

Davis stared at her.

God, she was beautiful. He had forgotten how beautiful she was.

He knew they chattered cheerfully throughout the picnic, but he did not know what they talked about or what they ate. All he remembered afterward was the way she looked, the way he wanted her—and how much he had loved her.

"I don't want to think about anything but this afternoon," Isobel said after a while and stretched out her arms to him. He fell into them with almost a groan of relief and a feeling of homecoming. "And I want to tell you something. . . ." Today she was going to tell him how much she loved him. She had decided she could not bear it, that no movie was worth not seeing him, worth missing the warmth and comfort of his arms and the wonderful touch of his hands. Even if he laughed at her, she was going to tell him.

But she had no chance to tell him because he was lying on top of her, pressing her against the soft white pillows, and kissing her long and searchingly, unbearably aroused. Then, still kissing her, he was entering her body, groaning his delight deep in his throat, tumbling her dark hair through his hands, and plunging wildly to a fast, uncontrollable climax.

"It's been too long," Davis murmured, lying across her, his face pillowed in the curve of her neck and shoulder.

"Far too long," agreed Isobel, triumphantly happy. She had him back—everything would be all right.

"I didn't give you a chance. Sorry. Too quick." He kissed the soft skin below her ear.

"Never mind," Isobel said confidently. "You will." She stroked his hair, his shoulders, and the long curve of his tanned back.

He turned his head to look at her. His mouth was soft, and his hooded amber eyes gazed into hers with first a look of adoration and tenderness and then with the darkening urgency of desire. "God, how I want you."

"Well," Isobel whispered, mouth curving into a secret smile, "here I am."

He rose to his knees, placed a hand on either side of her head, and leaned forward to kiss the tips of her breasts. He ran his fingertips lightly over her body, then parted her thighs, knelt between them, and kissed her with mounting excitement until he was rigid once more and Isobel writhed wildly against him, clutching at his shoulders.

He raised his head. "Wait," Davis cried gently. "Iso, wait, I don't want to—" Then his voice faded. Her legs were drawn up tightly against her. High up on her right thigh, too far around to be easily visible to her, were four blue marks. And a fifth, slightly distanced.

Fresh bruises, imprinted by somebody else's fingers. And he knew perfectly well whose they had been.

Davis felt cold. His brain darkened. His love was obliterated by indescribable rage. He hadn't thought it possible to feel such anger. He wanted to kill Isobel. His hands trembled on the warm flesh of her thigh, and he imagined them around her neck, sinking into her flesh, her eyes bulging with horror and her tongue protruding. Images of Isobel and Steve Romano together swam in front of his eyes. They were coupled together, laughing—like dogs. Like goats. And then there was Isobel with Hall Jennings. Oh God, the fucking whore. Why else would he lend her money, pay for her apartment, buy her a goddam Mustang? For all he knew, Hall Jennings had bought her the Maserati as well. She had used everyone. She had played him for a fool, all the time, and he had been planning to tell her how much he loved her.

The violence in him had to be spent. Davis reared back onto his knees, caught Isobel under the armpits, and twisted her flat on her face on the pillows, pinning her down with his hand hard across the back of her neck. He took her with fury, hating her, hating himself for hurting her, but unable to stop himself. It was, after all, better than killing her. . . .

In a vile mood, Isobel boarded a Mexicana Airlines jet for Guadalajara three days later. She had never been to Mexico before save for small trips across the border and had been looking forward to it; now she didn't care if the whole country dropped into the ocean and disappeared.

She leaned her hot forehead against the weather-blistered first-class window, stared numbly at the endless miles of sand and wind-blasted rock below her and tried not to think. Especially not think about Davis.

But that dreadful ride back to Marina Del Rey in the boat went on forever in her head: Davis's cool, distant profile turned away from her as he handled the wheel; his cool, distant remark—"I'm sorry, Isobel. That was definitely unnecessary roughness. But I promise you, I've not left any marks. . . ."

Back home, she had examined herself and understood exactly what he had meant.

God, how she hated Steve Romano.

She called for a vodka, drained it, and called for another, glaring at him where he sat, in an aisle seat two rows up, handsome as the devil and every inch the bandit chieftain, wearing bush jacket and khaki pants, terrorist cap pushed to the back of his elegant head, unabashedly flirting with the stewardess.

Isobel's bedroom at the Palacio Azul—the best hotel in San Blas and once the summer residence of a European ambassador to Mexico—was as big as a ballroom. It boasted twenty-five-foot cathedral ceilings, a pair of vast windows with intricate wrought-iron work and heavy wooden shutters, and two double beds. An enormous fan chuntered slowly around overhead, gently rotating the hot, moist air; double carved mahogany doors opened onto a central patio crowded with flowering shrubs and foliage and resounding with the squawks of parrots.

The Palacio Azul was probably one of the most romantic places Isobel had seen—but she had lost her lover and was here with the man she most hated in her life.

Lying in one of the huge beds, listening to vague slithering and rustling sounds as the nocturnal creatures of the old hotel came to life, she began to cry softly. As though by signal, the latch of her door rattled, and a voice hissed, "Hey, Iso, babe, let me in—it's Stevo."

Fuck you, Stevo, Isobel whispered into the busy darkness. She pretended not to hear. To be asleep. At least he couldn't get in—she had drawn both the heavy iron bolts, and the door was three inches thick. With grim satisfaction, she reflected that from now on, she need not knuckle under to Steve Romano. They would never throw her off the film now. . . .

"But can't you at least be polite to the man?" Bud Evers complained. "I thought you and Romano were supposed to be a hot item. Can't you quit the fighting? I can't take any more shit."

Poor Evers had enough problems. The weather was dreadful, the rain falling in blinding sheets. Half the second unit was stricken with diarrhea. The chief cameraman had been bitten by a mysterious, unidentifiable insect, suffered an acute allergic reaction, and had to be flown out by helicopter. There were constant problems with supplies. Film had been ruined by the damp. And the remaining crew members, all threatening to strike, were growing increasingly morose and drunk.

Between the scenes they managed to shoot, Isobel sat either on the steamy terrace of the Palacio Azul drinking tequila or when the rain held off, on the damp beach under the gray clouds, wondering despairingly whether she would ever be happy again.

The only ray of light was the sudden appearance of Refugio Ramirez, who was visiting the set to take publicity pictures of the actual shooting.

Ramirez had become an old friend. She owed a lot to him; she felt comfortable with him; and better yet, she could talk to him about Davis. "I guess it's all over," she half sobbed, sitting across from him at a rickety wooden table in a palm-thatched bar called the Coco Loco. She had drunk three huge rum concoctions and was feeling miserable. Across the table, Ramirez's toad face wore an expression of indescribable sensitivity and concern.

Later they wandered among the coconut palms down to the beach, the fronds rattling restlessly over their heads in the gusty wind. Far out at sea, the black mass of an approaching squall blotted out the stars.

"I feel so awful," Isobel howled suddenly and began to cry.

"Hey," Ramirez comforted. "It's okay, Iso. Come here . . ."

She turned her wet face into his warm shoulder and felt his hands stroking her back, so gentle and soothing. He murmured to her quietly, as though calming a distressed animal. His hands felt wonderful. Isobel felt her tears drying as he caressed her hair and his gentle, knowing fingers tilted up her chin so he could kiss her lips. She forgot he looked like a toad.

Then he took off his leather jacket, spread it on the sand, and eased her down onto it. She lay passively as he sat beside her, gathered her into his arms, and rocked her like a baby. He continued to murmur to her in a mixture of soft Spanish and English, the rhythm of his hands unbroken—but suddenly the buttons of her shirt were open and his clever artist's fingers were caressing her breasts.

He was tender, warm, and loving. Isobel did absolutely nothing to stop him as he pressed her gently back against the sand and began to make love to her.

He brought her comfort—and pleasure. She remembered Davis's saying that toadlike Ramirez had made love to every beautiful woman in Los Angeles and not believing him, finding the thought incongruous and even hilarious. Now it seemed perfectly fitting that he should have, for Ramirez was a lover in the best sense of the word. He was alive to every nuance of her body, and he wanted to give her nothing but pleasure. Making love with Refugio Ramirez, Isobel was even able to forget about Davis. She forgot everything but the sureness of those clever, tender hands.

Three days later, the morning dawned clear and sunny, and everyone was galvanized into action.

It was an enormous relief to be working. They worked from dawn to nightfall, taking advantage of every dry moment. The weather held through the week. And Evers worked them every day from sunrise to sunset.

Finally, there was just one key scene left to shoot. After that, they could go home and leave the second unit to take the final location shots of village and jungle.

At dawn, they loaded into three jeeps and set off down a muddy track through the coconut groves toward the fringes of the rain forest.

Isobel had dreaded this scene—her most important scene with Steve Romano. It was Maria's escape attempt, where she crawls away from the camp, starts to run for freedom, and is overtaken, overwhelmed, and subsequently raped by Enrique Diaz, the bandit leader. As the jeep jolted along the narrow, overgrown track, Isobel tried to psych herself into the role. She must get into Maria's head. How would Maria feel? What would be the level of her desperation? Maria had been kidnapped at gunpoint by this terrifying man; she had been harassed and terrorized; she was exhausted, half-starved, and half out of her mind. Her entire being was focused on survival, on escaping before they killed her.

And now, she might, just might, have done it . . . creeping out of her tent just before dawn—the men, who had drunk too much last night, sprawled around the campsite heavily asleep, the watch guard dozing over his automatic rifle. Quietly, very quietly, on tiptoe through brush and leaves, she moved like a deer in her filthy jeans and torn silk blouse. She felt so dirty, her hair hanging around her face in uncombed snarls, and so humiliated—she had even had to go to the toilet in front of an audience of sneering men.

A twig snapped underfoot; she froze. It had sounded as loud as a gunshot. She waited, listening to her heavy breathing and the pounding of her heart. Nothing happened. Relief. It was all right. . . . The camp was now hidden from view behind a tangle of bushes and tree branches still festooned with nighttime spiderwebs spangled with dew. By God, she was going to make it—she was going to get away. She would find a road where there would be traffic and people and she could get help. . . . Maria gave a small sob and dashed the tears away from her face. Please God, she was going to make it—she had to, *had to*—

"Hold it right there, Miss Collins."

Oh Jesus. She froze once more, hands clenched at

her sides, horribly aware of the gun she knew would be trained on her back. Her sob now was audible—a sob of pure terror, frustration, and fury.

"Turn around. Real slow."

And there he stood, on the edge of the clearing, lean and dangerous as a panther, spread-legged, a big-barreled .45 unwaveringly aimed at her chest. He watched her grimly over the gunsights. "You don't go no place." And he began to walk toward her—only it was not a real walk, more of a glide, like that of a large predator stalking its prey.

She watched him helplessly. Her voice crackling with fear, she said, "I'm not worth anything to you dead."

He held the gun in one hand now. He shrugged powerful shoulders. "The deal is, we get paid and then we send you back to Daddy. Dead or alive is up to you."

Tears of rage poured down Maria's grimy cheeks. "Fuck you!" she whispered harshly.

He approached within six feet of her and stopped. He looked her over, his expression compounded of anger and contempt and shot through with a cruel urge to dominate. "Your debutante friends ought to see you now," he said cynically. "You're a mess, Maria Collins." He holstered his gun. "And you leave when I'm ready for you to leave. Not one moment before." Suddenly he smiled, a cold, cynical smile, and, his eyes not leaving hers for one second, his hands dropped to his belt buckle and slowly and deliberately unhooked it.

It was at that moment that the anger, helplessness, and misery that had wracked her since her capture suddenly coalesced into a hot steel ball in her chest. By God, she would do some damage in her turn! She flew at him, taking him totally by surprise, slashing him across the face with her dirty, broken nails and aiming a powerful kick at his kneecap.

Eyes blazing, he caught her by the wrist and slapped her hard. "You little bitch! Oh Christ, you little bitch—" She twisted in his grip and landed a vicious elbow in his gut. She heard the painful, shocked wheeze of his breath, and he released her so suddenly she stumbled in the long wet grass. He was drawing his gun now. She lashed out at him with her feet, lunging at the same time for the gun, while he cracked her across the side of her face. She screamed in fury and brought her knee up between his legs. His lips white with pain, his eyes narrowed and evil, he raised both fists and smashed her to the ground before falling on her with his full weight. They rolled back and forth like squalling animals until at last, inevitably, he overpowered her.

He held her down in the bruised, muddy grass, panting hoarsely through his mouth, the blood dripping down his cheek from the wounds of her gouging nails. He held both her wrists doubled up behind her head and ground his knee into her diaphragm. "Oh, you cunt . . .," he whispered grimly, staring into her defiant face, "you little cunt. Are you ever going to be sorry for this!" Then with one deliberate movement, he ripped the remaining shreds of her blouse from her body.

"Okay," Bud Evers said calmly. "Cut!"

Steve Romano climbed painfully to his feet, wheezing in distress. He tentatively touched his wounded cheek. "Jesus Christ, I'm going to sue."

"Bullshit," Evers responded. "When you see that scene, you're gonna piss in your pants with excitement. We had three cameras rolling all the way through, and the hand-held camera got close-ups like you wouldn't believe. We didn't miss a thing. That footage goes back to L.A. by special messenger this afternoon, right to the lab. You were terrific, man. You were every woman's living fantasy. Better believe it."

Refugio Ramirez caught a good shot of Evers placating the surly, pained Romano. And he got another good one, of Isobel, still sitting in the mud, her clothing in shreds, grinning in triumph. The normally taciturn camera crew was staring at her with awe. The wardrobe girl was handing her a jacket with which to cover herself.

"She went crazy," Steve continued to complain, but with less vehemence, thinking of himself being a living fantasy. "The bitch ought to be put in restraints. If I get infected, I tell you, I'm gonna—"

"You had your tetanus shot," Evers said soothingly, "and the doc can give you a jab of antibiotic soon as we get back to town." He clapped his hand on Romano's shoulder, feeling him wince. "Listen, Steve, when this is released, there's not going to be a woman in the country—in the world—who won't be lusting after your body. You were fucking sensational. And if I'm wrong, then you can sue with my blessing."

Isobel rode back to San Blas beside Refugio Ramirez. "You okay?" he asked anxiously. "He got in a coupla good ones."

"Yeah," said Isobel contentedly, "I'm all right. Nothing a soak in a hot bath won't fix. And I got in some better ones." Funny, she felt okay about Steve Romano now. She had had her revenge. She grinned.

Back in the hotel, Bud Evers caught Isobel by the arm, dragged her into a dark, secluded corner of the bar, and ordered them both a shot of tequila. "You are one dumb, crazy broad," he told her threateningly. "If you pull a stunt like that again, you're fired so fast you won't believe it. If I hadn't gone right to work and groveled, told him how sensational he'd been, we'd be up shit creek. All because of you."

"You could have stopped it any time," Isobel said.

"What?" Evers stared at her in surprise. "And miss great footage like that? Now I know you're crazy."

Isobel smiled.

"And it turned out okay. Steve really was good. Better than I've ever seen him." He tipped up his glass and drained his tequila. "But you were better. No matter what I told Steve, that was your scene. It's going to do it for you, I think. Believe me, Isobel, you were fantastic."

Six weeks later, the movie was wrapped. Steve Romano's face did not become infected. Isobel decided to take a short vacation. She needed one desperately.

She had picked up some stomach bug in Mexico that she was having trouble throwing off. She was suffering from intermittent cramps and nausea, had lost nearly ten pounds, and had never felt so exhausted in her life. A course of megavitamins was needed, she decided. And iron—she was certainly anemic.

She went to the doctor for tests. Dr. Shapiro gave her a thorough physical and put her on a regime of vitamins and mineral supplements. "That'll put you right back on track."

"Well, thank God," Isobel said with relief. "I was afraid I might have picked up something serious in Mexico. Like a parasite or something."

"That's one way of putting it," Dr. Shapiro smiled. "But actually, you're as healthy as a horse, Isobel. Under the circumstances."

"Circumstances?" Isobel stared at him blankly. "What circumstances?"

Dr. Shapiro stared at her. "You mean you don't know?"

Her mouth dry, she asked, "Don't know what?" What hadn't he told her? What was *really* wrong?

She heard his voice coming from a great distance, against a vague background of tinny bells. "You're pregnant, Isobel," the doctor's voice said from far away. "I'd say at least two months."

6

The morning Sally Weintraub called Arran to say she had received an offer for her book, Arran realized how few real friends she had.

It was eight o'clock in the morning—eleven o'clock in New York. Arran woke to the sound of the telephone ringing and froze in terror. Please Fatso, she begged silently, answer it. But she knew Fatso would never hear—he was fast asleep in his little room behind two closed doors with his earplugs in.

Ten rings later, she forced herself to creep from her bed and pick up the receiver. "If I didn't know about your problem, I'd have hung up long ago," Sally Weintraub said. "You'll have to get over this, Arran. Now, listen . . ." And Arran listened in disbelief to the news that a well-known paperback publisher had offered a seven-thousand-dollar advance. "I talked them up from five," Sally said in a proud voice. "It's not bad for a first book, not bad at all. . . ."

She asked Arran if she ought to accept the offer.

"I guess so," said Arran. "Sure. Go ahead . . ." She was stunned that Sally should even ask her. Of course she would accept. Seven thousand dollars seemed an incredible amount of money. She listened uncomprehendingly while Sally outlined the terms of the contract, which would be in the mail any day now.

"Fine," said Arran.

"Well then," Sally said after a pause, sounding slightly nonplussed at Arran's nonchalant attitude, "congratulations. I'll be talking with you soon."

Arran made herself a cup of instant coffee and took it back to bed with her, telling herself that she had sold her first book and that she was a success. She found it all quite unreal. Her only reaction so far was guilt that she had not shown more enthusiasm over the phone. Sally, who had worked so hard for her and been so nice, had sounded rather hurt by Arran's lukewarm reception to the great news. But then . . .

Oh my *God*! Arran sat bolt upright, spilling her coffee all over her covers. "I sold a book. I am a success! I really am!"

She knew how hard it was to sell a book. She met disappointed authors every day. Even Helmut Ringmaiden had an unsold novel in a back closet. And she, Arran Winter, had written and sold a book—a novel that Sally Weintraub predicted would do well. "You're going to make some money out of it," she had said with confidence.

She was an author! A real, honest-to-God, live author! She'd be famous—and rich! Not rich like Isobel, of course, but a millionaire by her own standards. Arran leaped out of bed and dashed to the phone to tell her news to the world.

Then she sat with the phone in her hand, wondering whom to call.

Isobel was still in Mexico.

Christian was in Switzerland arranging her affairs.

Fatso was fast asleep and would be asleep until noon.

Helmut Ringmaiden's phone would be switched to the answering machine, as it always was this early.

Freedom did not have a phone.

She had hundreds of acquaintances, but so few friends with whom to share her exciting news.

Suddenly Arran felt very sorry for herself, sitting alone on the floor on what should have been the most exciting day of her life. In the end, for want of anyone better, she called Captain Moynihan. Luckily, he had just walked into the office. He was very, very happy for her and was generous with his praise. After offering his sincere congratulations, he told her there was even more good news—the house in Alameda had been raided. They had unearthed vast quantities of drugs and an arsenal of weapons, including a cache of M16 assault rifles. Arran would also be interested to know that a raving speed freak named Farley Holub— aka Jackhammer—had opened fire on the arresting officers and had been cut down. He was DOA in the emergency room, and very good riddance too. "He might have been your guy," Captain Moynihan said. "He had fallen way over the edge. Even his cronies thought he was bad news. . . . By the way, how's the counseling going?"

Caught unawares, she mumbled, "Oh, fine."

"Don't lie to me," said Moynihan. "Do something about it. Come on now—you promised."

Shit, thought Arran crossly, sitting cross-legged, still wearing her striped pajamas. But then, she could no longer be cross, she was so relieved. Of course it had been Jackhammer. She could feel it in her bones. If she closed her eyes, she could see a bloated oily face inches from hers, see his hot yellowish eyes and protruding hairy belly and smell his rancid breath. He was a sadistic psychopath, and she had sought him out again and again.

She promised herself solemnly that she would never do such a thing again as long as she lived. She had had a lesson she would never forget, and she would learn from it.

And she was a successful author!

She decided it didn't matter, not being able to reach Ringmaiden and Freedom on the phone; she'd surprise them with her good news and take them out to lunch to celebrate, with champagne and everything. They would close up the shop and go to Luigi's.

Suddenly, it was a wonderful day after all!

But by the end of the working day, she still had not told them. Ringmaiden arrived later than usual, redeyed and weeping. Old Bones had died in his sleep. "He was still warm," Ringmaiden told Arran wanly, "as if he'd wake up any minute."

"He went the best way he could," Arran attempted

to console him, "going in his sleep like that. He wouldn't have known anything about it. And he was very, very old. . . ."

Ringmaiden could not bring himself to dispose of his old friend. Eventually, Freedom and Arran had to drive to his apartment on Stanyan Street, load poor Bones into the back of his station wagon themselves, and take him to be cremated at the SPCA.

"We'll have to get him another dog," Freedom said seriously. "When he gets over it a bit, we'll get him a puppy."

Arran didn't have the heart to break her wonderful news, either that day, the next day, or the rest of the week. Ringmaiden brooded miserably in his back office, and Freedom, concerned, even managed to handle the cash register and telephone.

Ringmaiden wouldn't hear of a puppy. Nothing could replace Bones.

At the end of the week, however, Freedom managed to persuade Ringmaiden to accompany him to the pound—just to look. "Think of all those poor, doomed animals," he said sternly. "How can you not even look?" They returned with a large, neutered tomcat with grimy white fur and ragged ears. The cat had an evil disposition and a peculiar black patch over one eye. Freedom had already named him Sinbad.

"Why not a kitten?" Arran asked, mystified. "Didn't they have any kittens?"

"Of course they had kittens," Ringmaiden replied almost fiercely, "but kittens are cute. Everybody wants them. Nobody would have wanted poor old Sinbad here. They'd have put him down in another couple of days." He scratched the cat behind its ears, and Sinbad rewarded him with a contemptuous stare from flat, mud-colored eyes. "He has a lot of character," Ringmaiden concluded, rather defensively.

For some reason, the little incident made Arran feel more lonely than ever, and it was all she could do to stop crying. When Captain Moynihan called her in the afternoon to bully her yet again about counseling, she impulsively decided not to put it off any longer. "Yes," she told him, "I'll do it. First thing next week. I really do promise, this time."

Dr. Engstrom's office, apart from some bright examples of children's art on the walls, was a uniform beige: the rug, the chairs, the couch—which Arran couldn't quite bring herself to look at, because couches were for crazies undergoing psychoanalysis and she wasn't there yet, thanks very much—and even Dr. Engstrom himself. He had a long face, pale brown eyes, and pale brown hair and beard, and he wore tan slacks, penny loafers, and a beige cardigan with leather buttons.

Nobody could feel passionate about beige. The entire office pulsated with a calculated inoffensiveness that Arran found both irritating and depressing.

"You can sit wherever you like," Dr. Engstrom said, noticing her distaste for the couch, and laid a yellow legal pad on his desk. "Pull up a chair."

There were some grown-up toys on his desktop. In one corner sat a vertical frame about a foot high with a number of metal balls suspended from it. When one pulled back the outermost ball and released it, all the other balls were set clicking together—*click, click, click*—in almost perpetual motion. Off to the other side lay a pile of magnetic rhomboids that could be piled one onto the other into a structure resembling the Watts Towers in miniature. And there were several twisted steel wire puzzles to put together and take apart again.

There is nothing to be afraid of, Arran, nothing at all, she told herself firmly. Dr. Engstrom's going to help me, so I'll be normal and have friends and a social life like other people. So why did she feel so tight inside, so angry and defensive?

"Tell me about yourself, Arran," Dr. Engstrom said, regarding her intently through steel-framed glasses. "How old you are, where you live, where you were born, and something about your background. Parents, brothers and sisters, other relatives . . ."

Name, rank, and serial number. Arran complied.

She gave him the facts. Just the facts, unembroidered. She was childishly determined not to make this easy for him. Let it be as hard for him as it was for her.

" . . . and I have two sisters," Arran concluded. "Both older than I am. Isobel lives in Los Angeles, and Christian in Europe."

"How do you feel about them?"

"What do you mean?"

"I'd like to know your feelings. Do you love your sisters? Do you all have a close relationship?"

"Yes. We do. Very close."

"You must miss them."

"I do—yes." A sudden threat of tears, instantly subdued.

"And what about your parents? Are they living?"

"Yes. They live in England."

"Do you get to visit very often?"

"No."

"Why is that?"

"I can't afford it."

"Would you like to see them more than you do?"

"No."

A pause. "Tell me about your parents, Arran. You needn't say anything you don't feel comfortable about. Start with how old they are and where they live."

Arran leaned her head against the beige chair and closed her eyes. "They're the same age. About fifty. They live in a town called Market Harborough now. I've never been there, so I can't tell you anything about it."

"Do you call or write to them?"

"I send Christmas cards."

"How about your sisters?"

"Isobel writes. She sends them presents."

"Will you send them presents too when you earn some money from your book?"

"I—I don't know."

"Describe your mother, Arran. Is she like you?"

"I haven't seen her for a long time."

"How do you remember her?"

"It's kind of hard to—" Despite herself, Arran started

thinking about Mother, but she couldn't see her face, just a pale, featureless blur. "She's not very tall," she began, discomfited, "about five-four. She has light brown hair kind of like mine, but it's starting to go gray, and her eyes—her eyes are—" Good God, she couldn't even remember the color of Mother's eyes.

"How do you feel about your mother?"

"What do you mean?"

"Do you love her?"

"I suppose so. I've never really thought about it. I mean, she's my mother."

"Now describe your father."

The description came much more readily. "He's tall, with black hair. He's getting a bit fat. He doesn't look so good now."

"Did he look good before?"

"He was supposed to have been very good-looking. Isobel takes after him."

"What kind of work does he do?"

"He doesn't."

"How does he spend his time?"

"I don't know now. He used to write poetry."

"So you get your talent from your father." Dr. Engstrom smiled and began to play with the little steel balls that hit one against the other, *click, click, click, click, click.* "Does he publish his poetry?"

"No. He never has."

"Tell me more about your father, Arran. Take your time."

Arran's mind closed up. She set her mouth. He was a fool to think she'd talk about Father. She was a fool to have come here. She craned her neck to look at the face of Dr. Engstrom's little clock. She could go at 10:50. That was when her appointment was officially over. Of course, she could walk out right now. "I don't really have much to say about him."

"Just as you like," Dr. Engstrom said pleasantly. He was writing on his pad, in some kind of shorthand. Arran could normally read writing whether it was up, down, or sideways, but she tried unsuccessfully to see what he was writing about her. It made her feel angry that he was writing things about her—things he had surmised, probably quite wrongly, from the little she had said. "We'll get back to that another time. There's not much time left now, anyway."

He made an appointment with her for the same time on Thursday morning. "And after that, I'd like to have you come in at least twice a week. We have to get some momentum going before we make any progress. Three times a week would be better if you can manage it."

At fifty dollars a visit, you bet, Arran thought cynically. She smiled at him and said that twice would be all she could manage.

Dr. Engstrom nodded. "As you like. It's all up to you, isn't it." He gave her some homework to do. She was to think, very carefully, about her parents and be prepared to talk about her life when she was very young.

"Okay," said Arran.

"See you on Thursday then."

"Good-bye, Dr. Engstrom." Arran gave him a wide, perfectly genuine smile, almost liking him now because she knew she was going to walk out of here and never come back again.

"Feel free to call me anytime you want," Dr. Engstrom said.

"Thanks." Arran smiled again, shook his hand, and slipped out the door.

She called Captain Moynihan to tell him she had been good and had had her first session with the doctor.

She didn't tell him it was also her last.

7

"No!" Christian cried. "Oh no, no!" She was running down a long dark road, terribly afraid, but there at the end was Mr. Wexler waiting for her. She could see the outline of his trim body and neatly groomed head, see his arms stretched out for her to run into, but when she got up close she could see his face and it was a rotting skull and his hands were bony claws.

"Nooooooo!" shrieked Christian, trembling and sobbing. Then warm living arms were holding her safe, and Arran's voice soothed and reassured her . . . until the next night.

Sometimes it was not the decaying corpse of Mr. Wexler waiting for her. Sometimes it was even worse—she would rush into Mr. Wexler's waiting arms only to find, too late, that it was not him at all but George Winter, her father, standing there waiting to catch her. "You thought you'd got away, did you?" he would cry derisively. "You thought he'd protect you. Well, you'll never get away from me, never, never, never!" And with his shriek of contemptuous rage, there she was, back in the familiar box, the walls shrinking in on her and the lid grinding down, sweating, sobbing, and panting to draw breath.

Night after night.

"Christian, calm down. Please, be quiet now. It's all right, Chris—he can't touch you. There's nothing he can do to you. . . ." Finally, in desperation, Arran would say, "Chris, Mr. Wexler *is* still taking care of you—he gave you *a million dollars*!"

Arran was right, of course. It hadn't really occurred to Christian yet that she actually had money of her own. She decided that she could run a long way with 3.5 million francs, and for a long time. She would start by leaving her husband.

Of course Isobel thought she was mad, and told her so. "If you just walk out on him, Chris, he's not going to give you a cent."

"I don't want his money."

"Don't be wet. If you can work it out in a civilized way, he'll make you a nice settlement."

"I don't need a settlement."

"You're crazy. He can't be that bad. He seemed like quite a nice fellow."

"I can't stay with him another minute." And she refused to tell Isobel why.

John thought she was crazy, too. He could not understand her. After a long argument, with Christian adamant throughout, he looked her over coldly and told her that under the circumstances she could expect nothing from him and that she was behaving like a silly, inconsiderate child.

Christian arranged for her personal things to be stored and left the big house on Cheyne Walk with just two suitcases. On the plane to Zurich, to see Mr. Wertheim, she felt her spirits rise slightly for the first time since Ernest Wexler's death.

From Zurich she went to Monte Carlo, where Ernest Wexler's business was in the process of being taken over by an American syndicate and Pierre was preparing to retire to a little farm in his native Provence. She climbed the steep twisting roads and flights of steps just once to the Avenue Hector Otto, to stare at that old, shuttered house she had never liked. It had an alien feel to it now, as though she had never been there at all.

When she returned to her room at the Hotel de Paris, Christian felt lost and disoriented. Monte Carlo was so much a part of Ernest Wexler, and he was no longer here. There was no point in remaining, but it was impossible to leave. In the end, she stayed for three aimless weeks.

Christmas came and went. She ignored it.

At last, however, when Wexler had been dead for four months, she woke one morning feeling a new vitality. She knew she had mourned long enough; it was time now to begin her new life. She called Arran and Isobel. "I'm coming to California," she told them both, and she felt glad.

1974

Isobel met Christian at Los Angeles International Airport—a decidedly pregnant Isobel, translucently beautiful, wearing white *broderie anglaise* threaded with blue ribbon.

"Iso!" gasped Christian. "What a surprise!"

"Just four months along and showing already," Isobel said wryly. "Can you believe it!"

When she had recovered from the shock, Christian decided that she had never seen Isobel look better. Her face was tanned and healthy, and she looked rested—pregnancy suited her. But who was the—

"Sorry, Chris. That's my secret," Isobel said calmly.

"Are you going to marry him?"

Isobel shook her head.

"Why not? Is he married already?"

"No."

"Don't you love him?"

"Chris," Isobel said, gunning the Maserati onto the freeway heading for Santa Monica, "do me a favor and don't ask. Okay?" And Christian didn't. After all, she had refused to tell Isobel why she had left John Petrocelli. All through the following months, she scrupulously kept her word and asked Isobel nothing, although daily she expected Isobel to break down and tell her.

It never occurred to Christian that the father could be one of three and that Isobel herself had no idea which . . .

That terrible afternoon she had rushed straight home from Dr. Shapiro's office and arranged for an immediate abortion. Much as she liked Refugio Ramirez, and as restorative as his lovemaking had been, she would not, could not give birth to a little toad. Nor would she tolerate an infant Romano.

However, during the night she had suddenly woken from a restless sleep and begun thinking about that dreadful day with Davis in the boat, a day she had almost but not quite made herself forget. Well, she would never forget it now.

She might be having Davis's baby. . . .

In the morning she canceled the abortion.

When, inevitably, news leaked of the impending birth, the publicity department at the studio was delighted. The baby would be born soon after the release of *Ransom!*, and a pregnant Isobel Wynne was news. She must marry Steve Romano at once. They would work up a fantastically romantic story of a secret wedding in Mexico. . . .

"But I'm not going to marry him," said Isobel.

Steve himself asked rather smugly, "Iso, be honest now. Is it my baby?"

"No," snapped Isobel.

Refugio Ramirez shot endless photographs of her looking romantic, smiling enigmatically in soft focus, and sold them for a great deal of money. Like many Latin men, he found pregnant women enormously arousing and told her so frequently. Especially as she might be having his baby.

"I'm not," Isobel said firmly. "Forget it!"

She wondered what she would say when Davis asked.

But Davis never did. He was waiting for her to go to him, and she never did. But why should she? he thought, feeling sick with jealousy, when it was Romano's, not his?

The publicity department eventually came up wth the "counterculture heroine" angle, coupled with an air of mystery. SPUNKY ISOBEL GOES IT ALONE, announced *Silver Screen*. ISO STAYS MUM ON BABY'S DAD! cried the *National Enquirer*. "There's no reason why I can't be both a mother and a father to my baby!" *Ms.* magazine quoted her as saying.

She had to hire a secretary to handle the influx of mail. It ranged from hellfire and damnation on ruled dime-store stationery—"Yore a wanten hore and youl bern for all etenitty"—to proposals of marriage, lewd proposals in general, adulation for her courage, and an invitation to appear on a TV panel with Gloria Steinem.

Just as the interest in Isobel's baby seemed to be leveling off, new fuel was added to the fire.

Isobel went for her monthly doctor's appointment and returned later than usual looking pale. "Are you all right?" Christian asked with concern. "Is the baby—"

Isobel flopped into a basket chair and stared at Christian slightly wild-eyed. "Yes—no—I don't—Chris, it isn't just a *baby*."

"It isn't *what*?"

Isobel gasped, then gave a short, hysterical laugh. "It's *babies*. Oh Chris, I'm having twins!"

In the final months, the barrage of media attention grew out of control. There were numerous offers from manufacturers of baby products—baby food, car seats, diapers—for Isobel to become their sponsor. At the insistence of the studio, Isobel refused, even though the money would have been useful. *Ransom!* was slotted for a mid-June release, and all the baby business could backfire. "She's supposed to be a sexy broad getting it on in the jungle with a hard-assed bandit," the head publicist agonized. "We've got to cool it with all this baby shit."

In her final two months, therefore, Isobel was secretly moved from her home in Santa Monica to a large cool mansion in the hills. There was a high wall around the grounds, a locked gate, and a limousine with darkened windows. No longer could she use her beloved sports car. She made a fuss at first, but eventually had to admit that a hugely pregnant woman driving a Maserati looked a trifle ridiculous. Anyway, her swelling stomach now forced her to ride with the bucket seat so far back that she could barely reach the steering wheel or the foot pedals anymore.

For Christian it was a novel sensation to be taking care of Isobel for a change, monitoring her food and exercise, making sure she took her vitamin pills and got enough rest. She felt protective of Isobel—and sometimes experienced a pang of envy. She, Christian, had never even had a chance to be pregnant and have a baby.

If only Isobel would tell her who the father was.

If it wasn't Steve Romano, then who? Surely not Davis Whittaker. That had been over for a long time. Although nothing in Isobel's manner gave her any real cause for anxiety, Christian worried just the same. She knew that somewhere there was an unhappy secret. And then there was that other secret, her own secret, the one she tried so hard to forget. . . .

She began to have anxious dreams about Isobel's babies. "What's the bloody use?" Father shouted from the room next-door. "What's the point of going on? I'm crazy. I'm never going to be well—we should never have had a child!" "George," Mother said, "you don't know what you're saying. It was the war, George. You were wounded." "You know as well as I do I wasn't in the war. . . ." And Father's face loomed over Christian, grinning, spittle flecking his chin. His mouth opened wider and wider and wider as he laughed crazily at Isobel. . . .

Christian wondered whether she should tell Isobel that Father was insane. Iso didn't know. Christian was sure of it. But what good would it do now?

Apart from her late-night anxiety spells, however, Christian slipped easily back into the California life. She played tennis, toasted herself a deep brown on the beach, and began to enjoy a small social life of her own. Quite often the phone rang for her now, as well as for her glamorous sister.

One evening, a month before Isobel was due to give birth, Christian found herself talking, to her intense surprise, with Stewart Jennings.

"Christian," Stewart cried warmly, "I heard you were back!" Isobel had barely mentioned the Jennings family since that unfortunate business over Hall and their dinner together in San Francisco. There had also been a problem with Stewart, she remembered, something about Davis, but there certainly did not seem to be a problem now, and indeed why should there be? Christian listened to Stewart chat happily about Wellesley, about how glad she was to be home in California (those New England winters had been ghastly), and about how nice it would be to see her and Isobel again. "Actually, that's why I called. I'm graduating from UCLA and among other things, my folks are giving a little party for me. I *insist* you both come. I know you'll have heard about the silly gossip—people talk about anything, don't they?—but it's ancient *history* now! Do say you'll come. Mom and Daddy are absolutely dying to see you again."

Christian had never liked Stewart, had never trusted her, and she didn't think she'd like her or trust her any better now. She didn't want to go to her party.

But they went. Isobel, oddly, insisted on going. She had been hearing the rumors about Davis and Stewart; their names had even been linked cautiously in one of the columns. No matter what Christian said, it would give her a chance to see Davis once more. Suddenly she needed him dreadfully.

"I've got a bad feeling about this party," Christian said worriedly. "I think it's a mistake."

And the moment they walked through the door, Isobel knew Christian was right.

Stewart welcomed them effusively, a new, polished Stewart, with a warm smile, looking very pretty in pale pink silk. Davis Whittaker stood at her side. Seeing Isobel, his eyes widened in momentary shock, followed instantly by a flash of intense anger before his eyelids drooped protectively and his polite manners took over. His hand held Isobel's for precisely the right length of time to greet a welcomed guest. "Isobel! You look wonderful. I had no idea I'd be seeing you."

"She looks marvelous, I do declare," Stewart cooed. And smooth as silk, eyeing Isobel's bulk, she said, "Not long now, I guess!" She extended her long, delicate-boned hand to Christian. "How great to see you! My, this is just like old times. . . . And Steve! Dashing as ever."

Steve Romano strolled through the doorway, dashing indeed, shirtless, wearing a scarlet denim vest and tight black jeans. Christian saw Davis's nostrils flare white and watched him flash a murderous glance at Stewart, who simpered, "Well, I don't need to introduce you guys to each other, do I?"

"Of course not," Isobel said firmly. "We're old jungle buddies."

Noticing nothing amiss, Steve Romano greeted everyone with bland friendliness, kissed all the women, patted Isobel casually on the stomach, took two glasses of champagne from a tray, and drank both.

Hall and Margie Jennings, much stouter now, Hall nearly bald, greeted their newly arrived guests with a strained amiability and invited them to go through to the patio and enjoy themselves.

On the patio, Refugio Ramirez, looking naked without his cameras slung around his neck, was chatting with a willowy blonde half a head taller than himself. When Isobel, Christian, and Steve entered, he left her side summarily.

"You were the last people I'd expect to see tonight," he said flatly. "What the fuck does she think she's doing?"

No one who didn't know Isobel well would ever have realized that she was exercising tense control over herself. Christian didn't know how she could do it, holding court, billowing like a peony in her lawn chair, looking serene and happy, still captivating all the men, even if she was eight months pregnant.

Refugio Ramirez hovered at her side, more toadlike than ever. Davis Whittaker kept the full length of the patio between himself and Isobel at all times.

After an hour of amiable circulation, all the while

aware of the currents radiating through the party, Christian tracked Steve Romano down in the pool house, where on a glass-topped table he was serenely laying out two lines of cocaine.

"Well," he said genially, "hello there, sis."

"Hi. Steve, are you involved with all this?"

"With all of what?" He took a hundred-dollar bill from his wallet and rolled it into a narrow tube. He gestured toward the table. "Want a hit?"

"No thanks."

"Not into recreational substances?" He delicately inserted the rolled bill into one nostril, bent his head, and sniffed up a line of white powder.

"Steve!" Christian's eyes narrowed. "Listen to me. Something's happening. What is it? What did Ramirez mean, that we're the last people he expected to see tonight?"

Steve straightened up. "I don't know. Honest, I don't." And Christian believed him. Steve Romano was, despite his monumental faults, consistently honest, seeing no reason to be otherwise. "But you're right. Something's going down."

"I want to go home. I want to take Iso home." She had realized, with crawling fear, how much Stewart hated Isobel.

Steve did the second line and sighed. "You're right. But she won't go, you know. She's going to tough it out."

"Tough what out?"

"Did you ask Ramirez what he meant?"

"He wouldn't say."

"Well, I can guess, can't you?" He rolled his eyes and perfectly mimicked Stewart's wispy, affected voice. "Steve, darling, I *do* want you to be here tonight. Daddy's going to make a special announcement after dinner!" He stuffed his wallet back into his pocket. "She's talked like that ever since somebody told her she sounded like Jackie Onassis."

"An announcement—"

"I think you know as well as I do. And now it's after dinner. Daddy will do it soon. Then I can leave.

Thank God." He tapped the side of his nose. "I've got about enough juice left to get me through another half hour of this shit. Want to come with me to a real party?"

Christian shook her head.

"Suit yourself. You'll only miss out on paradise. You know," Steve said slowly, "Isobel is one tough lady in her way—I should know—but when it comes to the down and dirty, she's no match for pretty little Miss Jennings. She's not even in the same league."

"I'm going to keep this short," Hall Jennings said. He stood on the steps leading up to the rock garden and looked as though he were addressing a board meeting of Orient Pacific. Margie stood on his left, wearing something tentlike and golden, smiling self-consciously. To Hall's right, Davis and Stewart held hands. Stewart glowed with satisfaction. Davis, his body rigid, stared fixedly over the heads of the crowd.

A bevy of white-jacketed waiters scurried among the guests, filling glasses from magnums of champagne.

"Speeches don't belong at parties anyway," Hall continued, flushed and a little glittery eyed. "This is more of a toast."

He raised his glass.

Beside Christian, Isobel gave a sudden stabbing intake of breath.

"Ladies and gentlemen, good friends, everyone—it's my very great pleasure to tell you that we're not *only* celebrating Stewart's graduation tonight. As though that were not enough, Stewart has an extra surprise for you all and I know you'll be as excited and pleased as her mother and I are. She's made us very happy. Raise your glasses, friends, to Stewart and Davis Whittaker.

"Married just this morning . . ."

"Congratulations to you both," Isobel said calmly. "I hope you'll be happy."

Steve Romano was watching Stewart with a faintly derisive lift to his eyebrows.

"Thank you, Isobel," said Stewart. "I'm so glad you and Christian could be here. It wouldn't have been the same without you."

Davis Whittaker was looking at Isobel. Christian saw that glance—for a second unguarded—and flinched, for it held such anger and despair. And love. But it was too late now, and Isobel, smiling placidly at Stewart—God, but she was a good actress, Christian thought with admiration—had not seen.

8

"I didn't know before tonight," Christian said sorrowfully. "I never guessed. I should have. . . ."

"Love!" Steve Romano gunned his pewter-colored Mercedes 450 SL around the steep curves at outrageous speed. "Who needs it?"

Lying with her head back against the seat and her eyes closed, Christian couldn't help but agree. Love brought unhappiness and pain. She thought about Isobel and Davis—hurting each other every possible way they could, neither able to admit how much they cared, retreating behind their separate walls of unbreachable pride. She thought about her own small excursions into the realm of love. How quickly she had been disillusioned.

She opened her eyes, saw wheeling stars, and experienced a strong feeling of déjà vu and a pang of nostalgia for that innocent seventeen-year-old emotion that she had felt riding up into the hills in Tommy Miller's Mercedes after the tennis tournament. Now she was in a Mercedes again, riding up to the house of another man—her sister's ex-lover, possibly the father of her sister's children.

It hadn't concerned Isobel in the least. "Yes, do go to the party with him," she had said at once, and Christian had realized Isobel wanted to be alone. "Just watch out; he's a bloody satyr. But you can take care of yourself by now, Chris."

Then Ramirez had enfolded Isobel's bulk in his thick, hairy arms and planted her protectively in the passenger seat of his car. "Don' you worry," he told Christian seriously. "I'll take good care of her."

So now here she was, Christian Winter Petrocelli, riding up into the hills again—the difference from that first time being that she was not and never would be in love with Steve Romano, just as she could never be disillusioned by him because she had no illusions in the first place. She knew him much too well.

He was shallow, vain, and callous. He saw the world in relation to himself. The world was a great solar system, in which he played the part of the sun. He lived as he wanted, he took what he wanted, and he never made excuses or apologies. Christian both found comfort in and respected his sheer predictability. "I was a Shakespearean actor once," he had told her casually. "Made all of two hundred and fifty dollars per week. Then I said, fuck art, I want to be rich. So I did, and I am. It's great."

"You're honest about it."

He had given a sudden disarming grin. "Why not? Everybody knows I'm an egocentric shit. But I'm a *rich* shit!"

Steve's house was nothing like Tommy Miller's house, and Christian's vague feeling of déjà vu stopped right there. It was a curious blend of Spanish and Asian architecture. It meandered down the steep hillside on many separate levels, with balconies, decks, and sudden, surprising little gardens and pools, furnished and decorated with an eclectic, unself-conscious verve.

Steve installed Christian among brightly colored silk pillows on a rattan sofa overlooking the lights below and summoned the inscrutable Shiro, demanding champagne, caviar, melba toast, and cocaine. "As you've probably gathered," he said with a grin, starting to strip off his clothes, "the party is here, and we're it."

Shiro returned bearing a bottle in a silver ice bucket, two silver goblets dotted with moisture, and various arcane paraphernalia, including a black glass mirror, a golden reed, a jeweled snuffbox, and a wicked-looking knife with a jeweled handle and razor-sharp blade. He opened the champagne, filled the goblets, and re-placed the bottle in the ice bucket, tucking a white linen cloth around it. "Turn on the Jacuzzi as you go by," Steve called. The servant bowed in polite acquiescence.

"You'll like the bathroom," Steve told Christian. "It's my latest extravagance. I lie in it and pretend I'm Nero." He opened the snuffbox. "Pretty, isn't it? It's Turkish." Carefully, he spooned some white powder into a pile on the mirror. Then he took the knife and sliced and fluffed the powder until it lay in fine fragments, which he divided into four neat lines. "Your play," he told Christian casually and handed her the reed, which she surmised, on feeling its weight, was actually pure gold.

"I told you I don't do coke."

"But you do tonight. You need the energy. You're not getting any sleep tonight."

Just watch out; he's a bloody satyr. But you can take care of yourself by now, Chris. What in the world would Isobel say, Christian wondered with a mental chuckle, if she knew I was still a virgin?

"Put a finger on the other nostril, and breathe gently," Steve was saying. "Breathe, don't blow. And for mercy's sake, don't sneeze."

There was an acrid, medicinal taste in the back of her throat, and her lips felt numb. Her body was warmly fuzzy all over. She lay back among the pillows watching the white lights in the Valley, which looked hard and glittering. Steve sat watching her, stark naked, his body well formed and hard muscled.

Christian asked with mild interest, "Do you always run around the house naked?

"Usually. That's why I keep the heat turned up. You'd better peel off too. That's a Valentino, isn't it? We don't want to ruin it, do we?"

Christian laughed as she found herself thinking that Steve was only the second man to see her naked. She felt no apprehension over what she was doing and what was about to happen—just very curious, with a new, hard-edged awareness as glittering as the lights below. She felt very strong.

"Come on," Steve said, gathering up bottles and

glasses. "Let's go and make it in the Jacuzzi. I'm really into water-fucking."

A few minutes later, sitting spread-legged on Florentine mosaic tiles with Christian in his lap, he exclaimed, "Holy Jesus Christ!"

The white water seethed and hissed around her in a trillion tiny bubbles. She could feel each one as it burst against her skin. "What's the matter?"

"I never thought I'd be surprised again by anything for the rest of my life, but I'm surprised now. Christian Petrocelli, you're a virgin."

"Yes, I know."

"What a gift from the gods! I didn't think there were any virgins left over the age of eleven in the whole world, and you're a divorced woman of twenty-one." He twisted around, filled their glasses, and handed one to her. "This is a celebration. Cheers. Was your husband a fag?"

"No."

"What was his problem? Impotent?"

"You could say that," Christian nodded.

"Well," Steve said complacently, "his problem's my reward." He misquoted cheerfully: "Let me show you how I love thee. All one hundred and twenty-five ways. I told you it'd be a long night."

The cocaine had a curious effect, Christian discovered. It simultaneously alerted and relaxed her body. And with the warm surge of water around them, and so many tactile sensations all coming at once, she barely felt any pain at all.

She rested, still in his lap, her legs dangling over his thighs in the water, leaning back in the warm bubbles, feeling the length of him all the way up inside her, warm and strong just the way she had always hoped it would be, and feeling both linked to him and disembodied at the same time. He watched her brightly. "How was that for starters?"

"It was so easy."

"It's not meant to be too difficult. Later on, you'll even find it's fun."

He linked his hands around her hips and moved her

back and forth, shifting his thumbs and caressing her clitoris, peering intently through the roiling bubbles at her swollen, eager flesh.

"It is fun," Christian gasped, and then suddenly began to laugh. "It's *great fun!*" She grinned at him where he leaned back against the tiles, his soaking black hair plastered to his skull, the water beading on his brown face and streaming down his chest.

He grinned back. "I want to make you come, babe—it's really something, to come your first time. Watch my hands, babe," he instructed. "Watch what I'm doing to you. Think about what my cock feels like, up deep inside you. . . ." He rocked her on himself, back and forth, on and on, until Christian's body felt heavy and the pressure inside her built and the sensation increased and Steve's actor voice, husky now, told her explicitly what she was feeling, what he was feeling, and what he was doing to her body. Then everything was turning dark and falling loose, and she heard herself shouting and he was still there, hard as ever, pulling her down onto him. She collapsed across his wide chest, feeling tremendously proud of herself.

A short while later, he disengaged from her and half floated on his back in the gurgling water, his erection rising above the surface like a mast.

"Swallow me," he said. "There's a love—" And he guided her head onto him. "I'm going to give you a break—make sure I don't knock you up your first fuck." He sprawled across the steps, squirming in contentment, directing the motions of her lips and tongue. "Yeah, like that—terrific—go *on*, babe. . . . You know the three most common lies?" he murmured. "I'll call you tomorrow, your check's in the mail, and I won't come in your mouth. Well, I *never* lie. . . ." He caught the back of her head and pressed her hard against him, then flung his own head back against the wet steps as he came in long, energetic spurts, howling like a wolf.

An hour later. Or two hours. Or three. Christian had

reached a point of such intensely energized exhaustion that she felt outside of herself, as though she were watching two strangers coupling. She stared through the steam into the long mirror that ran the length of the bath. Two strangers, with long brown limbs, dark, straight hair, tanned faces, and long hazel eyes, gleaming golden in the muted light of the Jacuzzi. Those people look beautiful, she thought from far away, watching the curves of Steve's back and shoulders and his brown hands on her breasts. She had never thought of sex as being beautiful. . . .

"You're not my type at all," Steve murmured suddenly, his mouth an inch from her ear. "Isobel's my type. I like tits and ass. You don't have any. You're like a boy. I could be fucking my brother, you know that?" He slid his hands down to her narrow, athletic waist. "Or myself—what a turn-on!"

"We're alike in more than just looks and bodies," Steve mused later, as the gray eastern sky grew flushed with pink and the mountains across the valley stood knife edged and clear for the first and only time that day; soon the rising fumes from the freeways would blot them from view. "We both want to be free. We don't want ties. We tell the world to go fuck itself. You didn't love your husband, did you?"

"No," said Christian exhaustedly. "I never loved him."

"Love's a real killer," Steve said. "Love's a bind. You get fucked-up so fast—look at Isobel. Poor Isobel. I can even feel sorry for Whittaker, but not much. He's a tight-assed Yankee, and he's always hated my guts."

"I did love somebody. . . ." Christian began.

"Sure you did—the old guy who left you all the bread. But he was a safe bet, wasn't he. No one lives forever."

"It wasn't like that," Christian tried, though she could not remember telling him about Ernest Wexler. She wondered what else she had told him. But she was too tired to worry or to argue about it.

"You can't love somebody else and be free to be yourself at the same time," Steve said. "Love is a prison. You better look out for number one. . . ." Or that was what she thought he said, trying to untangle the words in her muzzy brain.

A sudden ray of sunlight fell across the tousled bed where they lay entwined. Christian felt herself floating down a deep, dark well. There was a warm rushing in her ears and a diminishing echo of a voice: "Better look out for number one . . . look out for number one . . ."

9

It was just like the 1930s, like a premiere at the height of Hollywood's golden age.

Searchlights rotated inside their drums outside Grauman's Chinese Theater on Hollywood Boulevard. Crowds of fans screamed and waved from behind velvet rope barriers erected on each side of a wide red carpet leading from the street to the theater entrance. An uncontrollable mob of press photographers and paparazzi frenziedly jockeyed for position as a succession of limousines pulled up to release their cargoes of celebrities.

A white limo nosed to the curb like a browsing Moby Dick, and there was an immediate hush. Instantly, by some magical instinct, the crowd of fans knew *this* was the limo they had been waiting for. After an expectant intake of breath, roars and cheers erupted as Steve Romano stepped out, looking devilishly handsome in a close-fitting white tuxedo over a black silk shirt. He waved cheerily to the crowd. Then he turned and stretched out his long, lean hand with casual grace. With an almost imperceptible heave, he tugged into the limelight the celebrity everyone had been waiting for and speculating about, asking over and over the most burning question of the year: what in the world would Isobel *wear*?

She lurched slightly on her very high heels, and Steve caught her under the elbows and held her steady. There was a moment of awed silence—then a burst of excited applause.

Isobel was truly immense—there was no point in attempting to camouflage the obvious presence of the twins—but she looked immensely magnificent. Her black hair was upswept into a mass of curls threaded with silver ribbon, her face framed by soft tendrils curling about her ears. She wore a gown specially created for her by LaVetta of Beverly Hills, known for her lavish one-time-only confections for the more flamboyant performers. It cascaded to the ground in tier upon tier of lightest black taffeta, cut very low in front to focus attention on her now truly awe-inspiring breasts.

Isobel and Steve stood beside each other, a fine couple, hand in hand. They waved and smiled. Steve turned and dropped an affectionate kiss on Isobel's smiling mouth, and the photographers went crazy. They demanded an encore. Steve obliged. Isobel hammed it up for the fans, closing her eyes, pretending to faint, fanning herself with her hand. They went wild. Isobel had a reputation now as a people's star. She was earthy and friendly and one of them. There was no shit about Isobel. She liked people and they liked her back and let her know it. A crowd of young girls with long straight hair, peasant dresses, and sandals held up a sign bearing a border of daisies and a message: WE'RE WITH YOU ALL THE WAY, Iso. People cheered.

In the theater, Isobel sat between Arran—who had flown down for the premiere and intended to stay on for the birth of the twins, and who, for the first time in her life, looked almost ethereally lovely in misty blue chiffon—and Christian, dark and spectacular in flame-colored silk. Bud Evers sat at Arran's other side, and Steve Romano sat beside Christian. Steve and Christian were linked regularly now in the press. They made good copy—visually, they were a well-matched pair, and there was something deliciously scandalous about their relationship. Imagine—fathering twins by one sister, and then romancing the other! The sisters still seemed to be good friends. Perhaps they shared him! But then, of course, it was all expected—this was Hollywood!

The five of them watched the film unroll with varying emotions.

Bud Evers felt overall pride for a job well done but

occasionally clicked his teeth in annoyance over what suddenly seemed poor cuts and opportunities lost.

Christian and Arran forgot they were watching Isobel and Steve and were drawn into the plights of Maria, her father, and the violent but fanatical bandit leader Enrique Diaz.

Steve Romano watched himself with clinical detachment, noting each expression, nuance, and shift in his interpretation of the role, wondering whether that slight softening he noticed under his clean-cut jawline ought to be taken care of sooner rather than later, and promising himself he would never act opposite Isobel again. She upstaged him once too often.

Isobel barely recognized herself. In the now famous fight sequence, she watched herself in another incarnation—thin and savage—as she struggled with Steve among the wet, tangled undergrowth of the Mexican jungle and tried to recapture the emotion she must have felt as she slashed and clawed at him, ripped his face, and drove her knee into his groin. At the end of the film, when Enrique had been gunned down by the federal police and Maria knelt beside his shattered body, resting her fingertips lightly on his bloody chest, staring dazedly at her father without recognition, so Isobel sat staring at herself, wondering, was that really me?

The end credits began to roll against the thin, ghostly sound of a reed flute. There was no reaction from the audience at all until the flute music began to rise in volume—then a murmur and collective gasp and a sudden thunderous burst of applause.

"I'd say we've got ourselves a hit," Evers murmured.

"Well, girls, here's to success," Steve said jubilantly, and the cork smacked explosively into the roof of the limo. He filled their glasses—Isobel's, Christian's, Arran's, and his own—and they all toasted success.

"Phew!" sighed Isobel, fidgeting in the deep, soft leather seat, which offered no support to her overburdened spine. Nowadays she found that to be comfortable at all she had to sit bolt upright, stand, or lie down. Her stomach jutted out in front of her, hard as a rock and very active inside. She felt thirsty and gulped half her glass at once. Steve filled it. "Celebrate," he said, adding, with unexpected and uncharacteristic generosity, "it's your night."

Isobel suddenly wanted to cry. The film was over. For better or for worse, it was launched into the world. It was going to make her career, and it had broken her heart. Very soon now her pregnancy would be over too. Then a completely new life would begin for her. She would become a different person.

Isobel the star. Isobel the mother. And Isobel alone . . .

A fresh platoon of photographers awaited them in the street outside the gates of the mansion where Cy Green, producer of *Ransom!*, was throwing his triumphal party. Isobel posed once again with Steve, with Christian and Arran, and alone. Then, inside the house, she posed yet again for the invited members of the press.

She drank more champagne and began to feel light-headed and spacey. The prickle at the back of her neck traveled softly down her spine.

She needed to go to the bathroom. "I have to go every few minutes," she told Arran irritably. "How would you like to have two huge people sitting on your bladder?"

Christian and Arran escorted her. Cy Green's vast guest bathroom was a labyrinthine atrocity entirely walled in mirrors. "Wow!" exclaimed Arran, exploring its mystic recesses, "have you ever seen anything like this?"

"It's grotesque," Isobel said, "and it makes me dizzy." She stared at endless, overlapping images of her elephantine figure. "Who needs to sit and watch oneself pee a million times?"

"Don't be so mundane," Arran chided, laughing. "It's the cabinet of Dr. Caligari! You go in as you, and you come out as someone else. . . . It's like the fourth dimension!" She threw out a slender arm and waved; a battalion of Arrans waved back.

Christian perched on the edge of a vast black onyx bathtub, which was surrounded by a plantation of dwarf palms. "I don't see why you bothered to go on location in Mexico. You could have shot *Ransom!* in here."

Arran peered up into the kaleidoscopic facets of the ceiling and watched an infinite number of Isobels pause in the middle of the black-and-white tiled floor and peer down intently at their feet.

"Shit!" said Isobel, watching liquid cascade into her Charles Jourdan shoes, "I guess I didn't make it in time. . . . Oh!" she added, in a strained, peculiar voice, "Chris? Arran? I think . . ."

"My God," said Arran, "it's the twins!"

After that things happened fast.

Christian left Arran and Isobel in the bathroom and ran downstairs to look for a phone. The first person she saw, waiting at the foot of the stairwell, was Steve Romano. He took one look at her face and knew without being told what was happening. "Don't tell me, I'll tell you," he said, quite calmly. "I should know; I have nine younger brothers and sisters. Go and call the doc, Christian, then bring her outside. I'll have the limo waiting and we'll get her to the hospital faster than an ambulance."

Christian finally reached the doctor at a dinner party in Beverly Hills. He had watched Isobel and Steve's glorious arrival at the premiere on the 11:00 P.M. news and heard them hailed by the newscaster as the new Gable and Lombard.

Steve and Bud Evers loaded Isobel back into the limo, and Steve insisted on escorting her, with her sisters, to the hospital. The limo driver was justifiably nervous. "It's okay, man, it's her first—it'll be hours yet," Steve announced calmly as they shot onto Mulholland Drive, a motley array of vehicles falling into convoy behind them as press and photographers chased after the hottest news story of the evening.

"I hear the film was a sensation," cried the anesthetist, a pretty woman in her thirties, as she adjusted the drip for Isobel's caudal anesthetic. "Congratulations!"

"I guess so," muttered Isobel, watching her gigantic pink stomach heave itself up into a point, then lump over to one side.

Dr. Wolz bustled in, still wearing his tuxedo. "If this is what you do for an encore, Isobel, I guess some people will do anything to attract attention!" He peered between her legs, said, "See you in the delivery room," and hurried away.

Moments later, the pain of the contractions diminished to a faraway pressure, Isobel watched a succession of ceiling lights flash by as she was wheeled down the passage. With little woolen socks on them, her feet felt warm and comfortable. They were the only part of her body she could feel. She could not see them because they were hidden behind the vast mountain of moving and struggling flesh that seemed to have nothing to do with her.

She had stopped worrying and stopped thinking.

Steve's babies, Ramirez's, or Davis's—who cared?

Although she had to admit she would rather not have a pair of toads.

Steve Romano, clearly the hero of the evening, held court in the waiting room, commanding the press and photographers, who were forced to cool their heels there. He played the welcome blitz of publicity for all it was worth.

"Wonderful! Beautiful!" Dr. Wolz cried, with as much pride as if he had fathered the baby himself. He held up a limp, faintly wriggling, grayish object for Isobel to admire. "Isn't she gorgeous?" It was female, then, thought Isobel faintly. Not long afterward, the boy appeared—tiny and shriveled, with a pointed head. "Here he is," enthused Dr. Wolz, "a fabulous boy! Terrific!"

The babies were washed, diapered, wrapped in shawls, and returned to Isobel. By now, their bodies oxygenated, they were pink and more human-looking.

She held them gingerly, staring at the tiny little faces, looking into two pairs of unfocused, dark eyes, and softly patting two heads of matted black hair that would, she was told, fall out and be replaced by blond, babyish fluff.

This was the moment she had looked forward to and dreaded for nearly seven months. The final moment of truth.

She looked searchingly into the faces of her children. Was their father Steve Romano, Davis Whittaker, or Refugio Ramirez? She didn't know. They just looked like babies who one day would grow up and be people.

She wondered whether she would ever know.

The story was carried in all the trades.

STAR'S MAD DASH TO HOSPITAL!

TWINS FOR ISOBEL!

And—IS STEVE THE PROUD DAD?—with a picture of Isobel and Steve together in a hospital room, Isobel radiant in lace and full makeup cradling two nondescript bundles, Steve smiling complacently.

Davis looked at it and read the accompanying print with no comment.

10

1976

Arran sat in the television studio waiting tensely for her turn to go on the air.

She was becoming something of a celebrity herself, now. Her first novel, *The Neighbor Lady,* had had respectable sales in paperback, but *The Night Caller,* her second, had sold into hardcover and was scheduled for a paperback auction, which Sally Weintraub confidently expected to realize a six-figure sale. She was also confident of selling the movie rights. It would make a provocative film—a lonely woman terrorized by calls in the night, the ambience of big-city alienation and indifference, and the progressive interaction between the woman and her psychopathic tormentor.

Writing the book had been cathartic for Arran. She felt that she had now written both her terror of the experience and the initial destructive urges out of her system. Her compulsion to seek out a Blackie, a GianCarlo, or a Jackhammer had diminished to the faintest of infrequent tremors. Best of all, there would now be no need to return to Dr. Engstrom. Her life was turned around.

As a congratulations present after *The Neighbor Lady* was published, Isobel had sent her a state-of-the-art, tomato red IBM typewriter upon which her fingers flew at twice the speed that they had on Helmut Ringmaiden's old Underwood. "Sheeyit," Fatso had remarked, looking at the awesome machine, an incongruous accent of high technology in Arran's shabby, old-fashioned room. "Can that there thing make toast?"

Fatso still lived with her, a considerate, tidy roommate and a quiet one too, save for afternoon trombone practice. Fatso's sister Helen was coming in to clean now and do some cooking. Arran felt cared for and secure.

She worked very hard day and night, and now she was reaping the reward of her labors. She had success, growing recognition, and this television interview on the weekly magazine program of the local CBS affiliate. After all, it was a great story—little North Beach hippie makes good! She had been featured in a personality profile in the *San Francisco Examiner*, with proud comments by Helmut Ringmaiden and Freedom. And the fact that she was Isobel Wynne's sister did her no harm either.

Hearing about the television interview, Isobel had been on the next plane. It was, after all, her particular area of expertise. "Darling, I'm so proud! You're going to be a big success. It's wonderful, but, Arran, love, *what are you going to wear*?"

Arran had looked blank. "What I usually wear."

Isobel had screamed in horror. "You can't wear jeans and a T-shirt on 'Weekly Magazine.' "

She had rushed Arran down to I. Magnin. After long discussion, she and the saleslady had settled on a five-hundred-dollar demure cotton dress with a ruffled front. It had good strong colors for the camera, and the pattern was neither too large nor too small.

Arran, as usual, found herself wilting before Isobel's determined onslaught, although her interest revived when buying shoes. "I don't want a pair of shoes," Arran said determinedly. "I want those." And she pointed to a pair of glossy, chestnut brown boots. "They'll look great with the dress, and I think they're beautiful."

Next came the battle over Arran's long, straight hair. "Who in the world cuts your hair?" Isobel asked.

"Fatso usually does it," said Arran. "He trims an inch off all round every couple of months."

"It looks like it," snapped Isobel and whisked her to an expensive salon off Union Square. The results were certainly sleek and glamorous, but Arran knew that her hair would look like a mess again within minutes.

She had also, no doubt from tension, developed a huge spot right between the eyebrows. "I *never* have zits," she cried in despair, certain it was a major deformity that everybody would notice and stare at—millions of people. To add insult to injury, once Arran got to the studio she learned that immediately following her on the program was Stefanie Lorenz, creator of a world-famous line of cosmetics and skin-care preparations, with two of her leading models. Their hair was styled like Arran's, but it looked so different on them.

Arran held her hand over her eyes and scowled into her lap. Why in the world couldn't Iso at least be here to hold her hand? But Isobel had refused. "Absolutely not, Arran love. This is *your* day."

"With us in the studio today," said the suave young man with the blow-dried hair, expensive European sports jacket, and mauve shirt, "is a young woman who, we predict, will be standing the literary world on its head before too long: Arran Winter—an amazing success story of a young girl, in this country for less than five years, working as a clerk in a local bookstore, who has written a best-selling suspense novel to rival *Looking for Mr. Goodbar.* Tell me, Arran"—he smiled at her genially—"when did you decide to be an author?"

"When I was about six," Arran replied, trying to remember all her important instructions. "Look at me," the young man had said, "or at the little red light on the camera. Don't try and watch the monitor." He had repeated, "Don't look at the monitor." Arran thus found her eyes drawn to the monitor screen as though by a magnet; she wished he hadn't mentioned it at all.

He was making some jocular remark now about knowing her own mind at a very early age. Arran's eyes slid to the monitor and she saw the side of her head. Her hair looked awful. Nervously, she pushed the carefully sculpted bangs off her high forehead. *Why* had they given her bangs? And she was bitterly disappointed about her boots. She had expected to be sitting in a chair with her legs visible; instead she sat beside the interviewer behind a high counter, and nobody could see the boots. . . .

"Arran, where does a writer find ideas? Do you have any particular secret formulas?"

At least the questions were simple and predictable. Arran talked about getting ideas, with which she never had problems, and about creating characters. "That's really easy—if you look approachable, people talk to you. I hear all kinds of things. . . ." Yet again, she touched on those long ago days in the Birmingham Public Library. "One's amazed at the rich material all around one."

"And what about routine. Is it important to work regular hours? And how many times do you rework what you've written?"

Arran discussed regular hours. "And I do about four drafts," she said. "The first one is rough; I just get the ideas down. In the second one, I develop the ideas. The third one is kind of a pruning—like throwing out the garbage. . . ."

The interviewer blinked. "I've never heard a writer refer to their work as garbage."

"They're talking about the finished article. I'm talking about work in progress. That's always an embarrassing mess," Arran stated candidly. "Any writer who says otherwise is probably lying."

"I see. Now then, a great many writers these days seem to include a lot of sex and violence. Arran, in your book—"

"Oh sure," said Arran blandly. "As much as possible. After all, it's what people always like to read about."

The interviewer raised his eyebrows. "Really? And you look so young. But surely, gratuitous sex—"

Arran launched happily into a dissertation on sex and violence in literature, including as examples *Romeo and Juliet, A Streetcar Named Desire,* and the Book of Esther in the Bible. She was so articulate and became so engrossed in expanding her theme that she forgot to

look at the monitor and the producer allowed her to
run three minutes over her allotted time. She was
disappointed when it was all over.

Back in the anteroom during a commercial break, she
was told, much to her surprise, what a great interview
she'd been. Such candor! Such honesty! Happy, she
looked in the mirror; her enthusiasm diminished
immediately— she might have been through a war
zone. Her hair stood up on end, and two buttons on
the front of her dress had popped open to expose a
half-inch of bra.

"Never mind," Isobel comforted. "You were waving
your hands around a lot. I'm sure no one noticed."

They sat in L'Etoile over a celebratory dinner. Christian was there too. It was the first time they had all
been together since the birth of Mark and Melissa.

"I hope it's not always going to take publishing a
book—or having a baby," Isobel said, laughing gaily.
She was staying at the Huntington Hotel on Nob Hill
with her latest fancy, a wealthy young congressman
from Orange County with one of these reversible names.
Arran could never remember if he was named Morgan
Randall or Randall Morgan. He had bland, blond,
conservative good looks and was obviously smitten
with Isobel. They were staying in town until tomorrow
night, after her book-signing party at Mogul Books.

Isobel was now a full-fledged star. She was working
terribly hard. She was doing two major films back-to-
back and had signed for a third, with shooting to start
almost as soon as the previous one had wrapped. She
was no longer represented by the Whittaker Talent
Agency, but had moved up to one of the majors—
William Morris, Arran thought. She wondered how
Isobel could do it all without falling apart. She had
moved into an enormous house now, a Southern-style
mansion, with a large staff and an English nanny to
take care of the twins.

She was always very, very busy. When she wasn't
actually working, she was partying with a succession of

rich, eligible men such as the congressman, a Mexican oil millionaire, or an Iranian prince. She endlessly bought clothes for herself and gifts for everybody else. The two-year-old twins owned every conceivable toy, and their closets bulged with outfits they would have neither the time nor the opportunity to wear.

Isobel herself was the Hollywood idol personified. She was thin, gorgeous, every detail of face, figure, and clothes perfect—although personally, Arran thought she was overdressed. She was also laughing too much, tossing her hair around too much, and drinking more than Arran ever remembered her drinking before.

Christian looked sleek, elegant, and tanned. Following her much publicized though amicable breakup with Steve Romano—"We're both independent people and feel it's time to move on"—she had spent a year traveling the circuit with French race-car driver Raoul Valmy.

"How exciting," Arran said, eyes wide. "But how horrible. What on earth do you do when he's on the track? I'd be terrified."

"I never go to the track anymore," Christian said. "I lie beside pools. How do you think I got my tan?"

Now she was ready to move on again. It had been thrilling, at first—but the thrill had faded quickly. In actual fact, Raoul Valmy was a terrible bore. He had three compelling interests in life: cars, sex, and himself.

He was a coarsely handsome young man of twenty-seven, with a tough, hairy peasant's body. During her time in his company, Christian had spent hundreds of hours lying about on various beds around Europe watching Raoul study himself in the mirror, tense and untense his hard buttocks, run his calloused, oil-stained hands complacently over his rib cage and flat, furry stomach, and caress his powerful thighs. After fifteen or so minutes of this self-admiration, Christian could tell from the regular motion of his muscular back and shoulders that he was now stroking his penis, proudly watching himself come to full erection. Then he would spin around and present it to Christian with the pride of a chef bringing a beautifully risen soufflé from the oven.

Definitely, it was time to move on.

She had never been a racing fan. When she watched the high-performance cars roar around the track, she could not tell Raoul's car from all the others. They would be past and gone in the blink of an eye. The sounds of roaring and revving engines gave her a headache. So did the smell of high-octane gasoline and overheated metal, and the endless press receptions and parties where Raoul would brag and puff out his chest and put on his macho stud act for all the goggle-eyed pit groupies.

Well, there was no reason why she should not do just as she liked. She could afford it.

She would be off after Arran's book-signing party, off to the next country, the next party, the next man . . . . It was wonderful to be so free.

Freedom had made a careful and artistic display of Arran's book in the window, incorporating the cases in which they had been shipped, with the title stenciled on the side, and some artfully placed clumps of straw. Sinbad ruined the display almost at once by climbing into the middle and purposefully sitting down. Freedom could have cried.

"Never mind," Ringmaiden comforted. "We'll sell them all before anyone's had a chance to see it."

"Do you think so? Really?" Arran could never believe that people actually wanted to buy her books. She was terrified that nobody would buy any at all—or even come.

"It's not even four-thirty," Ringmaiden explained patiently. "The party doesn't start till five."

"Do I look all right?"

"You look fine. Much better than on TV. Now stop fussing."

For tonight, she had resolutely dressed her way, despite Isobel's idea of what a famous author ought to look like. "If it's my night, I'm going to look like me." She wore a cotton shirt, belted with Freedom's gift—a multicolored, braided sash from an Indian store in Berkeley—and her jeans, although they were rolled to the knee to display the new boots.

The party was a smash success. Everyone was there: socialites, pillars of the community, and all the important press people. A succession of whiskered North Beach denizens wandering in for the free drink and food added a suitably eccentric, bohemian flavor.

For the first half hour, Arran sat at a little card table, religiously autographing books until there were no books left. Isobel ordered a hundred copies from Ringmaiden to give to her friends in Los Angeles.

Freedom, wearing his first three-piece suit, which he had purchased specially for the occasion that morning from the Junior League thrift shop for $17.50, circulated with champagne. The cases of champagne were a surprise gift from Isobel, as were the pâté and cheese from the expensive delicatessen up the hill.

Freedom was looking quite handsome, Arran thought. His hair was neatly tied behind his head in a ponytail; he had shaved his straggly beard; and in his suit, which was not a bad fit, he could almost be taken for a junior executive. Ringmaiden reported that he was over his terror of snakes and evil spirits and had even stopped having his LSD flashbacks. Freedom had begun to change. And he would change more. Within six years, he actually would be a junior executive and would be living in the suburbs with a wife and baby.

Ringmaiden himself was in his element, the center of a crowd of San Francisco literati, press, and reviewers.

Isobel looked fabulous, wearing her trademark black and white. She chatted vivaciously to an endless stream of admirers and well-wishers, the congressman sticking to her side like a burr. Christian, with brittle energy, answered questions about her affair with Raoul Valmy. The next day she would be well written up in the society columns, sowing endless envy and discontent in the hearts of a million housewives and secretaries who would give anything to live the romantic, glamorous life of Christian Winter. . . .

During the entire party, the flashbulbs popped nonstop until a columnist from the *San Francisco Chronicle* finally brought the three sisters together for a family photograph.

They posed, smiling widely for the camera, arms linked: a best-selling novelist, a movie star, and a news-making socialite.

"What's the secret?" they were asked. "What's the special ingredient that sets the Winter sisters apart from the common folk?"

They looked at each other, grinned, and raised their glasses in toast to one another.

Then, in quick succession, they replied.

"We vowed to be successful when we were kids," Isobel said, remembering that long ago night when she wore Stewart's blue party dress.

"We were motivated," said Christian.

"And we're sisters," said Arran seriously, "so perhaps it's in our genes," which raised a roar of appreciative laughter.

The subsequent story and picture were headlined: THE WINTER WOMEN. THEY HAVE IT ALL.

Part Five

1

1984

Arran sat alone at one end of a large oval conference table, the unwinking focus of ten pairs of expectant eyes. She was a guest celebrity and workshop leader at the Big Horn Writers' Conference at Timberline Ranch, near Sheridan, Wyoming.

Timberline, a turn-of-the-century stronghold of cattle barons, a massive structure of pine logs and native rock, had evolved in recent decades into a state-of-the-art conference center that handled groups up to two hundred. Now the huge old rooms with their rough-cast walls and flagstone floors, Indian rugs, heavy mountain furniture, and memorabilia including bear traps, antique weapons, and lowering moose heads contrasted uneasily with the new communications center, complete with computer terminals and Telex, copying, and printing machines. On the wide pine deck, there was now a luxurious hot tub that could accommodate up to twenty bodies. Looking at it all, Arran couldn't help but wonder how those rugged old mountain men would feel, confronted with Timberline one century later.

The Big Horn conference was an annual and highly prestigious event, attended by a select number of promising students, each of whom paid a great deal of money for a week of workshops and personal critique, beautiful surroundings, great food, and the opportunity to mingle informally with literary celebrities. Previous guest speakers and workshop leaders had included Truman Capote, Lillian Hellman, and John Irving. Arran's invitation to join such an illustrious group had both stunned and terrified her.

"Don't be foolish," Brad Stilling, the conference founder and director, told her sternly. "You forget you're a celebrity too!" But at least Brad, author of five scholarly novels, was everyone's idea of a literary genius, from his overlong gray-brown hair to the leather patches on his fraying sweaters.

"Nobody's going to take me seriously," Arran protested in vain.

"Nonsense. They'll all be hanging on your words," Brad reassured her in his well-modulated, classroom-tuned voice. "Anyway, you let them do most of the talking—sit there and be admired and look wise."

All very well for him, Arran thought morosely, but it was hard to look wise when you looked so much younger than any of the students. She went out at once to buy a pair of horn-rimmed glasses she didn't need.

Now, shivering inwardly with fear, the focus of attention, she reminded herself that she was twenty-nine years old, she had published four books, all of which had sold much better than Brad Stilling's books and two of which had been made into movies. She need be intimidated by nobody.

The electric clock on the wall said 9:05. Time to begin. She cleared her throat and adjusted the glasses on her nose. "Good morning," Arran said, trying to keep the tremor out of her voice. "I'm Arran Winter. . . ." And she launched precipitously into a brief introductory speech for those who might be unfamiliar with her work. "Tell 'em how great you are," Brad had told her. "Impress the hell out of them right at the start and they'll eat out of your hand."

She finished, a little breathless, and gazed around the table. It was now time to get down to business. "As you know, we work on two short fiction pieces every morning. Today we're looking at Walter's story" —she smiled down the table at Walter, a nervous young man with a huge Adam's apple that slid up and down in his throat like a tennis ball—"and then, after the coffee break, at Brenda's." Brenda was fortyish, with bulldog jowls, wearing a peasant dress and

Birkenstocks. Arran knew already that Walter would be quiveringly grateful for any advice received, while Brenda would be truculent and argumentative.

"Now then," she began, directing her clear gray gaze at Walter and speaking as calmly as though she led workshops every day, "we always ask the author not to say anything until we've finished; the work must be allowed to stand on its own." Suddenly, she noticed that they were all taking notes on their new yellow pads. She was speaking, they were listening—to her—and they were taking notes.

Good God, thought Arran, stunned. She felt immeasurably cheered. Perhaps Brad was right, after all.

By 1:00 P.M., when the group broke for lunch, Arran was quite enjoying herself. As she had expected, the grim-faced Brenda had wanted to wrestle every point into the ground. With an authority she had had no idea she possessed, Arran had ordered her to be silent, and the other nine students had backed her strenuously. Even Walter had raised his voice in protest, free of his embarrassment now that his own ordeal was over.

"But of course," Brad said, between bites of his cream cheese and alfalfa sprout sandwich. "They pay a lot of money to come here. They pay to hear you, not Brenda. And remember, when you're a success you're perceived as infallible. Consider yourself an oracle now, my dear."

And so the Big Horn conference, which she had attended so reluctantly and only at Brad's urging, began to be fun after all. The students were fully occupied from dawn to dusk with workshops, lectures, poetry readings, and a daily discourse by a psychologist on overcoming writer's block. Arran's mornings were taken up with her workshop, and during the afternoons she spent time reading and working on the next day's pieces. Still, that left quite a lot of free time until the evening, when, traditionally, the staff mingled informally with the students over cocktails and supper and

Arran found herself pleasantly besieged by admirers, all eager to buy her drinks.

It was heady stuff. "And quite right, too," Brad said. "It's a little reward—recognition for all those lonely hours pounding on a typewriter all by yourself. Enjoy it!"

On Wednesday afternoon, Arran was scheduled to talk about her own work to the whole conference, with the exception of the screenwriting group, who were off in the projection room with their director, Hart Jarrow.

Arran had never faced such an audience before. It was far more intimidating than a television interview, where, although speaking before millions, she would actually be aware only of the small group in the studio. She stared out at the blur of faces, felt the sweat break out on her forehead, then deliberately and ceremoniously put her glasses on. She was discovering that the glasses brought her a measure of psychological protection, as though she were facing a firing squad knowing she was wearing a bulletproof vest.

She began talking about early writing attempts, including her repertoire of funny anecdotes about the library and Mogul Books, and was rewarded with ripples of laughter and general relaxation. She moved on, relating how she gathered ideas, developed material, and established work habits. Then she touched on the handling of rejection. "You mean *you've* been rejected?" a woman asked disbelievingly.

She described how she had acquired an increasing reputation as a social crusader. "It wasn't planned. I wrote a suspense story about a lonely woman being harassed and threatened over the phone, and found that what I was really writing about were the problems of alienation and loneliness in a big city."

Her third novel had dealt with the frightening helplessness of the undereducated poor. When talking about it, Arran became emotional and indignant, forgetting her rapt audience, seeing only the miserable, sick face of Fatso's sister Helen, no longer a healthy chocolate brown but grayish against the hospital pillow. Helen's voice had been weary and querulous. Yes, she was well taken care of, she guessed . . . but that food! "Every day they brings this menu an' we gotta choose . . . an' Ah lost mah glasses an' cain' see for nuthin' what that menu say . . . then the food come an' they don' got nothin' on the tray Ah likes, Miz Arran . . ." This was when Arran realized with a jolt that Helen's problem had nothing to do with bad food or lost glasses. Helen couldn't read and was too proud to admit it.

"It was that basic," Arran told her audience, "but do you think anybody cared about her feelings? Hell, no!" She thumped the desk with emphasis, her fine brows drawing together into a scowl. "No one was going to take the time to read the menus to her with courtesy and tact. There was no time, they said, to let her keep her dignity. After all, she wasn't a human being, just an ignorant old black woman."

Arran collapsed back into her chair, overwrought, her hair standing on end where she had clutched at it in her fury. She peered at her silent, goggle-eyed audience and, suddenly, grinned. "Gosh, sorry," she apologized ruefully. "I guess I got a bit carried away there." She called for questions.

Everyone's hand shot into the air at once. . . .

"I hear you were a smash success," Hart Jarrow said at dinner. "Congratulations. I was sorry to miss it."

He sat down beside her, a vast plate of rare roast beef and gravy in one hand, a stein of beer in the other. "Word's out you're raising the social conscience where Charles Dickens left off."

Arran had been looking forward to meeting Hart Jarrow. She had admired his recent screenplay for *Marley's Year*, which had won an Academy Award. She was sure she would like him. Now, she blushed deeply. "Oh, please! That makes me sound like a real goody-two-shoes!"

Hart chuckled. It was a warm, deep-throated sound; if a bear chuckled, Arran thought, it would sound like that. In fact, Hart was definitely bearlike: brawny arms, shoulders, and chest, thatch of grizzled hair, heavy black brows. And underneath that plaid lumberjack shirt would be a matted black pelt. . . . Thinking about Hart's naked chest made her flush again. She said diffidently, "Well, I've always identified with the underdog."

"Can't imagine why," Hart grinned. "You don't look like any underdog to me!" He studied her fine face and huge, innocent eyes and resisted an urge to touch her soft brown hair, to feel the velvety texture of her cheek. He looked down at his enormous farmer's hands and felt oversized and clumsy, even oafish.

Later, they strolled together down the graveled driveway toward the horse corral and the lake, where Canadian geese were already gathering for migration. Except for the wind sighing in the pine trees and the occasional rustle of a sleeping bird among the reeds, it was very quiet.

Their backs to the ranch house and the intrusively harsh fluorescent lights still burning in the computer room, they stood side by side, leaning their arms on the split rails of the corral.

"What *would* they think, those old cattle barons, if they could see the place now?" Arran wondered. "You're from the West, aren't you?"

"Idaho," said Hart. "But my family are hardly cattle barons. We're potato farmers."

"Potato farmers. An unusual background for a screenwriter."

"I got a football scholarship to college," Hart explained. "Was supposed to major in agriculture, but took a couple of creative writing courses." He shrugged. "It went on from there. . . ."

"Good lord," breathed Arran, "whatever did your parents say when you ran away to Hollywood?"

He gave his bearlike chuckle. "Being good, solid, Bible-thumping Methodists, they thought I'd sold my soul to the devil." He shook his head ruefully. " 'Hart, boy—that there place is full of queers and pimps and easy women. I'll pray every night that God keeps you safe from temptation!' They've never set foot in L.A. and they never will, I guess."

"Not even for the Academy Awards?"

"Not even then."

"That's too bad. They'd have been so proud of you."

"Well, so they were, but in their own way—the best way for them—watching it on TV, with all their friends in for coffee and pie."

Hart kissed Arran good night at the door to her cabin. The air was cold now and smelled of pines. "You're one gorgeous lady. I didn't know there were any people like you still around." His lips were firm and warm. Arran rested her head on his wide shoulder. She had never been kissed that way before—romantically, sweetly, with tenderness. "How do you stay the way you are? So fine and unspoiled," he murmured into her hair. "So gentle . . ."

A man like Hart was what she needed, thought Arran—someone loving and strong who would protect her from herself. She would be *safe* with Hart. She wondered whether she had already fallen in love with him and shyly allowed herself to respond to his kiss. She felt almost unbearably happy.

The rest of the week passed swiftly. Arran seemed to drift in a haze of new delights. In the late evening, wearing thick parkas against the cold, thin air, she and Hart walked under the enormous glittering sky, hands linked, and talked about themselves.

Hart lived in the Napa Valley now, where he owned a small vineyard. It wasn't potatoes, but once a farmer, always a farmer, he said with a grin. He described the view from his house . . . the groves of live oak and madrona, the green vines sloping down to the valley floor, and the line of mountains beyond, where the colors shifted throughout the day from gold to green to misty blue to purplish black. "I could never live in the city again," he told her flatly. "Thank God I don't need to."

Arran told him about her new book—"a very city book, I'm afraid"—the story set in a shelter for the homeless in a grim part of town, its cast of characters including prostitutes, winos, and bag ladies.

"Could you work in the country, do you think?" Hart asked. "Or are you only energized by city streets? Do you have to be there, with your street people?"

"I do for this book, but perhaps," Arran said tentatively, "when it's finished."

She sat by her window for hours after he had gone, listening to the rising wind in the tall pines, watching the moon, thinking how the Napa Valley was not much more than fifty miles from San Francisco, thinking about going there to see him, dreaming of living in a vineyard with Hart. She hated to go to sleep in case she dreamed of anyone else. . . .

She woke with a jagged headache and the most numbing depression she had ever felt in her life.

Thank God today was Friday—her last workshop. She got through it somehow. She looked white and strained; her eyes were dark, smudged holes. The now standard adulation, far from being fun and flattering and her just due, rang false in her ears. Whom did they think they were fooling, for God's sake? She knew who she was, all right. She fought a compulsion to lash out, to sneer, to tell these untalented fools what she *really* thought about their pathetic little stories and poems.

After dinner, there was a party for all staff and students. A trio of colorful, whiskered old men wearing bib overalls and checkered shirts arrived in a pickup truck and played toe-tapping country music and reels on guitar, banjo, and accordion. When they left at midnight, there was a movement toward the hot tub, where the less inhibited threw off their clothes and clustered with giggles and shoves, chin deep in the steaming water.

By now, even Hart had drunk enough bourbon to quell his Methodist acculturation, and he lounged hap-

THE WINTER WOMEN 301

pily among them, naked as a jaybird, a fifth of good
Kentucky sipping whiskey close to hand.

Arran nestled against him in the water, her body
pale and delicate and diffuse through the cloud of
steam. She dropped her hand between his legs, cupped
his balls gently, and drew her long nails deliberately
along the seam of his scrotum. She heard his sharp,
indrawn breath and encircled her fingers around his
suddenly rigid penis. His big body tensed; his dark
shaggy head turned toward her. She couldn't see his
expression, but shafts of reflected light glittered in his
eyes. "Jesus," said Hart Jarrow softly.

Methodically, sensuously, she stroked him under
the water. Her headache was quite gone. She felt hard
and strong and cold inside. "I want to get out of
here," she said flatly. "We'll go to my cabin. Let's go,
Hart."

He had never heard her use that tone of voice, so
hard and arrogant. Against his will, he found himself
obeying, climbing awkwardly out of the hot tub, shield-
ing his erection with his hands, grasping for his clothes
and his bottle. Arran swung lightly from the water,
her body slender and beautiful and small breasted. It
was the same body, Arran's body, but it seemed unfamiliar to Hart's overwrought senses, as though inhab-
ited by a stranger. His first shock of desire had faded.
She was no longer his gentle, wide-eyed little Arran,
to be protected from the world. Watching her move
with a new, predatory stealthiness like a night-stalking
animal, he had an instinct that the world must be
protected from Arran.

"Come on!" she chided, tugging him across the
deck through the pools of white light cast by the
computer room windows. She refused to stop long
enough for him to pull on his pants. He felt foolish
and vulnerable and cold. "Hurry!"

Behind the closed door of her cabin, she led him to
the bed, sat down, encircled his hips with her slender
arms, and sucked on his deflated penis until he was
once again engorged. Then she drew her mouth away,
flung herself backward on the bed, opened her legs

wide, and teased her nipples into stiff erection in front
of his shocked eyes. "What's wrong, Hart?" she whispered, her voice coldly beguiling. "What're you waiting for? I'm ready. Oh God, am I ready!"

"You're drunk." Hart stared at her where she tossed
feverishly on the bed.

"So who cares?" She twisted upright in one lithe
movement, reaching out for him with greedy hands.
"Hart, come to me. Put it into me." She could feel
how shocked he was. Shocked stupid, the fool, because his darling, innocent little girl wasn't as innocent
as he had thought. She was corrupt and dirty—boy,
was she ever—she would show him how dirty!

Hart had wanted Arran more than he'd believed it
possible to want a woman—but not anymore. Not
now. However, to his shock and self-disgust, he found
himself huge and hard and pounding with lust and
then, helpless to stop, doing all the things she ordered
him to do to her, and enjoying it.

"Don't you like it this way, Hart?" Arran demanded,
writhing her buttocks against his loins. "Isn't it much
better? Jesus, the sensation! So much tighter. Go on,
go *on*—don't stop—do it, do it—I want to feel you
come inside me. . . ."

Later, she tore the belt out of his jeans and commanded him to beat her. "What the fuck are you? Are
you a man or not? I want to feel the leather on me,
Hart." She writhed, exposing breasts, belly, and spread
thighs. "Go on, for Christ's sake . . ."

When he refused, she attacked him, ripping at him
with her nails. Suddenly, he lost his temper and hit her
hard across the face, at which point she launched into
a terrifying and joyless climax, dragging his hand between her legs with a force he had never dreamed
could come from those smooth, gentle arms.

Later, feeling drained, used, ashamed, he dressed
silently and stood beside the bed staring down at her
where she lay curled on one side, looking up at him
with hard, gleaming eyes.

"You're sick, Arran," he said finally, his voice tightly

controlled to hide the revulsion he felt. "You'd better get yourself to a shrink damn quick."

Arran laughed at him. It was a dry, deadly sound. She watched him leave the room, heard the decisive click of the lock and the crunch of his departing feet. She fell asleep at once, sated and triumphant.

In the morning, she awoke with a feeling of dread that, on remembering, became sick shame. She hid in her room all morning until the arrival of the charter buses to take the students and staff down the mountain to the airport at Sheridan. During the whole ride, she sat with her face turned to the window, silent, pleading a migraine.

Her flight for San Francisco left at 1:30. By then, all she could think about was North Beach, her street, her block, her building, and the little apartment where she could lock the door, crawl under the covers, and, she hoped, sleep forever.

2

While Arran wept alone in her bedroom in San Francisco, Christian, unknowing, peered out through the postcard-sized window, at forty-four thousand feet saw nothing but a tiny rectangle of dark blue sky, through which they were traveling at twice the speed of sound, then leaned back in her seat and studied her flawless fingernails. With professional detachment, she reflected that her appearance was as technically perfect as it could be, from the crown of her burnished head to her immaculately lacquered toenails in the chestnut-colored Ferragamo sandals, including her sporty, sand-colored traveling suit by Pierre Cardin and the long beige, gold, and olive Hermes scarf wrapped softly about her throat.

By now, after ten years, she preserved her image of perfection and gloss without a great deal of effort. She regularly appeared on best-dressed lists, was frequently photographed for glossy magazines doing exciting things with fascinating people, and had been described by *W* magazine as a "Five-Star Woman."

Life was quite good, really, Christian decided, accepting a glass of champagne from a smiling flight attendant and flicking a not particularly interested glance at her seat companion, a robed Saudi Arabian who had not yet raised his eyes from the commodities trading page of *The Wall Street Journal*. He had nodded and smiled at her when he first sat down. He knew perfectly well who she was. Everybody knew who Christian was—at least, everybody who mattered. He would probably invite her to dine with him when they reached London—she was someone with whom it

305 THE WINTER WOMEN

was useful to be seen, even for a man as exalted and
rich as he undoubtedly must be—but Christian would
refuse. She had another invitation, a better one.

She was to join a house party at Cleeve Castle,
where a fellow guest would be Sam Stark, whom Christian had decided would be her next husband. She had
been careful when choosing her various companions
and playmates during the years, but there had been
one or two expensive mistakes, such as the Haitian
artist and the Swiss ski champion. And although it had
taken her a long time to make a dent in one million
dollars, thanks to Herr Wertheim's sensible investment
portfolio, once her money started to go, it drained
away as quickly and steadily as water from a bathtub.

She had had lots of fun, however, and not once had
she woken in terror from nightmares or felt the old
claustrophobic dread as the walls closed in. Of course,
she hadn't felt much of anything else except mild
enjoyment, Christian mused as the Arab folded his
Wall Street Journal and turned beady, expectant eyes
in her direction; but she was thankful for it. Too much
feeling was entrapment, and she wanted to be free.
She was free. She could do as she pleased, and for
now it pleased her to be flying to London in the
Concorde to meet Sam Stark at Cleeve Castle.

Cleeve was a vast property, for hundreds of years
the country seat of the dukes of Berkshire, now an
increasingly deadly burden on the shoulders of its new
owners, Sir James Upshott and his wife, Moira, who
had so far sunk two million pounds into its new incarnation as an amusement and safari park along the lines
of Longleat and Woburn Abbey and had helplessly
watched their money leach away, literally, into the
insatiable ground.

Looming over the River Thames, Cleeve Castle was
an Elizabethan monstrosity with battlements and tur-
rets and chapel and bell tower, to which Jacobean,
Georgian, and Victorian wings had been added over
the centuries. The formal reception rooms overlooked
a flagstone terrace from which wide flights of steps
swept down to the formal gardens and fountains that

in their heyday had rivaled those of Versailles, then to rolling acres of lawn, tree-lined avenues, and walkways, and finally to a now impenetrably overgrown maze.

There was an outdoor Greek theater immediately overlooking the river, where two hundred years ago the prince regent had staged little theatrical productions with his friends. There were stables for forty horses, carriage houses, gardeners' cottages, gatehouses at the ends of the mile-long driveways, and, most recently added, an Olympic-sized swimming pool and two tennis courts—one grass and one composition.

It was all too much for the Upshotts, who were coming to the unavoidable conclusion that if they did not escape as soon as possible from the debilitating grip of their "investment," they would be facing bankruptcy. When Sam Stark, Florida entrepreneur, property developer, and multimillionaire, proposed buying Cleeve and turning it into a luxury hotel, resort, and casino, their joy knew no bounds. Moira, who had once served with Christian on the committee of the Anglo-French Ball at the Hyde Park Hotel in London, telephoned her old friend at once. "Could you possibly come and be bait for us, love? He rather fancies you, doesn't he? It'd be such a help."

Being the bait in the bear trap of Cleeve Castle had actually suited Christian's own purposes very well.

It was a beautiful evening, her first at Cleeve, and warm enough for cocktails to be served on the terrace. Apart from the Upshotts, quiveringly anxious to please, their faces wearing identical expressions of smiling desperation, the company so carefully chosen to seduce Sam Stark included a cabinet minister and his very county wife who wore a baggy tweed skirt and a string of very good pearls and talked piercingly about horses; a partner from one of the leading merchant banks; a successful model whose gorgeous face smiled winsomely from the cover of the current *Vogue;* and the Honorable Geoffrey Beaumont, younger son of an earl and a keen amateur tennis player who had once reached the second round of Wimbledon.

When Sam Stark did not appear in time for dinner, James and Moira grew steadily more nervous.

As soon as two tables had been set up for bridge and everyone had sat down to play, he finally arrived. Christian heard the flurry normally involved with the arrival of Sam Stark: slamming of car doors; shouts; barking of dogs; and moments later the eruption into the room of the man himself.

Stark was a very big man, six-five, and flashily handsome, who had risen in the world by perpetually and ruthlessly exploiting the weaknesses and needs of others. He owned the multimillion-dollar chain of Stark-price discount and convenience stores throughout the South and eastern Texas; also his were shopping centers, resort property, an island off South Carolina, and, most recently, the fifty-six-story Stark Summit on Fifth Avenue, Manhattan, where the prices for the luxury suites and condominiums began at two million dollars.

He was also a determined and ruthless sportsman, and his athletic practices exactly paralleled his business methods. Sam Stark played to win no matter what. He was a keen racing yachtsman, where he had been known to force competitive boats onto the rocks or the beach rather than give way. On the tennis court, he had a power serve that was never modified whether he be serving to man, woman, or child.

Stark had a booming voice with which he dominated every conversation, an inexhaustible fund of off-color and ethnic jokes, and a taste for bright clothing. Tonight he stood in the doorway of the Yellow Saloon, where in another age the duchesses of Berkshire would retire after dinner to their embroidery frames. He had a large cigar clamped in the corner of his mouth, and he wore plaid slacks, an emerald green Lacoste shirt, and a salmon pink sports jacket. He should have looked ridiculous, but he didn't. He was built on too grand a scale; he would always look impressive. Now, he surveyed the gathered company with narrowed eyes, yelled greetings to all, dropped a half-inch of ash on the worn Aubusson rug, spotted Christian, and charged single-mindedly across the gracious room. "Chrissy! Jesus, it's good to see ya!"

Christian smiled and allowed herself to be swept into his huge embrace and kissed noisily. On and off during the remainder of the evening, she wondered when would be the most opportune moment to go to bed with him. She decided that it was too soon; Stark was not a man who valued anything that came easily. It had to be worth a good fight, in his book. . . .

The next morning brought another gorgeous day. After a luxurious breakfast of scrambled eggs, bacon, sausage, fried kidney, and tomatoes served buffet style in the baronial-sized dining room, Stark and the Upshotts disappeared for a tour of the property, the banker relaxed on the terrace with a cup of coffee and the *Financial Times*, the model returned to bed, and Christian explored the grounds and the stable block with the cabinet minister and his tweedy wife.

Lunch was poached salmon and a very good pouilly-fuissé, which Stark called "filly piss." While he laughed inordinately at his own joke, Moira and James smiled nervously, the model stared at him in blank incomprehension, and Christian told him curtly not to be so gross. He scowled at her across the table, then beamed. "Chrissy, you devil, you always know how to put a man in his place!"

Afterward there was tennis.

Christian and Sam Stark played against James Upshott and the Honorable Geoffrey.

Stark, a dazzling figure in blinding new whites, a professional-looking green visor, and sweatbands on his hairy wrists, was first to play. He aced the game with the power serve. After that, however, Christian really had to scramble to make up for his mistakes. When his shots went in, they were generally untouchable, but more often his play was erratic, and made more so by the lunchtime wine. He bounded, slashing, about the court; he poached shots that should have

been taken and easily won by Christian; and he yelled
in fury and frustration when he struck out or into the
net. Jimmy Upshott, winning yet another point and
seeing Stark's empurpled, ferocious face across the
net, began to sweat in terror. "You can't let him win
too obviously," Christian had warned. "You've got
to let him fight for it, or he won't think it's worth
it. . . ."

However, having lost the first set 4–6 and played
poorly in the second until the score was 3–5 against
them, Stark, extremely powerful but heavy and unfit,
began perceptibly to tire and Christian took full advantage of it. She salvaged the second set with clan-
destine cooperation from her opponents, and finally,
magenta faced, pouring sweat, and triumphant with
his win of 4–6, 7–5, 6–3, Stark was shaking Jimmy
Upshott's trembling hand across the net, smacking
Christian across the behind with his Prince Pro racket,
and proclaiming it a tough but good match—Jesus, a
real workout!

By Sunday night, it seemed that the sale of Cleeve
Castle was in the bag, although Stark would doubtless
drive a ruthless bargain for it. Christian's own immediate future was assured as well. Steadfastly refusing
him her bed, Christian was rewarded by an invitation
to visit his ocean-side mansion in Palm Beach the
following week, which she also graciously declined.
"I'll have to take a rain check. I have other plans."

"Like hell you do." Sam Stark was unaccustomed to
being turned down. "Cancel them."

Christian smiled. "I can't. I'm staying with my sister
in Los Angeles. She starts a new film soon, and this is
my only chance to see her for a while. She's giving a
party for me."

"A party? Well, for Christ's sake have her send me
an invite."

It was fascinating, Christian thought cynically, how
the concept of a Hollywood party, of meeting the stars
and celebrities, could seduce the toughest and most
jaded into groveling anticipation.

"What's the point?" Christian asked. "You'll be in Florida. You won't be able to come."

"What do you think the fucking Lear's for?" Stark scratched his fleshy, sunburned nose and glared at her. "I don't employ a whole buncha pilots to sit around on their asses in the hangar playing poker. If that's the only way I get to see you, then I'm coming to Isobel's party!"

"So you're going to be the next Mrs. Samuel Stark," Isobel mused, pouring more vodka. "Congratulations! That's terrific. How much is he worth? How many billions?"

"Can't remember," Christian said and yawned. She was weary, hung over, and suffering from jet lag.

"What happened to the last Mrs. Stark?"

"Couldn't take the fast lane anymore. Retired to a nice quiet place in Connecticut with lawns, flowers, and high walls."

"Went nuts, huh?"

Christian shrugged. "A straight diet of Stark would send anyone nuts."

"So don't stick around too long. Cut in and cut out and make damn sure you have a better lawyer than he does." Isobel stared admiringly at the huge diamond on Christian's finger. "You sure did all right with that. It's bigger than Liz Taylor's."

Christian nodded. "That's just what *he* said. . . ."

A month later Christian sat beside Sam Stark in the bar of the Marriott Hotel in Fort Lauderdale, Florida. It was Friday night, and the bar was packed with beautiful bodies looking for action. Disco music pounded relentlessly from batteries of speakers; colored lights flashed and revolved, turning the dancers' faces livid shades of cobalt blue, lemon yellow, and fire-engine red; gallons of expensive liquor were lubricating hundreds of thirsty throats; and various high-priced drug deals were being consummated with insouciant openness at the tables and in the lobby.

Stark, his voice a lion's roar easily heard above the

deafening racket, was telling a raunchy Polish joke to his assembled guests. Stark was celebrating tonight; just that afternoon he had concluded his purchase of a hundred acres of wetlands, now to be cemented over and covered by condominiums, a shopping mall, and a parking lot.

He had worked goddam hard the last few days putting it all together while Christian had spent her time in Lauderdale sunning and playing—but what the hell, she was a good kid. He'd do anything for her. "Waddya wanna do today, Princess, while the old man goes out and makes a buck?" he had asked her this morning. Christian had opted for a boat ride, so Stark had chartered a sixty-foot Hatteras, loaded it with his friends, food, and enough booze to float the *Queen Mary*, slapped Christian familiarly on the rear, and sent her off to enjoy herself.

It had been a hot and raucous day. Christian had drunk too much champagne and had spent most of the afternoon napping in the master cabin. She didn't really remember much about the trip, except, oddly enough, the skipper—and she even remembered his name: Ludo Corey, an arresting-looking man with deep-set, very dark eyes and blond hair bleached almost white. Once she had found him watching her with those inscrutable eyes and had felt uncomfortable. She knew he didn't like her or the other people, even though he had been the perfect skipper, maneuvering the big boat with expert precision, baiting fishhooks, opening bottles, and laughing at all their jokes. And Christian knew *they* would never have guessed his feelings. Nor would they have cared if they had guessed. But all the time she had felt his contempt, and *she* cared. She hadn't wanted him to think she was just like them. Because I'm *not*! Christian cried with silent intensity.

Now there was a disruption at their table as a waiter arrived with a plug-in phone through which Stark bellowed for several minutes before rising so precipitously he nearly knocked over six margarita glasses the size of soccer balls.

Complications. "Gotta go see some guys. Back in a couple hours. Take care of yourself, honeybun. Get to bed early. Get plennya rest for tomorrow, you heah?"

Christian smiled vaguely and waved to his broad back as he surged from the table. Tomorrow—what was happening tomorrow that she needed rest for? Then she remembered. Oh yes. Tomorrow she was getting married.

Tomorrow she would be Mrs. Sam Stark.

Christian sat on a bright green velour couch in the ladies' room staring into the mirror. Her reflection, framed by light bulbs, stared back, and for an eerie second she didn't recognize herself. The face in the mirror was familiar—it *was* her own face—but she no longer knew who was behind it. Where was *she*? Where was the real Christian Winter?

Watching the mask in the mirror made her feel disoriented and a little dizzy. It was several minutes before she was able to stand up. She told herself it was time to go back to the table. She ought to be polite to Sam's guests, although she doubted they had missed her.

Crossing the dance floor, threading her way through madly gyrating figures and splintered flashes of light, to her surprise Christian saw Ludo Corey sitting alone at the long bar. His pale head gleamed scarlet, then yellow, then bright blue. He wore a sleeveless black T-shirt and jeans. On impulse, she sat down on the empty stool beside him.

He looked up. "Hello, there."

"Hi."

He smiled politely. "Buy you a beer?"

"Sure," said Christian. "Thanks." Her mouth was dry and she felt very thirsty. A beer was just what she wanted.

"Salud," said Ludo. And he toasted, "Amor y pesetas."

They clinked glasses.

"And *are* you enjoying love and money?" he asked pleasantly.

"Of course," Christian said lightly. "And tomorrow I'm even marrying it! Lots of it!" She felt indescribably coarse the moment the words left her mouth.

"Well," Ludo said, dark eyes expressionless, "congratulations. Stark, of course?"

"Of course."

His mouth twisted wryly. "The demon developer who won't rest till he's cemented over the whole of the Everglades!"

Christian flushed, opened her mouth in crushing response, then closed it again because clearly there was no argument.

Ludo stared into his beer. "Excuse me. It's none of my business whom you marry. Or what he does with his money."

"No."

There was a tight little silence. Christian didn't know what to say next. She had to say something, because suddenly she couldn't bear this tenuous, rather hostile encounter to be over. She felt she would die if she had to return to her table with nothing kind or important expressed. Finally, just to keep some kind of conversation going, she said, "I'm surprised to see you in a place like this. I wouldn't have thought it was your style."

"I'm meeting somebody here."

And then she felt crushed and unaccountably humiliated. Of course he was—how could a man who looked like Ludo Corey not be meeting someone? How stupid she had been to think that he and she—oh, what in the world *had* she thought? "Aha," she said with forced airiness, "your drug connection!"

Ludo raised one dark eyebrow, but made no comment.

In despair, Christian set her half-finished drink on the bar and muttered, "I suppose I ought to be getting back to my group." But she found it impossible to rise from her stool.

"I suppose you ought," agreed Ludo. "I'm sure Mr. Stark wouldn't want his bride drinking with the hired help."

"He's gone for the evening." (Why tell him that?)

"I'm just with his friends." (See, they're *his* friends, not mine!)

"You mean the fun crowd on the boat today?"

Suddenly Christian felt as though she was about to cry.

"What's the matter?" Ludo asked. "Didn't you have fun? You seemed to be enjoying yourself, before you passed out."

"No," Christian whispered, hanging her head, not looking at him. "No . . ."

For the first time, Ludo turned fully to face her. He watched and waited.

Christian clenched her hands and pressed them into the hollow of her rib cage, warding off the huge blot of despair that was rising inside her, choking her. The tears suddenly spilled from her eyes. They poured down her face and splashed onto her cramped fingers. Ludo leaned forward and wiped her face with a cocktail napkin. "Come now, it can't be that bad. Think about good things. Think about Sam Stark. You must enjoy *his* company. Are you looking forward to married life?"

"No!" Christian blurted helplessly. She dabbed at her face and began to shred the soaked napkin into doughy balls.

"Then that's easy," said Ludo. "Don't marry him."

She stared at him in dull surprise. "What do you mean?"

"What I say. Don't do it. Your life's yours, you know. Just yours, your very own. You don't have to marry him if you don't want to."

"But it's too late," Christian said miserably, thinking of the ponderous machinery of a vast wedding now moving implacably into high gear; of the huge party planned for tomorrow; of all the invitations sent and accepted; of the guests arriving from all over the world; of the gifts pouring in; of the honeymoon—oh God, the honeymoon; and of the years ahead. She felt suffocated. She struggled for breath. She felt more trapped than she had ever felt before in her life—buried alive under tons and tons of weight and darkness. "Oh!"

she panted, trying to breathe, seeing darkness all round her except for the pinpoints of brilliant color reflected in Ludo's eyes. "Oh God," gasped Christian, as the music clashed discordantly in her head, rising in volume, sour and off-key, faster and faster.

She clutched at her ears and screamed, her mouth an O of silent terror. She felt a powerful arm around her shoulders. A calm voice in her ear said, "It's okay. You'll be all right. Come on, you're getting out of here."

The sound pulsed sickeningly around her, and the lights spun. Heavy, hot bodies reeled into her. She would have fallen without that strong supporting arm. She knew she was walking, but she couldn't feel her feet. She whimpered with panic.

Then, somehow, she was outside. It was dark and quiet, and the air was moist and soft. Ludo walked her down to the end of the hotel dock and sat her down on a bench. He sat beside her and held her hand. "You're crazy if you marry Sam Stark," he said bluntly.

Christian looked around her at the newly emerging world, and saw bright reflections in black water and a line of palm trees, highlighted in blazing, unnatural green. She glanced at Ludo, then away in embarrassment. "I'm sorry. I haven't done that in *years*."

"What happened?"

"Sometimes I have—attacks. Claustrophobia. When I feel all boxed in."

"I see." Ludo began gently and expertly to massage her neck and shoulders, feeling the tense muscles slowly relax. "You'd definitely better not marry Stark."

"But how can I not marry him now?"

"There can't be a wedding," Ludo said reasonably, "if the bride doesn't come."

"I guess not," Christian agreed, and instantly felt a peculiar churning inside her, as though the tight ball of despair were shifting, even breaking up to admit thin chinks of light. "But what'll I do?" She had no idea. She had lost the ability to think for herself. She had lost herself.

"You can come with me if you want," Ludo said

casually. "I'm supposed to deliver a sailboat to San Juan."

She stared at him. "San Juan, Puerto Rico?"

He nodded.

"You're sailing from here to Puerto Rico by yourself?"

"It's what I do for a living," Ludo said easily. "Deliveries and charters. But this time I was supposed to have a crew. The guy I was waiting for tonight. I've been waiting three days now. Guess he won't show up. Want to come instead?"

He sounded quite serious. Why not? Christian thought impulsively, oh God, why *not*? Then she slumped back in the seat and sighed. "How can I? Anyway, Sam will be back soon. He's only gone a couple of hours."

"Then we'd better go now," said Ludo, getting to his feet and holding out a hand to pull her up.

"Now? But—"

"Go to your room, pack a few things—as little as possible, but a jacket and sweater and sneakers if you have them—and write him a note. Tell him you're not marrying him after all." He made it all sound so simple. "He's a tough fellow—he'll get over it. Then take a cab—here—" He wrote an address on the back of an envelope and gave it to her. "Go round the left side of the house and across the yard down to the canal. The boat's tied up at the dock. I'll wait for you until one A.M."

So she was running again, running, the way she had run all her life. But this time there was a difference—she was not running away, she was running *to* something.

With a feeling of immense lightness, Christian gazed around the plush hotel room and found it absolutely alien, as though she were already long gone.

She wrote Sam a note on hotel stationery, put it in an envelope, dropped her enormous engagement ring inside, and sealed it. She changed into slacks, shirt, and tennis shoes, then packed a sweater, a bikini, a poplin jacket, some toilet things, and her immigration card and passport into a tote bag.

She began to chuckle happily, thinking of what she was walking away from, and how easily—all the jewels, furs, and clothes in the world; a three-million-dollar condo in New York; and one of the richest men in the country. She felt only freedom. Isobel would think she was mad! Well, Iso would be right because Christian was dumping all of it to sail to Puerto Rico with a total stranger. She would be alone with him on the high seas for weeks. She would be trusting her life to him. Unquestionably, she was crazy. But was she? Really? Because somehow Ludo Corey was no stranger. Because somehow the moment she saw him she had recognized him as somebody vitally important in her life, as somebody she might have known well in some other life, long ago.

She closed the door quietly behind her. Then she rode down in the elevator, crossed the busy lobby, and vanished into the humid night.

The grass was damp underfoot as she crossed the dark garden. She could clearly see the black silhouette of the boat's mast and crosstrees against the star-studded sky, hear the gentle squeak of mooring lines as the boat rocked gently in the placid water, and, as she approached, see the pale blur of Ludo's fair head where he sat quietly waiting in the cockpit.

He took her bag for her, and she swung lithely on board.

Below, the cabin smelled of wood shavings from newly built cabinets and lockers, of linseed oil, and of varnish. The tweed bunks were still sheeted in plastic covers. A brand-new boat. Ludo showed her where to stow her few possessions, how to operate the butane stove, and how to work the light and instrument panel. Then he left her boiling a kettle for instant coffee while he went on deck to start the engine.

The boat quivered rhythmically under Christian's feet. She heard Ludo scrambling up to the bow to release the lines. Then the engine settled into a gentle purr, and they were moving forward. The kettle whistled, and Christian filled the coffee mugs. She returned to the cockpit. At Ludo's suggestion, she topped off the mugs with rum.

He was sitting at the wheel, his face eerily lit by the red glow of the compass light. Christian sat beside him. They sipped their hot rum and coffee. Neither spoke very much during their long ride down the canal, into the harbor, and out to the channel. When they did speak, it was almost in whispers, as though Sam Stark might hear and still stop them.

Christian leaned far out over the side of the boat, staring at the arching black satin ribbon of their bow wave.

And then, at last, they were out in the ocean, passing Bahia Mar and the long golden beaches, passing the last channel marker, and breasting the swells of the Atlantic and the warm, tumbling waters of the Gulf Stream. . . .

3

Now ten years old, Mark and Melissa were beautiful children. Melissa had inherited Isobel's cleft chin and Mark had not, but they both had their mother's thick, black, curly hair—and the same tawny brown eyes. They were bright and aware, and from an early age knew that their mother was important and that they were important too. At four years old, Melissa began to bare her teeth at total strangers in a fiercely ingratiating grimace. "My million-dollar smile," she would explain breezily.

They were charming children when they got their own way, when everything went right, and when they received their customary adulation, attention, and presents. But when things did not go right, they would scream with anger, purple in the face, until matters were corrected. Christian and Arran thought the twins were ruinously spoiled.

"What in the world are they going to do with all those new toys?" Arran had sighed as long ago as the twins' fourth birthday party. "They can't begin to play with them all."

Beautifully dressed—Mark in a miniature suit of shorts and jacket, with bow tie, white kid shoes, and argyle socks; and Melissa a picture, from the blue bow in her curls, frilly lace blouse, and starched blue pinafore, to the toes of her little white Mary Janes—the twins sat side by side at the head of the huge dining table. Around the table were planted twenty-five other little Hollywood princes and princesses, all bloated and silent, having gorged on rich pastries and frosted birthday cake, now staring glassy eyed at a mountain of gaudily wrapped and beribboned packages. After Mark and Melissa opened the presents, the next distraction would be Kooky the Clown, who would squirt water from the plastic daisy in his lapel, fall over his enormous shoes, and make little animals out of balloons. Finally, rides would be offered by Mrs. Brewer and her Shetland ponies, already waiting patiently in the front garden.

The actresses talked shop in a corner over wine coolers or Perrier. The Hollywood wives worked seriously on their drinking. Suzi Blumenthal, married to the head of Omega Studios, had lost her shoes and wandered blankly from group to group, loosely clasping a glass of straight Beefeaters gin and slopping liquid onto the powder blue rug. Soon she would pass out, be taken home by the chauffeur, and her child, a persistent thumbsucker with permanently wet pants, would be returned later by someone else's chauffeur.

With each passing year, the elaborateness of the twins' birthday parties had escalated, to reach epic proportions by their eighth. And between birthdays, the gifts showered in regularly. Whatever the twins decided they wanted they received at once and in abundance, from the very latest in electronic games to life-sized stuffed tigers from Neiman-Marcus.

"You're spoiling those children absolutely rotten," Christian said in exasperation.

"I'm only making up to them what we never had."

"You can't, because they aren't us. Anyway, they've always had *everything*."

"I want them to be happy," Isobel said stubbornly.

"Well, they're not," Christian said equally stubbornly.

Isobel refused to speak to her after that for several months.

Arran felt very sorry for Mark and Melissa, who she felt never had a chance to be children. She no longer attended the awful birthday parties but always stopped by Isobel's mansion whenever she was in Los Angeles on business, swept the children into the back of her rental car, and took them to the beach, where, away from the excess and the tension—yes, there was a lot of tension in Isobel's house—and after the whiny demands for trendy restaurants, action-packed movies, and flashy video arcades had been solidly refused—"not my kind of thing," Arran said firmly—they would frolic in the waves, eat sandy hot dogs, and poke around in the seaweed just like real children.

On returning home, however, they would no sooner step inside when once again they would become fractious and impossible. "They need to go to bed," Arran would say. "They're tired."

But Melissa would bare her teeth in the milliondollar smile, which curdled Arran's blood, and cry, "I don't need to go to bed, do I, Mommy?"

"I won't go to bed." Mark would lower heavy lids and thrust out his lower lip. "Try and make me."

"You're only young once," Isobel would say with an indulgent smile, and, exhausted, they would stay up until midnight.

Their eighth birthday party was held at the Savoy Hotel in London, while Isobel was in England for the premiere of her latest film. Afterward, they had special box seats for *Cats*, and went backstage after the performance. During the next few days, they went shopping at Harrod's, were photographed continually for the press, and were interviewed on a BBC children's news program, where they were asked, "Is this your first trip to London?"

Melissa smiled graciously. Because her new teeth had not yet grown in properly, she had learned not to open her mouth so wide. "Oh, yes," she gushed, "and I think England's just *lovely*!"

In fact, it was not their first trip, although they were quite unaware of it.

They had spent two months in London when they were three years old. Isobel had been filming at Pinewood Studios and had taken a big flat on Cadogan Place, a pretty street overlooking private gardens, where, immaculately dressed in scarlet rubber boots and little camel-hair coats from Jaeger, the twins were taken each morning and afternoon by Miss McTavish, the London nanny.

During those two months, Isobel drove up north to visit her parents for the first and only time.

She had not seen them for almost eight years. She wrote to Elizabeth to announce her arrival and rang the bell just as she had said she would, at four-thirty, in time for tea.

It was a raw March day with blustering, icy wind and occasional bursts of driving rain that made Isobel long for the placid, cloudless blue skies and sunshine of Southern California. She wore a fur-lined leather overcoat with high-heeled black leather boots and a mink hat pulled down over her ears, and still she felt frozen half to death. She had forgotten how cold it could be in England.

She drove slowly down the dingily genteel street of redbrick, half-painted housefronts and a few forlorn, leafless trees, thinking that back home in California the mimosa would be blooming.

The net curtains of number 57 stirred slightly as her long, fawn-colored Rover pulled up outside.

Elizabeth Winter opened the door to her, unsmiling. "What a surprise, Isobel."

"Didn't you get my letter?"

"Oh yes, but still . . ."

Isobel sighed. Had she really expected a welcome?

She was led, as formally as if she were a distant relative or a stranger collecting for charity, into a small, cheerless front room where Elizabeth installed her on the slippery brown sofa she remembered, now impossibly shabby with greasy arms and worn-through patches. The brown carpet was threadbare. The room was freezing cold.

What in the world had they been doing with the money she had been sending regularly? Couldn't they have bought a few little comforts?

Elizabeth was wearing an old gray flannel wrap-around skirt and a long shapeless gray cardigan with pockets that she bunched up in front of her with nervous hands. "I'll go and see if there's anything for tea. And your father will be up from his rest in a minute."

Isobel heard the distant sounds of running water and the soft chink of crockery. And then the door pushed slowly open, and there was Father looking in at her.

Her first reaction was one of shock. He had aged so much. She instinctively sought his eyes on the old, remembered level, but Father had shrunk, his face was shriveled though fleshy at the same time, and he had a little potbelly.

"What are you doing here?" he asked rudely.

"I wanted to see you. It's been a long time."

"Do you think so? It hasn't seemed long to me. . . ." His voice was the same, as melodious as ever, and just as cruel. He stared at her coldly, then shrugged. "But now you're here I suppose you'd better stay to tea. Not that there's very much. Mummy and I can't afford a lavish spread every day, though we do the best we can. It won't be up to your standards."

"I don't eat tea anyway, thank you," Isobel said, feeling all the old anger rising uncontrollably to the surface and knowing she was quite helpless to stop it. She realized that she should not have come. She should have stayed away and just continued to send checks to assuage any guilt she felt for deserting them. As Father drew closer and dropped, with an old man's stiffness, into one of the chintz armchairs that had once had a pattern of autumn leaves but was now faded a lifeless muddy brown, she caught the sweetish smell of gin on his breath and knew at once what her money was buying.

Isobel heard an offstage clanking noise, and then Elizabeth appeared pushing a sagging trolley with a squeaking wheel, lifting the legs awkwardly over the frayed edge of the rug. There was a thick brown earthenware teapot on the trolley, a plate of white sliced bread spread thinly with margarine, three Marie biscuits on a saucer, and a small plate bearing half a tired-looking sponge cake. Elizabeth poured out the tea and handed a cup to Isobel. Then she handed a cup to Father, who suddenly rose and left the room without a word, returning as Elizabeth was offering Isobel a biscuit. He staggered a little as he sat down.

Elizabeth did not seem to notice, or at any rate, she paid no attention. "Shall we have a fire?" she asked brightly. "It's a little nippy today."

"Why?" demanded Father aggressively. "It's only half past four. Won't be dark for an hour. What's the big occasion?"

"All right, dear. I just thought—" Elizabeth looked nervously at Isobel, who shivered in her fur-lined coat and said that she really felt warm as toast.

While she sipped her first cup of tea, which was not quite hot enough to warm her insides, Father made two more trips out of the room, returning progressively more unsteady. From sulky aggression, his tone changed to a maudlin whine. "Anyway, to what do we owe the honor of this visit? Mummy and I were quite sure that by now we had quite been relegated to dim memory. You must have better things to do than to visit your dreary old parents."

"I don't come to England often," Isobel said defensively.

"Well, as you see, we struggle on. We do our best with what we have."

"Yes," said Isobel, feeling sad and angry and wishing she hadn't come. She should have had more sense. Of course nothing would have changed. "I brought some pictures of the children," she said stoically, taking an envelope of photographs from her purse. "They're your grandchildren," she reminded Father. "They look just like you." Once this would have been true, but Father was now a sagging old wreck who in no way resembled the handsome man of her childhood. "Aren't they lovely?" she asked, smiling tautly. "Aren't you proud?"

"Proud?" Elizabeth regarded Isobel with genuine astonishment. She didn't even glance at the photographs of the children, standing grinning in Cadogan Gardens in their little Jaeger coats. "Proud? How can

I be proud? Isobel, you aren't married. The twins are illegitimate. You should see what they say about you in the papers, the names they call you. Father and I are deeply, deeply ashamed. Luckily, of course, nobody here knows you're our daughter. . . ." She shot a nervous look through the net draperies at the bleak, darkening street, plainly afraid the sleek car outside would draw unwelcome attention. "Isobel, we can't possibly think of them as our grandchildren."

Father returned from another trip out of the room, wiping his lips. He fell into his chair and knocked over his untouched cup of tea. Mother, uttering little cries of distress, wiped up the mess with a dish towel, glaring at Isobel as if to say, "There, see what you made him do?"

"Not surprised, though," George Winter said belligerently. He pushed at the trolley with his foot. "Take this bloody thing away, Liz. Our actress said she doesn't like tea. More used to champagne and caviar. Oh no"—his voice became louder—"not s'prised, not at all, knew what would happen when she went away." He thrust his face close to Isobel's, his breath thick with gin fumes, and sneered, "Hollywood! Easy money and easy sex. You can't live around perverts without it rubbing off."

"George," Elizabeth whispered, "please."

"No, I won't *please*. I'll say what I bloody well like. This is my house," he shouted at Isobel, "and I'll say what I like."

"Isobel, why didn't you marry their father?" Elizabeth ventured.

"Prob'ly married to someone else," George slurred thickly. "All the same, these Hollywood gigolos. *If* she even knows who the father is . . ."

Isobel wanted to scream. She got to her feet. With effort, she controlled herself. "I think I'd better go."

"What's it matter in the long run though?" George continued. "Whoever it is, you'll regret it."

"No, I won't," Isobel said defiantly. "Mark and Melissa are mine; they're beautiful and bright and sweet and I love them."

"Will you still love them when they're not bright and sweet and beautiful? When they go crazy, like me?"

Isobel stared at him scornfully. "They won't go crazy. Why should they?"

"Because they're my grandchildren. They look like me. You said so yourself. You look like me too, Isobel. You'll be the same."

"Oh stop it, Father," Isobel said wearily. "You don't know what you're saying. You're not making any sense. You're drunk."

"Isobel!" Elizabeth said in a shocked voice. "How dare you speak like that to your father!"

Isobel compressed her lips and put the photographs back in her purse.

"Be quiet!" George Winter roared at his wife, whose face instantly broke pitifully apart. "Of course I've had too much to drink. I always have too much to drink. I'm a bloody drunk. I started drinking because it helped my head," he explained to Isobel in a reasonable voice, obviously wanting her to understand. "It made my head soft and fuzzy—it stopped it hurting and stopped me falling inside my head, over and over and over. . . . I'm mad, you see. I have a disease of the brain." And then he added, with obvious satisfaction, "Soon you'll get it too."

Elizabeth leaned forward in violent negation, but Isobel held up her hand to forestall her. "Don't say that, Father. You have some bad spells, but you're *not* mad. You've got it all wrong. You were wounded in the war. Don't you remember?"

"No," Father replied calmly, "because I wasn't."

"Of course you were, George," Elizabeth cried fiercely. "You were shot down in your plane. You were so brave. . . . Don't you remember all your medals? And the king pinning on the—"

"You know as well as I do where those medals came from," George snapped accusingly. "You bought them lock, stock, and barrel. I saw the name inside the box before you threw it away—Colonel Edward Cummings, D.S.O. They were Army medals, not even RAF. Wrong bloody service. You couldn't even do that right," he accused bitterly.

Elizabeth shrank back in her chair, eyes wide with misery. "But the king—"

"How could I go to Buckingham bloody Palace? I was crazy as a loon. I'd probably have had one of my fits. . . ."

One of my fits—just like Christian used to say— Isobel felt something inside her tear and begin to bleed. "I don't believe a word of this, Father," she said hopelessly.

"Then don't believe it," George Winter said, "but it's true. I wasn't shot down. I never went up in a plane. I was never even in the RAF. I wasn't fit." His eyes glittered. "I was born crazy, just as you and your sisters were born crazy. It'll happen sooner or later, the way it happened to me. To your children too—you can't escape. You can't. . . ." His face had become the color of dough, a bright red spot glaring on each cheekbone. His voice sank to near inaudibility. "You hear whispers, you know. Then they start talking and talking at you, and then they start to shout and you can't hear what they say or understand them, and it makes you angry and you shout back at them, and then you begin falling. And falling. Over and over and over. And you take a drink or two because it's a comfort and then another drink until you're either mad or drunk, all day every day, and you wonder how long you can stand it—"

"George!" Elizabeth screamed as he tottered to his feet and swayed dangerously, about to lose his balance and crash into the trolley. "Oh George, let's go to bed. Let's rest. Mummy will take care of you. Please, my darling, come with Mummy and let's have a little rest now."

George Winter pointed an accusing, shaking finger at Isobel. "You all went away. You left me alone."

"You're not alone, George," Elizabeth crooned.

He paid her no attention. "It was all your fault. You made the others go away. Christian . . . and my Arran . . ." He began to stagger from the room, then turned and glared at Isobel over his shoulder. "You'll be sorry, Isobel, just you wait and see. Sorry you had those—those—" He gestured impotently with his hand, searching for the right word, and gave up. "Just you wait and see. . . ."

Isobel drove through the darkness and rain back to London as though she were an automaton. She had no idea where she was until she suddenly found herself in the middle of the Knightsbridge roundabout, just a quarter of a mile from home.

It couldn't be true, of course. It just couldn't be. She refused to believe it . . . but then she remembered Mother's stricken face as her carefully constructed edifice of lies was torn down in front of her, and she knew that of course it was true. Father was crazy, and Mother had covered up for him, lied for him, and invented a whole fantasy world for him to live in where, as a disabled war hero, his madness was not only acceptable but even a matter for pride.

The first thing she did upon entering the flat was to pour herself a large vodka over ice. Then, feeling steadier, she went to the twins' bedroom. Miss McTavish had already put them to bed, but despite her stern protests, Isobel woke them up, terrified for them, searching in their drowsy brown eyes for the seeds of madness, then taking them back with her to the living room to play. They became so overexcited that Miss McTavish, furious, wasn't able to get them back to bed again until long after midnight.

That was the beginning, for Mark and Melissa, of inexplicable but delightful wakenings, frenzied midnight games, and 2:00 A.M. snacks in the kitchen with Mommy.

For Isobel, it was the start of a vicious cycle of overprotectiveness, overindulgence, and insatiable anxiety. She would wake in the night sweating with fear and rush to the twins' room, lean over their beds, stare down with panic at Melissa, who always slept on her back, arms flung out, breathing noisily through her mouth, and at Mark, quiet, exquisite, curled on his side, little fists knotted under his chin. As she gazed at the flushed, healthy cheeks, the tangled black hair, and the sturdy little limbs, the burden would lie on her shoulders like a lead cape, and she would feel very, very lonely. Oh God, what had she done, cheerfully having these children just in case they might be Davis's—what dreadful birthright had she bequeathed them, and how much longer did they have before the onset of madness?

Back in Los Angeles, she rushed them to a famous neurologist, demanding a brain scan. The preliminary test results were all so normal, the doctor said, that a scan was not indicated.

"You must," Isobel cried.

"My dear Miss Wynne, Mark and Melissa are healthy, normal children, somewhat advanced for their age. Forget it!"

But she was not reassured. Supposedly, Father had been brilliant when he was young.

For the first time, Isobel began to wish she were married after all, so that there would be somebody else with whom to share the burden. She would take a glass of vodka to bed with her at night and lie sleepless, staring at the ceiling, lonely and frustrated. She grew brittle with nerves and worked harder and harder, but the more money she made the more the expenses mounted and the more she spent. There was no saving for the rainy day that surely must come. It was like running on a treadmill.

Year followed year in a whirling, nervous rush. She felt permanently tired and always lonely. If only she could confide her news about Father to her sisters, but she dreaded what the knowledge would do to them, especially to Christian. She couldn't tell them. . . .

Now, however, packing for Christian's huge wedding celebration in Florida, at which she and Arran would be maids of honor in lime green and coral crinolines, Isobel decided that Christian seemed better balanced these days than she had ever been. To Isobel's knowledge, she hadn't had a claustrophobic fit in years. She seemed to have stopped running away, too.

Then the phone rang. Isobel answered it even though it was quite late, at least eleven at night.

Sam Stark's furious voice was so loud she thought the receiver would explode in her hand. With sinking dread, she listened to what he had to tell her.

"She just up and left. She's gone. She with you?"

So Christian had run away all over again.

4

Ludo Corey leaned his forearms against the wheel, rested his face against his hands, closed his eyes, and decided that he had gone out of his mind. Below deck slept Sam Stark's ex-fiancée, whom on a whim he had persuaded to abandon a marriage and life of luxury and sail to Puerto Rico with him—a total stranger.

But yet—not a stranger . . . In some curious way, he had recognized her at once as somebody for whom he had perhaps been unconsciously waiting all his life. And he knew she had recognized him. He had been fair to her; he had warned her about what to expect. "It'll take a couple of weeks minimum getting to San Juan, and we'll be out in the Atlantic. This is no fun, island-hopping cruise through the Bahamas. It's a delivery, I have a deadline, and I'm not stopping."

Christian had been perfectly agreeable. "I've never been out of sight of land in a boat. It'll be fun." And the thought of spending weeks at sea with him had not daunted her a bit.

That first night, even though inexperienced, she had been helpful and increasingly efficient, listening attentively to all he told her and asking sensible questions. Ludo set a course to clear the northern cape of New Providence Island. "You ever steer by compass?"

Christian hadn't, but she was a fast learner, and she took the helm while Ludo clambered up and down adjusting sails. She enjoyed herself. She stayed in the cockpit for two or three hours, until the steep plunging motion of the Gulf Stream waters got to her and with a horrified gulp she rushed for the rail.

Ludo sent her below to rest. "Most people throw up

first night out," he said reassuringly, "particularly if they've spent the day drinking booze and eating rich food. And the Gulf Stream is pretty mean." He stayed in the cockpit, aware of lights coming on and going out below as Christian prepared for bed, then curled up in a sleeping bag in the cabin. Then there was just the darkness, the sound of wind and water, and Ludo, with a wry grimace at his own craziness, wondered where fate was leading him this time.

Their third night they ran into heavy weather, and the wind built up steadily until Ludo had triple-reefed the sails. Still, they moved over the boiling sea as though flying, surfing from wave crest to wave crest under racing clouds and sudden blasting squalls. Neither of them was able to sleep much. The automatic pilot was unreliable in high seas, and the wheel had to be manned constantly. They lived on hastily heated cans of soup and beef stew, crackers, canned ham, Spam, and instant coffee with the occasional swig of rum to revive their flagging energy. At night, they spelled each other in two-hour watches.

Christian would sit at the helm while Ludo slept like the dead on the seat beside her. She'd stare up at the wheeling stars and the small black triangles of sail slicing through them like the fins of a giant fish through a sparklingly iridescent sea. She had never felt so exhausted in her life—muscles she never knew she even possessed were aching cruelly—and she had never been so happy.

By now she had lost her alcoholic bloat; her eyes were clear; her body tuned and fit. She found herself forever hungry. Accustomed to a daily diet of champagne, caviar, smoked salmon, and filet mignon, she munched canned ham and stale crackers, washed it down with Kool-Aid or warm beer, and relished it.

She and Ludo said little those first few days that didn't relate directly to sailing the boat. But with the easing of the wind and the decreasing swells, they talked guardedly of themselves.

By now, Ludo knew whatever Christian felt ready

to tell him about her life, her family, and Ernest Wexler.

Christian knew a little about Ludo too, but not very much.

Ludovico Jimenez had been born in San Juan, in a dingy barrio below the fortress of El Morro. He remembered very little of his early life except continuous hunger and regular abuse from a slatternly, fat woman with black hair, presumably his mother, and more abuse from the stream of men who passed through her life.

He was about seven, he thought, when he ran away from home for good, to become a feral child living out of garbage cans and sleeping in alleyways, one of a gang of juvenile thieves. With them, Ludo learned to work the tourists in the rich Condado Beach district, and, during rush-hour traffic on the Baldorioty, he would appear at car windows with a little tray of Chiclets, eyes blurred with professional tears, and plead with the trapped driver. He was hungry, so hungry, sir; his mother was sick; his sister needed an operation; please, sir, buy some gum? And when, as often as not, the driver reached for his wallet, sorry for the poor, little, starving waif, it would be snatched by lightning-fast fingers, and the waif would be away, vaulting over moving cars, agile as a cat in the traffic, while the driver could only sit in his seat and curse.

Eventually, Ludo was rounded up, viciously biting and squalling, in a periodic sweep by the authorities to get the growing number of savage little boys off the streets. To his fury and dismay, almost within the hour Ludo found himself being bathed in disinfectant by two stalwart nuns. He had never had a bath in his life, and here were these women holding him down in the evil-smelling water and scrubbing every part of his body. It was humiliation such as little Ludo had never dreamed of, and he was determined to have his revenge. However, things took an odd turn. As the water turned a greasy brown and Ludo's body in contrast grew clean, so did his matted, infested hair. The filthy, black-eyed little urchin had hair of the purest, softest gold, *"como un ángel,"* breathed Sister Annunciata in awe.

It was actually the hair of no angel but of a Scandinavian sailor who had once spent a brief time in his mother's bed. Sister Annunciata and Sister Immaculata, however, preferred to believe in angels and were deeply impressed with its beauty. Ludo, who had had no idea he owned such an asset, stored their admiration away in his crafty little brain for future use.

Originally, he had no intention of staying longer than one night in the Catholic orphanage. He remained for the first few weeks, however, because of the food. He had always been hungry; having enough to eat every day seemed a ridiculous fantasy. But his first night, after the dreadful bath, there was a meal of beans and rice, fried plantain, a piece of chicken, and a glass of milk. Ludo had never eaten chicken. He hunched his skinny arms protectively around his plate, his teeth bared in a snarl at the other children lest they dared try and take it from him; then he devoured it like an animal, within seconds. But the next day there was more food. And the next . . .

Later, he stayed because of Father Corey.

"Corey," said Christian. "That's your name."

"Yes," agreed Ludo. "It is now."

Father Corey was old and vague, had food stains on his shabby soutane, and wispy white hair that constantly ruffled like a cockatoo's feathers. He was courteous and gentle with Ludo, who began, after a period of deep mistrust—for he had never met with gentleness before—to follow the old priest around in fascination.

It was Father Corey who told him that he must learn English, that English would open up a new world for him. Ludo had picked up a little English during his forays to Condado Beach. He knew enough to steal. But learn English properly? How could he? He was an ignorant, stupid, illiterate little thief. He had been told so frequently. "How could a boy like me learn English?" he asked scornfully.

"Easily," said Father Corey. "You're young. Now me, I'm much too old to learn good Spanish. Do me a favor and try."

That night, in what Ludo realized later was a stupendously cunning move, Father Corey took him to the movies. Ludo would never forget that evening. The film was English, *A High Wind in Jamaica*, a thrilling story of shipwreck and pirates. It was the most beautiful experience of his life. He sat motionless and entranced, the Hershey bar Father Corey had bought him melting in his hand, watching billowing sails and surf crashing on golden beaches. But because he didn't speak English, he was unable to understand a word of what was said, and because he didn't read, he couldn't rely on the Spanish subtitles.

That night Ludo dreamed that he, too, had a sailing ship, that he cruised the islands through clean blue water and spanking white waves under a golden sun. He too was a pirate captain, stealing treasure.

The next day he began, single-mindedly, to learn everything the parochial school could teach him.

When Ludo was fourteen, Father Corey arranged for him to go to a Jesuit boarding school in Miami. "You have a good brain, Ludovico. You'll have to work hard, mind, but you can do it. You learn everything they can teach you, learn to speak English like a gringo, and then come back and show me. Make me proud!"

Ludo hated the school. The work was brutally hard and the discipline so strict he felt he was in prison. He ran away three times. But in the end he stuck it out because he had promised Father Corey.

At seventeen he graduated from high school, in the top ten of his class, and returned at once to San Juan. He had not seen the old priest in three years, and recently his letters had been sparse and shaky. He could not wait to see his friend, to shout, just like an American, "Hi, Father, how ya doing?"

But he never had the chance because Father Corey was gone.

Ludo was crushed by the shock of abandonment, numb with distress. He listened while they told him, so sensibly, that Father had, after all, been ninety-three years old and no one lives forever, that his passing had been painless and easy.

Ludo stared at the old priest's grave, his eyes hot and hard, his hands clenched in his pockets. "How could you do this to me?" he whispered in rage. His heart was breaking. "I had so much to tell you."

"I know," Christian said softly. "I know—it was the same for me . . . almost." But at least, she was thinking, Father Corey never sold you for ten gunships. . . .

"I took his name, though. I didn't think he'd mind. I never really forgave him for dying," Ludo said, with a quirk of his lip. "But he was far more of a father to me than anyone else had been."

For a while, they were both silent, staring over the dark blue sea with its marching crests of whitecaps.

"What happened then?" Christian asked.

Ludo stirred and flexed his shoulder muscles. "Then? Well, then there was Vietnam."

To a seasoned street warrior like Ludo Corey, the Vietnam War did not offer any surprises or any horror with which he had not been familiar since birth. He was no stranger to tropical diseases, dysentery, internal and external parasites, leeches, and spiders the size of dinner plates. He had been an accomplished knife fighter since he was five years old and had no compunction about killing someone who threatened him. He lost no time in mastering the incredible new range of weapons now available to him. And soon enough, he realized that the Vietnam War offered an unprecedented opportunity to make money.

By the time he was nineteen, one year after he enlisted, Ludo was captain of a patrol boat on the tangled, lethal waterways of the Mekong River. He related a few of his more conventional adventures to Christian; he did not tell her about the commodities he would move on his boat, about his forays, collections, deliveries, and fringe benefits. He took risks and was well paid. It was ridiculously easy. And always in the forefront of his mind was a tall-masted, white-hulled sloop, sails taut and perfectly trimmed, tearing across the dark blue Caribbean waters or the tumbling green Gulf Stream, himself alone at the wheel.

Ludo was not greedy. He just wanted his boat. He worked hard, stayed alive, and left the military with an honorable discharge and sixty thousand dollars cash over and above his pay. Soon he had the boat. He named her *Espiritu Libre*—Free Spirit. Now he could realize his dream of supporting himself with fishing charters and deliveries, and he allowed Christian to believe that that was where his story ended.

Old habits die hard, however, and there was no Father Corey to talk to.

In 1974 he was living in Miami, owned a good boat, and was bilingual, expert with weapons—and bored.

He was uniquely qualified to be a smuggler.

His capital began to build extraordinarily. He stashed his money in various accounts in the Bahamas and the Cayman Islands. Soon, Ludo realized, he might have enough capital to set himself up as a legitimate businessman—if he wanted. He began to feel complacent. He had skirted the edges of a dangerous profession, made enough money, and was now in a position to extricate himself.

He decided to do just that. But by then it was too late.

One evening, two pleasant-looking young men fell into step on either side of him as he left the Dinner Key Marina in Coconut Grove, Miami.

One had dark blond hair and a short, stubby beard; the other had brown hair and a mustache. They were clearly in good physical shape, appeared to be about twenty-five years old, and wore sailing clothes.

"Hi, Ludo," the blond said, smiling. "We have a friend who wants to meet you and buy you a drink."

Ludo looked from one to the other. "Thanks, but I'm busy."

They allowed him a glimpse of the heavy-duty handguns they wore in shoulder holsters under their light parkas.

"Well now," Ludo said resignedly, "on second thought, why not?"

In a trendy fern bar, all bare wood, stained glass, and tubs of flowers, where a huge red and blue parrot jeered from its perch above the bar, he met the man who called himself José Estevez.

Estevez was a small, pale man with weary, dark eyes. He spoke quietly, with a Cuban accent, and seemed to know everything about Ludo. He was polite and firm, and it clearly never entered his head that Ludo might turn down the offer he made.

Ludo said he'd think about it. He wasn't sure whether he wanted to make regular trips to Colombia. He didn't know whether he wanted to go to Colombia at all.

José Estevez, looking patient, pointed out to Ludo the serious personal disadvantages of not doing as he was told.

Ludo understood perfectly then. He sighed and nodded, and after that, as black-haired Vic Jimenez, he was back in business as a courier and pilot among the islands off the Colombian coast and the inlets, keys, and mangrove-fringed lagoons of western Florida. Between trips he sailed as blond American Ludo Corey all over the Caribbean and the Bahamas in *Espiritu Libre*, listening and watching and reporting on the movements of José Estevez's opposition.

He made a comfortable living, taking each day as it came. Sometimes there were dangerous days, but these were relatively few so long as he stuck to the rules. Ludo was still not greedy, and he did not want to die, although as each day passed he thought he would mind dying just a little bit less.

On the fifth afternoon out from Fort Lauderdale, the Bahamas long behind them, the open Atlantic stretching ahead to the coast of Africa, Christian lounged comfortably in the helmsman's seat, the automatic pilot engaged, watching the wheel move gently from side to side as though nudged by ghostly hands. The wind had eased, and the boat was riding the sparkling blue waves with a jaunty air, as if knowing that hard times were past.

The hot sun beat down on Christian's tanned back and shoulders. She felt thirsty and would have gone below for a drink if she had not been feeling so lazy and happy—and if she had not been watching Ludo sleeping.

He lay flat on his back on the starboard seat, his head just inches from her bare right thigh. He wore nothing but ragged Levi cutoffs, Topsiders on his feet, and a waterproof watch on his left wrist. He looked much younger when he slept. The deep, rather bitter grooves framing his mouth smoothed out, and his lips softened and parted slightly so that Christian could just glimpse the sharp white edges of his teeth. She carefully studied his thick, dark eyelashes and the sun-bleached, almost white hairs on his forearms. Salt had dried in streaks on his chest and shoulders. She suddenly wanted to touch him.

Staring at the tumbled gold hair just inches from her fingers, she reflected that she had been living with a man under the most intimate physical contact for nearly a week and had never touched him in anything but the most mundane manner. He must be so tired, she thought, after the past few days. Watching the patterns of light and shadow chase across his sleeping face, she impulsively reached out her hand and caught a strand of his hair between her fingers. Christian knew by now that Ludo could move into fast action from a position of total inertia like a highly tuned sports car reaching sixty miles per hour in three seconds, but she didn't know that even in sleep he could distinguish between a casual touch and a calculated one; sometimes his life depended on it.

There was no change in the rhythm of Ludo's breathing, and he didn't appear to move a single muscle. Bolder, Christian stroked the tangled thick hair back from his forehead, her touch a gentle, cool caress.

Suddenly, she found alert dark eyes looking up at

her. Seeing him watching her when she had been so sure he was asleep, Christian dropped her hand and flushed with embarrassment.

"No," Ludo said seriously. "Don't stop."

Christian didn't look him in the eye, but brought her hand back up and watched her fingers thread through the glossy strands of his hair. She watched them twist and knead with deliberate, feline movements all their own, smoothing the sweat-dampened hair at the nape of his neck, then flowing along the firm, sun-warmed flesh of his jaw. She lightly touched the brown stubble on his upper lip and chin. Very gently, she touched his lips, watching her fingers trace the outline of his mouth with amazement, as though they moved of their own will. He reached out his hand and held her loosely by the wrist. He tugged her gently but firmly down onto his chest.

Christian found herself floating in an unreal, sun-spangled haze of blue and gold and glancing light. Ludo's hands moved on her neck and shoulders, slow and smooth, then slid down to span her lean waist. She bent over him, seeing twin miniatures of her face reflected in his eyes, so dark the iris was a mere shade lighter than the pupil. His eyes were questioning. I want you, they were saying, but do you want me? Do you want this? Her eyes were answering yes. She reached behind her back and untied the straps of her bikini.

Seconds later, her bikini bottom and his shorts lay in a small heap on the floor of the cockpit. She knelt over him, naked, and watched his hands cup her breasts and then gently caress her nipples. Neither of them said a word. She leaned forward and kissed him for the first time. His lips were firm and salty and opened under hers. His hands slid across her back as he maneuvered their hips and thighs on the narrow seat. Christian felt a flooding gush of warmth throughout her body, a heavy sensation of melting; she sighed deeply and slid effortlessly down onto him, knowing she had never felt this way before, never. She had not known it was possible to want someone so totally. She

lay on top of him, her hands locked tightly behind his
neck, his body locked deeply into hers, and raised her
head to look at him. He watched her, a ghost of a
smile lifting the corners of his mouth.

"I love you," said Christian.

Ludo smiled. It was a beautiful, happy, young smile
that she had never seen before. He didn't tell Christian he loved her too, but she didn't expect him to.
Not yet.

In fast-falling darkness and a rising storm, Christian
and Ludo sailed under the grim fortress of El Morro,
for centuries the protector of the city of San Juan.

The surge swept in through the narrow harbor entrance in powerfully breaking swells, and they swept
with it, Christian staring up at the stained yellow walls
towering hundreds of feet over her head and then
nervously down to the jagged rocks, so frighteningly
close. But then they were through and breasting evenly
across the gentle wavelets of the harbor. Christian
lowered and furled the mainsail; Ludo stood at the
helm, eyes alert and searching, happily confident, coming home. "We'll get cleaned up," he said, smiling at
her over the folds of sail, "and then go out and get a
steak. Or maybe an honest-to-God American hamburger. What do you think?"

It was marvelous to be on solid land again after more
than two weeks at sea, marvelous and slightly strange.
Christian found the ground moving under her feet.
And the one thing for which she was ravenous was
fresh red meat: a steak—oh perfect—and a bottle of
good wine to go with it. . . .

They sat thigh to thigh in the taxi, Christian with
her arm around Ludo's waist as he leaned forward to
talk to the cabdriver. He wore a thin white cotton
guayabera—the casual shirt frequently worn by Latin
men—over loose white pants. Through the cloth, she
could feel the heat of his skin and the smooth sliding
slabs of muscle. If she was near Ludo, she found it
impossible not to touch him. Over the past two weeks,

they had made love an average of four times a day. She thought about making love now. Holding him lightly, she stared over his shoulder through a windshield half-obscured by holy pictures, plastic roses, baby shoes, and a bobbing rubber alligator and instead saw images of Ludo's bent, bright head, naked shoulders, and tensed arms. Then rhythmic glimpses of that thick column of flesh plunging into her overtook the other images. She gripped him spasmodically and—oh God—could feel herself beginning to come, right now, in the taxi. She groaned and took his hand and clenched it between her thighs, buried her face between his shoulder blades, and gasped and clutched at him while he continued, in a shaking voice, to give the driver directions.

They pulled up outside a small restaurant in the Punta Las Marias district, not three blocks from the beach. Ludo paid the driver while Christian stood, shaken, under an acacia tree, listening absently to the tropical night sounds: the rasping buzz saw of crickets and the shrill chorus of tree frogs over her head; the nearby booming of the surf on the reef; and a rumble of thunder. She flinched as the sky suddenly ripped in half with a purple-white lightning bolt, revealing massed ramparts of cumulus clouds. Then the rain fell on them in solid, warm sheets, the drops the size of marbles. They were soaked before they reached the door of the restaurant.

All through their first dinner, they talked of inconsequential things, sitting very close, drinking wine, laughing a great deal. Tanned as a gypsy, wearing a pair of Ludo's sailcloth pants and one of his shirts belted tightly around her waist, a spray of scarlet bougainvillea in her dark, shining hair, Christian looked exotic and blooming with health and happiness. Her tanned cheeks glowed dusky red each time she felt the warm touch of Ludo's hand on her thigh. She ate her steak with huge appetite, thinking with satisfaction how nobody—absolutely nobody in the world, not even Arran and Isobel—knew where she was. She had stepped apart, out of reality, out of time. She wondered whether Sam Stark had tried to find her and hugged herself with childish glee that it had never occurred to him to look for her on a small sailboat in San Juan.

They left when the storm ended. The dark streets were steaming, the trees dripping, light glinting on deep puddles. The sweet scent of the blossoms rose in the newly freshened air, and the little tree frogs, happy to be wet, shrieked in the branches over their heads. They took another taxi, back to the boat.

The cabin was humid, moisture glistening on the woodwork, the overhead hatch closed, a sudden violent rattle of hail pounding the deck over their heads. Ludo stood with bent head, barefoot, staring hungrily at Christian where she lay naked in the double bunk, waiting for him. He stripped off his clothes, not taking his eyes from her body, and flung them carelessly behind him.

For a long moment they did not touch each other, Christian staring as hungrily at him, thinking how beautiful he was without clothes, how compact and sleek, and how every moment not in actual physical contact with him was sheer torture, but prolonging the agony so that touching him again would be the greater joy. She quivered under his dark gaze, knowing what it meant now to be in heat, like an animal, and finally stretched out her arms. "Come to me! Come here, Ludo!"

He smiled at her, his face breaking into that smile that would always be hers, then joined her in the bunk. They enfolded. . . . Christian closed her eyes.

She lay under him, her long legs wrapped around his shoulders, her bare feet braced against the low ceiling, his hands linked under her hips straining her against him while she kissed his eyelids and clutched at his tangled hair. He plunged on and on inside her until she sensed the growing, frantic force between them, heard his breathing quicken and rasp in his throat, and felt the sweat break out on his body and his muscles grow rigid and lock into spasm while he poured his whole being into her, while she saw darkness and whirling lights and moaned his name over and over, lost.

Afterward he lay beside her, very quiet and still, eyes closed, the sweat drying on him in the cool breeze from the newly opened hatch, which they had to remember to close soon, against the coming of the next pounding squall. Christian raised herself on one elbow and looked down at him. She wished she knew what he was thinking.

She would not have wanted to know.

Ludo was wishing they were still far out in the middle of the Atlantic Ocean.

Emotions flickered through his mind like fox fire. He had never felt like this before. For Ludo, sex was a violent and necessary bodily appetite, easily satisfied because women had always been attracted to him, and then forgotten until the next time. He had never been inclined, ever, to become involved, and it was just as well. In his sometimes violent and always roving life, there was no place for it. Now, there was Christian. What was he going to do with her?

At first, he had rationalized that it was just for the trip; they would arrive in San Juan and go their separate ways and that would be that. Good-bye, good luck, and I'll think of you sometimes. But now, parting from Christian was no more possible or realistic than cutting himself in two.

If only their voyage had never ended; if only they could be still out there, with just the wind and the ocean to worry about, safe.

Tomorrow he would have to pick up his life again. He would have to make phone calls: first to the owner of the boat to report safe arrival; then to his friend Miguel, a charter-boat owner, who always kept Ludo's little Fiat while he was away; and then . . . and then he would call his contact, a waiter at the Condado Palace Hotel. Then would come, sooner or later, the departures, the lies, and the dangers—that other life, in which Christian had no place, in which it was criminally unfair of him to involve her.

He felt a chill of fear, but let no trace of it show,

knowing she was watching him. He had been afraid before, but never like this. Now he was afraid for another person, and he knew that sooner or later, he would have to send Christian away.

No question—she would have to go.

But oh, dear God, please not yet.

5

These days Arran poured nearly all her energy into work. There was very little of her day that was not directly work related. When she was not sitting at her desk typing on Isobel's beautiful red IBM, she was interviewing or researching.

Socially, her life was stagnant, her old friends dispersed.

After the death of his sister Helen, Fatso rediscovered a long dormant but still very real hatred of white people. His anger was unbreachable, even by Arran. He disappeared from her life into an impenetrable black world, and she never saw him again. Helmut Ringmaiden retired, and Mogul Books was now a trendy import shop selling llama-fur slippers, Afghan caps, and Mexican serapes. Freedom, now answering to his real name of Bernard Root, was finally finishing his bachelor's degree at San Francisco State University.

Nor did Arran have much contact with her sisters at this time. Isobel was working as hard as she; Christian had, to all intents and purposes, disappeared. She had walked out on her wedding to Sam Stark, Florida billionaire, and had resurfaced in Puerto Rico, the traveling companion of some unknown man named Ludo Corey, who Isobel was sure must be a drug smuggler. "What else could he possibly be?"

Arran worried horribly about Christian, even though she had sounded so happy the one time Arran talked to her on the phone. Come *on*, Chris, she'd wanted to cry—a drug smuggler? And she was even more anxious because Christian had cut herself off so completely—no phone, no address, no way of reaching her. Suppose something *happened?* She felt abandoned by her sister, resentful that perhaps Christian didn't trust her enough, and, shamefully, jealous. Yes, jealous. Christian was in love and happy, and she, Arran, was bitterly jealous. Sadly, she wondered whether she would ever be in love herself and decided probably not . . . not anymore.

She was so terrified of repeating her humiliation with Hart Jarrow that she avoided men almost entirely and shunned personal relationships. Now when the dark impulses hit her—for it seemed that, far from being exorcised by her appalling experience with Jackhammer, they had just gone into hiding all this time, waiting and gathering strength—she would climb into her battered old Toyota, drive down to the industrial area south of Market Street, and spend a few hours at the Eleven Hundred Club.

The club was frequented by sadomasochists of all sexes, and Arran would be unwillingly but irresistibly drawn to its rambling depths beneath the warehouses and to the professional indifference and ruthless competence of the prostitutes who worked there. She developed her favorites: Gus, a bodybuilder with a shaved skull who worked at a meat-packing plant during the day, and Sandro, half–West Indian and half-Greek, who was endowed like a donkey. She would prowl through the luridly lit rooms with their offerings of beating and bondage, her body aching after the assaults of Gus and Sandro, and feel, for a precious few hours, free and cleansed.

The following day she would wake weeping with shame and despair and vow never never to go to the club again. She would clean up her act. She would live like a nun. The ever present possibility of catching some deadly disease hung over her head like the sword of Damocles. Never again, she would swear to herself, never, never again.

A month later, desperate with stress, she would be back, ringing the hidden bell, five hundred dollars cash in her purse for a night of abandonment in a dark cellar with strangers.

*   *   *

The early evenings were the most difficult times for Arran, which was why, even though her research was finished and her book completed, she began to spend more and more time at the St. Andrews Center for the Homeless down on Ninth Street, where up to 150 homeless men, women, and children were daily given a hot meal and safe, warm lodging for the night. Finally, she started to volunteer her services on a more or less regular basis.

She began to grow personally involved with the street people, who, once they trusted her, accepted her almost as one of them and talked to her freely—people such as Gooch, a street-smart fifteen-year-old familiar with every crash pad and source of free meals and handouts in the city; Jim and Mac, drug-blasted victims of the sixties, who clung together for protection with the closeness of Siamese twins; Mrs. Delaney, an evil-smelling old crone convinced there was a Martian plot to prevent the second coming of Jesus; and Mr. Frolich, a kingly professional beggar of eighty, a double amputee with the face of a poet, always accompanied by his massive, tender-eyed German shepherd Loftus.

She also grew friendly with other volunteers. There was Dr. Johnny Garcia, an intense young Guatemalan who ran the Clinica Dolores on a side street off Mission. He stopped by the center twice a week to treat with no charge any complaint from skin eruptions to dysentery. And there was Humphrey, a three-hundred-pound homosexual who owned a leather bar down the block called The Dungeon. He was in charge of the kitchen. Each afternoon at five o'clock sharp, Humphrey would arrive sweating and panting, dressed in a black-leather quasi-Nazi uniform and dragging an enormous vat of homemade soup. He shopped at the farmer's market for fresh produce every day. His ambition was one day to open his own little French country restaurant.

One night, Arran met Devlin. "Dev's here," Johnny Garcia said. She was standing behind the counter arranging cups of coffee, tea, and milk on trays. "He wants to talk to you." But before he could tell her who Devlin was or what he wanted, his attention had been claimed by an elderly man with a horrible boil under one ear.

Perhaps Johnny thought she already knew Devlin? But when he came up to her, she knew she had never seen the man before in her life. If she had, she would have remembered him.

He was a handsome man whose every feature was so strikingly at variance with the rest, from the sheaf of glistening white hair to the unmarked, youthful face to his ancient, questing dark eyes, that he could have been anywhere from thirty to sixty. He wore an old black turtleneck pullover, which was unraveling at the sleeves, and a pair of faded jeans. He had the kindest smile Arran had ever seen.

"You must be Arran," he said warmly. His voice was rich and deep. "I've been looking forward to meeting you. Johnny's told me a lot about you, and I have a favor to ask. Let me buy you a beer after everybody's been bedded down."

By nine o'clock, Dev and Arran were sharing a booth at La Rondalla, a Mexican bar and restaurant on Valencia Street. Above their heads looped an elaborate and permanent array of tinsel and paper Christmas decorations: silver bells, angels, Santa Claus and his reindeer, angels blowing dusty golden trumpets.

Dev munched hungrily on tortilla chips. "Here's what it's all about," he said, and he began to explain his project. "I'm planning to make a film about the center and the people who depend on it, hopefully to be aired on public television, to attract attention and raise some money. We'll show the day-to-day running of the place with on- and off-screen narration, have interviews with the staff—and with some of the people too, if possible, like Mr. Frolich. He'd enjoy it and would be a marvelously colorful character. But"—he smiled—"we need a professional script, and we can't pay the writer any money."

"Of course I'll do it," Arran said at once. "I'd be glad to."

"Oh great!" Dev's dark eyes sparkled. "That's terrific . . . because from what I hear about your work, you're the one we want. . . ." He began to lay out the format and guidelines for her. "Do you think you could put together a short outline or treatment for me to look over by next week?"

Beguiled by Dev's energy and the sheer magnetism of his personality, Arran decided she probably could. "Who'll narrate?"

"I will. At least, that's the plan at the moment, for want of anyone better."

Arran didn't think there could be anybody better and told him so. "You'd be perfect. You have a good voice. Are you an actor?"

Dev seemed to find that very funny. His eyes crinkled with amusement. "Aren't we all?"

Slightly nonplussed, not understanding the joke, Arran said, "Well, you certainly know something about film."

"I went to film school once."

"Where?"

"USC."

"I'm impressed. So did George Lucas and Steven Spielberg."

Dev smiled. "I was a little before their time. . . ."

A cheerful, fat woman wearing a scarlet Indian-style costume plunked down two more bottles of Dos Equis and refilled their platter of tortilla chips. "Of course, not wanting to push my luck," Dev said, "I have another project going—with Johnny. It's just a concept now. We're looking for the space and the support." An undertone in his voice told Arran that this was even more important to him than the film.

"What kind of project?"

"A sanctuary for refugees, Hispanic refugees who can't go home for political reasons. People with no money, no resources, no medical care . . . probably non-English-speaking . . ." As though thinking aloud, he verbally examined his scheme and Arran listened.

"Perhaps we'll do another film, depending how the first one goes, but in any case, a good writer on tap is like a pot of gold . . . if you're interested, of course."

"I'm always interested," Arran said, deciding that Dev was unusually socially aware for an actor, or filmmaker, or whatever, and then that his face was one of the most beautiful she had ever seen. She studied his long, glinting dark eyes, and the crescent-shaped laugh lines on each side of his mobile, expressive mouth. He obviously smiled a lot, as though there really was joy in the world.

Arran felt a sudden wave of bleakness sweep through her from head to foot, followed by a familiar tense rage. He was too good, too kind, too special, and far too wonderful to be real.

When the waitress returned, she said abruptly, "I don't want another beer. I want a scotch on the rocks."

She drained it, straight down. The whiskey hit her empty stomach with the impact of a grenade. She crunched aggressively on a tortilla chip and stared at Devlin with narrowed eyes.

"I wish I'd read one of your books," Dev was saying, apparently finding nothing remarkable in her behavior. "Johnny has. He says that you pack quite an emotional punch, and that you have a real feel for the people you write about."

"I suppose," Arran said absently, looking around for the waitress, making little wet circles on the table with her empty glass. She needed another drink.

"You've a sympathetic manner and people talk to you."

"People have always talked to me."

"That's a gift."

Arran shrugged. She didn't want to talk about writing. She did not want to talk at all. She wanted . . .

"Did you always plan to be a writer?"

She shifted in her chair. "I don't know. I guess it just happened."

"I wish I could write better." Devlin sighed. "But I never will. I'll just have to keep borrowing other people's talents." He leaned across the table and took her by the hand. Arran flinched. "I appreciate your helping us. It's going to make a real difference—"

"Then get me another drink," Arran demanded, taking her hand away as though burned.

Devlin glanced at her thoughtfully and, with a small gesture, summoned the waitress, who arrived at once. Arran knew Devlin would always get instant attention, wherever he went.

"Tell me," he said slowly, watching her drink, "what do you do when you're not working?"

"I eat and sleep."

"No friends? No boyfriend?"

"No."

In a gentle voice, he asked, "Arran, how old are you?"

"Thirty."

"You look much younger."

"I know. People always tell me that. It's a bore."

He smiled. "Excuse me."

"That's all right." She stood up. "Let's go."

Devlin stood up too. "If you're ready."

"I'm ready. We'll go to your place. Where do you live?"

"Nowhere you can go."

"What the hell do you mean?" Then before he could tell her, she said, "Well, okay, we'll go to my house."

They were out in the street now, and he was holding open the door of his old Volkswagen squareback. She sat down; he sat beside her in the driver's seat and slammed the door; then she turned on him before he could start the engine, her eyes narrow and dangerous, all reaching hands, voracious teeth and lips, groaning in her throat with her need. Surprised by her attack, Dev fell back for a second, but then, with surprising strength, for he was neither a big nor a seemingly powerful man, he caught her by both wrists and slowly but surely forced her back into her seat.

"What's the matter with you?" Arran raged. She tore one hand free and cracked him across the mouth. "Aren't I good enough for you? Don't you want me?"

He recaptured her hand and pinned her wrists. Her body arched against him, taut as a bowstring. "What's the matter?" she jeered. "You a fag?"

"No."

"Could have fooled me. What's the problem, then?"

"No problem. Sex just isn't on my list." He gripped her tighter than ever, feeling the hysterical tension quivering in her forearms.

"It's on everyone's list one way or the other."

"But not mine. You ought to know that."

"Know what? Can't you get it up?" Arran demanded coarsely.

"I thought Johnny told you. I'm sorry. I was sure . . ."

"What the hell are you talking about? Johnny told me *what*?"

"That I'm a priest," Devlin said cheerfully, panting slightly with the exertion of holding her.

"Oh shit." Arran closed her eyes and slumped in her seat. Dev released her. "Then why don't you wear a goddam collar?" she muttered.

"Because sometimes, at the center, people feel threatened by uniforms." He waited quietly. Finally, Arran began to laugh. She laughed until the tears began to pour in rivers down her cheeks. "Oh God, a fucking priest!"

Dev took her into his arms and turned her soaking face into his neck. "You're a beautiful girl, Arran," he told her calmly, "an enticing one, and quite, quite drunk. I'm going to take you home now; you're going to sleep well; and tomorrow, or whenever you feel ready, we'll talk."

6

Mark Wynne was unaware of being exceptionally privileged. He had a big house, a huge swimming pool, and a movie star for a mother—but nearly everyone he knew had those. He went on vacations to Hawaii, Mexico, the Caribbean, and Europe, just like the other kids in his set.

Actually, he felt somewhat underprivileged. He did not have a father, although most of his contemporaries were, at any given time, also between parents—mothers and fathers seemed to change around with such bewildering rapidity. Neither was he very happy, but somehow he didn't really expect to be happy. Home was, well, not a terrific place to be. He didn't enjoy school either because, although very bright, he wasn't popular. He decided it was because the kids were jealous that his mother was a bigger star than anybody else's mother; for some time now they had called him a snob and wouldn't play with him, which made him mad, so he punched some of them out. Then they called him a mean bully as well as a snob. They always came to his parties, though, because they were so much better than anyone else's.

When Bryant was transferred into his fifth-grade class, Mark did not have a single real friend. Bryant was back in Los Angeles after three years in New York with his mother. He didn't know he wasn't supposed to like Mark Wynne. And if he had, he wouldn't have cared.

Bryant was an independent child, sophisticated for his age. His parents were separated. His father was a shadowy, rather formal figure who worked very long hours, seldom smiled, and made Bryant feel uneasy. His mother played a lot of tennis, went out to lunches with other women, had her hair done, and was always going to meetings to arrange parties for diseases, like the Arthritis Ball, the Cerebral Palsy Tea, or the Muscular Dystrophy Luncheon. Mother—she didn't like him to call her Mommy anymore—would dress up to the nines, stare at her lovely blonde hair in the mirror, complain bitterly about the mess Kenneth, her hairdresser, had made of it, squirt herself with Giorgio, and dash off in her powder blue Mercedes to meet all the other ladies who had also been to Kenneth and dressed up.

Bryant couldn't imagine what went on at these functions, but Mother told him they were terribly, terribly important. Well, of course they were—Mother was an important lady. He was reminded of that all the time. Mother was important, and Father was a bastard, and as soon as Mother's lawyer had "taken Father to the cleaners" she and Bryant would be back in New York in the flick of an eye.

Bryant felt none too happy about that. He had enjoyed New York, but he liked Beverly Hills better. He liked the sunshine, the flowers, and the spaciousness, and now, he liked his new friend Mark.

Mark in turn liked Bryant, and not just because, as a friend, Bryant was the only game in town. His liking had something to do with Bryant's airy self-possession; a lot to do with Bryant's looking something like himself, enough to generate a comfortable feeling of tribal fellowship; and somewhat to do with the sad fact that Bryant's birthday was on Christmas Day, which made Mark feel dreadfully sorry for him. Feeling compassion was a new and rather pleasant feeling that made Mark feel warm and generous and even more inclined to like Bryant.

They had something important in common, too. They both wanted to play the piano and were both frustrated for opposite reasons.

"My mother won't let me take piano," Bryant said,

"because my dad plays. She doesn't want me to do anything like my dad."

"That's dumb."

"Yeah. Real dumb, 'cause I'm like him anyway. Granny's eighty and doesn't play with a full deck"—he tapped his forehead significantly with his fingertip—"and she even thinks I *am* my father."

"I have a Steinway Grand at home," said Mark. "I had lessons last year." But he didn't want to learn anymore. Mom had spoiled the piano for him, as she spoiled everything. It seemed the moment he had told her he would like to play the piano, the Steinway had arrived in the living room and lessons had immediately been arranged with one of the leading teachers in California.

Somehow, the excitement and the joy had gone for him. He had a good ear and good hands but was a listless student, as though to spite himself. After a few weeks, he never touched the beautiful piano with its gleaming mahogany casing, soft-as-silk ivories, and rich, mellow sound. Suddenly, he no longer cared. "I'll be *damned* if I'll learn." Now, he just played "Chopsticks" on it with Melissa.

He didn't understand why he felt that way.

It was like when the Shetland ponies had come for his fourth birthday party. He had asked for one to keep, and his mother had given it to him, just like that.

And the dog. He had wanted a dog so badly, and Mom had said, "Mark, look what the good fairies brought for you." And there it was, the most beautiful puppy he could ever have imagined—Mom said it was an Afghan—prancing across the hallway toward him, its nails ticking on the marble, but it wasn't *his* dog. He had wanted a scruffy, shabby, ordinary dog, something dirty, a bit smelly, even with fleas—a *real* dog, not this pretty, nervous, delicate thing. He had screamed and screamed in rage, and Mom had looked terrified and said if he didn't want this dog, then what did he want and she'd get one right away.

Mom tried so hard, but—and this was a difficult,

rather grown-up thought that Mark was wrestling with— she tried *too* hard and always took the fun out of things. And then he got angry and miserable and yelled, and Melissa would yell too, and Mom would look frightened.

Now here was Bryant saying he wanted to learn the piano but wasn't allowed, and it gave Mark a great deal of satisfaction to rebel against a mother, even if she wasn't his. "Come back to my house after school and play *my* piano. I'll show you the notes, too," he promised grandly. "And I've got all the lesson books and stuff."

Bryant loved going to Mark's house. He loved the Steinway and he even liked Melissa. "Dunno why," Mark said. "She's a real asshole."

"No, she's not an asshole," said Bryant, and Melissa would have developed a crush on him if he hadn't been six months younger than she. As it was, she followed him around constantly, trying to impress him. Bryant was delighted; secretly, he was lonely and would have liked a brother or sister. But when he'd asked his mother some years ago if he could have one, she'd said, "Over my dead body." So he pretended that Mark really was his brother and Melissa his sister. He wanted to go back to New York less and less.

The third time he went over, he met Mark and Melissa's mother, Isobel Wynne, the famous movie star.

He and Mark were sitting together at the Steinway, Bryant laboriously fingering through the Minuet in G from the *Little Music Book of Anna Magdalena Bach.*

Isobel parked right outside the front door, not putting the car away because she was in a big hurry. She rushed into the house—God, she had half an hour to change and get back to the studio for the publicity photo session—and heard the hesitant notes from the living room.

Entering, she saw her son in duplicate, sitting at the piano. Two heads of thick, black curls. Two pairs of sleepy-lidded, golden brown eyes. Identical mouths.

For a second she mistrusted her own eyes. Oh God, thought Isobel, who had had several lunchtime drinks, surely I didn't have *that* much.

The boys looked at her. Mark said, "Hi, Mom."

"Hullo, there," said Isobel.

"This is my friend from school."

"How nice!" Isobel sighed with relief and smiled at the child. What a handsome boy! Goodness, he was the image of Mark—how cute! "What's your name, dear?"

The boy stood up politely. "I'm Bryant Whittaker. Mrs. Wynne, you sure have a nice piano. . . ."

Isobel felt disoriented for the rest of the day. Emotions she had thought long buried came tumbling back. She had of course known that Davis and Stewart had had a son. The child had been born in December, seven months after they were married. It had been like a slap in the face, realizing that Davis had been making love to Stewart possibly even the same day that he had made love to her, Isobel. She had tried not to think of them together, but it had been impossible.

A nightmare memory of that wedding party exploded into her mind, as clear as though it were yesterday: Stewart, the bitch, looking like the cat who'd eaten the canary and two months pregnant with little Bryant, holding Davis's hand while Hall Jennings made his pompous little speech.

But according to gossip the marriage had been as good as over within the first year. And now, at last, Stewart and Davis were getting divorced. The thought was irresistible. Suppose now, after all these years, she went to Davis and said . . .

What?

"Hello, Davis!" She imagined herself cheerfully sitting down in that opulent swivel chair on the other side of his broad executive desk. She would cross her legs seductively and smile her million-dollar smile. "It's so good to see you again. It's been so long. And guess what? You know my twins, Mark and Melissa? *Well. . . ."*

Davis would listen, cold as only he knew how to be, and would say, "How interesting, Isobel. Quite ironic, wouldn't you say?" Or perhaps he'd respond, "If you want money, you'll have to see my lawyer. I'll be as generous as I can under the circumstances."

She arranged for dinner with Refugio Ramirez. She sought him out now and then, for he was the only person who really understood her and the only person with whom she could talk about Davis. She had a desperate urge to hear Davis's name spoken aloud by someone else, even in discouraging terms.

They were eating dinner at a small Mexican restaurant in an unfashionable part of town that served, so Ramirez swore, the finest huachinango north of Manzanillo. Ramirez was now immensely fat. He sliced his fish very carefully, dabbled it in the garlic-butter sauce, rolled it in a tortilla, and popped it in his mouth with a sigh of pleasure. "I ain't seen the dude in months. . . ."

Davis was now a loner and an automaton, working sixteen-hour days and at night returning alone to the hotel room where he had lived since Stewart left him. He was one of the most successful and wealthiest agents in Hollywood and had earned the reputation of one who would drive a merciless bargain. "But you know how much he used to enjoy the wheeling and dealing? What a kick he got out of squeezing a little more out of the deal for a client? How it was like a game, and how good he was at it? Well"—Ramirez shrugged chubby shoulders—"now he's better than ever, but he don't enjoy it. It's no game. He don't enjoy anything anymore. Of course, it was that tight-assed cunt he married that fucked him up. And she's hitting him for everything he's got over this divorce. He'll be lucky to get away with the clothes he's wearing."

Part of Isobel simply bled for Davis. Sitting at the dinner table with Ramirez, listening to that greedy little man mumbling through his mouthful of tortilla and fish about how unhappy Davis was, she was tempted to leap to her feet and drive impulsively to Davis's hotel, where she would rush into his arms and make up to him for the last eleven years, make it all better again. . . .

"He don't make it easy to be a friend anymore, and that's a fact," Ramirez complained, wiping his mouth on a napkin. "I stick around, but I'm the only one and I don't know as I'll do it much longer. The dude just don't give a shit."

Isobel stayed right where she was, in her chair. Davis wouldn't want her. Not even now, hearing about the twins. He wouldn't give a shit. Why should he suddenly start to care now after all these years? He had never tried to find out whether they were his children when they were born.

Late that night, exhausted, her mind teeming and unable to rest, Isobel paced her huge bedroom, glass in hand. At last she went to bed and stared blankly at the moving light patterns on the ceiling. She slept uneasily. . . .

And there she was, standing beside Davis in the Jenningses' garden, and it was not Hall Jennings standing on her other side but Father, who was making a long rambling speech about two good old families, the Winters and the Whittakers. The speech went on and on, rising in pitch, faster and faster, ending in a fit of terrible laughter. "That girl's father's quite mad, you know," one of the guests said in a concerned voice. "They should never get married. Think of the children . . ."

"Yes, Davis. By the way, my father has a degenerative brain disease. It could come out in Mark and Melissa."

"Don't come to me," Davis said wearily. "See my lawyer. He'll arrange for the medical expenses."

The wake-up call came at 4:30 A.M.

Isobel struggled out of bed like a zombie. She felt sick and hung over. Her head was splitting in two. Sitting in the back of the limo driving to the studio through chilly darkness, she placed two Excedrin tablets in her mouth and washed them down from her Thermos of black coffee.

"Jesus God," said Guy, the makeup man, staring at her puffy white face and swollen eyes. "I'm sure going to earn my money today. You look like shit."

Isobel collapsed drearily into the chair and listened, while Guy's clever fingers massaged and kneaded her jawline, to his usual lecture about how she had to take care because she was well on the way to ruining her looks. Today, as never before, the lecture hit home. Soon, if she went on like this, she would be ugly and her career would be over.

She would be a has-been, a failure.

Then, with maudlin self-pity, she decided she already was a failure. She had certainly failed as a woman and as a mother.

"Stop that, Isobel," Guy said sharply. "If you cry, you'll ruin everything."

Isobel grimaced and made herself not cry. Instead, she thought how, hell, she *was* a good mother. At least she tried. The kids lacked for nothing. They had everything in the world—except a father, of course. Then, mused Isobel, perhaps they should have one. Maybe she *should* get married after all. The more she thought about it, the more it seemed to answer all her problems. And with the right man, perhaps she would even stop thinking about Davis.

Isobel grew slightly more cheerful. Mentally, she scanned her list of men friends to see whom she would choose. . . .

7

For Christian, the days and weeks passed in a sun-spangled happy dream, a sensuous, tumbling haze of honeymoon.

Sam Stark might have existed in another lifetime, a lifetime she did not care to remember. It was over, irrelevant.

It had even been difficult to bring herself back to earth long enough to call Arran and Isobel to tell them she was safe and happy. Isobel had been shocked and quite angry with her. "You're *where*? With *whom*? Chris, you're insane. You don't know anything about the man at all. . . ."

"Yes, I do," Christian murmured gently.

"Now listen, tell me exactly where you are. Give me a number where I can reach you. You need to come back to reality."

"This *is* reality, Iso." And she couldn't give a number. How could she when they didn't have one? She was glad about that. She wanted no one intruding on her dream just yet, not even her sisters.

"I'll let you know when I get a number," said Christian, then said an affectionate but firm farewell and returned to the dock to help Ludo clean up.

Later in the morning, Ludo's friend Miguel brought around the little white Fiat. That afternoon the owner collected his boat, which Ludo and Christian had scrubbed from stem to stern and rendered immaculate. He presented Ludo with a fat check for the delivery, which they then proceeded to spend.

They drove to the southeast corner of the island, not many miles but a whole climate removed from the teeming rain forest of the central cordillera, where the mountain El Junque sat under a permanent shawl of clouds. Their new location was in a region of heath and mesquite and dwarf shrubs, rolling, grass-covered hillsides, and views across the flat, burning blue sea to the little islands of Vieques and Culebra. They would walk on the beach at sunset, arms linked, bare feet making twin tracks in the soft white sand. And they would swim in the hotel pool, the most bizarre pool Christian had ever seen in her life, the bottom painted in psychedelic swirls of blue, yellow, and scarlet, so that one seemed to swim through rainbows. Their room overlooked a sandy lagoon ringed with rock, where brilliant fish darted in the turquoise water. They made love almost all night in the biggest bed they had ever shared.

After four days on the coast, they drove up the steep shoulder of El Junque. Ludo wanted her to see his island with him now, all of it, because it would be their only chance—although she did not know that, of course. They spent a week together in a hideaway known only to a few, where the old, cool colonial rooms opened directly onto broad stone patios and galleries overhung with wide tiled roofs, where the lush vegetation crawled in tropical abandon around windows and walls, the petals of the flowers opening, Christian was sure, before her very eyes. They would sit, the only guests in the dining room, eating long afternoon meals of guinea fowl, wild rice, and fruit, their table decorated with hibiscus and gardenias, while outside the hot rain fell in long straight sheets.

At last, homecoming.

Ludo drove the Fiat in through the gates of the small sport-fishing club near Mayagüez where he kept *Espiritu Libre*.

They passed the tennis courts and the little club-house. He honked his horn and waved to Beto, the manager, who leaned through the window to wave back. And they drove down to the dock where the white-hulled sloop moved softly against its moorings, its reflection mirrored precisely in the motionless, bottle-green water.

Later, Ludo inflated his Zodiac dinghy, and they motored out of the harbor into the calm sunset waters of the Mona Passage. The sun was sinking into long streamers of violet clouds. They sat in their dinghy and stared at the black silhouettes of the palms against the crimson-stained water. Ludo opened the bottle of Spanish champagne he had brought especially for the occasion and filled two plastic glasses. "Welcome home," he said to Christian, and cursed himself for a fool.

They would have just two weeks more before the honeymoon was over for good.

Ludo had been called to the phone early in the morning. He was gone all day. He didn't tell Christian where he was going or when he would be back, but she didn't mind. She spent the time doing small chores, taking a load of laundry into the village, and shopping for their supper. She bought a barbecued chicken, lettuce, tomatoes, and a bottle of white wine. After lunch she took her new mask and fins and drove the Zodiac across the harbor entrance to a reef where the snorkeling was particularly good.

When she returned to the boat in midafternoon, she found two strangers sitting in the cockpit talking intently in rapid Spanish. They were both native Puerto Ricans: black haired, olive skinned, dark eyed. To her intense shock, she realized one was Ludo. She stared at him foolishly. Why in the world had he dyed his hair? Why did he look at her in that detached, almost angry way? She stared from one man to the other, waiting to be told what was happening.

Ludo greeted her with a hard, distant smile. He told her to pack her things quickly and then his companion, whom he introduced merely as Tonio, would drive her to the airport in Mayagüez, where she could take the shuttle flight to San Juan.

Stunned, Christian asked, "Why?"

"I have to go away for a while."

"Where?" Understanding nothing and suddenly frightened, she followed him down into the cabin, where their half-prepared supper waited on the galley counter. She watched him take clothes from a locker and pack them into a small flight bag. "Ludo," she said helplessly, "what's going on? Please, won't you tell me what's happening?"

Ludo didn't look at her. "I'm sorry. . . . Christian, you have to go now."

"What do you mean?" She stared at him, at this hard-eyed, black-haired stranger. It was astonishing how the hair color changed him. He looked somehow smaller and swarthier. And when she had first seen him talking with Tonio, even the planes of his face were altered because different muscles were called into play. His Spanish muscles . . . She didn't know this man. He wasn't Ludo anymore.

He was wearing his white guayabera and a cheap blue cotton jacket. As he zipped his bag closed, she saw the handgun lying beside it on the bunk. A 9 mm Walther, she noted dully. Businesslike . . . "Oh God, Ludo, where are you going?"

"I'm sorry," he said again, still not meeting her eye. "I thought we'd have longer together."

"But I'll see you in San Juan."

"No."

"You mean you're telling me to go away? Really go? Leave you?"

He nodded.

The color drained from her face. Engulfed in a wave of hideous weakness, she sat down limply on the bunk beside the gun. "No," Christian whispered, feeling drained and sick. Then, suddenly stabbed through with a new hardness of her own, she said stubbornly, "No, I won't."

"You must. Don't make this any worse."

"I'll make it as bad as I have to. Ludo, the only way you can make me leave you is to tell me you're tired of me and you want me to go—and make me believe you."

He turned to look at her at last. His face was set

into alien, harsh lines. He stared down at the gun and then back to her face. "Oh fuck," said Ludo, who seldom swore.

"It's all right," Christian told him, feeling an enormous, icy calm spreading through her body and sealing off all emotion so that she didn't have to feel love and didn't have to feel afraid—not yet. "It's all right. I'll go to San Juan. I'll find a place to stay. I'll call Miguel and let him know where I am, and I'll wait for you. I'll be there when you come back."

He looked at her helplessly. "I don't know when that'll be. And I might never—" He couldn't finish.

"I don't care how long. And there's nothing you can do. I'm not going to leave you." She set her jaw. "I'm never going to run away again."

Christian didn't cry until the next night, when she lay alone in her hotel bed, stared at the white ceiling, and wondered what Ludo was doing now, where he was—and who and what he was.

Then she cried as though she would never be able to stop, lonely, frightened, missing him desperately.

8

Looking back, it appeared to Arran that her long, meandering, and frequently interrupted talks with Father Devlin actually merged into one dialogue that took place over a six-month period in sundry locations: in coffee shops, at the center, in bars, even interlaced with script sessions for the film.

There was never a formal "talk," as Arran had vaguely feared there might be. There was no sitting stiffly in a rectory parlor among odors of furniture polish and sanctity. Father Devlin had neither the time nor the inclination for such niceties. He was a hardworking inner-city priest, his duties running the full gamut from the spiritual solace of the sick and dying, to leading the illiterate or non-English-speaking through the intricacies of filling out government forms, to literally wiping up blood after bouts of horrifying violence. He saved souls intermittently, on the run between crises.

He reminded Arran of a juggler spinning an almost infinite number of plates on their rims and never letting one fall. He had added her to one end of the row, and each time she faltered and trembled and threatened to topple, he would be there to touch her with his magic and his energy and set her spinning safely once again.

Eventually, she found herself talking quite freely about Father's madness, his fits of violent anger, and how it had been at home. "There was always a lot of tension. We never knew what would trigger him off. Of course, I had the easiest time. I didn't get in his way so much."

"What about your sisters?"

"Isobel used to annoy him terribly. She was always so vital. He seemed to hate having someone so energetic and alive around him. Isobel was always wanting to do things, to be something more, to be the best. By the time she was in her teens, it was one head-on collision after another. But she's the most generous of all of us. Even though he seemed to really hate her, she's the only one who's stayed in touch. She went to visit them, and she's always sending them money, even though they never thank her. She bought Mother a car last year. Of course, it was different for Isobel. . . ."

"Why was that, do you think?"

"Because she was—wasn't—"

"Wasn't what?"

"Damaged."

"I see," said Father Devlin. "And how about Christian?"

"Oh—Chris." Arran's mouth tightened in worry. "She was always terrified of Father. He used to torment and humiliate her, tell her she was stupid, and call her 'Miss Mediocrity.' She'd have nervous attacks and run away. She was always running away. She's never gotten over it—she's still running."

"Where is she now?"

"Oh God, I wish I knew. She's living on a boat in the Caribbean somewhere and won't give an address or contact or *anything*." She related the very little she knew about Ludo. "Isobel thinks he's a drug smuggler."

"Hmmm." Dev looked thoughtful. "So poor Christian was driven half-crazy. What about you?"

"Me?"

"You were damaged too."

Arran looked furtive. "What do you mean?"

"You said that Isobel was the only sister who was not damaged."

"Did I say that? I didn't mean it like that."

"All right." Dev let it slide. "You and your sisters are very close, aren't you?"

"Oh yes."

"Arran, do your sisters know about your sex life?" he asked bluntly.

She stared at him, shocked. She wasn't sure which shocked her more, a priest talking about sex or the thought of telling Chris and Isobel. "Of course not!"

"Why not?"

"I *couldn't* tell them, Dev. Never."

"Don't you think they'd understand?"

She paused. "They might," Arran muttered. "But they'd be so . . ." She trailed off into silence.

"So what? Shocked? Disgusted?"

"Well, yes. Of course."

"Do you think they wouldn't love you anymore? Something like that?"

Arran hugged herself across the chest and looked down. "Yes," she said. "Something like that. I suppose."

Father Devlin let it go. For the time being.

Another time. Evening at the center.

Dev was rubbing flea powder into the rump of Mr. Frolich's big German shepherd Loftus, who was itching badly and had chewed himself raw. "Your mother now," Dev said thoughtfully, "what did she do when your father used to bully your sisters? Did she take their side?"

"Oh no. Never." Arran shook her head emphatically. "She'd always take his side against us. She always protected Father."

"Protected?"

"Yes. Mother did everything for him. He was as much a child to her as we were." She paused. "Probably more."

"But she wasn't protective of *you*. Does she like children?"

"I suppose so," Arran said dubiously. "I mean, she used to work with war orphans and adoption societies and things. Before she married."

"Was she upset when the three of you left home?"

"I think she only pretended to be," Arran said shrewdly. "She was probably glad, because after we went she had him to herself. . . ."

By now, Dev's black jacket and trousers were liberally covered with white powder. He brushed at himself and coughed. "Well now, back to you. You were your father's favorite daughter. Why was that?"

"Because I wasn't a rebel or a runaway, and I wrote, like he did. He always said I understood him. He'd read me his poetry." Then, compulsively, she told Dev about her father's endless romantic war stories. "He absolutely believed he'd done all those things."

"How do you know he hadn't?"

"Because when I worked for the library, I found these old boys' adventure books—the Biggles series, about the RAF—and there were Father's stories. He'd make them a little different each time and get them confused, but he'd definitely taken them from those books. He'd even used some of the same names."

"So you don't think he was ever in the war?"

Arran shook her head. "I don't know how old I was when I started to feel that it was wrong and phony, that things had never really been the way Father said, that it was fantasy. . . ."

"What do your sisters think?"

"They don't know. I've never said anything."

"Why not? Wouldn't it have been a good thing to talk about it?" Devlin put the powder aside and allowed the complaining Loftus to go. The big dog immediately shook himself, releasing a fine white cloud over both of them. "Damn!" coughed Father Devlin, and he sneezed precipitously.

"Why didn't you ever tell your sisters?"

"Dev! I *couldn't!* Isobel was always so loyal and proud of him. She'd never have believed me. And Christian—she'd have been even more frightened of him. Sometimes she seemed so close to the edge herself."

"You're very protective of your sisters. Especially Christian."

"Christian's fragile."

"Well," Dev said matter-of-factly, "she seems to be happy now."

"If only she'd let us know where she is. And what's happening . . ."

"She might not want to be found, even by you. Perhaps she's afraid to confide in you."

"That's stupid," Arran said scornfully. "Chris could tell us *anything.*"

"Then if you feel that way about her," Devlin said mildly, "why can't you tell her—and Isobel—about yourself?"

Arran stared at him stonily. "That's different."

"Why? Your activities are too disgusting for your sisters' delicate ears? I doubt it. I think you're doing them an injustice. And depriving yourself of their support."

Arran remained mulishly silent.

Devlin rose stiffly to his feet. "All right, Arran, let's drop it. But you might think on this a while. There are an awful lot of secrets in your family. Everybody seems to be protecting everybody else. Does anybody really talk about anything important?"

It had been a difficult evening. For the movie, Arran had arranged a live interview with Mrs. Delaney, who had immediately launched into a diatribe about Jesus, alien spaceships, and the two Martians she had seen outside the liquor store on Sixth Street that very afternoon. "And wasn't that their flying saucer parked right there, looking for all the world like a 'seventy-eight Buick?" she demanded in outraged tones, spittle flecking her whiskery chin.

It had taken a long time for Arran to calm the old woman down, and now she felt tired. The coffee shop where she sat with Dev was steamy, warm, and fragrant with smells. She felt relaxed, and without knowing just how it began, she found herself telling Dev about Blackie Roach.

Dev watched her fingers grip her coffee cup, white and tense.

"Soon after he was killed, I went to Los Angeles to live with Isobel. . . . And then I moved to San Francisco. I was really happy for the first time. I loved it, and everything was going so well for me. I had a job and some friends, but. . . ." She went on to tell him about GianCarlo Vaccio. And after GianCarlo, the motorcycle gang in Oakland. "And then I started getting these phone calls"—Arran's face went waxy pale—"disgusting, horrible calls. Oh God, I was so frightened."

"So you saw the danger in time," Dev said. "Did you ever wonder why you'd been deliberately taking such risks?"

Arran looked down at her knees. "I just felt—I had to. It made me feel—clean for a while. I know how crazy that sounds."

"Not really," said Dev. "Anyway, then you decided to get help. That was smart."

"But I couldn't go through with it." To her horror, she felt tears prickling behind her eyelids. "It seemed so phony, sitting politely in a tidy office talking about stuff like that. What can this guy do anyway, I thought, except bounce back to me what I tell him in the first place? And I knew I'd lie to him. I didn't want him to know. I didn't like him. . . ."

"Then you were right to leave. You weren't ready."

"And anyway, I didn't think it would ever happen again. I was sure I was cured. Until—"

"Until what?"

"Something happened—something so bad—" But she couldn't, simply couldn't bring herself to talk about Hart Jarrow. "I started going to the Eleven Hundred Club."

"Oh," Devlin said peacefully, "that place."

Arran stared at him, truly shocked. "*You* know it?"

"Arran," he responded patiently, "I'm not blind or deaf. Of course I know about the club. I know everything that goes on in my territory—it's my business to know. Anyway, one can't crusade for the light," Dev said, with his glinting smile, "if one doesn't understand the seduction of the darkness."

"But you're a *priest*."

"Thanks for reminding me. But remember, I was not born a priest, I became one. I was out there in the real world for quite a long time."

Arran blushed and looked down at her knees again, fighting back impossible images of Father Devlin in the Eleven Hundred Club. He watched her with a quizzical expression, perhaps guessing her thoughts. After a moment he asked gently, "What happened to drive you to the club?"

Shrinkingly, and halting many times, she told him.

Dev listened to the whole miserable story of Hart Jarrow and didn't seem at all shocked. He went to the counter and came back with two more cups of steaming cappuccino. Arran stared gloomily at the little flakes of chocolate on top of the frothy cream. "I don't know what happens to me. Whenever things are going really well for me, I have this urge to destroy it all. . . ."

"But not for much longer," Dev said gently. "Not for much longer, I promise." He was silent for quite a while, then said, "People talk to you, Arran, and people talk to me too. Day in and day out, week by week, year after year. The stories are always different, and they're always the same, too. After a while the patterns develop. They're easy to recognize. Your story has happened before many, many times; it'll happen again. Listen."

His voice grew soft but resonant, with an almost hypnotic quality. "A young girl grows up in an unhappy home. There is a harsh, dominant father, a passive mother. At first things aren't so bad; the father likes the girl more than he likes her sisters and isn't unkind. But as the girl grows up, more and more she's her father's favorite."

Arran wanted to stop him then, but she seemed curiously powerless to say anything. That beautiful, melodious voice had fascinated her.

"As soon as she's old enough, the girl escapes. She goes far away, leads her own life, and becomes a success. But she never allows herself to relax and enjoy the rewards of her success. Whenever things get too good, she has to give herself a huge slap on the wrist. She punishes herself because she feels guilty. She knows she doesn't deserve success and happiness, because she's dirty. And after a while it's not enough just to punish herself; she needs to make other people feel dirty too."

Now, she could bear it no longer. "Stop!" cried Arran. "That's enough. Please."

"But she shouldn't feel guilty," Devlin continued. "Why should she? She did nothing wrong. She had no choice and no control. Children never have control. She was ashamed to tell anybody what was happening all those years ago, and even if she had, no one would have believed her. She was badly damaged. She has lived with shame and anger all these years because she would die if anyone knew, especially her beautiful, talented, so perfect sisters."

"Devlin," Arran said in a low, furious voice, "stop this right now or I'm leaving."

"No," Dev said, holding both her hands across the table, not tightly but firmly. She knew how strong he was and knew that if she tried to get away his grip would be unbreakable. "You're not leaving, because there's a happy ending to the story. You see, she's intelligent, she realizes at last that it's all right to be angry, that she doesn't even have to feel dirty. . . . Now, perhaps she can stop punishing herself. What do you think?"

Arran slumped passively in her seat, looking at nothing. "He never raped me or anything."

"I don't suppose he did. I expect he used emotional blackmail. That's the most usual."

"You talk as though it happens every day."

"It does, Arran," he said gently. "It doesn't make it any better, but it does."

"He'd come to my room almost every night," she began, her eyes wide and glassy. "At first, he'd just want me to hold him and kiss him and tell him that he was wonderful and that I loved him. He'd read his poems to me, and he'd tell me his war stories, and I'd feel so sad and ashamed for him. But then, after Isobel and Christian had both gone for good, he'd start . . ." Her voice trembled. Dev swept the coffee cups to one side and gripped her wrists. "He'd start wanting to look at me naked. He'd want me to undo my—my blouse so he could look at my—"

"Breasts," said Dev.

"Breasts," Arran repeated obediently and shuddered. "And then he'd touch them and want to kiss them, and he'd suck on them and call me his little mother. And then—then—he'd turn out the light—and make me get on the bed and—I can't."

"All right." Dev held her hands tight.

Arran closed her eyes, then caught her breath and resumed, in a weird, stumbling, half-dead voice. "And then he'd feel me all over and tell me that I was his precious little pearl, that he was opening up his pearl, and he'd put his fingers into me and rub my—my—"

"Yes—"

"And at first"—her face twisted in shame, the words straining through clenched teeth and stiff lips—"at first, just at first, I liked it. I even felt proud that he liked me and not my sisters. Oh God, I did. And then he'd feel me and I was wet, you know, and he'd tell me how he wanted to make me come, and then he'd— he'd—" Her voice changed again. She looked him straight in the eye, her own eyes suddenly dark and hard as agates. She rose slowly to her feet and demanded, "Let me go."

"Not yet."

"All right then. You want to hear it all? You want to hear the best part? I'll bet you do, you fucking eunuch." Her voice sounded like a fingernail on a chalkboard. "How's this, then, Mr. Priest? Father fucking Devlin? My father would go down on me. He'd suck my cunt and stick his tongue up my ass; then he'd stick it in my mouth and shove his hand up me, and you're so right, Father—I started going with types like

Blackie Roach because they'd fuck me stupid back and front and really work me over and it was the only way I'd ever feel clean. And now, if you'll excuse me, I have to go because I have a date. His name's Gus, he's six-six, weighs two-eighty, and has a cock ten inches long." Her voice rose to an eerie, thin wail. "Later on, we'll probably have a three-way circus. Do you know about circuses, *Father* Devlin? I'll have three guys inside me at once. Do you know how that's done, Father? And then—will you let me *go!*"

"Shut up," Dev said calmly. "We're leaving."

His arm around Arran's shoulders was like a bar of iron. He gripped both her elbows. With concerned but incurious faces, the other customers watched the priest walk the distraught girl to the door.

"I'm going to the club," Arran spat at him, once they were out on the sidewalk, "and you can't stop me."

"Yes, I can," Dev said imperturbably.

"How?"

"Because I'm taking you somewhere else."

She glared at him suspiciously with glittering eyes. "Where? To church? To exorcise me?" She sneered.

"To somewhere all this energy of yours can be turned around and put to good use . . . by someone who needs all the help he can get." And he drove her to Johnny Garcia's clinic.

There was a long line of people there. A teenage mother sat silently holding a lividly bruised baby. The boy beside her said over and over, "I dunno how it happened. I tell ya, I *dunno* how—" A heavyset middle-aged man had blood caked over his forehead and one eye. An older woman clasped a wailing child. A very pregnant woman sat holding her swollen belly and weeping softly.

The line went on. A dozen people, all ages, all poor, all in distress.

Johnny came into the room from behind a curtained alcove. He looked drained and exhausted. There were streaks of blood on his white coat. "Arran's come to help," Dev said.

Johnny looked first at him and then at Arran, and his drawn face relaxed a little. "Thanks," he said sincerely. "It's a bad night."

For the next three hours, Arran boiled instruments, took histories, and quieted frightened children. At midnight, she and Johnny delivered the baby to a shelter for abused children.

She did not think once about herself.

She went to bed very late and slept well.

9

1985

Isobel stared morosely through the tinted window of the limo at a landscape of beautiful rolling golden hills. She was on her way from San Francisco International Airport to the Napa Valley for three weeks location shooting on *The Vintners*, a period piece set during Prohibition, in which Isobel played the rebellious wife of a patriarchal Italian winegrower.

The film was supposed to be thought provoking and deep; Isobel did not know about that so much, but at least the clothes were elegant. It was being directed by Jerry Agnew, an English director who was very hot right now, and had been written by an autocratic, eccentric, Academy Award–winning genius named Hart Jarrow.

It was Isobel's best part in three years and she should have felt good, but things were generally sour these days, and she had progressed no further in her search for a father for Mark and Melissa. Her latest official romance was a convenience arrangement with Lawrence Sanzone, her costar in *The Vintners*, who, after one of their well-publicized "dates," would drop her home with relief at 10:00 P.M. and dash back to his current muscular eighteen-year-old surfer boyfriend. If people only knew, she would think with a sigh, how unromantic a movie star's life *really* is!

In her room at the Old Vine Inn, self-consciously quaint, decorated with an abundance of Laura Ashley wallpaper and fabric, Isobel swept the silver-framed photographs of the landlord's Scottish ancestors off the bureau and replaced them with her picture of the three little Winter sisters, thinking with a small pang how much Melissa resembled her at that age, took a large swallow of vodka, and flung herself disconsolately across the antique four-poster bed. She had two hours to take a nap before the limo would carry her to Hart Jarrow's ranch for a script meeting and dinner.

She had demanded to know why he couldn't meet them at the hotel.

"Because he prefers we go there," Agnew said. For him Hart Jarrow occupied a pedestal somewhat higher than God.

She didn't think she would like Hart Jarrow.

The limousine turned east off the Silverado Trail and lurched up the hillside along an uneven asphalt road, through two tall stone gateposts, then up a winding track between rolling acres of mature vines. Hart Jarrow owned sixty acres of vineyard; he grew pinot noir and chardonnay grapes, which he sold to one of the major wineries. Hart left his property in the valley only when it was absolutely unavoidable; as one of the most successful and highly paid screenwriters in the country, he could afford to live where he wanted and to call his own shots. He did both emphatically.

Well, good luck to him, Isobel thought sullenly as the driver hesitated at a fork in the road and took the left one, which almost immediately proved to be a bad choice. Moments later, they stopped in a farmyard where a boy was rubbing down a tall white horse while, from the radio of a muddy pickup truck, Kenny Rogers sang about a gambler knowing when to walk away from the table. A burly farmhand wearing filthy jeans and a stained Stetson and carrying a fifty-pound sack of steer manure under each brawny arm paused beside the driver's window and jerked his head laconically to the right. "Through the archway. Can't miss it."

Through the arch they went, between a cluster of barns and buildings, and then out onto a wide sweep of circular graveled driveway fronting a low-lying, gracious Spanish-style house with white adobe walls, red-tiled roof, and a wide, cool veranda hung with baskets of fuchsia.

Three men sat at a picnic table littered with shooting scripts and notepads. Jerry Agnew; Lawrence Sanzone, her costar; and another man, with an intelligent, angular face and an Asian cast to his features. He greeted Isobel with a charming smile and a small, gracious bow from the waist.

"Mr. Jarrow, I presume," said Isobel.

"Jules Yamada," corrected Sanzone, introducing him as a gallery owner and collector of Japanese art who had driven him up from San Francisco. He did not have to explain that the suave Mr. Yamada was his latest lover. Isobel wondered what had happened to the surfer.

Isobel nodded hello to the trio, accepted the offer of a drink from the smiling Mexican maid, and sat down in the proffered chair, her spirits rising as she admired the lawns, flowers, tiers of green vines, and wooded hillsides sloping gently down to the misty valley floor. Her mood improved still more with the infusion of strong liquor. Mellowing, Isobel even decided they made a charming and sophisticated picture: the talented young director; the actor, handsome and virile in his oatmeal-colored jacket and trousers from Banana Republic; the cosmopolitan art collector, not at all the cute boy she had been so certain Larry Sanzone would bring; and, of course, Isobel herself, in her casual but chic lavender jumpsuit by Cardin. The whole scene reminded her of an advertisement for expensive scotch.

Then the farmhand who had given her driver directions reappeared, clumping across the gravel in well-worn cowboy boots. He had changed his clothes and was now wearing a clean pair of jeans and a blue-and-white gingham shirt with Western snap fastenings. He approached the table smiling, hand outstretched. "Hi, Jerry. Hi, everyone. Welcome to the valley. I'm Hart Jarrow." His gray-green eyes took in Isobel's flamboyant presence with sardonic resignation. His big, work-roughened hand held hers for the precise length of time dictated by politeness and not a moment longer. "Everybody taken care of for drinks?"

Jarrow called for a beer, then settled in a chair, spread his long legs, and sighed with comfort. "Okay then, guys—let's get down to business."

Throughout the evening, Hart Jarrow was polite to Isobel but made it quite clear that he had neither the patience nor the time to tolerate the affectations of a movie star. Isobel found herself rising to the bait and attempting to impress him with both her wit and her lack of Hollywood pretension.

From the first, Hart was emphatic about his hatred of Hollywood.

"I never go near the place if I can help it," he told her flatly over the mesquite-barbecued strips of tender steak. "I don't care if I never see it again. It's crazy and destructive. It turns people into monsters."

Isobel decided not to argue the point. "I don't blame you if you own a place like this. Of course you wouldn't want to leave it. And it must be wonderful to make your own wine." This prompted a brief discourse from Hart on varietals, generics, and mini-climates.

During dinner she sampled both his own estate-bottled chardonnay, which she praised effusively, and the pinot noir. She was rewarded at last by a smile of genuine pleasure. However, Hart Jarrow was not a one-topic conversationalist, Isobel realized, listening to him talk with apparent knowledge to Jules Yamada about his netsuke collection, and in his own way he was a fine-looking man. Her interest became aroused. She covertly studied his powerful body and strong, chiseled face, decided she was going to enjoy working with him, and felt her first little thrill of sexual interest in years.

After dinner, Hart walked her back to her car, his big warm farmer's hand holding her arm very lightly, and told her he looked forward to working with her too. He smiled, and his teeth gleamed white in the darkness.

She thought about him in very sensual terms all the way back to the Old Vine Inn.

Their final night in the valley, after shooting had successfully wrapped, an Italian countess gave a party for the cast at her Florentine-style palazzo in the hills.

Isobel called Arran in San Francisco and begged her to drive up. "For God's sake, it's only sixty miles." But Arran was evasive and made excuses. Her new book was going well; she couldn't spare the time; she had promised to volunteer at the clinic.

"Clinic? What clinic?" Isobel demanded, and she listened with annoyance while Arran told her about Johnny Garcia's Clinica Dolores.

"All right then, Mother Teresa," she said tartly, "you don't get to meet him after all."

"Who?"

"Hart Jarrow. Arran, I've *told* you about him. And just perhaps—if things turn out right—he's going to be your brother-in-law!"

Isobel thought she heard Arran give a short gasp and with a feeling of pleasure, congratulated herself on having at last impressed her stubborn little sister. However, after a short pause, Arran merely said with her customary vagueness, "Well, that's lovely, Iso. Sorry I can't make it. But things are really busy down here." Isobel heard a kiss blown into the phone and blew one back herself. Oh, damn the girl. But she couldn't be cross with Arran for long—she was too happy.

It was one of the most perfect evenings of her life, thought Isobel, who had not had a perfect evening in a long time. The floodlit castle could be an illustration from a fairy tale; the people all looked beautiful and exotic; the scent of flowers was everywhere.

Isobel had drunk a great deal of champagne, but she felt light as air and not the least bit drunk as she wandered across the velvety lawns with Hart at her side. She found him an enthralling, exciting, and incredibly sexy man, the more so because so far, apart from the lightest of good-night kisses on the cheek, he had barely touched her. They had spent hours in each other's company every day, but there had been neither the time nor the opportunity for personal talk or exploration. But now the film was wrapped. There would be time now. . . .

He was looking particularly impressive tonight, Isobel decided. He was not wearing his customary jeans and cowboy boots, but tailored white pants, a bell-sleeved, white cotton shirt open at the throat, and a marvelous brocade vest. The anticipation swelled inside her body— tonight surely they would at last make love. What kind of a lover would Hart Jarrow be? wondered Isobel. And she answered herself—the best.

They wandered into the orchard at the foot of the lawn, into warm, loamy darkness under the spreading branches of plum trees. Hart caught Isobel to him and turned her face up to his. He was so tall she had to strain against him on tiptoe. He said nothing, but kissed her long and thoroughly, his hands hot against her bare back. Isobel felt small, dainty, and romantic. "I've wanted to kiss you since that first dinner at the ranch," Hart muttered into the carefully tousled, inky masses of her hair.

Later that night, in his bedroom, Isobel stared drowsily over his naked shoulder, outlined in silver by the rising moon, and gazed down into the moonlit vines and the dark mysterious depths of the valley below. She sighed with contentment, for it had been as wonderful as she had suspected it might be. Hart was a gentle, considerate lover, but with the power and stamina to satisfy her over and over again. He had made her feel like a goddess as she came three times in his arms, deliciously, her fingers clutching, head arched back into the pillows, luxuriating in the heat of his lips on the straining tendons of her throat, his hands warm on her swollen breasts. So good, oh yes, so good—she couldn't remember feeling so good since . . .

She caught herself in a small burst of anger and exasperation. Why in God's name think about Davis

Whittaker now of all times? And she found herself wondering whether, perhaps even now, at this time of night, he would be sitting alone at his big desk in his enormous office. Did he still have her picture on the wall?

"What's the matter?" Hart asked sleepily.

"Nothing," Isobel murmured. She decided that if what she was feeling for Hart Jarrow was not actually love, then it came close enough, and that he'd make a marvelous father for Mark and Melissa. How they'd love the ranch! She'd bring them here for a long visit after school was out in June. Of course that was more than two months away, but she didn't want to rush things with the twins. In the meantime, she wanted Hart more or less to herself—surely she deserved some happiness! She snuggled contentedly against the curves and angles of his big body, feeling him relaxing, settling for sleep, and then, with a sigh, fell quietly asleep herself.

"I don't want to go to any shitty old farm," Mark said sulkily. "It's Bryant's last week in L.A."

"Me neither. I'm not gonna go to any old farm," echoed Melissa.

"You'll love it!" Isobel looked into two pairs of angry brown eyes and explained exactly why. "There's a lake, and horses—"

"So? Big deal." Mark and Melissa looked at one another, and their strong black brows drew together fiercely.

But Isobel was determined. "I'm taking a week off, and we're having a vacation all together."

"I don't like Mr. Jarrow," Melissa sulked.

"You hardly know him," Isobel protested. "And anyway, he's coming down for your birthday on Saturday." Then she added, weakly, "I expect he'll bring some great presents. . . ."

As usual, having decided the children needed the wholesomeness of country life, Isobel had gone all the way. She had purchased, at vast expense, a matched pair of palomino ponies for the twins' birthday. She couldn't wait to see the excitement on their faces. And how glad she was that Hart would be here too. It would be a real family outing.

The twins opened a mountain of packages after breakfast, including two enormous wooden crates containing scaled-down but fully functioning Ferraris just like their mother's, although the only gift Mark seemed really to like was the set of shark's jaws that Christian had sent from a place called Puerto Plata in the Dominican Republic. He immediately hung the revolting things around his neck and would not be parted from them. Isobel felt jealous and told herself not to be so petty. In the midst of her new, exciting life with that fascinatingly dreadful Ludo, it was clever of Christian to remember the twins' birthday at all.

Afterward they drove to the San Fernando Valley in Isobel's Mercedes for the surprise, the twins in the backseat looking bored, wearing brand-new hand-tooled Frye cowboy boots. Hart sat silent in the passenger seat looking trapped.

They were welcomed at the Valley ranch by a leathery blonde woman in riding breeches who clapped Mark and Melissa on the shoulders and boomed heartily, as though they were winning contestants on a TV game show, "Boy, kids, does your mom have a surprise for *you*!"

The ponies were brought up. Their golden coats shone. They were frisky and charming, tossing their pale manes and tails, staring at the new people with liquid, intelligent, dark eyes.

"You first—up you go, young man." And Mark was thrust into the saddle.

Isobel watched ecstatically. Hart, resigned, waited for the inevitable disaster as the boy bounced around the arena, stiff and uncomfortable, the reins clamped in his hands, feet flapping in the stirrup leathers. "Better get him before he falls off," Hart told the blonde woman laconically. "He's got no business on a pony like that. The kid can't ride. . . ." But it was too late. The pony flicked its tail, tossed its head, skittered nervously to one side, and Mark was on the ground, shaken and furious and trying hard not to cry.

"Leave him alone," Hart commanded as Isobel, with a short scream, was about to rush to the rescue. "He's okay." And while the blonde woman caught the frisky, cross-looking pony and made soothing noises to it, he knelt down beside Mark in the dust and began to speak to him, calmly and too quietly for Isobel to hear what he said. Mark raised his head belligerently, his mouth opened in angry retort, then closed it. She saw him meet Hart's placid gaze with a thoughtful expression and nod slowly. Then suddenly he smiled, almost shyly.

Isobel's eyes were misty. Hart was wonderful with children! Oh God, he would be the perfect father.

The twins accepted Hart with gusto after that. Around him they were well-mannered and respectful, and even anxious to please. And they thoroughly enjoyed their visit to the ranch, where they had horseback-riding lessons every day, helped out with stable chores, swam in the lake among reeds and frogs, and nobody minded if they got dirty. In the evenings, Hart would sometimes let one of them sit up in front of him when he rode his big white horse down the hill and through his vines.

They both cried when it was time to leave.

The next month was blissful for Isobel. She felt young again, stopped drinking except for a little wine at dinner, and felt healthier than she had in years.

Hart was also a wonderfully satisfactory lover, and she reveled in feeling like a real woman. It was such a change to be spoiled and pampered and treated as though she were porcelain.

But then, for no real reason, things started to go a little awry. Isobel would find herself growing impatient with Hart for such silly reasons. For instance, *why* should it matter that Hart refused to kiss any part of her body except her lips, face, and breasts? "You're always wanting me to go down on you," Isobel pointed out, "so why won't you do it for me?"

"I just don't like to," Hart said pleasantly.

It was no big deal. So what? thought Isobel. He just doesn't like to. But later she would wonder, well *why* not? Did Hart think women were dirty? Did he find a woman's sexual organs actually unpleasant? Eventually, she decided that he did, and it made her angry.

And then, there were the continuing arguments about money.

Isobel loved to spend money. She was always giving expensive presents. Whenever she was depressed, she jumped into her new Ferrari, rushed down the hill, and went on a shopping spree as therapy. Hart was always complaining about her extravagance, which made Isobel angry. After all, it was *her* money.

He was also frank in his dislike for her house. "Well, I think it's beautiful," Isobel said. "You don't know what it means to me, having a house like this. You don't know how I had to fight to get where I am."

She tried to explain to him about Father and Mother and the drab ugliness of her early life. But Hart did not understand. "For God's sake, Isobel, my parents worked like slaves sixteen hours a day. Your father got by without working at all. Don't talk about being deprived."

But there was more than one way of being deprived, thought Isobel, wondering whether Hart would ever understand her. She was finding that, despite the sensitivity of his writing and his apparent understanding of women, Hart's own attitudes and those of his characters were not necessarily the same. She couldn't help but remember that Davis might have ended by despising her, but he had always, always understood her.

The real turning point came when Isobel returned from a shopping trip with Arran in San Francisco. She had spent a huge amount of money—but it was worth it! "She's going to be on the Johnny Carson show," Isobel cried proudly, "and God knows what she'd have worn if I hadn't gone to help out."

But for once Hart had not accused her of overspending. He said instead with numb surprise, "You mean Arran Winter's your *sister*?"

"Of course," said Isobel. "I'm sure I told you. I've been trying to get her down here so you two can meet. You'd get on so well."

Hart said in a muted voice, "We've met already."

"You have?" Isobel exclaimed. "Oh well, then, you know how great she is!" She smiled fondly. "Maybe next time—"

"No," Hart said flatly. "Don't do that. Your sister's a seriously troubled young woman."

"She's always been a bit eccentric," Isobel agreed, but, she thought, *troubled*? Surely not Arran. What could she have said or done to justify such deep disapproval? She couldn't understand how anybody could not like Arran. Then she felt enraged by Hart's not liking Arran. How dare he!

The rift between them grew wider.

Their relationship took another dive—although it took her a while to realize it had not only dived but ended—over *Roper's War*. He had flung the script in the wastebasket as though he had every right to dictate her career. "You're doing it just for the fucking *money*!" he yelled. Well, what if she was? She needed the money, and, in any case, it was *her* decision!

Isobel told herself that he didn't want her to make a mistake, that he cared for her and was proud of her being a real actress. But she knew secretly that *Roper's War* was just an excuse. He had been looking for a suitable way out, and now he had found one. He stormed out of her house, and she knew he would never come back.

He left the twins in a state of imminent mutiny—they had expected that Hart would be their new father.

He left Isobel with a hollow feeling of fright and a $250,000 Guido LoVecchio bronze horse.

To make herself feel better, Isobel bought an absolutely beautiful but outrageously expensive Venetian glass bowl for the hall table.

Mark got into a fight with a neighbor's child and gave him a black eye.

Melissa started stealing money from Isobel's purse.

Mademoiselle threatened, tearfully, to quit. Isobel gave her another raise and she stayed, but very reluctantly.

Then, *Roper's War*. A heavy work schedule and less time to think. She was glad to be working so hard, although she disliked every moment of the film.

She began to drink vodka again.

She saw a dreadful photograph of herself on the cover of one of the tabloids, haggard and puffy faced at the same time, with the damning caption, ISOBEL'S CAREER DOWN THE TUBES? She washed down three Valium with a glass of Stolichnaya and went to bed.

Her life was going into a tailspin, collapsing all around her, and she seemed helpless to do anything to stop it.

And then the phone call. "Isobel—your father is dead. . . ."

He was dead because he was a crazy drunk. He had killed himself. Was that what lay ahead for her? Yes, it probably was. And for the children too.

She had never felt so afraid in her whole life.

10

HELP!!! MISSING!!!!

50-ft. motor/sailer *Serena*. Gulf Star. White hull, blue topsides. Reg. Boca Raton, Fla. Dep. Governor's Harbor, Eleuthera, 3/14. Dest. Georgetown, Gt. Exuma. Crew: Stanley Quimby, 47; Elaine Quimby, 45; Roxanne Quimby, 22. REWARD! Any information as to whereabouts of this boat . . .

Christian stared at the faded Polaroid photograph of the Quimbys. The three of them were sunburned the shade of lobsters, grinning into the camera, wearing party hats, and raising glasses garnished with slices of fruit and little umbrellas. Where were they now?

"Davy Jones's locker," Ludo had said shortly, "with bullets in their backs—if they were lucky."

There were other similar notices on the bulletin board in the bar of the Peace and Plenty Hotel, Georgetown, Great Exuma. Christian read them while Ludo haggled amiably with William, the vegetable man, sitting at a table over glasses of beer. The Peace and Plenty was a place where sailors gathered, and William was a regular supplier of fresh produce to boats. Ludo always sought him out because not only did he have wonderful fruit and vegetables, but he also knew all the latest gossip. He and Ludo would discuss who was going where, from where, and with whom. And which boats had set out and never arrived.

Christian shivered slightly, despite the intense heat, reading about the Quimbys—a happy, unsuspecting family in a seaworthy boat, in the wrong place at the wrong time, meeting the wrong people. "New name, new registration, new paint job," Ludo had said. "She'd make a useful mother ship. . . ."

"What does Ludo Corey *really* do for a living?" Isobel had asked suspiciously during one of their infrequent phone calls.

Christian had talked cheerfully of charters and deliveries, as though just by talking she could make herself believe it too—believe that the real Ludo was the one drinking beer with William, talking about papayas and about whether to buy ten pounds of tomatoes or fifteen for the week-long trip back to Mayagüez, and not the sharp-featured, black-haired stranger, who spoke fluent gutter Spanish and moved with controlled violence, a dangerous man who carried a knife and a gun and was expert with both.

As though it were yesterday, Christian could remember the shock and the horror of that first time he had left her alone.

She had stayed in a little bed and breakfast hotel in Ocean Park for three weeks, going to the beach just after dawn to sit on the damp sand, watching the early morning joggers, gazing at the light patterns of the sunrise on the tall downtown hotels, finally just staring out to sea. At midday, back in her room, she would sleep. Then, every late afternoon, she would take a taxi to a different area of San Juan and walk the streets, searching for him. She never managed to sleep much at night.

On the twentieth morning, walking down onto the beach, she found a man sitting at the water's edge, his back to her, his chin resting on his hunched-up knees, the early light gleaming rosily on his burnished hair. She sat down beside him, the wavelets lapping around their feet, and after a moment he put his arm around her in silence and drew her tightly against him.

After that, there was a long respite, with months of safety to get to know each other again.

They sailed *Espiritu Libre* around the coast to San Juan, where they berthed for several weeks at the

Club Nautico and Ludo helped Miguel with fishing charters, leaving at dawn with parties of raucously happy, sunburned men looking forward to a day of serious beer drinking and, they hoped, a good session in the fighting seat with a dorado or marlin at the other end of the line. It was a happy, rather aimless period, but Christian was always aware that Ludo was waiting for something—a phone call, a contact, news. That time there had been no call. They returned to Mayagüez and soon afterward went to sea, cruising slowly through the Bahamas as far north as Cape Eleuthera.

But a day or two after they returned, Ludo was gone again, slipping away from her, a whole world away.

Once he had returned from a trip looking gaunt and ill, with a half-healed wound curving across his ribs. "Oh God," said Christian helplessly. She began to cry.

"It's okay," Ludo said brusquely. "Just forget it."

But how could she forget it?

Another time he returned looking drained, with dead eyes; he cleaned his gun and put it away in grim silence.

Whatever you're doing, Ludo, Christian would think, over and over, how many more times before it kills you?

Now, turning resolutely away from that ominous notice board, Christian reminded herself with a determined hope of her secret. She had never had such a secret from Ludo before.

It had begun a month ago, anchored in six feet of water off Long Island—an ironic name for a sandbar that appeared totally uninhabited—when Christian had deliberately not taken her birth control pill. She was not going to take any more pills. She was going to get pregnant. If she had a baby, then surely Ludo Corey would have to dispose of his terrifying alter ego, Vic Jimenez. If he had a family, he would surely not risk his life—or a long spell in prison.

And he had a perfectly good job waiting. Just last

month Miguel had cried, "Hey, man, when the hell you gonna come work with me full-time? I'm workin' my ass off, man."

Christian had thought longingly of harmless fishing parties, families and children out for day sails, or longer trips to the Virgin Islands.

That night off Long Island, as soon as the sun dropped below the horizon, a sea mist rose eerily from the water. The huge moon, which hung like a big silver dollar above the sand dunes, grew blurred and vague until its outline was gone but its light diffused evenly through the mist.

Ludo and Christian sat on deck drinking rum and grapefruit juice as though in a translucent shell, unable to tell where water ended and air began. It had been *then*. Christian felt such a powerful almost explosive need for Ludo that for a second she felt weak with shock. And then not weak at all. She set her glass down and turned to him. She unbuttoned his shirt and ran her hands over his smooth chest, the rough line of new scar tissue a sudden stark confirmation of her fears. She unfastened his belt buckle and reached for him, finding him fully erect. She straddled him, feeling such urgency she almost cried with frustration at a moment's delay, needing him inside her that minute, that second. She sank onto him, aware of every millimeter of his skin, feeling him deeper inside her, surely, than ever before, while his hands tightened around her buttocks and they stared into each other's eyes in the milky light. Now. It was the right time and the right place. Make me pregnant, Ludo, Christian demanded silently, make me pregnant *now*. . . . And they commenced a brief savage thrashing as though they were fighting, locked, to the death.

Afterward they rested together, exhausted, until he roused, carried her below, and made love to her all over again, slowly and thoroughly, for hours. Now, a month later, her period was two weeks overdue.

They left Georgetown, southbound. It was incredibly hot. Christian sat at the helm, piloting the boat through the reefs back in the direction of Long Island,

her head aching under a brassy glare of still, solid
heat, one hand on the throttle at dead slow, the other
on the wheel, eyes straining at the compass through a
reddish blur while Ludo leaned over the bow watching
for the treacherously lethal coral, which could rip the
bottom from the boat in seconds. She found herself
smiling, despite the discomfort of the heat.

By the time they sailed into Cockburn Harbor, South
Caicos, she was sure she was pregnant. She wondered
what to do because she didn't want to tell him just yet.

But on the way back to Mayagüez, the weather
turned bad. For three days, they fought the wind and
high seas all down the coast of the Dominican Republic, then plunged across the screaming waters of the
Mona Passage under storm sails until the boat broke a
stay with a crack like a gunshot and they had to make
the final eight hours to the Puerto Rican coast under
power alone. The motion was lurching, uncomfortable, and directionless. Christian was violently ill, but
Ludo would never suspect anything other than seasick-
ness to be the cause.

Back in Mayagüez, he was preoccupied with boat
repairs, and the following month he was away on a
charter for Miguel. So far he had noticed nothing.

But at the end of August, when Christian lay flat on
her back and examined her naked stomach, she found
a small round bulge, the size of a partially buried
grapefruit. It seemed to have appeared overnight. She
laid her hand protectively over it and found it hard
and warm. She reckoned she must be more than three
months along by now. She could wait no longer. She
must tell Ludo now.

She waited for the perfect moment, deciding as they
ate dinner at a local restaurant overlooking the crimson-
stained sunset water of the Mona Passage—now deceptively calm and placid—that it would be tonight,
back on the boat. And to her unutterable happiness,
Ludo had just told her that there would be no more
trips as Ludovico Jimenez. She would have no more
terrified nights thinking unthinkable thoughts, gnawed
by unnameable fears. He would be safe. He would run

a charter business with Miguel, and they would be a safe family. She hadn't even had to use her secret weapon.

He kissed her on the way home, standing under the fragrant trees. "How many times are you going to come tonight?" He was amused, flattered, and thrilled by her insatiability for him and by the ease with which he could bring her to climax.

And then the news from Isobel. A sudden stifling return of old fears, the more shocking because so unexpected. A sudden terror that however far she ran Father would still be there waiting for her, one way or the other. Irrational and shameful because now she had Ludo and the baby. It would be all right. She was part of a new family.

But she was part of nothing.

"Are you sure?" Ludo said coldly, his face bleak. "How far along are you?"

"Three months."

"You could still—"

"No!" Christian cried savagely, thinking of their precious little baby being cut or siphoned out of her body, suddenly hating Ludo.

Then blow followed blow.

He told her curtly that when she returned from England, "you'd better take a hotel room. I'm not sure where I'll be."

And Christian knew, with absolute dreadful certainty, that it was all over. After tomorrow she would never see him again.

Several times over the past year when her muscles had cramped with tension and rage, Arran had very nearly rushed straight for the murky solace of the Eleven Hundred Club. One was the time when, so happily, Isobel had announced that she planned to marry Hart Jarrow. But each time, a phone call to Dev—her lifeline—had helped her to substitute some different form of action—usually a stint helping Johnny in the clinic—until the stress eased.

Now the humiliating episodes came less and less

frequently. She began to feel in control of herself at last. And Dev had gradually been stripping away the layers of guilt, anger, and horror for her.

"Do you think your father really is crazy?" he had once asked thoughtfully. "Or is he merely a great manipulator?"

That had never occurred to Arran before.

"He was certainly in the hospital for a long time, whatever the reason. But is it possible," Dev mused, "that he later took perfectly sane advantage of his situation? Your mother was devotedly waiting on him hand and foot, sheltering him from the world and allowing him full rein with his war hero fantasy. If things didn't go exactly his way, all he needed to do was throw a tantrum, like a child."

Confused, Arran found she almost preferred to think of her father as insane. If he was insane, then there was an excuse for what he had done to her.

Devlin understood completely. "Of course. And I'm afraid that's a burden you're going to have to learn to live with by yourself. There are no miracle cures. You can't expect it ever to be made up to you, and you're left knowing he did something terrible and got away with it—it's horribly unfair. But remember, if your father's sane, you never have to watch yourself and worry. Nor need your sisters."

Late in August, Johnny Garcia asked Arran for a date—a real date for a movie and supper, not just a quick pizza between clinic sessions, or a beer or coffee to discuss plans for the sanctuary.

It was the first real date Arran had ever had. She worried about it terribly.

"It's all right," Dev said. "It's Johnny. He's your friend."

"I'm scared."

"Well, don't be. Go out and have a good time."

They went to see *Indiana Jones and the Temple of Doom* at a rerun theater downtown. They both thoroughly enjoyed the movie. Then, a happy choice, Arran took Johnny to Luigi's in North Beach, where she was accepted as family, or very near, and as a celebrity at that. They were given a hero's welcome. Pietro visited from the kitchen, resplendent in his chef's hat, and later Luigi himself brought a bottle of Strega to their table. "She's a good girl," he told Johnny with a mock scowl. "You keep your thieving wetback hands to yourself. I'm saving her for a nice Italian boy."

The level of the bottle sank steadily until Luigi and Johnny were old buddies swapping jokes. The other tables were all empty.

Very soon it would be time to go. Johnny would walk her home. Then what? Arran began to feel terrified. What would he do? What would *she* do? She listened for the rising darkness inside her. Oh God, she didn't want to spoil everything.

She kissed Luigi and Pietro good night. Her palms felt wet. Johnny went to fetch her coat. And then they were outside. It was cold, a night of clammy summer fog. Johnny put his arm around her to keep her warm.

She wished Dev were there. But then it occurred to her that Johnny was very like Dev. He was passionate, zealous, and devoted to the causes he served. He too had seen everything the world could offer; he was a solid, real person; and he cared about her. She suspected, with a flash of warmth, that Johnny could handle anything she dished out to him. He would never humiliate her and tell her she was sick and walk away.

She felt safe.

They stood in front of her apartment building door while Arran searched for her key. Then Johnny pulled her into his arms. He kissed her very gently on the lips. "This is for now," he said gently, as though something fine but very fragile was growing between them that must not be rushed. He touched her cheek with his fingertip and then was gone, loping around the corner on his long, springy colt's legs.

The next day she refused to allow herself to think about Johnny until after her lunch at the Washington Square Bar and Grill with the fire chief. Then, her notes typed, relaxed and sleepy from the rich food and the lunchtime wine, she lay flat on her back on her bed, laced her hands behind her head, and dreamed about Johnny Garcia. She heard the phone ring, but it wouldn't be him so she didn't answer it.

At 7:15 she played back her messages.

Then Isobel's voice, a shock like a seismic jolt, and the ground falling away. A sensation of dark, greedy hands reaching up for her to drag her down once and for all.

Thought she'd gotten away from it all, did she? Thought she could walk away and forget all about it?

Well, Father wasn't about to let her do something like that. He was jerking her chain, showing her just how crazy he was after all, and demonstrating what was waiting, at the end of the line, for her too—a bottle of gin and lungs full of fumes in a closed car. . . . Because she was just as crazy. Of course she was— look at the things she did! "You're sick, Arran," reminded Hart Jarrow.

Dev, breathed Arran, Dev, be there for me. But he was not at the center, his office, or the clinic. Johnny Garcia wasn't there either; he was out making calls. . . . She waited for half an hour, then could wait no longer.

Arran left the building at a run, got into her car, and headed back to that place she had known all along she would go back to one of these days. She would never get away. She was as mad as Father.

As she swung out onto the Embarcadero, a bolt of pure anger drove through her body and she almost swerved into a concrete abutment. Father had destroyed her. The son of a bitch had always gotten away with everything. Now, he had gotten away with everything forever.

Part Six

1

"Can anyone tell me why we're all so afraid?" Arran glanced first at Isobel, then at Christian, neither of whom would look her directly in the eye. "We are afraid, aren't we? All of us. *Why?*" And then, still shaken with self-disgust, she said, "I know why I am. Do you?"

"It's terribly late," Christian said uneasily. "We ought to go to bed."

"Mother's going to tell us something," Arran went on. "Something she thinks we need to know—but I think secretly we all know what she's going to say. Don't you think we should talk about it?" *"There are an awful lot of secrets in your family,"* Dev had said. *"Everybody seems to be protecting everybody else. Does anybody really talk about anything important?"* Suddenly, Arran felt determined that certain things should be said now, while they were too weary and vulnerable not to be honest.

"Oh why not? I don't think I could sleep, anyway. I'm too tired." Isobel refilled her glass. Christian and Arran both glanced covertly at the almost empty bottle; both their minds issued the same warning cry: Iso, you're drinking too much.

Isobel intercepted the glance. She said defiantly, "Well yes, I'm boozing. So what? It's been a rough day."

"Okay," Arran sighed. "I guess we all have our different ways of dealing with things," uncomfortably aware that she especially had no right to criticize Isobel, or anyone else. *God*, if only Dev or Johnny had been there for her. She squeezed her eyes closed and clenched her fingers into fists, bitterly angry and disappointed with herself for being so weak, such a failure. No, of course she couldn't blame Isobel for simply being human.

"This whole business about Father hit me at a bad time," Isobel was explaining with a wry smile. "Everything seems to have gone wrong in my life at once. I feel out of control." She took a large swallow of her drink. "So, sure I'm frightened. How wouldn't I be? Hart's gone and I'm on my own again. I'm making a horrible movie. My career's going down the tubes. The kids are turning back into monsters. I—Oh shit!" She gave a nervous laugh and rattled the ice cubes in her glass. "So I drink. So what . . . wouldn't you?" *I drink like Father . . . and soon I'll be drinking to stop the voices in my head, just like Father, and I'll end up killing myself like Father. I'm not just frightened. I'm terrified.*

"I'm tired," Christian said purposefully. "I want to go to bed." With a meaningful frown at Arran, she added: "We *all* should go to bed. Perhaps tomorrow—"

"If you say it'll all look better tomorrow after a good night's sleep," Isobel muttered, "I'll scream."

Christian shook her head. "No. I wouldn't say anything like that."

"I know this is dreadful for you," Isobel said enviously, "but at least you can go back to Puerto Rico, back to your boat and—"

Christian stood up abruptly, twisting her hands into the hem of her striped fisherman's shirt. "No."

"What?"

"I can't go back. Not now."

"But, Chris, surely Ludo—"

She shook her head slowly from side to side in a desolate gesture, staring at the floor. "Ludo's left me."

"Oh, no! Oh Chris." Isobel and Arran stared in dismay.

With brittle bravado, straining not to show the hurt, "I'm pregnant, you see, and he didn't want the baby." *But that's only part of it, the admissible part that other people can understand. Because I can't tell the truly frightening part, that it makes no difference, Father's being dead, no matter what Iso says. Father's still there inside my head and he always will be. Ernest Wexler kept me safe for a while; then I put Steve Romano and all the others between me and Father; and at last Ludo— and I was so sure that Ludo would always protect me. But now Ludo's gone and I'm alone.* "We should never have had a child," Father had said that night long ago.

"A baby! Oh *no!*" Isobel cried involuntarily in a peculiar tone of despair. "Oh poor Chris!"

Arran listened to the charged silence in the room. Isobel now looked angry as well as frightened, knowing she'd said too much. Christian looked down at her hands bunched in the striped fabric. Arran poured herself a drink—*nobody talks about anything important*—and asked curiously, "What do you mean, Iso? Being pregnant isn't the end of the world. These days you have options. You should know."

"It's not that," Isobel began. "You don't understand."

Christian cried, "But I *want* to have the baby!"

"Then what's the problem?" Arran demanded, sensing something concealed, something that needed shaking loose. "This is the eighties. Even if Ludo *has* left you, it's not exactly a disaster being a single mother." She added reasonably, "You can afford it, too."

Christian looked as though she was about to say something, but checked herself.

Isobel reached involuntarily for the vodka bottle, then thought better of it.

Arran glanced expectantly from one to the other. "I want to say something. May I? I want to say I think you're both lying. You're throwing up smoke screens. Of course, you have problems—don't we all—but it's more than that."

A pause. Then Isobel said in a husky voice, "Well?"

"You're afraid, Christian's afraid—and I'm afraid too," Arran confessed. "You see, I lost control of myself after I heard about Father. I did something I didn't want to do and hated myself for doing, but I couldn't stop it." She added under her breath: "I've never been able to stop. . . ."

Christian sat down again. She and Isobel were watching her, absolutely silent, waiting.

Well, it had to be said. Arran drew a deep breath. She looked at her hands, which were shaking slightly, and stuffed them into the pockets of her jacket. "We were afraid before Father died, but we're much more afraid now—afraid for ourselves. You see, I know about Father—just like you. About his . . . oddness. I guessed a long time ago it didn't have anything to do with a head wound, because so much didn't fit. I'd listen to all his war stories—I always remember stories—and they'd never be the same the second time around. When I worked in the library, I found he'd actually lifted the plots from a boys' adventure series. I did a bit of checking then. I found there never was a Ludgate Manor Aerodrome. As for the medals, they couldn't have been his—one of them wasn't even given by the RAF. Mother must have bought them for him at a military surplus shop or something. . . . Father's name wasn't in any of the records, either, because he was never in the Air Force at all. He never fought in the war. He wasn't the way he was because of a head wound."

Then, carefully, she lobbed her rock into the middle of their quiet, waiting pool, listened to the hollow splash it made going in and the weighty echoes that followed.

"Father lost his mind. Father was mad."

There was a long ringing pause.

Finally, Isobel, white faced, said, "I thought *I* was the only one who knew—Father told me himself, years ago. When Mark and Melissa were three years old."

Christian said in a small voice, "I knew too. One

night, when I was sick—when I was little—I heard them talking through the wall. Father was shouting how crazy he was and how he should never have had children. I didn't know what it meant at the time." Involuntarily she clasped her hands over her abdomen, as though protecting her own unborn child.

"Yes. Well—" Arran straightened her soiled gray skirt over her knees and tried to banish sudden images of Father's gloatingly expectant face next to hers and then, horridly, of Gus's glistening, brown body. She put her hands over her eyes in a futile attempt to shut it all away. "For years and years I've done things I'm sure sane people don't do—and I'd be scared to death thinking I was crazy just like him. And now he's killed himself and it seems like the final straw." She took a deep, shuddering breath. "It made me think, one day it'll be me. . . ."

In his will, Ernest Wexler left Martin, his chauffeur, enough money to start his own rental car company—a longtime dream. Martin had prospered and steadily expanded his services, his fleet of vehicles now ranging from a bulletproof stretch Mercedes to a nondescript workman's van with luxury interior fittings. He specialized in celebrity escort and protection: snatching rock stars from back entrances at stadiums, hotels, and airports under the noses of their rabid and often violent fans, and smuggling heads of state and sensitive political figures through cordons of demonstrators.

Shepherding a movie star and her family through the mechanics of high-visibility bereavement with the lowest emotional wear and tear was just another job to Martin, and a simple one at that.

At 11:00 A.M. the following morning, driving a funereal Daimler limousine with tinted windows, he picked up the Winter sisters at a side entrance of the Dorchester, bore them out of London with the minimum delay, then headed north on the motorway. Arriving at Sheffield, he escorted them smoothly through

the knot of reporters who had waited patiently outside
Elizabeth Winter's house for Isobel's arrival; an hour
later, he conveyed a whey-faced, swollen-eyed Elizabeth and her suitcases into the Daimler. He then deposited mother and daughters into the comparative
privacy and comfort of a suite at the Great Mid-
land Hotel and took himself thankfully off to a good
pub he knew that served fine shepherd's pie and draft
ale.

The cremation took place the following afternoon,
after a stark little service conducted by a very young,
very flustered Church of England minister, uncertain
of the protocol for a suicide and overwhelmed by the
presence of a celebrity. All this, combined with the
intense heat, had given him a fierce red rash across his
sweating cheeks.

Isobel was the only member of the family who had
brought suitable clothes for a funeral. She wore a
black sleeveless linen dress by Chanel, high-heeled
patent-leather sandals, and huge dark glasses over her
tired eyes. She had lent the dress's matching jacket to
Christian, who wore it over a red-and-black-striped
tank dress—the only dress in a wardrobe now consist-
ing of shorts, jeans, bathing suits, and oilskins. The
shoulders of the jacket were moderately padded, the
lapels long and narrow. With her deep tropical tan and
long brown legs Christian exuded an aura of swash-
buckling glamour. In contrast with her sisters, after a
foggy San Francisco summer, Arran seemed ethereal
and magnolia pale but wanly elegant in the Saint
Laurent suit that, having brought no luggage at all,
she was forced reluctantly to wear yet again.

A battery of cameras flashed, clicked, and whirred
as the sisters emerged blinking into the brassy sunlight
and stifling heat of the memorial gardens, where the
grass lay dry and brown underfoot and the parched
flowers wilted sadly in the borders. The excited voices
rose in clamor, the reporters and cameramen surging
around the Winter sisters, so incongruously glamorous
in their drab surroundings, and the poor little minister

flapped his hands and attempted ineffectually to stop a family tragedy from being turned into a media circus.

Elizabeth Winter, the forgotten widow, stood virtually ignored in her shapeless, brown polyester knit. She clasped the ornate urn Isobel had bought, which now contained George Winter's ashes. "Disgusting," she muttered to no one in particular. "Just disgusting."

"This way, Iso—" *Click!*

"Iso, did you know your father was depressed?"

"Are you still dating Lawrence Sanzone?"

"Are you planning to marry in the near future?"

"How did you feel when you heard your father had killed himself?"

"Let's have one of you girls standing together."

Click! Flash!

"Look at her," Elizabeth complained bitterly to Arran, "showing off as usual. That girl always has to be the center of attention."

"It's not her fault, Mother. She doesn't want this any more than you do."

Isobel handled it all with professional calm. Dealing with the press was second nature to her, although this time she was thoroughly glad of the stalwart presence of Martin at her side and the stolid touch of his hand on her arm. Finally, heading steadily and firmly toward the gates, she announced, "You'll have to excuse us now. This is a time of private family sorrow. I know you'll understand."

"So dreadfully undignified," complained Elizabeth. "I'd have thought at least at her own father's funeral—"

"Mother, it's just as bad for her," Arran said.

"She shouldn't feel she must put herself forward. She has no right. No right at all."

Oh dear, *poor* Mother, thought Arran sadly; for Elizabeth Winter not only was being denied her rightful part as heroine of the tragedy but had been firmly relegated to a minor supporting role.

Half an hour later, Martin having successfully eluded any press who might be following, the Winter sisters and their mother sat comfortably enfolded in the soft gray leather seats of the Daimler as it sped eastward. Still furious, Elizabeth cradled the urn against her flat chest and stared rigidly at a BBC afternoon broadcast of "Gardening Club" on the television set, where a gnarled old man in rubber boots strolled between beds of chrysanthemums and Michaelmas daisies. Christian and Arran watched too; it was a relief not to have to talk. Isobel lay back against the seat with her eyes closed, ostensibly asleep.

They had a long way to go—halfway across the country to the Norfolk coast, where Elizabeth planned to scatter the last mortal remains of George Winter on the weed-choked runways of the old RAF aerodrome near Ludgate Manor, although, as Martin had muttered discreetly to Christian, "You know, the place doesn't exist. Never has, either."

"I know. What'll we do?"

Martin said kindly, "We'll think of something."

He was as good as his word. By six o'clock in the evening he had installed them in a small but attractive family hotel surrounded by flower gardens in a coastal village called Brancaster *and* demonstrated an amazing gift for creative diplomacy.

"Bit of a problem, Madame," Martin said, as though he had just received the news, "but it seems Ludgate Manor Aerodrome's a restricted area now; an American missile base. No civilians allowed."

Elizabeth looked shocked, sniffed, and thrust her lips in and out in obstinate denial.

"Why don't you scatter him in the sea instead," Martin suggested gently. "He can be with his mates then, with all the blokes who bought it flying back from raids over Germany. . . . He might like that even better."

And so, at 7:00 A.M. next morning, at high tide, he drove them up the track above the dunes. By now Elizabeth was in full approval of Martin's idea and might even have thought of it herself. "Yes, the planes went over this way," she said, nodding emphatically. With the absorbed face of a high priestess, she stood on the edge of the bluff above the gently whispering sea, where the surface already glared under the newly risen, burning sun. George Winter's store-bought medals lay at her feet; she held out the urn in both hands as though making an offering.

The cold waters of the North Sea received the last mortal remains of George Winter with placid indifference, and bore him away without a trace.

2

"We can serve you lunch in the garden if you like," the girl said. "The dining room's ever so stuffy."

"That would be nice," said Isobel.

No air moved at all in Brancaster. The brassy sun, lacking definition, hung heavily in the sky behind a grainy, amber-colored haze.

The picnic table was set up under the wide branches of a chestnut tree on the lawn. Under the thick clusters of yellowing leaves, the shade was dense and cavelike and almost as hot, but still preferable to sitting in the blinding, all pervasive glare. Behind a vine-covered fence, the women could hear the muted shrieks of small children splashing in a swimming pool.

Lunch was cold poached salmon with mayonnaise, salad, and slices of thin brown bread. They drank a pitcher of lemonade. Elizabeth picked at her food and said nothing at all, her expression fading gradually through shades of exaltation to bewilderment. Finally, the young waitress cleared the plates and served coffee. Elizabeth stared at her cup as though it were an extraordinarily rare object of immense value. Suddenly she announced, "He's gone. George's gone."

There was absolutely nothing to say. Sitting beside her mother, Isobel gently patted her hand.

"Thirty-five years," Elizabeth said in a strained voice. "He was mine for more than thirty-five years. He could have had anybody, you know—any girl at all—but he chose me. . . ."

She fell silent again, and they didn't have the heart to intrude on her reverie. She sat there, lost and withdrawn. Perhaps she was once again walking with young, handsome George Winter through green fields in the summer of 1944. "I was worthy of his trust," Elizabeth went on, bobbing her head in emphasis. "I took care of him all that time—such a privilege. I nursed him, protected him, and shielded him from the world. No matter what they said or did . . . you'll never know what it was like."

After a long pause, Arran said, "Yes, Mother, we do know. We know what you must have been through. We know all about it . . . don't feel you have to say any more."

Elizabeth jerked up her head. "What *do* you mean?" Her face smoothed out and grew blank. It was the same evasive expression they remembered her wearing when they had lived too long in one place and people were starting to notice, to gossip.

Isobel glanced sideways at Arran. "Let Mother tell us if she wants to."

But Elizabeth looked from Arran to Isobel and asked in a hard, brightly impersonal voice, "Tell what? I don't understand."

Isobel gave a small sigh and shifted in embarrassment. It was painful, putting such things into words. "Well, you said there was something we should know."

Elizabeth set her head, birdlike, to one side.

"But please don't feel you need tell us, Mother, because we know already."

Something flared momentarily in Elizabeth's eyes. Her expression shifted. She looked genuinely surprised. "But you *couldn't* have known. We were so careful. . . . You *couldn't*—"

"Oh, Mother," Isobel said gently, "don't you remember, Father told me *himself*!"

Elizabeth looked astonished.

"You must remember. When I came to tea, and showed you the pictures of the children. He *told* me . . . that he had a mental disease. You were *there*. You heard him."

Elizabeth shook her head impatiently. "He didn't know what he was saying."

Isobel pushed the thick hair back from her hot forehead. "And Christian knows too. She heard you and Father talking about it long ago. Arran has known all the time. She had more of a—rapport with Father."

"Yes," said Elizabeth in a cold voice, "she would have." Angrily, she turned to Isobel. "I don't understand you. What are you saying? Did you tell your sisters your father was *mad*?"

Isobel looked down at her hands, embarrassed and confused.

"Because it's not true. It's a horrible lie. I admit your father was once in a mental hospital—but he got well again! Of course he did! My husband was *not* insane."

From behind the fence an adult voice cried encouragingly, "Come on, Caroline, swim to Mummy . . ." Christian listened, and thought about teaching her own child to swim. She thought of sturdy little brown limbs thrashing the water, and Ludo not being there to watch and smile. She wanted to cry.

"I know he'd get a little confused," Elizabeth went on, "and he'd lose his temper sometimes. He was a little unstable after his surgery. They had to cut some nerves when they took the shrapnel out of his head."

"Mother," Arran pleaded. "Don't go on pretending. Don't you understand? You don't have to pretend anymore."

Christian sat miserably silent, distracted by little Caroline and her mother. The baby had been a precious miracle which would keep Ludo at her side, which would save them—now there was not only nothing to save, but all the old fears were crowding back into her mind: she was crazy just like Father, and she had no right to pass that on to her baby. She wondered what she was going to do. She had no idea. She wanted to crawl away, to crawl into darkness, and go to sleep forever.

The mother on the other side of the fence called out, "There's my clever girl!" There was a lot of splashing and cooing. Christian felt sick.

Mother was extremely angry now, making fierce assertions about Father's indubitable sanity and demanding responses that Isobel and Arran found increasingly difficult to make.

At last, Arran pointed out with relentless logic: "Then why did we move around all the time? Why all the excuses? Why did you make sure we never saw any friends or family, *unless* Father was . . . sick, and you didn't want anyone to find out?"

There was a long silence.

Finally, Elizabeth said, "No, they couldn't find out." She pushed her lips out in her timeworn gesture of obstinacy and shook her head vehemently. "Oh no. But he *wasn't* insane." She turned again on Isobel. "That's wicked to say!"

The sisters looked at one another mutely. Isobel shook her head slightly. Leave it, her eyes said, it's pointless. But Elizabeth's lips were compressed and the light of battle gleamed in her eyes.

"You're right, Mother, it's wicked," Arran said, "so let's drop it now, it doesn't matter anymore."

And Isobel in turn, attempting to save the situation but managing to make it much worse, said, "Of course he was drinking heavily. Perhaps—"

Elizabeth's reaction was explosive. She gripped the edge of the table in convulsive fingers and jerked to her feet, face scarlet with rage. "What are you saying now? That my husband was a drunk? An *alcoholic*?"

Isobel slumped in her chair, appalled. "Oh God, no. Mother, no!"

"*How dare you!*" Elizabeth raised a flaccid but powerful arm and slapped Isobel violently, leaving a livid red imprint across her cheek.

Isobel stared up at her mother, shocked speechless.

"How dare you," Elizabeth said again in a shaking voice, looking ready to hit her again. Arran leaped to her feet and grasped her mother's shoulders. Elizabeth gave a convulsive shudder, then folded back into her chair, her angular body bending in sections like a carpenter's rule. She leaned forward, put her big-knuckled hands over her face, and rocking back and forth, began to cry. "I won't listen. I *won't* listen to these lies about your father. He wasn't insane, and he wasn't a drunk." Then abruptly she raised her head and glared around the table. "You don't believe me. Any of you. Do you?"

There was a ragged pause. Arran drew a breath. "Of course we do, Mother."

She was too late.

"All right then," Elizabeth cried, breathing loudly through her nose, "all right. Even though I promised him I'd never tell—that I'd take his secret to my grave. But rather than have you believing lies about your father, I'll tell you now."

Then, into the dense, expectant silence under the chestnut tree, she dropped her first bombshell of that extraordinary day.

"You're right, of course—George did not fight in the war. He wasn't wounded. But nor was he insane or a drunk."

Her eyes unfocused, her voice a near whisper, Elizabeth confessed: "He was a drug addict."

Christian began to laugh helplessly. She laughed until the tears ran down her cheeks. She bit down on her knuckles, the tears still streaming, Elizabeth's droning voice fading in and out. . . . "Of course it wasn't George's fault—*they* made him one. He had electric shock therapy after his breakdown, and then they put him on tranquilizers and pep pills. It got out of control. George never had any willpower. He couldn't stop—he took more and more until he was taking huge amounts, cocaine to take him up, and gin to bring him down. . . ." Elizabeth gave a long raw sigh and picked at her fingernails. "In those days they'd have called him a dope fiend. I couldn't let him face the disgrace."

She stood up with a certain dignity. Then, in a characteristic switch of mood, as though she had been discussing nothing more disturbing than tonight's expected thunderstorm, she announced placidly, "Well, I think I'll go and lie down until teatime."

Christian also spent the afternoon in bed with Isobel seated by her side. Christian could not stop laughing.

"My father was a drug addict, and my lover's a drug smuggler. It's so neat and tidy. So ironic! Don't you think?"

Isobel had managed to cajole some ice from the kitchen, in short supply on a day like this, and held it, rapidly melting, against her smarting cheek. "Come on, Chris. Stop it. You're exhausted. You've got to rest. Think of the baby." For Isobel, Christian's baby had become a life raft in a wild sea. After her mother's astonishing revelation, Isobel felt lost, her equilibrium destroyed. She clutched gratefully at the thought of the baby, something *real,* something she could understand and deal with.

Soon Christian's uncontrollable giggles turned to sobs. "I guess I don't have to worry about the baby anymore—that's wonderful. The poor little thing can't be *born* an addict. But Ludo's gone on another trip and he'd *promised* he'd never go again—he was angry about the baby."

Isobel laid her dripping ice bag on Christian's hot forehead and made soothing noises. She felt terribly sad and sorry for Christian, but at least in believing Mother's story a whole range of anxiety and fear had been cut away for her in one stroke. Of course, Ludo was gone, but Christian could always find another man. She would fall in love again—though, that's what I told myself, Isobel thought forlornly, and I never have . . . not really.

"Do you think Ludo's punishing me?" Christian asked pathetically through her tears. "I want the baby so badly—"

"Of course not," Isobel said determinedly, "just give him a chance. It was probably the shock. He was overreacting." She pushed a tissue into Christian's limp hand. "And don't forget, he's been living like a gypsy for years. Think of the readjustment. You probably terrified him. When he's had a chance to get used to it, go back there and find him and it'll be all right."

"But this time he's not coming back," Christian said dully. "He's going to get killed. I can *feel* it. He can't go on being lucky forever. I'm so frightened for him."

Christian looked up at her sister, overwrought, her eyes dark-circled. "If he's killed, the baby's all I'll ever have of him."

"Hush," Isobel said comfortingly. "Try not to worry about him. You can't help him. Just think about the baby and be sensible." She wiped trickles of ice water from Christian's neck with a towel. "Go to sleep now. . . ."

Arran had gone to the beach to swim, wearing a glaring purple satin one-piece suit, an end-of-season reject that was the only one in the local shop to fit her.

However, the tide had retreated so far she had not had the energy to tramp across the sand to find the water, and instead lay flat on her back, arms outspread, staring up into the colorless sky.

For a long time she thought of nothing at all, concentrating on the heat as it penetrated her body, letting it become a part of her, feeling it as it pulsed through her veins. Finally she was ready to think about Father's being a drug addict and not mad after all. I need *never* be like him, she thought with calm logic; my life is my own and what I do with it is my choice. And it's really *most* unlikely I'll ever kill myself. She felt immensely comfortable and shut her eyes, staring at the translucent redness of the insides of her eyelids, listening to a pair of sea gulls fighting shrilly over some disputed treasure. She thought sleepily how thankful she was that Mother had not carried the secret to her grave after all.

Then she sat up abruptly, eyes wide open.

Mother had emphatically *not* been intending to tell them about Father's drug addiction. Absolutely not, and she never had. The confession had been dragged from her under duress. Isobel had told her what Mother had said: "There's something you three need to know . . ."

There was another secret. What could it be? Arran couldn't imagine.

She wondered uneasily when they would find out.

*   *   *

By evening it was still too hot and breathless to stay in
either the hotel or the garden. They walked along the
path above the dunes, where the closeness of the sea
brought a slight hint of freshness. The tide was coming
in now, the waves lapping sluggishly at the sand, leaving coils of oily foam. The sky was purplish black to
the east, and lightning flickered on the horizon.

Elizabeth strode along in the lead, wearing a faded,
old-fashioned, but incongruously youthful floral sun-
dress. She had never moved gracefully and now, as
always, she walked with awkward, plunging strides,
looking neither right nor left.

Arran and Isobel followed, walking abreast, both
silent. Christian brought up the rear, the dark thoughts
flitting through her mind like bats.

At the spot where she had tossed George's ashes
into the sea, Elizabeth halted abruptly and turned to
face the murky eastern horizon into which, forty years
ago, she knew the planes had flown on their forays
from Ludgate Manor.

Christian flopped down gratefully on the coarse grass.

It was there, staring over the lead-colored sea at the
now ceaseless flickering of the lightning, that Elizabeth smiled vaguely and said, "I suppose you think I
should have told you earlier about George's drug problem." She sounded as casual as if she were talking of
hay fever or hammertoes. "But George couldn't bear
anyone knowing. It would have upset him dreadfully.
He was so ashamed of his weakness."

Isobel demanded, "Were you telling the truth,
Mother? *Was* he really on drugs?"

Arran recalled the wild swings of mood, the bursts
of deep depression and disorientation, the rages, the
manic restlessness. It appeared obvious, with hind-
sight. "Yes, of course, Iso."

"But *was* he, Mother? I want to hear you say it.
Mother, look at me."

Elizabeth turned crossly. "Of course I'm telling the
truth. Why should I lie to you? It's been hard enough,
God knows, to talk about it at all."

The anger coiled inside Isobel like dark smoke. She

could feel it seeping from every pore of her body. How could Mother have let her suffer so much for so long, all for nothing? She wanted to lash out, to hurt, to force Mother to see what she had done—even though she was quite aware that her anger was pointless, that Mother's perspective was so skewed she would never understand. Isobel said chokingly, "So because it might upset him if we knew the truth, you let us think Father had a hereditary mental disease."

"I did nothing of the kind," Elizabeth countered. "It was you who decided that in your own distorted, wicked minds."

"Mother! Jesus!" Isobel's chest felt constricted, as though laced tight with iron bands. It was a struggle to breathe and even more so to speak. "Do you have the slightest *idea* what it's been like for the last seven years? My God, I've worried myself sick over Mark and Melissa! There hasn't been *one day* when I haven't watched them and wondered and waited. And you never said anything, even though you'd heard Father tell me *himself* he was insane."

Elizabeth wrinkled her nose in distaste; she didn't want to think about Mark and Melissa.

"I can't tell you what it's been like," Isobel cried, "and now I find I needn't have worried at all—"

"Of course not," agreed Elizabeth. "Why should you? It wasn't your problem. It had nothing to do with you."

"What?" Isobel looked blank. "Mother, what do you mean?"

It was then that Elizabeth Winter broke her news. In a gently reproving voice, she said, "It's time you stopped calling me that. I'm not your mother." Her mouth curved into a smile. "And my husband was not your father," she announced with infinite pleasure. She turned to face Christian. "Nor yours."

Far away a small child whined with tiredness as it trailed up the path from the beach dragging a pailful of seaweed and shells; a dog barked; sea gulls wheeled and whooped; over a car radio Cyndi Lauper breezily told the world how girls just wanted to have fun . . .

but in their own reality, all was deep silence and suspended time.

The angry flush drained from Isobel's face. She stared at Elizabeth and her hands, vehemently outstretched as though to shake her mother into forced admission of the harm she had done, sank slowly to her sides. Christian, long limbs sprawled on the grass, gazed at Elizabeth through narrowed eyes turned black with bewilderment. Arran glanced from one to the other of her sisters, and then at her mother, who now seemed suffused with good humor. The moment of dense silence stretched and stretched. Their ears rang with it.

Then Isobel said shrilly, "I don't understand." And Christian whispered, "I don't believe you!"

Arran said, "You'd better tell us about it, Mother."

No one moved. The sisters stared at Elizabeth, waiting. Afterward Arran found her muscles had been locked into position so rigidly that her neck felt painfully stiff.

For the first time in her life Elizabeth found herself the focus of undivided attention. It seemed to bring her great satisfaction.

"Tell it from the beginning, Mother," Arran said.

But Elizabeth would not be rushed. She told her story in her own way, the second set of revelations blending almost seamlessly with the first, and focusing as always on George Winter.

"George was always much too sensitive. He could never have survived the ugliness of war; George was an artist; a poet. He wanted the world always to be beautiful. When his call-up papers came, I suppose something inside him snapped, like they say. He didn't know who he was, didn't recognize his parents, didn't even recognize me. He sat on his bed, couldn't dress himself, and cried and cried. He wet himself. He was as helpless as a baby.

"But I never deserted him," Elizabeth went on in triumph, her eyes shining. "I stayed at his side all through his year in hospital, and afterward. He *needed* me so. I was the only one he would talk to. He couldn't have survived without me. Margie's parents wouldn't let her see him—they were ashamed. And then, when he was finally discharged, we were married and I took him away . . . to take care of him and make him happy. Just the two of us, always. He was all the baby I ever wanted—he was my boy!

"But George wanted children." Elizabeth's eyes clouded with hurt. "He wanted a family although it was impossible—you see, he couldn't—wasn't able to—you know."

She flushed rosily. "Not that it mattered to me. I loved George. It made no difference at all. . . . Those sex things have never mattered. Anyway, I still had my contacts with the adoption agencies. There were lots of children. So many children born in the mess after the war. And to please George I arranged to adopt two little girls. . . . *Your* father"—she turned to Isobel, the triumphant bringer of bad news—"was a German prisoner of war who stayed on afterward working as a farm laborer; your mother was an Irish maid. And as for you," she said to Christian, "your mother was some little slut in London; she said your father was an Italian waiter."

Arran asked quietly, "What about me?"

"You." Elizabeth looked at her for a long time, eyes dark with remembered betrayal. "Your father was so pleased with his new family—two pretty little girls, and one even looking like him. He was content and relaxed, and able, after a while, for a few weeks, to go to bed with me. For the first time . . ."

From the blackness in the east came the first long, deep drumroll of thunder. Arran found she had been holding her breath for a long time. She exhaled sharply. "So I wasn't adopted."

"No. You were not adopted, and after you were born," Elizabeth said bitterly, "he always loved you the best, not me. Even though I gave him everything—no sacrifice was too great. I shielded him from the world as I'd always done, from the shame. . . ." Her voice sank. "Nobody ever guessed." Then she looked around, from Isobel to Christian to Arran. They were all mesmerized by the truth. "Close and thick as thieves," Elizabeth cried at last. "Through thick and thin, always plotting, head to head, making plans, caring for each other—sisters together, so close, and all the time"—she began to laugh—"you're not even related! Not one of you!

"You're not sisters at all!

"You don't belong to anyone. . . ."

3

Ludo Corey was climbing doggedly up through deep darkness toward the light, with the blind tenacity of the first seaborne creature that crawled from the water onto dry land billions of years ago. But with the gradual lessening of darkness came the increased awareness of pain. The pain grew until it pounded through his body in hot waves with each pulsebeat.

He knew he could not tolerate that pain and he turned resolutely away from it, sinking again, with utmost relief, back into darkness.

Later, he knew he was climbing again. He was much closer to the surface now. He remembered the pain and instinctively reached out for Christian, who would be there and who would take the pain away.

The next time he was closer than ever, aware of more than just pain and darkness, a confused jumble of images unrolling in his mind. He didn't understand the images yet, didn't know whether they sprang from memory, reality, or nightmare. He wasn't even sure whether his own role was that of onlooker or participant. He saw himself on a boat—a fast boat, narrow beamed with a long racing hull. It was night. He was sailing the boat through enormous cresting swells and he knew that he was afraid; he could taste the urgency and fear in his mouth. Then a sudden flood of blinding light—another boat grating alongside, its sharply raked bow towering impossibly high over his head. A figure of a man—himself or someone else?—seen as a black silhouette against blue-white light, a jerky marionette that flung up its arms, folded in the middle, and then dropped out of sight.

Something clattered to the floor of the cockpit; Ludo knew it was a gun. The man had dropped his gun. It was the first sound he had consciously heard, and now . . .

He blinked in confusion. The boat was gone. He was in a room. The light was muted and yellowish. He watched a blurred figure in white push a rattling metal trolley toward him.

Then without warning the pain struck. He screamed for Christian, somehow knowing he made no noise at all. The white uniform swam closer. He saw a pair of eyes, huge; the face seemed all eyes and then very soon, like magic, the pain was gone again and Ludo slid gratefully away.

The next time, he came back all the way. A man was sitting beside him watching him closely. He knew the man but couldn't remember his name yet. But where was Christian? He felt a pang of intense disappointment. Didn't she know he was here, that he needed her? Why hadn't she come?

Seeing he was conscious, José Estevez smiled and said, "Welcome back."

Ludo stared at him in bewilderment and tried to moisten his dry mouth. Estevez held a water bottle to his lips, with a straw. "Just small sips now."

After a moment, Ludo managed to speak, in a small weak croak. "Where am I?"

"Dade County Hospital, in Miami. You're badly hurt, but you're going to be okay."

He couldn't move his head and his eyes ached, but now he was aware of a spidery confusion of tubes and bottles and machinery. In front of him a huge, fat, white cocoon seemed to stretch away to infinity. Estevez was saying, as though somehow Ludo's own carelessness was to blame, "You weren't supposed to get hurt. You should have been out of the way, up on the fly bridge, when the Customs boats intercepted."

Ludo closed his eyes wearily. He had not known it was possible to feel so weak, or so exhausted.

"But you did a fantastic job." Estevez went on enthusiastically. "You brought that boat in, even in those weather conditions. A thousand kilos."

More than a ton of pure cocaine. Ludo was glad Estevez was happy, but personally he couldn't care less. All he wanted was Christian. And now the pain was coming again.

Estevez, for all his preoccupation with success, noticed the sudden sheen of sweat on Ludo's pale face. He rose, went to the door, nodded to the guards posted outside, and peremptorily called for the nurse.

Ludo asked fretfully, "Where's Chris?" He needed her so badly. And then he suddenly remembered: he had sent her away. He felt hollow with fright. Why had he sent her away?

And then he remembered that too. Oh God. She was having a baby. She'd looked so beautiful, telling him. She'd been so proud and happy, so sure he'd be pleased too, but all he had seen was little Ludovico Jimenez, not much more than a baby himself, starving, bruised, his little body crusted with scabs, foraging for food among the garbage. He had felt nothing but revulsion. He had accepted Estevez's last assignment after all: to hurt her. And then she had gone.

The nurse came in. She was young and pretty with black curls under her cap, and friendly brown eyes. The blue-and-white pin on her chest said she was Rosalia Castillo, SRN. She stepped to his side and adjusted the mess of tubes running in and out of his body. "You'll be comfortable in just a few seconds." Her voice was nice too—but she wasn't Chris.

Estevez was saying, "She went to London. You want her? We'll find her. She can be back here tomorrow."

But already Estevez's voice was growing hollow and fuzzy.

"Yes please," breathed Ludo with terrible effort, as the morphine took him, "I want Chris—"

Then everything lifted and swung and the dark waves once again closed over his head.

4

"I always wondered why we were so different," Isobel said. "Now it seems obvious."

The thunder crashed right over their heads and the drenched garden suddenly burned a sizzling magnesium white.

The three Winter women sat in Isobel's room, staring out through the big picture window at the storm.

It was very late now.

When the spell had been broken and the real world once again broke into their private bubble of suspended animation, none of them dared think or even speak beyond essentials. They had hurried back to the hotel, seeking their rooms, each instinctively wanting to be alone to confront Elizabeth's extraordinary revelation.

For Arran, still her parents' daughter, there were formidable adjustments to make. For Isobel and Christian, the thoughts, expectations, and attitudes of a lifetime had been turned end over end.

Elizabeth had retired early, eating dinner in her own room from a tray. She had apparently made a good meal too. "The poor dear lady," the waitress said. "It does your heart good to see her with a bit of appetite."

"But *do* you think it's really true?" asked Christian, for the third time. It was such an astonishing thought, Mother and Father suddenly having no physical connection with her whatsoever. She was aware of an unexpected sense of loss coupled at the same time with a huge excitement. I'm free! Christian exulted. The baby's safe—really safe. Then she felt guilty for her happiness. It was as though she rode an emotional roller coaster, first up, then down. Images crowded into her head—Father, his face glowing red in the firelight, reading aloud in his beautiful voice to Mother, who was knitting something long and beige and watching Father at the same time, her eyes shining (yes, there had been good times)—and superimposed upon Father and Mother were other faces—that of a very young, rather perky little girl, swept away by the excitement of the big city and the bright lights, and a flashing-eyed handsome boy who looked very like Steve Romano.

Christian knew beyond a doubt that the girl wished she could have kept her baby, that funny-looking, rather swarthy, very un-English-looking little girl. She would have been so sad, having to give the baby up. Of *course* she had been sad. Sentimentally, Christian wanted to think the best of both her real parents, and to love the image she was creating of them. Then, abruptly, she felt disloyal to Father and Mother and thoroughly guilty again. She sighed. One thing was certain, the necessary adjustments would not take place in a day.

Isobel said, "She's got our real birth certificates in a safe-deposit box. She said so, and we can easily check. She couldn't fake that." She was unable to feel angry with Mother anymore, just sorrow for opportunities lost. Isobel had once loved Father but her love had been scornfully rejected. She would have liked to be able to love Mother. It was such a waste. Poor Mother. Isobel could see her now, visiting the adoption agency, wearing her best outfit (probably beige) and an unbecoming hat, and being presented with a lusty, squalling, black-haired Irish-German baby girl to take home to Father. How she must have resented the three of us, Isobel thought, when all she really wanted was to have Father to herself. She must have *loved* breaking her news—that Father was not Father after all.

However, apart from the sadness and a certain wistful nostalgia, Isobel mainly felt a huge relief. Now she could look at Mark and Melissa and just see a pair of healthy children—difficult, perhaps, but normal, no longer potential victims of mental disease to be over-protected and stupidly indulged. I'll be a sensible mother now, Isobel promised herself; no longer a fussing, hysterical idiot. And I'll stop drinking so much. Things are going to get better now.

"What about *us*, then?" asked Arran. "How do we feel about not being sisters anymore?"

"I don't know." Christian looked perplexed. "It's so strange, not being who you thought you were. Thinking for your whole life you had sisters—and then suddenly finding you don't anymore . . . I wonder, will that make a difference?"

"I don't see why it should," said Isobel.

"It will though," Arran said. "But that doesn't have to be a bad thing." She went on slowly, as though feeling her way: "At first, I felt sad and deprived. I'd thought I'd lost a family. But now—I'm not so sure. I can't help thinking, instead of sisters I've got two incredibly close friends."

"Sure," agreed Isobel. "Nothing's really changed. We've always been close, we still are and always will be. We haven't lost anything."

"Actually, we've gained," Arran said firmly, "because you can talk to friends. I mean, really talk. Without being afraid of hurting them . . . You can tell friends things you mightn't want to talk about with a sister." She felt that she could really do that at last. One need not be overprotective of friends. It was like receiving a sudden, unexpected gift. Arran thought happily, I can tell them my problems and they can tell me theirs and there don't need to be any more family secrets . . . although there would be one secret she would never tell to either Isobel or Christian; no one but Devlin would ever completely understand Arran's own relief on hearing of Father's addiction. That not only was her fear of inherited insanity gone, but that now there was a reason for what he had done to her—or at least an excuse. It was a comfortable peg on which to hang her anger, until at last the anger itself melted away.

"I think we ought to drink a toast," Christian said suddenly.

"Good idea," said Isobel. She poured vodka into their bathroom tumblers, and raised her glass. "Well. Here's to"—she groped for the right words for an unimaginable situation—"to us. To the Winter sisters."

"The Winter women," Arran amended.

They solemnly clinked glasses.

"What are we going to do about Mother?" Isobel had asked just before they disbanded for the night. "Now that Father's gone, what *will* she do?"

But in the morning, Elizabeth seemed surprisingly tranquil, as though she too had experienced catharsis and emerged the stronger for it. Isobel and Arran found her in the breakfast room, seated across the table from an elderly gentleman with a gray mustache and a military air, animatedly telling him all about her revered George.

"Such a brilliant man. He would have gone to Oxford and read English. He was going to be a poet," she explained earnestly. "But it was so tragic. He was called up just before the end of the war and was wounded in the head—quite badly, I'm afraid. He was a fighter pilot—his aerodrome was around here somewhere. It's an American missile base now."

"I think she's happier now than she's ever been," Arran said softly. "Father will grow a little more perfect every day until he's just the way she always wanted him and she's living out her complete fantasy; who's to know it isn't all true? He can be a real war hero at last. And think, Iso—she'll never have to pretend anymore or make excuses or keep moving house. She's free too!"

"What an odd thought," Isobel said, spreading butter on a dainty little triangle of toast, "but you're probably quite right. She—"

"Excuse me! Miss Winter?"

They both looked up.

The young waitress's eyes were round with excitement. She focused on Isobel. "Miss Winter, is your

sister's name Mrs. Petrocelli? There's a phone call for
her. From America."

Having delivered her message, she rushed back to
the kitchen to tell the news to Cook; that yes, she was
sure the Winter family were celebrities after all—what
with limousines and people ringing from America! And
hadn't she always been *positive* the pretty dark one
was Isobel Wynne?

Isobel and Arran sat side by side on the beach under a
windy gray sky. The heat wave had broken with a
vengeance. The tide was out and the sand stretched in
cold corrugated ruts to the horizon and the steely line
of the North Sea.

Arran thought Isobel looked very un-Hollywood today. She was wearing a pair of jeans and a T-shirt and
was barefoot. Her face was curiously youthful and
vulnerable without makeup.

"So Ludo was an undercover agent with the DEA.
What a turnaround," Isobel said.

"Seems so," said Arran cautiously.

Isobel and Arran had left Christian in her room to
finish packing. Martin had already made her reserva-
tion, first class on British Airways, departing mid-
morning the next day. She had been radiant ("He
wants me back!") and then terrified. "Mr. Estevez
said he was hurt. If Ludo couldn't talk to me himself,
it must be bad. Oh God, suppose he's dying."

"Of course, he's not dying." Isobel had reminded
her sensibly, "he's been shot in the thigh. And it's not
surprising he wouldn't be able to talk. He'll be in pain
and they'll have him sedated."

"How did they know where to find her?" Arran
asked Isobel now.

Isobel shrugged. "It can't have been too difficult.
They have their methods."

"Hm." Arran stretched out her legs and stared at
her brand-new white sneakers, which she thought made
her feet look enormous. She wore a pair of brief
yellow shorts, also from the local beach shop, and a
navy sweater borrowed from Christian, which was much

too big and which she suddenly realized must belong to Ludo. It gave her a start, thinking about wearing Ludo's clothes. It was an uncomfortable intimacy. Surreptitiously she sniffed at the woolen sleeve, then dropped her arm with a flush of embarrassment thinking of Christian perhaps doing the same thing, desperate for a reminiscent trace of her lover. How strange—if he married Christian, this totally unknown man would be her brother-in-law. But no, she thought with confusion, of course he wouldn't because Christian was no longer her sister. She hoped so much that Christian would be happy, but whatever happened now she thought it would be all right for her in the end. Even without Ludo. She's been pushed into the wrong slot all her life, Arran thought. No wonder she was always so insecure—but now Christian had clearly found both a place for herself and a life-style that suited her. It seemed extraordinary and rather ridiculous now, thinking she'd been a jet-setting socialite and playmate to the rich and famous. Now, if only Isobel could be happy too . . . If anyone deserved happiness, it was Iso.

Arran said suddenly, "I think you should go with her."

Isobel blinked. "What?"

"You should go back with Chris to Miami." Arran watched the metallic line of the North Sea, which was widening perceptibly as the tide began to come in. She said slowly, "She needs you much more than Mother. She's in quite a state."

"Of course I can't do that. I can't leave you alone with Mother. It's not fair."

"Yes you can," said Arran, suddenly convinced that this was exactly what Isobel must do. "You have to go back to work anyway in a couple of days. And listen"—she broke out in a sudden impish grin—"she's *my* mother, not yours. And I think I'd like to spend some time wth her alone . . . see what she's really like now she's out of Father's shadow. I realized I have no idea what she's like—I've only ever looked at her in relation to Father."

"But then what'll you do? Honestly, Arran—"

"I've got a great idea. I'm surprised we haven't thought about it before. I'm going to call Margie Jennings, and I'll bet you she'll want to come over and keep Mother company for a bit. Margie's always been in love with Father, she'd probably give anything for a chance to talk about him again, and think how superior Mother can feel!"

"I wouldn't feel right," said Isobel, firmly.

"Try. Think about Chris. Listen, we don't know for sure that Mr. Estevez *is* with the DEA. Suppose he was with the . . . others. He was just a voice on the phone, saying Ludo was in hospital in Miami and wanted her. He could be anyone."

"God." Isobel looked startled. "I hadn't thought of that."

"It's not likely, but it's possible. If you were with her though, being *visible*, she'd be much safer."

Isobel nodded. "Okay. I'll go. But I still don't like leaving you."

Arran shrugged. "It's not as though it's forever. I'll wait for Margie, make sure everything's all right and Mother's settled for a while, then I'll go back to San Francisco. Maybe next week, or the week after. I'll call you at home."

"Home." Isobel rested her chin in her hands and stared pensively out to sea, her thoughts obviously now taking another tangent altogether. A depressing one. After a while, she went on: "I'm not looking forward to going home. It's stupid of me, especially as I ought to be so happy now. But somehow all I can see are the problems. And now that Hart's gone—"

Arran said, "Hart Jarrow was never for you."

Isobel sighed. "No, I guess not. One of these days, you'd better tell me about you and Hart."

"Yes, one of these days I will," Arran said, suddenly knowing that at last she could, without fear—that Isobel would not stop loving her! "But not today."

"No," Isobel agreed thoughtfully, "not today. I knew he wasn't for me as soon as he said those mean things about you. It made me *furious*."

Arran smiled wryly. "Did he say I was sick?"

Isobel nodded indignantly. "The jerk. And of us all, you're the one who really has it all together."

Arran thought how one day she would also tell Isobel exactly how she had *not* had it all together, but that could wait too. "Well, he was right, you know." Thinking how it was only a year since the Wyoming seminar, but how much longer it seemed. A whole lifetime away . . .

"But things are different now," Arran said.

She wanted to confide that she'd met someone, someone who made her feel happy. *Well, why not?* "I've met a terrific man," she told Isobel with pride. "Two terrific men, actually . . ."

How she had agonized, all during that dreadful flight to London, dirty and wretched and smelling of Gus and Sandro and all the others. Johnny would never want her again. Oh God, when he found out he'd be sick. He'd die of shame for her. But if I don't tell him, she thought now, he'll never know. And it'll never, never happen again.

Arran made a rough calculation in her head. It was approximately 3:00 A.M. in San Francisco. She would go back to the hotel and call Johnny. How wonderful— she felt free and strong enough to call Johnny on the phone—just like that! Or maybe wait until the next morning, after Isobel and Chris had left. It would be something to look forward to, even if he cursed her up and down for waking him up. But serve him right! When else could she be sure of finding him home?

"I'm glad, Arran," Isobel said sincerely, "I truly am. It's time you found a nice man." She sighed again. "I wish I could. The kids need a father so badly."

After a pause, "Isobel," said Arran, "you already did find a nice man. A long time ago. Remember?"

Isobel didn't reply. She stared out to sea. The line of white water was much closer and clearly now not white at all, but a scummy, yellowish brown.

"The right man, too," Arran added.

Reluctantly, Isobel spoke. "You mean Davis?"

"Of course."

Isobel sighed. "I wish I'd known it then. But how could I have known? Except in romance novels, how often is the first man you meet the one you fall in love with forever? It just doesn't happen."

"It does sometimes," Arran said. "You're still in love with him, aren't you?"

Isobel snorted. "How could I be? Of course I'm not."

"Liar."

"All right then, *yes*!" snapped Isobel. "But it never would have worked. He never loved me. I was just a property to him."

"If you believe that, you're more idiotic than I thought," Arran said. She thought, amazed at herself: listen to me—I'm telling Isobel what I really think, even if I have to be rude. I wouldn't have been talking like this last year—I'd have been polite and agreed with her, and things would have just gone on as they were. She added, "Blind, too."

Isobel demanded, "How do you know *anything* about Davis and me?"

"Because I'm *not* blind. And I'm a professional observer. Remember?"

"I suppose it all seems so simple to you."

"Sure it does. It's so obvious. Davis loves you very much. Why else do you think he's acted the way he has? He loved you so much he couldn't stand it."

"Hah."

"It's true. The problem is, Davis and you are exactly alike. So damn proud and afraid of being vulnerable that you have to go on and on hurting each other. Even Steve Romano could see that. He told Chris so."

"Goddam Steve Romano!" Isobel exclaimed. "Shit. It wasn't his fault. I knew what I was doing."

"Don't you think Davis understood?"

Isobel shrugged.

"Of *course* he did," Arran said patiently, as though explaining to a very small child. "But he wanted you all for himself and he was terribly jealous. He couldn't help it. Listen, we ought to get up. We'll get wet."

"Well anyway, there's no point talking about it. It's been over for years." With forced gaiety, Isobel added, "And it's not as though there aren't plenty of other fish in the sea." She clawed up a handful of gritty sand and flung it into the encroaching water. "And the kids really did like Hart. No reason why they can't like somebody else just as well."

Arran said bluntly: "They'd like their own father a hell of a lot better."

Isobel spun to face her. "What do you mean?" Then, seeing Arran's expression, she whispered, "How did you *know*?"

Arran opened her eyes wide; they were the same chilly gray of the North Sea. "I've seen Mark and Melissa, and I've seen Davis."

"Oh God," muttered Isobel, "that obvious?"

"Yes."

"Do you suppose he knows?"

"I'd be amazed if he didn't. Iso, call him when you get back. Listen, you can make a fresh start now. Meet with him. Tell him you love him. What've you got to lose?"

Isobel said in a stifled voice: "I'd rather die!"

"You're a coward."

"I've got my pride."

"And a lot of good pride does you. When you're alone in bed and you're drinking too much and your kids are getting in trouble!"

Isobel stared at Arran, white around the mouth. "I never thought I'd say this to somebody I cared for. Ever. But fuck you, Arran Winter! You're a *bitch*."

"And you," Arran snapped in frustration, "are not just a coward, you're a fool!"

5

The last time Chris and I flew together, Isobel thought now as the wide-bodied British Airways jet lumbered down the runway at Heathrow and ponderously took to the air, was fifteen years ago, when we first went to Los Angeles.

She closed her eyes, feeling the heavy vibrations permeate her body, determinedly not looking back, not anymore. She must look ahead. She told herself the world still waited for her. She was still young and beautiful, and now the burden of those dreadful years of fear had been, incredibly, lifted completely from her shoulders. She was safe; she was free; she was lucky—so lucky! But if *only* Arran hadn't started talking about Davis . . .

She felt terrible thinking about what she'd said to Arran, and even worse that she hadn't even been able to say good-bye properly. Somehow she hadn't even had the grace or the guts to kiss her sister good-bye. Her own—Oh God! Now that the ties of sisterly duty weren't there, perhaps Arran wouldn't even be her friend any longer. Isobel wouldn't blame her either. Arran had looked angry and so disgusted. Oh hell! Isobel hoped the plane would level out soon, so the cabin attendants could start serving drinks.

As she had so long ago, on their first flight, Christian sat with her nose glued to the window, staring out at the humid grayness of cloud. Her hands were tense on the armrests. She had been tense the whole morning, alternately irritable and withdrawn. She had shouted in frustration at Martin during that interminable drive ("Can't we go any faster than this? We'll never catch the goddam plane . . . never!"), even though Martin took the huge car through the country lanes at top speed and knew every shortcut. Despite the heavy rain, they actually made the trip in less than three hours, drawing up at a baggage entrance of Terminal Three an hour before the plane was due to depart. Then Martin led them through a labyrinth of back stairs, passages, and freight elevators, finally depositing them in a small private lounge. He had left them then, but not before hugging Christian, now fretful and close to tears, and patting her on the head as though she were a small child. "Take care of her, Miss" were his parting words to Isobel. To Christian, he added, "He'll be right as rain, you'll see."

It was raining in Miami too. Heavy sheets of warm tropical rain steamed on the tarmac.

José Estevez was waiting for them immediately inside the terminal; a smallish, unassuming man in a lightweight suit carrying a plastic raincoat. He told them he was head of undercover operations, Southeast region, Drug Enforcement Administration, and showed identification to prove it.

"Ludo's doing just fine," he told Christian reassuringly. "Well stabilized. He's expecting you."

In the car, a nondescript sedan of indeterminate color, Christian gave way to a sudden panic. She clutched Isobel's hand, white as a ghost. "He sent me away. He doesn't want the baby. I can't see him, I can't. Iso, what am I going to *do*? I look terrible! I should have changed." She was wearing the white jeans and striped fisherman's shirt she had worn on her outward journey the week before. Only six days ago, but it seemed like forever.

"Don't even think about it," Isobel said. "Who gives a shit about clothes at a time like this?"

Dade County Hospital was a hospital like any other, infinitely anonymous, a jumbled impression of glaring lights, disembodied voices paging doctors, rubber soles squeaking on shiny linoleum floors, the smell of industrial strength disinfectant.

They rode up three floors in a huge, crowded gray steel elevator then followed Estevez down a long corridor, stopping at last before a closed door.

The door was no different from any other, except that an armed guard stood to either side of it—and Ludo Corey was behind it.

"Go on in, Chris. I'll wait here with Mr. Estevez."

Christian turned agonized eyes on Isobel. "Iso— *please!*"

Then the door was open. Isobel and Christian went in, followed by Estevez.

He had been watching the door.

A haggard man with rough black hair, dark eyes burning with expectancy.

Isobel saw the light flare in his eyes, and hoped that Christian saw it too. Christian, beside her, was rigid, her hands clenched at her sides. She whispered, "Ludo . . ."

Then in an explosive burst, she went on: "Oh my God, my darling, you're all right. Oh my love, I was so afraid."

With an eerie feeling, even though she knew Ludo didn't move—couldn't move, wrists taped down, needles taped to his wrists—it seemed to Isobel as though a lithe, healthy golden-haired man met Christian in the middle of the room and enfolded her in his arms; that they came together in a swooping rush of such intensity that the air was driven from the room.

She blinked in momentary confusion . . .

Then there they were, together on the bed after all, Christian caressing Ludo's naked shoulders, kissing his face, his lips, his rough hair—but so softly and gently, so as not to hurt him.

She heard Ludo say in a weak voice, "Oh Chris, I'm sorry. Forgive me, about the baby. I never meant—"

Estevez said to Christian, "Not more than ten minutes. He's got to rest." Turning to Isobel, he asked,

"Miss Wynne, maybe you and I can go get a cup of coffee."

That evening, sitting beside the window in their hotel room, Christian was exhausted, elated, and seemed to glimmer translucently as though lit from inside. Isobel was very happy for her. As for herself, well . . . she decided she had never felt so desolate. Never before had she seen such single-minded love, and never before had she been so aware of her own aching emptiness.

The next day, when she, Isobel, had left for Los Angeles—for there was no reason for her to stay on here now, she knew she would only be in the way—Christian would move to another hotel, closer to the hospital.

"He told me, Iso. He told me why he hadn't wanted the baby."

"Well, why?" Isobel asked wearily, her mind on other things now. Mundane things, like calling maid service to do something about her clothes, and then room service, to send up a bottle of vodka.

"It's so stupid. I couldn't believe it." Christian giggled with a touch of hysteria. Clinically, Isobel noted the signs. Christian was about to disintegrate. She needed a hot bath and about sixteen hours of sleep. "When he thought of a baby, he said all he could see was himself, when he was very little . . ." Christian described Ludo's pathetic vision of little Ludovico Jimenez. "But I told him, this was my baby, *our* baby. It would be treasured and loved."

Christian began to cry, and then to laugh through her tears. "He said he didn't know how to love a baby, because he'd never had any parents. He was a bastard. I said I was a bastard too! Oh Iso, I love him so much . . . I'm so happy I could die."

"That's wonderful, darling," Isobel said heartily. "I'm so very happy for you!" She was sure she sounded absolutely convincing, and she meant it, every word. But perhaps she was too convincing—perhaps a wrong note had crept in somewhere—for Christian suddenly glanced suspiciously at Isobel. Then, with a pang for her own selfishness, Christian belatedly remembered her talk with Arran late the night before, and what she had promised to do.

"I think I'll take a shower," Isobel was saying now.

The moment Isobel closed the bathroom door, Christian hurriedly left the room and went down to the lobby to use the public phone.

It was seven o'clock in Miami; only four in the afternoon in Los Angeles.

She made two phone calls. One was to Charlene Hoover, who agreed reluctantly to Christian's request only after long and dubious argument. The other was to Refugio Ramirez, who (once she had tracked him down at a restaurant called La Casa del Sol) whooped in delight to hear Christian's proposition, and cried, "Sure, baby—you're on. I always wanted to drive one of those motherfuckers."

The next morning, Isobel could not afford to look the way she felt. She dressed for her trip to California with mechanical care in a black Chanel suit and hid her dark, circled eyes behind huge sunglasses. Christian was very sweet and considerate, however. She ordered a special farewell breakfast, and noting Isobel's depleted condition, had done various chores, such as calling the limo service in Los Angeles to arrange for Isobel to be met at the airport.

Despite everything, however, Isobel felt gritty, tired, and leadenly depressed throughout the uneventful but interminable flight across the country. She still had a fierce hangover: she'd sat up in bed the night before drinking vodka and staring at Christian's sleeping face—so fresh, so young and smiling, so obviously dreaming of Ludo, the baby, and happiness ever after that Isobel could have hit her.

At LAX, the driver—a narrow face under a gray peaked cap, a scrawny body—requested her baggage tags and politely escorted her through the terminal, past all the staring faces, the wave of turning heads, and the whispers—"Look, Mom, isn't that Isobel Wynne?" and "Hey, how 'bout that! A real star, our first day in L.A.!"

The midafternoon was glaringly hot, as brazenly smoggy as Isobel could ever remember. She wilted miserably during the short walk to the long white car with the blacked out windows. Her purse and tote bag felt as heavy as lead.

"Air conditioning's on full," the driver said, holding the door open for her. Isobel thankfully plunged inside, collapsing onto the deep, soft seat—only to find she was not alone.

She saw a well-cut light gray suit, a bent dark head, an opened briefcase, a sheaf of papers. Without looking up, the man said, "Welcome back. I hope it all went well. Excuse my not getting out, but—"

Isobel gasped. She said in a choking voice, "Davis Whittaker, what the fuck are you doing in my car?"

The door slammed behind her. A squat figure flung itself into the driver's seat. The driver's door slammed shut and the stretch Cadillac took off with a muted roar and a squeal of tires.

The expression in Davis's amber eyes ranged from shock to bewilderment, to fury. "And what the hell kind of game is this?" He rapped on the glass partition. *"Driver!"*

Refugio Ramirez half turned and grinned cheerfully from under his incongruously too small chauffeur's cap.

"Oh my God!" gasped Isobel. "But that's not— Where's the other—I don't *believe* this." The limousine tore down Century Boulevard, weaving dangerously in and out of traffic, and then onto the San Diego Freeway, where Ramirez proceeded to drive as though the Cadillac were a Maserati. Isobel and Davis sat helplessly in their seats, pinned down by the fierce acceleration. "Listen," Isobel cried, glancing at Davis's furious face, "this is *not* a game. It's a mistake. It's got to be a terrible mistake. Stop the car right now!" She shouted, "Refugio! What the hell are you doing? Slow down—"

Ramirez paid no attention.

"No use—the intercom's dead," Davis said. "Some mistake!"

"But of course it's a mistake. Do you think I'd *plan* something like this?"

Davis said caustically, "Well, somebody did."

"Who, then? *Why*? Ow!" They were flung roughly together, as Ramirez took a curve at seventy-five miles per hour. Davis's briefcase and papers spilled onto the floor. "Jesus Christ!" he shouted. "Goddam it, Ramirez—"

Two semis, a pickup, and a Greyhound bus were left behind as though standing still, then they were tailgating a black Porsche Turbo until, intimidated, it moved into the middle lane. Finally, they were holding position alongside a hopped-up old Mercury full of Mexicans who seemed to want to drag. There was some frenzied yelling back and forth in Spanish.

Davis pounded angrily on the glass behind Ramirez's head. The fat little photographer did not turn around, but lifted his pudgy hands from the wheel and waved them negatively in the air.

"For God's sake leave him alone," said Isobel. "Why *were* you at the airport?"

"I was meeting Julie Farlow. She's been shooting a special in New York. She was coming back through Miami."

"But Davis, I've been out of the country. How was I supposed to know *that*?"

"You tell *me*."

"But the driver was expecting *me*, not Julie Farlow. And he showed me to *this* car! Your car, not mine. I don't understand! And what about Ramirez? He's wearing the other guy's hat!"

"Listen, Isobel," Davis said grimly, "you can't duck out of this one. Charlene told me just this morning Julie needed to see me urgently and wanted me to meet her plane." His eyes narrowed—"Charlene . . ."—and then flashed dangerously. "So you two planned this farce *together*. Jesus, what did she think she was doing." With an unpleasant expression, Davis said, "That damn woman's overstepped her boundaries for the last time. I'll fire her for this."

"I haven't spoken to Charlene in years." Isobel was half-sobbing with anger. "It wasn't me!"

Then, suddenly, it was all clear. "It was Christian!"

"What?"

"It *must* have been," Isobel cried in rage. "Chris called the limo service for me this morning—or pretended to. She knows Charlene and Ramirez. She did it. Davis, I had nothing to do with this. You've got to believe me. *She* set me up. God, I could kill her." As the doubt began to replace the suspicion in Davis's hard eyes, Isobel said thoughtfully, "But it's not like Christian to think of something like this. And especially not now, when she's so involved in her own affairs."

Davis said bitterly, "I wouldn't have thought it of Charlene either."

"*Arran*!" Isobel whispered through white lips. "It was Arran. She planned it all, and got Chris to call Charlene, and somehow persuade her to . . ."

Davis demanded, "Why?"

"Because she was angry. We'd had an argument. A fight, really."

"What about?"

"Never mind. It was nothing."

"But I do mind. I mind a lot. It seems to concern me as much as you. Tell me."

Isobel bit her lip. "All right! If you must know: Arran said I should call you when I got home."

Davis looked at her coolly. "What for?"

"How should I know?"

"Come now, Isobel. Not good enough. What were you supposed to tell me?"

Isobel laughed jarringly then, close to hysteria. "That I *loved* you! Can you believe it?"

"And why ever would you say something like that?"

Isobel glared at him. Davis had never seen her look so angry or seen her eyes such a burning blue. He remembered as though it were yesterday the first time he had looked into Isobel's eyes, that night at the Jenningses' party. As though it were yesterday, he felt his body flood with desire for her. It was fifteen years later and his feelings were as intense as they had ever been. He was as angry as he had ever been, too, remembering how casually she had taken his love and used it for her own ends. He hated her as violently as he had that brilliant, blue afternoon twelve years ago on the boat.

"Why?" snarled Isobel. "Because it's bloody well true, that's why." Her face was dead white, except for blotches of color high on each cheekbone, eyes brimming with tears that she brushed away resentfully with the back of her Chanel sleeve.

Davis thought automatically that Isobel could always cry gracefully. Not for Isobel the ugly squared mouth, the running nose, the red, swollen eyes. As always, he mentally applauded her professionalism—but, he suddenly realized, she's not acting this time.

"I loved you since I first saw you," Isobel yelled, suddenly very English in her extremity, "and a bloody rotten time it's been. What did you care? You've never seen me as anything but a goddam property! *Product!*" she sneered, the tears now raining unheeded down her cheeks. She grasped the lapels of his elegant jacket in her hot wet hands and shook him. "And you never even *tried* to find out whether Mark and Melissa were your children! Hell, no. What did you care? I hate you, Davis Whittaker. You've ruined my life. Now please tell that *bloody* man to stop the car and let me out. I won't stay here another second. I had nothing to do with this, I don't want to be here, and I'll get home on my own if I have to *walk*!"

At the wheel, Refugio Ramirez grinned and purposefully pressed down on the gas pedal. By Jesus, this was fun! It was great! Driving this huge white monster down the freeway at ninety, he felt flooded with an exhilaration that was better than sex! Even better than food . . .

Suddenly they were stuck behind a top-heavy Winnebago with Minnesota license plates, determinedly traveling fifty-five mph in the fast lane, impervious to any harassment of lights and horn. "Fucking tourist," Ramirez snorted in disgust. He swerved out and overtook the Winnebago on the right, cut back in really tight, and gave the finger to a furious red face peering out the passenger window.

In the backseat of the Cadillac, Isobel lost her balance and fell helplessly across Davis's lap. "He's crazy!" she cried. "Or drunk! Make him stop!"

In Ramirez's rearview mirror, far far behind, there was now a flickering suggestion of color through the smog—red and blue flashing lights—well, he thought smugly, he'd be almost in Santa Barbara before they caught up with him!

"Don't worry, it'll be okay," said Davis absently, feeling her familiar weight, her familiar shape, aching for her all over again. "I know about Mark and Melissa." The limo lurched again and he tightened his grip protectively about Isobel's shoulders. He could feel her hot wet face on his naked throat. ("Dad, this is my friend Mark Wynne," Bryant had said shyly that day Davis had picked him up from school, and looking at Mark, seeing a duplicate of Bryant with the familiar Whittaker eyes and mouth, Davis had felt a twisting in his gut and a feeling of desolation, knowing he could never hold Mark in his arms and call him son—and now Bryant was gone too, back to New York to live with Stewart.)

Davis had felt drained and empty. Life stretched ahead, interminable and deadly. Now, with Isobel literally flung into his arms after all these years he found himself blessing Ramirez's reckless driving, hoping the wild ride would go on forever, and finding himself automatically kissing her hair and asking, "What do you mean, you've always loved me?"

"Forget it," Isobel said in a choking voice. "It doesn't matter anymore."

"But it does," Davis said, catching the point of her chin and forcing her to look at him. His eyes bored into hers. She looked up at him defiantly, hair tousled, her careful makeup ruined. "Why didn't you tell me before?"

"Why should I? You didn't love me."

"Oh God," said Davis. Gripping her by her wild,

black hair, holding her tightly against his body, he said, "Say it again, Isobel. Are you telling the truth?" Isobel twisted and struggled against him but he held her firm. "Tell me."

Her eyes flashed murder. "Oh *damn* you, Davis. Yes, I loved you. I've always loved you. I still damn well love you. *Now* will you let me go, and let me out of here."

"No," said Davis, and leaned forward and kissed her. Her face and lips tasted of salt tears. He felt her muscles tense against him and whispered, an echo of that first time they made love, "Please Isobel—don't fight me now." She gave one last furious sob and he felt her body grow limp. Then her mouth opened under his. Her fingers dug convulsively into the flesh of his back. He caught a glimpse of her closed eyes, the lashes tangled and wet, before his own world shifted and lost focus. His last impression, before he gave himself up to Isobel and to warm gasping thankful darkness, was of a persistent wailing noise, which he ignored, followed by a gentle well-sprung rocking motion as the limo slowed and finally came to a full stop and finally of beautiful colored lights flashing rhythmically behind his head.

Vaguely, he wondered why Ramirez had stopped; but it really didn't matter.

He kissed Isobel again. "And I love you too, more than I can say. Welcome home."

We invite you to read this compelling
excerpt from

AMETHYST
by Mary-Rose Hayes

A dazzling novel of love and prophecy

Coming soon from E. P. Dutton

Everything seemed different at midnight.

Even the smallest sounds were exaggerated. The darkness, which pressed upon them as though it had actual weight and seemed filled with listening ears and watching eyes.

Jess, Gwynneth and Catriona clustered together, needing the reassurance of each other's presence, listening to the sound of each other's quickened breathing.

Only Victoria Raven seemed at home in the midnight dark, but the young women remembered she was accustomed to wandering the bleak passages of Castle Dunleven, her beloved home.

She was sitting cross-legged on the floor, wearing a man's plum-colored silk dressing gown with black satin lapels, her incredible silver hair falling loose over her shoulders. She held a small flashlight in her lap, the beam glancing upward so that her face, lit from below, was all cheekbones and eye sockets.

The ouija board lay in front of her. "Not a real one, but it'll do," said Victoria.

She had made it from a square of white cardboard on which she had inscribed the letters of the alphabet in a half circle, the numbers one through nine including zero, the words "yes" and "no."

"I feel creepy," murmured Catriona, and moved closer to Jess's side.

"That's part of the fun," Gwynneth said stoutly.

Then Victoria pulled the extraordinary amethyst ring from her finger. "It was a gift from my brother Tancredi," she told them. "A family heirloom."

449

They stared at the enormous gemstone with fascination. The stone was breathtaking, both for its deep purple coloring and for the intricate, multifaceted cut which cast flashes of violet light across their faces.

"Well, then?" Victoria glanced from face to face. She placed the amethyst centrally on the board, and rested the tip of her index finger lightly upon the glittering stone. "Shall we start? You have to put your fingers on the ring too for the energy flow, but very gently. . . ."

Victoria smiled slightly, a mere tightening of the corners of her mouth, and closed her eyes. She sat absolutely still for some time. Feeling rather foolish, the others stared down at their fingers resting obediently on the amethyst, which seemed to glow inside as though lit by purple fire. They didn't know what to expect. Gwynneth stifled an irresistible urge to laugh.

Finally, "Somebody's here," Victoria said quietly.

There was a dense silence. Afterwards, suggestible Catriona would insist a sudden gust of wind had rattled the windows, and all of them, in retrospect, would be sure the gem had actually quivered under their fingers.

Jess wondered why she was taking part in this charade. Unlike Catriona, she didn't believe in prediction. Nor did she find this goulishly comical as apparently Gwynneth did. A creature of light, she felt oppressed by the dark furtiveness and if she hadn't known better, she might even have thought she was afraid. But of course that was ridiculous. She was Jessica Hunter. She wasn't afraid of anything.

Gwynneth, firmly denying the deep-rooted mysticism of her Welsh blood, took refuge in the humor of it all. She had her own role to play; she was "Good Old Gwynneth Jones," a sensible girl who did not believe in ghosts. She thought about her father the vicar, a narrow-minded righteous man whom she had always loved to shock. Well, she thought with satisfaction, he would be shocked now, all right!

"Who is there?" asked Victoria.

Slowly, deliberately, the amethyst began to move, flinging geometric lavender shapes around the walls.

Nobody pushed it. "Not then, anyway," Gwynneth said later. "It moved by itself. I'd swear to it."

Catriona gave an involuntary cry of fright.

"Hush," Victoria said sternly.

The gem moved to *S*; then *C; wheeling, spelling, faster and faster, gathering power before swinging to rest in the center. S-C-A-R-S-D-A-L-E.*

"My God," said Gwynneth.

Victoria said calmly, "My father."

After a tense pause she added, "I'm not surprised. It used to be his ring."

Catriona managed, "You mean, it could have— summoned him."

A slash of purple light angled across Victoria's cheek. "I don't know."

Jess sat back on her heels and thrust her hands into her pockets. "I think we should stop."

"Oh come on." Gwynneth glanced from Jess to Catriona and back to Jess, saying in a too loud voice, "We don't really believe it, do we?"

"Quiet!" murmured Victoria.

"Yes," Jess agreed. "Or someone might hear."

Catriona flinched, thinking of the sinister, listening shade of Lord Scarsdale. Suddenly she wouldn't have minded if Miss Pemberton Smyth, the headmistress herself, had broken in upon them.

"Sorry." Gwynneth pulled the skimpy bathrobe over her bony knees and put her fingers back on the stone.

There was a long pause in which Victoria seemed to be mustering her forces. "Father," she said finally in a remote voice, "where are you? Tell us what it is like there."

The answer came in a thready, wandering search for letters. *COLD. DARK. FAR. . . .* and then there was a long spinning succession of aimless circles.

"Will you answer our questions?"

IF I MUST.

"I ask you to, Father."

Scarsdale did not deign to reply. The stone rested idly.

By now a frighteningly complete image of Lord Scarsdale had crept into Jess's mind. She saw a lean dark face; cold eyes and a thin, bitter mouth. He doesn't like us, she thought; he'd never like anybody . . .

Victoria looked up. Her eyes seemed strange and dark, the pale irises swallowed by the widely dilated pupils. "Catriona, you first. You were the one who asked for this."

"Oh no. Not me. Please—somebody else . . ."

"Go on. He's waiting."

"I—" Catriona gulped, flushed, then, "how?"

"You concentrate," Victoria said patiently. "You think about what you want to know. Just that and nothing else. And then you ask."

"That's all?"

Victoria nodded.

"Oh. I see—" Catriona's voice trembled nervously: "Lord Scarsdale, please, I want to know—" and then in a rush, "will I marry Jonathon Wyndham?"

The reply was instantaneous. *YES.*

Catriona exhaled with delight. Gwynneth nudged her in the ribs. "There you are, ducky. The handsome prince sweeps the beautiful princess onto his white horse and they gallop away into the sunset."

"Oh, thank you!" Catriona smiled mistily down at the amethyst. "Thank you so much!"

Victoria asked, "Don't you want to ask anything else?"

"I don't need to, now."

"She's going to live happily ever after," said Gwynneth.

"But will she be happy?"

Catriona looked up. Something in Victoria's voice scared her. "Of course I will . . . won't I?"

Victoria shrugged. "Don't ask me." She inclined her head to the board. "Ask the ring."

Catriona bit her lip. In a timid voice she asked, "I'll be terribly happy. Won't I?"

There was a long pause. Catriona looked anxiously at Victoria who sat, still as a statue, eyes closed. She whispered, "Why doesn't he answer?"

"Hush," said Victoria, "wait." Haltingly the stone began to move.

HAPPINESS IS BOUGHT AT GREAT COST.

"Great cost?" gasped Catriona. "What does that mean?"

"Ssh. He's not finished."

AFTER YOU LEARN THE DARKNESS.

The stone came to rest. Catriona stared at it, horrified. "Darkness?"

TRUST IN YOUR OWN RESOURCES.

"But—what resources? D'you mean money? Lord Scarsdale, I don't understand." She was almost in tears now. *"Won't* we be happy?"

Then they all felt the stone grow dead under their fingers. Its haunting light seemed to fade.

"I—" Catriona gazed at Victoria, eyes huge. This wasn't the kind of fortune telling she was familiar with, no kindly gypsy telling her she'd marry Prince Charming. "He didn't say—"

"He's finished," Victoria said gently. "You have to work it out for yourself, now. If you marry Jonathon, perhaps you'll have to give up something important to you."

"But nothing's important compared to Jonathon."

"Then I don't know. You'll find out."

Catriona set her mouth stubbornly. "I don't care if there is great cost. I'd give everything, anything! to marry him!"

There was a thoughtful pause. Then Victoria asked, "Gwynn, would you like to go next?"

Gwynneth gave a small, nervous cough. She hadn't expected these peculiar, ambiguous answers. She felt an overwhelming urge to get out of this room. The future, she decided, was much better off left alone.

Then she thought, ah, come on. It was just the four of them, scaring the hell out of each other for fun.

Victoria prompted, "Come on, Gwynn."

What would she ask? Something harmless . . . just in case . . . She closed her eyes and wrinkled her nose in concentration. "Don't take too long," Victoria advised. "He'll get bored and leave."

Gwynneth sighed. She asked, safely, "Lord Scarsdale, will I enjoy my life?"

The answer was offhand and uninformative.

SOMETIMES

"You have to be more specific."

"But I don't—"

"Oh, come on," begged Jess. "Ask anything. Ask if you'll be rich."

"All right," said Gwynneth. "Will I be a millionaire? There!"

There seemed no question about it. The stone moved in a determined diagonal toward *YES*.

"What? That's stupid." Gwynneth stared at the board, where the letters suddenly seemed to swim gently as though detaching themselves from the paper. She challenged, "All right, how will I earn my money?"

WITH IMPECCABLE BONES

Gwynneth found her mouth had fallen open, and she closed it with a snap. Bewildered, she asked, "Bones. . . .?"

But the gem lay still.

"He's finished. Don't press him," Victoria murmured.

"Oh bloody hell," Gwynneth muttered, then mentally kicked herself. She didn't believe in this stuff. Of course she didn't. And of all the ridiculous notions, thinking of herself being a millionaire because of impeccable bones. It was the dumbest thing she had ever heard.

"I suppose it's my turn," Jess said unwillingly. One enormous question had formed in her mind, the one question she refused to ask. If the answer was yes, then the fabric of her life would be torn apart; if no her disappointment would be terrible. I'm believing this after all! she thought with dismay; I don't want to! It makes no sense! So she decided to ask something safe, a question to which she already knew the answer: "Where will I live after I settle down?" thinking confidently, the Cotswold country of England, of course, for wherever else was there in the world?

As Gwynneth had done, she watched the glass spell out the unlikely answer:

IN ANOTHER COUNTRY
"Another country? Where?" asked Jess blankly.
VERY FAR AWAY
"I don't believe it," Jess said firmly. "Why?"
TO SEE MORE CLEARLY
And then, once again, the glass was still.
"To see what more clearly?"
Victoria sighed. "That's all. He won't say any more."
"Well of course not, because he doesn't know," Jess snapped. "He can't know."
"He knows."
"This is stupid." Jess dismissed Lord Scarsdale's prophecies.
Victoria chided halfheartedly, "Don't." Then she fell silent, sitting very still, eyes glinting under half-closed lids. The silence stretched out. Jess, Gwynneth and Catriona found themselves holding their breath. Finally, in a low-pitched, almost dreamy voice, Victoria said, "Scarsdale, tell me what can you see for us all. What will happen to us twenty years from now?
Afterward they all remembered the sudden tingle of electric shock running from their fingertips up their arms and falling, cold, on their hearts. The gem was moving violently, sweeping back and forth with stabbing thrusts, hurling glittering showers of amethyst light across their faces.
They watched, transfixed.
YOU WILL BE TOGETHER AGAIN BUT YOU WILL BE ONE LESS.
When they realized what that could mean, someone, perhaps Catriona, gave a short scream. Then the stone streaked off the board and thudded loudly against the wall.
Suddenly the room was very, very dark.

About the Author

Mary-Rose Hayes has led an exciting and some-what nomadic existence—as a London fashion model, a secretary at an Arizona dude ranch, a sailboat deckhand, a librarian in war-torn Northern Ireland, a TV script editor, and a newspaper travel correspondent, all of it serving as background for her career as a novelist. Born in England, Mary-Rose Hayes currently lives in San Francisco.